IN THE BLOOD

A Jefferson Tayte Genealogical
Mystery

by

STEVE ROBINSON

THOMAS & MERCER

Published by Thomas & Mercer, Seattle

www.apub.com

Amazon, the Amazon logo, and Thomas & Mercer are trademarks of Amazon.com, Inc., or its affiliates.

ISBN-13: 9781477818527
ISBN-10: 1477818529

Cover design by The Book Designers

Library of Congress Control Number: 2013920525

Printed in the United States of America

IN THE BLOOD

A Jefferson Tayte Genealogical
Mystery

Other books in this series

For Karen

Prologue

1803. Helford Passage, southwest England.

Mawgan Hendry was dying. If he'd seen it coming, he might have had some chance to prevent it. As it was, all hope against such sudden and decisive brutality faded into the night with his first laboured breath.

On the river's inky swell, Cornish fishing boats continued to chatter and creak uneasily, though Mawgan could no longer hear them over the blood pressure drumming in his ears. He clawed desperately at his neck, drawing skin under his nails, tearing and ripping until his raw flesh burned. But he could not free himself. His fists lashed wildly to no effect. His feet became suddenly weightless, kicking and thrashing in frenzied panic like a crazed marionette until laboured breath became no breath at all and he was still.

A strengthening easterly wind cut into the throat of the Helford River, lashing rain at Mawgan's startled face, bluing and congested under the dim glow of the jetty lantern. His eyes grew dark as the empty night, bulging in their sockets as he dropped forcefully to his knees, thumping hard onto wet pontoon boards. He sensed unconsciousness was moments away, and for all his brawn he could not fight it. Between his thumb and forefinger he grasped a silver crucifix that hung loosely from his neck as he prayed for deliverance.

But deliver us from evil!

Then a voice whispered in his ear, cold and threatening.

'You know what I've come for.'

Mawgan shook his head, jerking his neck in quick, erratic spasms. At first he couldn't think, and then he knew. *The box...Lowenna...* He shook his head again, defiant. He tried to glimpse the figure bearing down on him, his head uncomfortably close, but the man's strength restricted him—denied him.

For thine is the kingdom!

'No matter,' the man said.

Mawgan caught the flash of a wry smile teasing at the edge of his assailant's mouth. He felt an ear press close to his neck, as if the man were listening for something. Waiting.

Then it came.

As the pressure increased and Mawgan's hyoid bone fractured, he saw his assailant fully at last when the man forced their faces together. He saw the man's eyes narrow, his jaw relax, slowly parting his lips in a moment that seemed akin to some exquisite pleasure, like he was savouring the intimacy, absorbing the delicacy.

And the power, and the glory!

As Mawgan's heart beat for the last time, he could think only of Lowenna, his love. The love that was now lost to him.

For ever and ever.

His body went limp, arms dropping heavily to his sides, hands like dead weights.

Amen.

Chapter One

An air horn screamed through the dark, and Jefferson Tayte's eyes shot wide open. In that same instant he watched his knuckles turn white on the wheel as a rush of adrenalin surged through him—tingling, pulsating; a burst of energy that began at his core and raged violently across his entire body. He'd never felt more awake than he did at that moment. The sound came again and the air inside the car resonated, buzzing the dash. He swerved just in time, narrowly avoiding the eighteen-wheeler that blocked his view as headlights dazzled him.

The piercing lights quickly passed. Behind him, the drone of the air horn faded at last, along with the uncomfortable pounding in his chest. He took a deep breath and forced it out again, still bolt upright in his seat, still clenching the wheel. He glanced down at himself and took in the straining buttons on his white shirt and the heavy thighs that were tight inside his loose-fit tan linen trousers.

'Gotta shape up, JT,' he told himself. He reached across to the passenger seat and scooped up an almost empty bag of Hershey's miniatures. *Goodbye, Mr Goodbar!* he thought as he popped the glove box and slammed the chocolates inside.

The dim beam of his own vehicle's antiquated headlights shed a soft glow on the quiet road ahead. He squinted into the night and ran a clammy hand through the sweat on his brow, pushing his fingers back through a dense crop of dark, unkempt hair. An approaching road sign told him he was still heading in the right direction, towards Boston, Massachusetts—his destination for a meeting he'd hoped to avoid because he knew his bear of a client was not going to be happy with what he had to tell him.

Something about the assignment didn't add up. Now his preoccupation with it had almost killed him. His mind was a torment of unsolved riddles. *Eleanor Fairborne…the children…why can't I trace them? What happened to them?*

Chapter Two

Tayte's client was a busy man, and breakfast meetings were to be expected if not always welcomed, although apart from the company, Tayte could think of few better places to enjoy a fine Tuesday morning than on the terrace of Walter Sloane's luxury penthouse condominium. Tayte was used to travelling to see his clients, but today he was weary from the 450-mile drive from his home in Washington, DC, and the near-death experience he'd had a few hours back. Long night drives left him drained, but it was better than flying.

Sloane's condo was in South Boston, a few miles from his client's business epicentre in the downtown financial district. It was one of four corner residences that enjoyed total privacy, boasting views across the Old Harbor towards the Harbor Islands in the east and north to the photogenic Boston skyline. Tayte was sitting at a smoked glass and aluminium table close to the balcony, overlooking Carson Beach. He dunked another croissant in his black coffee and continued speaking to his client.

'Somewhere close to a hundred thousand loyalists left America at the end of the War of Independence to remain subjects of King George III of England. Most went to England, others to Ireland, Scotland, and Canada, particularly Nova Scotia.'

He unfolded some more of the genealogy chart on the table. Tayte still used charts for show. Clients liked them; they liked to see the family tree grow as he revealed more and more of their past. 'Some of the family didn't make it through the war,' he continued. 'Both parents and grandparents were already gone before it started—life expectancy back then for Massachusetts was only about sixty years.'

He traced a finger across the chart, moving through several generations until he arrived at the first American-born ancestor of his client's wife. 'William Fairborne,' he said, 'James Fairborne's brother. He moved away long before the American revolution began, finally settling in what's now West Virginia, and there's nothing so far to suggest the brothers kept in touch.' He closed the chart again and shook his head, surprised at his own findings. 'Seems unusual,' he added. 'People don't often run away from money.'

Walter Sloane was a man who made Jefferson Tayte look fit. He appeared to be at work already, nose buried in the *Boston Business Journal*, a stack of national papers beside his elbow. He looked up. 'Maybe they fell out.' His voice was gritty with an undertone of sub-bass that distressed the air as he spoke. 'If that's who my wife got her temper from, they probably kicked him out!'

'Whatever the reason,' Tayte said. 'With only daughters following and James Fairborne moving the rest of the family back to England, that was the last of this particular Fairborne line in America. James Fairborne returned to a comfortable estate and a baronetcy for his loyalty.'

Sloane turned another page and slurped from a thin bone-china cup, his fingers clumsy on the delicate handle. He clanked the cup back onto the saucer. 'So where do we go from here?'

Tayte took a large bite from his croissant, dripping lukewarm coffee down his suit, but gave no indication that he noticed the spill. His free hand riffled through a black notebook beside the chart. 'James Fairborne and his family left America in…August 1783,' he said. 'I've traced James back to that time—to the southwest of England.' His niggling questions about Eleanor Fairborne and the rest of the family rushed back at him, interrupting his flow and causing his client to stare at him expectantly.

Tayte quickly continued. 'A county called Cornwall,' he added. 'Seems they arrived there...' His words lacked conviction. He knew he was speculating that the rest of the family had made it. Without records to back things up, he couldn't know anything for sure. 'But either I've got the wrong Fairborne, or...' His words trailed off again as he questioned the possibility in his own mind. But he knew he had the right man. What he couldn't understand was why James Fairborne's records continued beyond 1783, but the rest of his family's did not.

Tayte stood up and finished his croissant. He went to the edge of the terrace and looked out over the balcony, pointing down over the beach to the harbour. 'The *Betsy Ross* sailed from somewhere down there.' He spoke slowly, as though confirming things to himself. He knew the brig had sailed. He'd seen the departure entry in the Ship Index. 'They set up in England...' He stopped again, still puzzled. 'Things get a little hazy from there.'

Tayte gazed out at the expensive views of tall skyscrapers and high-rises on one side, then to the contrasting sea on the other. His mind raced with possibilities. *Think, JT!* It was a clear day, just a little blurred towards the horizon. He pinched the inner corners of his eyes, tired and gritty, in case it was his vision that was blurry, but the horizon remained as diffused as his thoughts.

Walter Sloane closed his paper and slapped it down with the rest, focusing Tayte's attention. 'Well, you need to get over there and talk to these people. Confirm things. Half a job's no good to me.'

Tayte was afraid that was coming, however much he'd expected it. His mouth cracked nervously at the edges as he snorted the beginnings of an uneasy laugh. 'Well, there's a lot more I can do from here...' He closed his eyes, silently reprimanding himself, wishing he could take the words back. His chin dropped to his chest. *So unprofessional.* If his university peers could see him now—Jefferson Theodore Tayte, on the brink of killing yet another perfectly good assignment because he was afraid to fly.

The job was nearly finished. He had a briefcase full of records and transcripts: births, marriages and deaths, covering everyone directly descended from William Fairborne to the present day. From that first American-born ancestor, he'd gone back to William's father and *his* father, who originally settled in America, arriving from England back in 1712.

Most of his clients had no interest in the families of their ancestor's brothers or sisters to any great extent. They only wanted to trace their direct ancestry—their own roots. But he had to get clever; he had to open his big mouth and convince Walter Sloane that it would be great to trace the Fairborne name back to England again through William's brother, James.

Well, he'd done that. Now a simple job he had been on the verge of wrapping up had become a total mess. His charts were full of question marks for James's wife, Eleanor, and their children; for his sister, Clara, and her husband Jacob. And one big question mark concerning whom the current Fairborne line in England descended from. Complications had certainly arisen. Questions he knew he couldn't answer in his usual stay-at-home way had presented themselves. He knew he had to go to England. How else could he finish the job in time? He sat down, suddenly uncomfortable in his coffee-spattered suit, which was more creased than usual from the long drive.

Sloane leaned in across the table, stone-faced. 'I hired you for this because someone told me you were the best.' His words were calm but firm, and Tayte gave no argument. 'I could have gotten Schofield for half the price!'

The man leaned closer still. His eyes widened until his brows looked like they were about to slide off the back of his smooth, well-oiled head. 'I'm not paying you to sit around on your fanny tapping keys and making phone calls all day.' His knuckles pressed into the glass tabletop, spreading to twice their usual size. 'Get your ass to England, Tayte. Find out what you need to know and get back here and finish the damn thing!'

Tayte blamed his tiredness, itself a byproduct of his fear: *pteromerhanophobia*. He thought they could have come up with something easier to pronounce, but figured the idea was that by the time you said it properly, the flight would be over.

Sloane got up, grating chair legs carelessly against the buff limestone flooring. 'You've got one week!' He raised a single stubby digit so there was no misunderstanding. Then he turned in the direction of the French doors that led back into the condo, pausing as he knocked into a telescope. 'Keep me updated,' he called back. 'Leave a message with my PA if I'm busy.' He glared purposefully at Tayte. 'Don't you fail me!' he warned. Then he disappeared inside.

One week. Genealogy had never been an easy business to earn a living from. The popularity of Tayte's profession had perhaps never been greater, but that popularity had pulled the competition wriggling from the woodwork. Now it was eating at the pie he used to enjoy with relatively few like-minded friends, back when there was plenty to share. If business had been better, he might have told the man exactly what to do with his chart. One week wasn't long in light of what he had to go on. He knew it would be tight. He also knew he was kidding himself if he thought he could walk away from this one. He had to find these people. There were bigger issues at stake.

Then there was the mention of Schofield. *That upstart!* The kid had been breathing down Tayte's neck for a few years now, and much as Tayte hated to admit it, he was starting to get to him. A technological whiz kid, Peter Schofield had jumped straight out of high school and onto the Internet with nothing more than his blonde, pearly toothed looks and a truckful of charisma, seemingly fuelled by the singular ambition of knocking Tayte off his top spot. He'd told Tayte as much at a recent genealogy convention.

'You're a forty-something who's had his day,' Schofield had said after the usual banter had fallen into decay. He was flaunting the latest copy of *Genealogy Today* magazine, with an annoyingly cocky portrait of the new wonder boy on the front cover.

'Yeah, right,' Tayte replied, feigning a smile. 'And that's thirty-nine.' He'd kept walking, past Schofield's stand, discouraging any further exchange.

'Oh, come on.' Schofield ran ahead and thrust the magazine in Tayte's face with both hands. 'This!' He poked aggressively at his own image, creasing it. 'This is what they want now, man!'

Tayte held out a hand, still walking. 'There's no substitute for experience in this game, kid,' he reminded Schofield. But all he got back was that grinning magazine cover, dancing arrogantly in his face, telling him he'd better watch out. He never could forget Schofield's parting jibe.

'Least I know who my own folks are!'

It was way below the belt and it hurt. After twenty-plus years of searching, all Tayte knew about his parents was that his mother had an English accent and that she'd abandoned him when he was just a few months old. She'd been good enough to leave him a photograph at least; he liked to think that she couldn't bear the idea of him growing up not knowing what she looked like. He'd kiss her image goodnight at the end of every day, and she'd watch over him from the bedside table as he slept. That's what he liked to think she had in mind, but who knows? He didn't even know his date of birth, not that birthdays ever meant much to him. They were a sore reminder that although he was adept at finding connections for other families, he wasn't good enough to find his own.

He shook his head to dispel the memories and collected his things from the table: pad, pen, the incomplete chart. *It's just a plane,* he told himself as he stuffed everything into a shabby leather briefcase that was as travel-worn as his suit. But he could already feel the sweat glands in his palms getting to work. He rose to leave, taking a last gulp of coffee and helping himself to a chocolate pastry to cheer himself up.

Chapter Three

The rushing sound coming from the circular vents above him told Jefferson Tayte that he was getting all the air American Airlines would allow. He twisted them again, just to be certain. Then he checked his seat belt, already knowing it was as tight as he could bear it. It was creasing his second linen suit of the day, this one a shade paler than the last.

A brief sleep in the passenger seat of his torch red 1955 Ford Thunderbird had barely refreshed him, but he was used to it. The car boasted 4.8 litres of V8 muscle with manual three-speed overdrive, but without headrests it wasn't meant for napping. He'd had the car since he started pulling pay checks, and even though it was on its third reconditioned engine, for all its faults he absolutely loved it. Running on whitewall tires with a white hardtop and enough chrome to shame a custom Harley, it looked a little ostentatious when he pulled up to see a client, but he didn't care. That car was his only family.

A suitcase nearly as shabby as his briefcase was testament to a lifestyle of stopovers at cheap motels, which had imposed a diet of fast food and a snacking habit that had contributed to his appearance over the years. Travelling prepared had at least saved him a trip back to DC to pick up a flight, and a few provisions from the shopping lounge at Boston's Logan International Airport had serviced any needs his suitcase couldn't provide for. He always carried a valid passport. He figured having it with him meant he could go anywhere in the world if he wanted to, even if he had no intention of using it.

Looking around the cabin he noticed it was half empty and wondered what the absent passengers knew that he didn't. Then the encounter he'd been trying to avoid since he first sat down happened. He caught the eyes that had been drilling into the side of his head from the window seat and the woman's voice suddenly burst the air, as though she'd been holding her breath all this time, waiting to get an introduction out.

'Hi, I'm *Julia*—Julia *Kapowski*.'

Her voice was nasal with a grating edge, and she hung on to her words as though afraid to let them go until she'd thought of something else to say. She was grinning childishly, like she was meeting someone famous and was their all-time greatest fan.

Tayte twitched in his seat, recoiling intuitively. Her accent was easy to place. *New York City*, he thought. *Queens—maybe Brooklyn.* A hand shot across the empty seat and the woman's face beamed with the widest smile Tayte had ever seen. He was thankful for the space between them. He shook the hand and offered an uncomfortable nod. 'JT,' he said.

The woman wriggled in her seat. 'J…T…' She repeated his initials slowly, as though buying herself time to work out what they stood for. 'Well…the *mysterious* kind!'

Mysterious? Tayte thought she'd never finish the word. *I really don't need this.* His lips tightened, saying nothing to provoke further conversation, but she was off.

'You know, you look a lot like my *last* husband.'

Tayte imagined she must have gone through a few. He just nodded politely.

'You *do*, it's almost spooky.' She turned to face him. 'He was a cuddly man,' she mused. 'Tall, too.' Her knees edged closer, straining beneath a dark trouser suit that was as sharp and raven as her hair. The body language told Tayte that he would not be allowed to face his fears quietly.

The woman continued to stare at him. 'You have *nice* eyes.' She sounded very sincere.

Tayte felt trapped.

'Did you know you had nice eyes? I bet you didn't.'

Nothing about Tayte felt nice.

'I bet you're a *kind* man. Kind men usually have nice eyes. Well, that's my experience.'

She went quiet. Tayte could feel her studying him again.

'They're a nice shade,' she said. 'A girl could *drown* in there!' She giggled, then at last she turned away and pulled a magazine from the holder in the back of the seat. 'My *dog* has brown eyes too,' she added. 'Not so nice as *yours*, though.'

Tayte was thankful for that at least. He didn't know if she was coming on to him or just liked to talk. He figured it was the latter and weakly smiled. Then he closed his eyes, fixed a song from *Les Misérables* in his head, and pretended to sleep.

This would be Tayte's second flight ever; the first was twenty-five years ago and he remembered it like it was just last week. He was four-teen, taking a flight to Vermont from Washington National Airport, as it was known before it was dedicated to Ronald Reagan in 1998. It had been a promising winter vacation, but it was ruined by the sicken-ing worry of the return flight home. Everyone on the plane had said how lucky they were, and that the storm hadn't really been that bad. Planes are designed to deal with lightning strikes. He'd looked up the statistics and discovered that every commercial plane in the States is struck, on average, just over once a year. He also knew that the last time a plane had crashed because of a lightning strike was back in 1967, when it hit the plane's fuel tank. But none of that put him any more at ease. He remembered reading that you are many times more likely to be struck by lightning than you are to be in a plane crash—all he knew was that he'd very nearly experienced both events together.

The passenger safety announcements came and went. The video screen in the headrest in front of him was blank again, reflecting unruly black hair that needed a cut and a comb, and a tired, sagging face in need of sleep. He knew he should have paid closer attention to the announcements, but they made him think of all the negative situations that could occur. He pictured himself fumbling beneath his seat for the lifejacket and wearing the oxygen mask that would drop from the hatch beside his air nozzle as the plane plunged and they lost cabin pressure. That led to an image of him sliding down the inflatable escape chute, arms crossed on his chest as he sank into a freezing sea. *Yeah,* he thought. *A great help.*

He looked out the window beyond Julia Kapowski, who was thankfully buried in the duty-free pages of the inflight magazine. There were a few clouds, but the sky was otherwise clear. He almost began to relax in spite of his thoughts and memories, but then he heard the jet engines pick up, and he continued to squeeze the armrests.

A voice over the intercom said, 'This is your captain speaking.' Tayte tried to switch off—shut himself down until it was all over. He only heard snippets as the voice continued: 'Taxiing…runway… cleared for takeoff.' Already far too much information.

The plane jolted as it began to move, and Jefferson Tayte's toes curled. He took some comfort from the odd bump or two as the plane's wheels caught the ridges in the asphalt, letting him know he was still connected to terra firma. Then the plane stopped and he knew they were at the end of the runway. A lump came to his dry throat as he waited. He thought he would have forgotten the little details, but he could already feel the impending rush of speed and the effect it would have on his body as powerful unseen hands pushed him back into his seat and held him there. Then it came, and if he'd had any loose muscle left in his body to clench, he would have.

'Whooosshh!' Julia Kapowski slapped her magazine onto her lap and jumped in her seat.

Tayte jumped with her.

'Don't you just *love* the takeoff?'

If only she knew.

Ten seconds later and that part at least was over. When Tayte opened his eyes again, the plane was safely in the air and climbing—although *safe* was the exact antonym for how Tayte felt. If he had the stomach to look out the window again, he would have seen the Boston Harbor Islands diminishing below, but his butterflies began to fight one another now, turning his stomach into a boxing ring. Then the engine note changed. The raging violence of exploding gases out on the wings, courtesy of Pratt & Whitney, settled down and a *bong!* sounded around the cabin as the seat-belt light went out. None of which gave him any further comfort.

He checked his watch—a cheap digital affair with glowing red digits that he'd had since the '80s and was still fond of, in a retro kind of way. It read 11:40, and he couldn't believe they'd only been up ten minutes. A quick calculation told him that it would be 22:30 UK time when they arrived. Tayte couldn't stop himself from rephrasing the sentence with the word *if* instead of *when*. He needed something else to think about.

He reached into his jacket and pulled out his travel documents, looking for the onward train journey details. He picked out the highlights: London, Paddington to Truro. The departure time was 23:45. That gave him more than an hour to clear the airport and get to the train—an overnight sleeper that would reach Cornwall approximately seven hours later.

As he put the tickets away and the plane began to level, he recalled how close he'd come to jacking it in, even as he stood there at the departure gate, ticket shaking in his hand. He always had backed out when the f-word came up—always found some excuse why he couldn't *fly* here or *fly* there. But not this time. Despite his client's insistence, he wasn't into this game just so some rich entrepreneur's wife could have a nice birthday present. This assignment was all about finding a family that someone did not want to be found, and that made the whole thing far more personal than Walter Sloane could know.

If you can't find this *family,* he told himself, *how the hell do you expect to be good enough to find your own?*

Tayte settled back and began to think about James Fairborne and his family again, wondering what they were like, piecing their lives together from the records he'd found. He compared journeys: a couple of months being blown about in a wooden tub, guided by the stars at the mercy of the Atlantic Ocean, versus seven hours in a relatively comfortable seat surrounded by the best technology modern science could provide. The plane was steady now. He had no idea how high they were and he cared even less. It was just like riding a Greyhound bus, cruising on some smooth interstate. He felt pathetic as tiredness caught up with him and he began to drift.

Chapter Four

Named in honour of the woman credited with having made the first flag of the American Union, the *Betsy Ross* was a 110-ton brig, bluff-bowed with a flat transom stern and both masts square rigged for speed. She carried cargo primarily, trading in anything saleable along the busy coastal waters of the Eastern Seaboard between Boston and the Indies to the south. In August 1783, however, she had a very different itinerary.

Sitting in the dock at Boston harbour, some seventy feet in length, she appeared to Katherine Fairborne as a ramshackle of heavy cordage and patched sailcloth, which did not instil confidence. Yet Katherine understood the importance of the day well enough. She had watched her father closely in the weeks that had built towards this cool yet fine morning, filling her journal with reflections of excitement and anxiety in equal measure. Now she wished nothing more than to get underway so that she might continue to record their adventure.

Katherine was sixteen and the eldest of three children. She was draped in a dull and heavy woollen cloak that concealed all but her face and its frame of golden ringlets. So as not to miss anything of the scene she would later paint with her words, she had positioned herself strategically at the quayside. Her father was to one side of her with her brother, little George, who was just five, and her mother was to the other side with her sister, Laura, who was twelve. Her aunt and uncle were also with her mother, and all Katherine could hear from that direction was the wag of Aunt Clara's tireless tongue.

Little George, whose head barely reached the belt buckle of his father's breeches, was so slight a child that it was difficult to believe he was there at all. The illusion was aided somewhat because he was the image of his father, dressed in a shorter cut of the same dark brown greatcoat. George was watching the cargo being carried onto the *Betsy Ross,* arms crossed and standing perfectly still, mimicking his father. Katherine thought his expression was far too serious for his years.

'What are they putting onto the boat, Father?' George said. He looked up for the answer, blinking against the glare of the sunrise and the intense effect it had on the sea.

James Fairborne continued to study the activity before them. A ramp stretched up from the quayside to the deck of the *Betsy Ross,* along which a seemingly endless line of men carried an assortment of crates and barrels.

'Seed, I believe—flax,' he offered. 'They use the plant fibres to make linen.'

'How long will it take to get there?'

James turned his head to the sea. 'There's a big ocean between here and England,' he mused, gazing out past the northern edge of Spectacle Island, which appeared in relief against the early sun. He gazed far out, beyond the shelter of the harbour entrance between Deer Island and Long Island Point, where it opened into Massachusetts Bay. Beyond that, like a promise, the Atlantic waited.

James answered slowly, perhaps in awe of the journey ahead. His expression was flat and distant. 'Over three thousand miles to England.' He squatted, giving George a smile and his full attention. His tone lifted. 'The master supposes we'll make about sixty miles a day. Can you work it out?'

Katherine smiled as she watched George act out his notion of a man in great thought. His eyes narrowed to a squint as they fixed

DUAL

Haya,
Nice to finally
meet you.
Kate Tharp

on a faraway space, high in the rapidly lightening sky. But it seemed that George could not work it out, so he continued to pull faces until his serious expression at last betrayed him. Then he grinned at his father, who laughed heartily and ruffled the lad's hair.

'It will take seven or eight weeks,' James said. 'If the weather is with us and God permits it.'

Katherine had been too distracted to notice her uncle until he entered the scene. He was a barrel of a man, adorned with enough lace to drown himself. He needed no greatcoat to combat the morning chill.

'James, I must speak with you,' he said. His voice was low and gruff, as befitted his portly appearance, and his jowls quivered as he spoke. 'I have concerns, James.'

Katherine watched her father's expression sour.

'It's this boat,' her uncle continued. 'Is it big enough for such a voyage? Is it *strong* enough? That is to say, is she capable?' He motioned in the direction from which he'd come, and his eyes settled on his wife's cradled belly. 'To own the truth, I'm concerned for the child.'

'Jacob, do not distress yourself,' James said. 'I am assured she is a craft worthy of the passage and it will not be her first Atlantic crossing. She has a good crew.'

'Yes, but only fifteen in all. Is it enough for such an undertaking?'

'She carries a carpenter *and* a sailmaker.'

Jacob Daniels nodded his approval.

'We should count ourselves fortunate,' James said. 'We have the means to charter such a fine vessel where others do not. And to have found her already converted to take us.' He put a hand on Jacob's shoulder. 'Return to my sister and comfort her. Clara will be in need of your support.'

Katherine's eyes followed her uncle's return, catching her mother's eye as she waved discreetly back to avoid disturbing the flow of the one-sided conversation Clara was having with her.

'I'm just not comfortable with it,' Clara continued. 'I like to know where my things are. I like them where I can see them, and that's not on the other side of the world.'

Eleanor continued to nod, smiling politely. A moment later she said, 'Do excuse me.' She raised her petticoats and followed her gaze towards her husband, passing Jacob midway as he tipped his head and touched the emerald brim of his beaver-felt tricorne.

With Eleanor gone, Clara turned to Laura to continue her monologue, but Laura too had left her.

'Well, I don't know. I'm sure I don't,' Clara said.

Little George had seen the gathering break. He rushed past Katherine, heading straight for Laura, and Katherine knew that his toothy smile and bright eyes spelled trouble.

Eleanor drew close to James as she arrived beside him, sinking her cheek into the soft ruffles of his cravat. 'Tell me again that this is all for the best,' she said. 'Tell me that our lives will be just as they were.'

'They will be better!' James held her shoulders, easing her away, yet keeping her close. 'You pay too much attention to the worries of my sister and her husband.' He searched her eyes briefly, moving in again when he seemed to find that place he was looking for. His tone softened. 'We must remain loyal to our sovereign, God bless him and keep him safe. There is nothing here for us now save our own persecution.'

'But so far away?' Eleanor said.

James brushed her cheek and kissed her forehead. 'Do not trouble yourself,' he added. 'All is set. Everything we have of value is safely arrived in England, where it awaits us. We go to a magnificent estate there, too, and a familiar business to continue. We can thrive in England, Eleanor! These are exciting times.' He let her go and began to pace the quayside, frothing with enthusiasm. 'Instead of copper, we'll mine tin. There are no richer deposits to be found anywhere in the civilised world than in Cornwall.'

Two blurs arrived between them, circling in a figure of eight before dashing off again.

'Give it back,' Laura yelled, snatching at a bright yellow ribbon that danced tantalisingly out of reach.

James shook his head, though his expression was as playful as the scene. His eyes lifted towards Katherine then, drawing her into the proceedings that she had previously felt distanced from, like a biographer writing about the lives of others.

'I think you had better round up your siblings and teach them a little decorum,' he said.

A stranger approached, though his apparel stated his business. 'Captain Grainger's about ready for you, sir,' he said.

No one on the quay watched them leave, and Katherine Fairborne was in no doubt that few cared they were going as the brig heaved and creaked through the calm of the early morning tide towards the sunrise. Yet she continued to stand with her family on the deck of the *Betsy Ross,* looking back at Boston harbour's quiet quayside, reflecting, as she supposed everyone was, on the lives they were leaving behind. Above her, sheets of sailcloth calmed momentarily, limp and flapping, then all snapped full, drawing the breeze, ushering them headlong into an uncertain destiny.

Katherine could barely control her desire to rush off and find her writing box, but she waited, and in doing so she saw a change in little George that disquieted her. He looked close to tears, pale of complexion and rigid as the portside rail he clung to. He was tight lipped as though imprisoning his emotions; she could see that the thrill of the adventure had deserted him. Now it seemed that fear had replaced it, watching like mischief beside him, sharing dark thoughts and painting darker pictures that were perhaps very different from their father's ideals.

George snatched at his father's hand, edging closer until there was no space left between them. 'I don't think I want to go, Father.'

James Fairborne tightened the bond between them. 'Be strong, lad,' he said. 'Be strong.'

As they cleared the harbour entrance, turning hard to starboard into the Black Rock Channel and the open sea, Katherine at last broke away, climbing the steps to the upper deck and descending through the hatch into the great cabin where her writing box and journal waited.

Journal of Katherine Fairborne.
Thursday, August 21st 1783.
The day has finally arrived and we are at sea with several weeks ahead of us and the promise of little else to do but watch the ocean and listen to it break against the boat. Father is being positive, but I sense he is uneasy about the crossing and our new lives in England. I will miss my friends and will write to them all as soon as we land—no doubt with exciting tales of adventure that will make them all pitifully jealous.

Everyone is being sick apart from Father and I—I do hope poor George will soon acclimatise and recover his usual temperament, not least because the matter affords the crew a degree of merriment that upsets Mother. I am sure, however, that they will all soon settle down to their duties as the demands of the voyage dictate.

Of the crew, I have noticed one in particular. As he guides our course in the weeks to come, I know he and I shall become good friends. I have already caught his eye and I must confess to enjoying his attentions.

Chapter Five

Somewhere over the Atlantic, American Airlines Flight AA156 from Boston, Massachusetts, to London's Heathrow Airport began to judder. *Bong!* The seat-belt lights lit up around the cabin, by which time Jefferson Tayte's strap was already tight. The comfortable innocence afforded him by the state of half-sleep he'd been in for the last couple of hours was over. Another judder shook his seat, reaffirming his now lucid state. He peered down the aisle to see a leggy stewardess buckling up and knew this was going to be bad.

Julia Kapowski must have seen Tayte startle back to life. 'Turbulence!' she said. 'It's just turbulence.' Her eyes lit up, and as though sensing his anxiety, she said, 'Here, sweetie, let me hold your hand.'

Tayte reacted just in time, crossing his arms like a sulking schoolboy as she moved in. 'Thanks. I'm okay.'

'*Hey!* Suit yourself.' Kapowski settled back in her seat and looked out the window.

Silence descended between them like an uncomfortable two minutes on Remembrance Day. When it was up, Tayte offered an apology.

'Sorry,' he said. 'But I'm okay. Really.' He knew she meant well.

Kapowski's smile returned. 'Don't like to *fly*, eh? My first husband didn't like planes either. Said they scared the *shit* outta him!' She put a hand to her mouth. 'Excuse me. That was just his way.'

The captain's familiar voice gave the usual greeting and then proceeded to confirm that they were indeed experiencing turbulence. By the time the announcement had finished, Tayte had heard the word more times than he cared to, and if he didn't already know that turbulence was 'a state of flow in which the instantaneous velocities exhibit irregular and apparently random fluctuations'—he did now.

Who is this guy?

He figured the captain's idea was that if you knew what you were experiencing and knew what caused it, then it wouldn't scare you. But the logic was flawed to Tayte's mind. He knew *exactly* how Dirty Harry Callahan's .44 Magnum worked, but he'd still need a change of underwear if it was pointed at his head. When the lesson finished, the captain signed off with that well-oiled phrase, 'There's really nothing to worry about…'

Yeah, right. Tayte could picture the cheesy grin on the pilot's face as he said it.

Another violent jolt saw Tayte's fingernails stabbing back into his armrests, preceding the sweat beads that broke across his brow as the plane suddenly dropped. He felt lighter, then heavy again as it levelled out. His stomach churned. He still couldn't believe he'd passed on lunch, however dire the offerings placed in front of Kapowski had looked, but he was glad now that he had.

It was all going so well.

At one point he'd even come close to real sleep, drifting to the rhythm of the riddles he had no answers to, convincing himself over and over that he had the right James Fairborne despite the obvious incongruities. His research had been meticulous. He was confident of his findings no matter what further issues they raised, and now, of all those concerns, there was one dominating question that stood on the shoulders of the rest and kept waving at him: who is Susan Fairborne?

He knew as much as records allowed, but he expected them to show James Fairborne and his wife, Eleanor, with their children,

Katherine, Laura, and George. Instead, he'd found James and his wife, *Susan,* and two completely different children: Allun and Lowenna. The copy of the transcript in his briefcase was very clear. James's marriage to Susan Forbes on Saturday, March 12, 1785, was unquestionable. *So what had happened to the rest of the family? Why were there no records? Why was James the only Fairborne who had left a paper trail in England?*

Tayte knew well enough that records are sometimes lost or filed incorrectly. Names were frequently misspelled, either because they were written in some difficult-to-read, idiosyncratic style, or simply because the scribe recorded the information badly. Any combination of such errors made finding records more difficult; sometimes people were genuinely untraceable. But so many without a trace? Only one person out of seven in a family with records intact? It was too much for Tayte to write off as coincidence.

Something else had started to puzzle him too, but he could no longer think straight. The plane was perceptibly banging now, as well as moving in all dimensions. Tayte couldn't remember the last time he'd had any religious inclinations, but he suddenly found himself thinking, *Dear God, get me through this!* He pictured his Ford Thunderbird, all alone in some strange parking lot, and wondered whether he would ever see it again.

It was some time later when Tayte became aware that something else was annoying him—something he couldn't quite put his finger on. It felt like an injection stabbing into his right arm, just below the shoulder, only the injection kept coming and the applied force grew until he felt himself rocking from side to side under the weight of the heavy needle that just kept jabbing and jabbing into his arm.

No records… The injections became painful. *What happened to them?* He began to feel desolate. *Eleanor? The children?* A cloudburst of despair washed over him and he sensed the answer was not good. The injection came again, but he no longer cared. He began to sob at the sheer hopelessness. Then over the sobbing he heard another voice. *The nurse?*

'Hey!' The voice was familiar.

The needle jabbed into his arm again only now it felt more like a knife. His arm went numb, squeezing and pumping, like the nurse was checking his blood pressure.

'JT…Hey!'

The despair left him as suddenly as it arrived. He shocked back into his seat to a rush of air vents and the muddled chaos of people standing all around him, struggling over each other to get their bags from the overhead compartments.

'I thought we'd *lost* you.' Kapowski was perky in her seat, a sharp fingernail still poised to give him another jab. 'You slept like a baby for the last two hours. 'We're *there* already!'

'Where?' He was still dazed from the heavy sleep that had finally caught up with him.

'Heathrow, dummy! You missed the best bit.'

'Best bit?'

'The *landing!*'

Tayte let out a sigh and rubbed his eyes. 'Sorry. I was dreaming.'

'Oh! Anyone special?'

'No. No one special.' He stumbled over the words. 'Well, maybe,' he added, feeling the need to correct himself. 'It's—well, it's something I'm working on.' He stood up, eager now to get off the plane. 'It's a little complicated.'

'Oh, don't mind me. I'm not the prying kind.'

The passengers were clearing. Tayte reached into the compartment above their seats and pulled out a familiar briefcase that he hoped had enjoyed the trip more than he had. 'Can I get your bag?' he asked.

'I'd like that, I really would,' Kapowski said. 'But I travel light.' She reached into her jacket pocket and pulled out a card. 'Look me up if you need anything,' she added, winking as she handed it to him. 'I'm in town the rest of the week.'

Tayte knew he wouldn't use it, but he took the card anyway. 'Thanks,' he said, slipping it beneath the flap of his jacket pocket without giving it a glance.

The aisle had cleared. They were the last few on the plane. 'Well, nice meeting you,' Tayte offered. Then he went for the exit, still half asleep and scarcely able to believe the flight was over and he was still alive.

Outside, the taxi rank droned with the chatter of diesel engines. It was raining and cool, and the air under the canopy shelter was heavy with the smell of exhaust fumes. Tayte made his way towards the black cab at the front of the queue, opened the passenger door, and followed his bags in.

'Pad-ding-ton Station,' he said, forcing a neutral accent that sounded a little too phonetically correct.

The cabby looked mildly confused. 'Paddington?'

'That's right—Paddington.'

'You do know there's a rail link that'll get you there in half the time for about a third of the price?'

'No, I didn't. Good of you to say, but I'm here now.'

'Okay, mate. It's your money.'

The cabby turned back to the wheel and pressed a few buttons on the meter.

Tayte checked his watch. 'I have a connection to make at a quarter to midnight.'

'No problem, pal. It'll be quiet once we clear the airport.'

Tayte settled back and stretched out his legs, still tense from the flight. Beyond his own reflection in the glass window, which now told him he was in need of a shave as well as a haircut, it was too dark to see anything much: other cars, grey buildings, an outline of trees that were no more than damp shadows beyond the street lights. As he sat listening to the clickety-hum of the engine and the rush of tire rubber against the road surface, he reflected again on what else had started to puzzle him.

He considered the facts. James Fairborne had remarried. The question was why? And just over a year after arriving in England? Divorce seemed unlikely, though not impossible. But why would Eleanor have gone in the first place if things were already rocky between them? Then there was the question of the lack of records for Eleanor and the children, and for James's sister, Clara, and her husband, Jacob Daniels. No death records, no further marriage record, and nothing at all in the IGI—the International Genealogical Index, otherwise now known as Family Search. According to recorded history, they had all simply vanished.

He felt certain the *Betsy Ross* had made it to England. James Fairborne's arrival was proof enough of that, and there was nothing in the Lloyd's Register of Shipping to suggest the *Betsy Ross* hadn't completed the voyage. But it concerned him that there was no information about the brig at Falmouth; nothing in the Ship Index to register her arrival. All he knew for sure was that she sailed from Boston in August 1783 and that James Fairborne had been buried in the parish of Mawnan in Cornwall, England, in 1829, having lived there for forty-six years and to an above-average age of eighty-one.

Tayte even considered death at sea, against the odds that everyone in the family apart from James had died due to some illness or accident, and knowing that only half such deaths were ever reported in the first place. But that route came to a quick end when he discovered that records of births, marriages, and deaths at sea only existed for a few British ports before 1800, and Falmouth was not one of them.

The further back in time you went, the less information there was. But to find no records for any of them was too much coincidence for Tayte, who was beginning to suspect that someone had been playing with the past and had done a very good job of hiding these people. *But why?* The sense of despair from his earlier dream on the plane told him that no good had come to Eleanor and her children. For now, it was the only thing he could think of to account for James remarrying.

'Never been to America myself,' the cabby said, breaking into Tayte's thoughts. 'Where 'bouts you from?'

'Washington, DC, home of the Redskins.'

'Oh, I know.' There was a pause. 'What's the DC bit stand for?'

'District of Columbia. It's between Richmond and Baltimore.'

The cabby's head was shaking before the sentence was out. 'Nah, sorry.'

'Two hundred miles southwest of New York?' Tayte offered, figuring everyone knew where that was.

'Oh, New York, New York. Yeah, 'course I heard of that…so good they named it twice!'

'That's the one.' Tayte was stupefied.

They stopped at a roundabout and Tayte thought he heard a chuckle over the clicking indicator relay. Then they were off again, cutting out in front of a white van. The cab's rear window immediately began to glow with the flash of headlights as distant obscenities split the night.

The cabby shook his head as the van sped past. 'Can't remember who sang it though,' he said, dismissing the near accident. He caught Tayte's eyes in the rearview mirror. 'The New York song?'

Tayte nodded back. 'Right.' His tone was one of agreement, feigning distraction. He wasn't going any further down that road. Then what started as a low, semi-tuneful hum beyond the screen in front of him quickly built into the worst rendition of Gerard Kenny's 1978 disco hit, *New York, New York,* that Tayte had ever heard. He couldn't believe the cabby was actually singing.

Nice to see a man happy at his work, he thought as he settled back. He smiled to himself and hoped the entertainment wasn't extra.

Chapter Six

On the A389 in Cornwall, heading southwest away from Bodmin on the western edge of Bodmin Moor, a beat-up, electric blue Mazda 323 hatchback sped through the darkness, main beam pumping light out into the void. It was late. There was no other traffic around, and the last road sign the driver had passed told him that Truro was twenty miles away. Another thirty miles and he'd be back in Helford—safe.

The driver slapped the steering wheel to the bass line of a punchy tune that was playing too loud on the cheap car stereo. He sat forward in his seat, still high, energised by the evening's activities. A sizeable grin split his face.

'I can't believe it!' he shouted, hard against the music. 'I can't believe I fucking did it!'

He looked down at the Tesco bag in the passenger seat footwell, knowing what was inside. He wanted to touch his ill-gotten prizes again, to prove they were real and that he really had pulled it off. Bodmin was behind him now, but he was still back there in the moment, savouring the buzz of the snatch. It had been far easier than he'd expected. Now, at last, it felt like things were finally coming together.

By the time the driver arrived at his intended destination, the night had deepened to its darkest reaches. A small rowboat had been necessary for the last leg of his clandestine journey, and now, as he sat grinning at his star prize, he was still buzzing from the thrill of his night's work. His eyes narrowed and sharpened on a silver crucifix that dangled from his left hand, swinging gently in harsh torchlight, suspended from a thick leather cord that was almost brittle with age. The light from the torch bounced off the crucifix, casting bright crosses against dark and angular walls. In his right hand was a tan leather-bound book, cracked and faded.

He knew the museum would miss them in the morning—of course they would. But what did that matter to him? No one would be able to connect him to the theft. No one yet knew what he knew.

'Not like it's stealing, really,' he said to himself.

It had taken time to gather the truth, piece by piece. It had taken a long time. His elation soured. It was a sudden change, like a resting alligator snapping without warning at a meal that had strayed too close.

'It's taking too much time!' he shouted. His words echoed around him, and then just as suddenly he was calm again.

A gratifying thought occurred to him, twisting his mouth. His gaze dropped to the ground as he tried to focus on a sandy spot just beyond his sprawled out legs. 'How can you steal something that's rightfully yours?' he asked. It wasn't everything he felt belonged to him, but it was a start.

He needed more.

'*You* know what I'm looking for,' he said, directly addressing that spot on the ground, like he was talking to some imaginary friend. He dropped the little book into a side pocket of his three-quarter-length black leather jacket and sighed. A half-empty ale bottle rested beside him. He took another slug, draining it back. He gazed at the familiar label: *Cornish Knocker,* a favourite that served him well on occasions like this.

'They have to pay!' he shouted, coiling as he launched the spent ale bottle into the darkness beyond the soft glow of his torch. The bottle smashed against jagged rock and the pieces fell, tinkling amongst the remnants of previous visits. The sound cut the still air, echoing against cold hard surfaces, shrill and piercing.

He stirred the air with the leather cord, and the silver crucifix spun low circles over the ground. 'Call it an anniversary present too, if you like!'

Damp sand shifted beneath his feet as he made his way towards a narrow slit of moonlight at the mouth of the cave, a beacon amidst dark rock barely wide enough to fit through. He followed the torch beam to a foaming edge of lapping water, then went through to the rowboat that awaited him on the other side.

Chapter Seven

Wednesday.

Tayte paid the cab driver who had brought him from the train station in Truro and wondered if he'd arrived at the right address. As the car pulled away, disturbing the bright morning, he found himself at the end of a short driveway looking through a cloud of roadside dust. Beyond was a double-fronted Georgian house that he figured must be on the outskirts of the village he'd just come through—Mawnan Smith. That was a mile back, and there were now very few other buildings around. Even the road had narrowed until, to Tayte, who was more used to the wide multilane freeways back home, it resembled little more than a track. A sign stuck out towards the road at the end of the driveway that read St Maunanus House—Bed & Breakfast, refuting his doubts.

Tayte had no idea what he was in for. His hurried brief to the woman at the Cornwall Tourist Board before he left Boston was for simple accommodation for five nights, as close to Mawnan as he could get. He started along the driveway, crunching loose gravel underfoot, and then stopped himself. It seemed a little early. Curtains were still drawn behind white sash windows in some of the upstairs rooms. He checked his watch. The digital display read 08:11, and he was glad he'd taken the time to freshen up at the station and get some breakfast, or it would have been even earlier.

He looked beyond a glistening lawn of dewy, well-kept grass, through pots of pink and white geraniums and large tubs containing palm trees. *Palm trees?* Not something he considered synonymous with England, but they were definitely palms. The view led his eyes through a jungle of colourful abstract precision to the front door, which had panels of stained glass tulips in the top half, glowing in the early sunlight.

Nice, he thought. *Peaceful.* But why did he feel so intimidated? *Too peaceful.* He began to wish he'd been more specific with the Tourist Board; wished he'd asked for a hotel—something less personal. He turned away, having decided to take a stroll and come back at a more sociable hour. Then a bell jangled and the door behind him opened.

A cheery voice sang to him. 'Hello!'

He turned back to see a woman standing in the doorway. She looked to be in her early fifties, slim, with blonde hair styled high off her forehead. She wore beige jeans and a sage-green sweatshirt beneath an apron on which she was hurriedly wiping her hands.

'Saw you on the drive there,' she said. 'I wasn't expecting you so early. You must be my American.'

Tayte wondered if his appearance was really that transparent. He eyed his comfy beige loafers and the white shirt that was pushing out through the jacket of his travel-creased suit and realised it probably was. He reached the door and the woman stepped back into the porch, inviting him through.

'Good morning,' Tayte offered, stepping inside. 'I was about to take a walk down the lane. It seemed a little early.'

'Oh, that's okay. People turn up at all sorts of times. Expect the unexpected, that's what I say. Mr Tayte, isn't it?' She led Tayte through into the hallway. 'You're my third American this month and it's barely started,' she added. 'Always busy early September. Especially when the weather's nice like this. Drops off in a week or two, though.'

If Tayte hadn't already eaten, the aroma that confronted him as he walked through into the hallway would have been too much to bear: bacon, eggs, sausage, and mushrooms. He passed an open doorway and saw a middle-aged couple sitting at a large table tucking into their breakfast. Their tanned skin was testament to the fine weather. Another two places were set, but as yet empty.

'Good morning,' the two at the table said together.

'Morning,' Tayte replied, offering a polite smile.

'That's John and Barbara,' his host said. She lowered her voice to a whisper, which grew louder again by the time she'd finished speaking. 'Lovely couple. Two of my regulars. Always come this time every year.'

They passed another doorway on the left and his stomach audibly groaned as he peered into the command centre and caught the bacon smell full on.

'Your room won't be ready for a few hours yet, I'm afraid,' the woman continued. 'But you can leave your things. You don't want to be lugging those about.'

She stopped at the foot of a full-turn stairway of stripped and waxed pine. 'Where are my manners—I'm Judith, by the way. You can drop your bags just there.' She indicated a space beside the stairs where a few coats were hanging. 'I'd say you could leave them in your room, only the couple that have it haven't left yet.'

'That's fine.' Tayte put his bags down. 'I don't want to keep you from your guests. How about I come back around midday?'

'Midday would be super. Just give the bell a good pull and I'll be there.'

'Thanks.'

They made their way back to the front door and Tayte gave a nod and another smile to the guests in the breakfast room as he passed. Ahead, the porch was lit with colour from the stained glass in the door and higher up in the frieze on the windows.

'There *was* just one thing,' Tayte said, one foot into the porch. 'Which way is the church?'

'Well that depends. There's St Michael's up in the village, and there's a Methodist church near that. Then the other way there's the parish church *and* a Catholic church. We're well catered for spiritually.'

Four churches. Tayte wasn't sure where to begin. 'Which is the oldest?'

'That would be the parish church of St Mawnan.' She turned to a narrow table by the front door and picked up a pile of pamphlets. She riffled through them and pulled one out. 'Here you are, take this,' she said. 'It's a walking guide of the area. Save you getting lost. Oh, and this is a good one. *Cornish Smugglers.* It'll tell you all about our shady past.'

'Thanks.' Tayte smiled and slipped the pamphlets into his jacket.

Judith stood in the porch and pointed down the driveway. 'Turn right as you leave the drive—a left takes you up to Mawnan Smith, that's the main village—then just follow the road. You can't miss it.'

'So this *is* Mawnan?'

'Yes, that's right. It's a hamlet, really. We're part way between the two, I suppose. Neither here, nor there. It's all Mawnan as far as the postman's concerned.'

'Is it far to the parish church?'

'No, only about ten minutes. If you want to go a bit further, there's a lovely walk down to Helford Passage. Just pick up the coast path. It's well sign-posted. That should take you about forty minutes from the church.'

Tayte held on to the smile he'd been wearing a little too long. 'Well, thanks again,' he said.

Beyond the drive, to the right as directed, the road continued straight for a few hundred metres until it became lost to a copse of trees. The sun was already warm on Tayte's face as he made his way there, observed from a distance by several horses on the other side of a post-and-rail fence. To the other side, cows grazed nonchalantly in a field behind a Cornish hedge of rock and earth, hidden beneath a barrier of lichen and the subtly fading late summer purples of leggy foxgloves and wild scabious, glistening with dewy gossamer in the morning sun. It could still have been midsummer; there was no sign yet of autumn's onset.

As he arrived at the copse, beneath the shade of its tangled tree-tops, Tayte began to wonder what he might find at the church. Would there be a headstone in the graveyard for each of the missing death records? One each for Eleanor and her children, another for Clara and Jacob Daniels? The recurring question began to circle in his mind again. Round and round it went, like a starving buzzard looking for an elusive prey.

Why can't I trace them? Why are there only records for James?

In January 1784, not six months after the *Betsy Ross* had sailed for England, James Fairborne was alone. His great estate on the exposed Cornish headland, where Falmouth Bay meets the Helford River, had become his desolate tomb. He had not left the house all winter, serviced in those months by a single manservant. All other staff had been dismissed immediately upon his taking up residence.

The Elizabethan manor house was a dark place. It was seldom lit at any time save for a single fire by which James Fairborne sat every day and well into the night, brooding. Occasionally the flicker of his manservant's candle could be seen pacing the long gallery as he went about his limited duties, the light from the candle scarcely distinguishing the shrouded furnishings and ornaments. Less often, a candle glowed for James Fairborne when he retired for the night, but only when he went to bed at all.

James Fairborne would continue to sit alone in his own personal darkness, constantly troubled by what lived there. Such plans had been laid. Now he could do nothing but wait. The more time passed, the easier it would become. He knew that was the way of such things. A few more months, perhaps. That would surely be long enough. Then the cloud would lift and light and life would once again fill Rosemullion Hall. And for James Fairborne, life's journey would begin again.

Chapter Eight

Mawnan parish church was built in 1231. Dedicated to Saint Maunanus, a sixth-century Celtic saint after whom the village of Mawnan was thought to be named, the church stood one hundred metres from the coastal footpath to the south of Falmouth. Tayte looked up at the church tower, sitting high above the mouth of the Helford River, and then turned his attention to the lych-gate ahead, peering along a shingle pathway that led to a blue church door. The gate itself was supported on either side by two deep stone walls that carried a tiled roof over a granite coffin rest in the centre. He looked up and read the words painted over the gate: *Da thymi nesse the Dhu.* Then a gentle voice spoke to him from within.

'It is good for me to draw nigh unto God.'

Tayte startled and peered into the shadows, to the stone benches that were shaped from the walls beneath the lych roof. 'Excuse me?' he said.

A slight, fair-haired man rose from the shadows. He was dressed in black trousers and a navy blue fleece jacket. The white of his dog-collar immediately gave his calling away. He looked older than Tayte suspected he was. His hair had receded and was thinning, but his face still held a youthful freshness.

'The inscription you were reading,' the man said. 'Cornish… from *The Life of Meryasek.* It means 'it is good for me to draw nigh unto God.'

'Oh, I see. Thanks.' Tayte feigned a painful clutch at his chest and smiled. 'You set my ticker running there.'

'My apologies,' the man said. 'I'm Reverend Jolliffe. There are no services today, but you're welcome to look around.'

Tayte extended a hand. 'Jefferson Tayte.'

The reverend's hand was small in Tayte's. His skin felt cold and dry. He opened the gate and Tayte went through.

'I expect you get this all the time,' Tayte said. 'But I'm looking for some graves.'

'We have many graves, Mr Tayte.' The reverend waved a slow hand to either side of him as they walked. Headstones scattered the lawns. 'There are many more beyond the south wall.'

'Graves from the late eighteenth century,' Tayte added. 'Early nineteenth, maybe.'

'An old family member?'

'Sort of. It's what I do—for other people.'

'A family historian? We have many enquiries.'

The reverend stopped walking and Tayte could see by his semi-perplexed expression that he had something to ask.

'Tell me, Mr Tayte,' Jolliffe said. 'Visitors often ask me about such things, but I'm afraid I'm shamefully close to useless when it comes to your profession. How does it all work? I mean, how do you manage to connect everyone together?'

The question was one that Tayte had grown accustomed to answering. 'It's really not all that complicated,' he said. 'Documents like birth, marriage, and death certificates hold more information than most people think. Take a subject's birth certificate. From that, as I'm sure you know, you can find the names of someone's parents, the mother's maiden name, the father's occupation, and address. In its simplest form, you just repeat the process for each parent, going back through time.'

'I'm sure it's not as straightforward as all that,' Jolliffe said.

'Well, perhaps not, but that's the idea. It gets a whole lot trickier the further back you go, and much of it's about confirming your data, but there are all kinds of indexes to help point you in the right direction. Deciphering old texts can be a challenge too, but you get used to it.'

'You must have a third eye,' Jolliffe said.

Tayte smiled to himself. 'I guess. A degree in palaeography helps too.'

'I should tell you that we keep no parish records here before 1900,' the reverend said. 'The older records are stored at the record office in Truro now. Have been for some time as I remember. But of course, you would already know that.'

Tayte recalled numerous telephone conversations with a girl called Penny Wilson at the Cornwall Record Office, bringing to mind her soft tones. He wished the records *were* there.

They approached the blue door that led into the main body of the church. Ornamental hinges covered the door in wide fans of swirling black ironwork, like sculpted leaves. Tayte's eyes drifted right and then rose with the church tower to its battlements. On each corner, surrounding a white flagpole, two-metre-high stump pinnacles rose to the sky, like spires pointing the way to heaven.

'The tower is over six hundred years old,' Jolliffe said, noting Tayte's interest. 'And there's said to have been a structure here before that.'

Tayte didn't want to get sidetracked by an architectural history lesson. 'I'm interested in a family that settled in the area in the late 1700s,' he said.

The reverend raised his eyebrows.

'James and Eleanor Fairborne in particular. Then there's Daniels. That's the name James's sister took when she married. Clara and Jacob Daniels?'

'Daniels…' Jolliffe gazed skyward, following his raised brow as it furrowed in thought. 'I really couldn't say, but Fairborne is a familiar name to most around here. If it's the same family, they have the estate on Rosemullion Head. Lovely views.' He looked suddenly distracted.

'You really must take in the view from our south door. It looks out across the estuary to Nare Point. Quite breathtaking at times.'

'Thanks, I'm sure I will.'

The reverend appeared lost to the scenic images conjuring in his mind as they made their way in slow steps around the church tower. They passed another blue door, this one below an arched window. Above that a further arch was slatted to facilitate the bells.

'So, the Fairbornes?' Tayte continued. 'Any buried here?'

'Oh yes, Fairborne...I think not.' The Reverend Jolliffe pondered a while. 'No, I don't recall any. Their land falls within this parish, all within the Deanery and Hundred of Kerrier, but I suspect their family members are buried on the estate. Quite typical for well-connected, well-financed families with enough land for it.' The reverend gently nodded. 'A most impressive estate, too.'

Now on the church's south side, Tayte began to understand why Jolliffe had led him this way. He looked out over long shadows, across the tops of memorial headstones and stone crosses, changed and worn by time and stained by lichens. Through a framework of trees, he could see an untroubled Helford estuary, then across a silver-foil sea the view encompassed a jutting headland beneath a clear and bright sky.

'You're welcome to look at our headstones, of course,' the reverend continued. 'Take as long as you need. We have a great many for a church of such relatively small proportions. Although...' Jolliffe paused, smiling suddenly, like someone who was about to give away a gift, knowing that the recipient would be overjoyed with it. 'As you're looking for something specific...' He spoke slowly, teasing. 'You might find it more productive to come inside and take a look at the books.'

'You keep plot records here at the church?' Tayte said. He couldn't believe his luck.

'We do.'

'Then please, lead on.'

Chapter Nine

Tayte waited beside an octagonal stone font inside the church, looking up at a stained glass window that bore the images of three saints framed by a single Gothic arch. Similar arches mirrored the length of the church to either side of the main aisle, and above him the ceiling was high and vaulted, painted white with dark wooden beams in stark contrast. Reverend Jolliffe had disappeared behind a blue velvet curtain to fetch the promised book of burials, and Tayte remained surprised that the church still kept them. Most were centralised in regional offices, and he considered that the book's presence in the parish church might explain why he hadn't been able to access this information from back home.

The velvet curtain twitched and Jolliffe pushed through, thrusting the book before him. He blew off the dust and thumped it down on a nearby table.

'Here we are,' he said.

'Chronological order?' Tayte asked.

'Of course.'

Tayte thumbed the pages, which opened with several records going back as far as the sixteenth century, with an increasing number of records for subsequent centuries as he expected. The seventeenth century came and went, and he slowed as he began to see dates from the eighteenth century.

'Genealogy's like a jigsaw puzzle,' he said. 'You just have to know where to find the right pieces.'

His eyes continued to scan the pages, watched intently by the reverend until he reached the year he was looking for—1783, the year the Fairbornes arrived in England. Between then and 1785, James Fairborne had re-married. Tayte turned back a few pages to the start of 1783 and checked the entries again, listing name, address, age, and occupation. For each entry, the date of death and the burial date were there with the plot location, but there were no listings for Fairborne, and none for Daniels. It seemed the reverend knew his plots well.

Tayte closed the book. 'Thanks,' he said. 'You've been a great help.'

Jolliffe gave Tayte an angelic smile. 'Not at all. I expect you'll find what you're looking for on the Fairborne estate. Plenty of history there to dig into.'

'Sure,' Tayte said. 'Well, thanks again.' He made to leave, heading along the church aisle. Then he turned back and said, 'And the estate? Rose—'

'Rosemullion Hall,' the reverend cut in. 'It's on Rosemullion Head. You can't miss the manor house once you get out there.' He walked briskly now, more sprightly than Tayte had seen him move before. He led Tayte with a strong grip by the arm to the south door and pointed out to his right. 'There's a gate,' he said. 'Just around the corner behind the cremation plots. Go through. Then follow the lane to your left until you come to the coast path. It's clearly signed.'

Tayte followed the reverend's enthusiastic hand movements.

'Turn left for Rosemullion Head,' Jolliffe continued. 'Then keep going for about half an hour. Lovely views along the way, too,' he added, taking in his own familiar view. 'Right takes you to Helford Passage. That will take a little longer, but well worth the effort.'

Tayte paused at the south door, one foot on the threshold. He knew he couldn't just walk up there and expect the family to let him prowl around their crypt. He was a total stranger, why would they? He recalled a time when he'd tried that approach before, back when he was still green and full of beans. His right hand wandered down to his thigh, feeling the scar tissue through his suit trousers as he recalled the encounter with one of the dogs that had chased him off the grounds. 'I don't suppose you know how I could get an appointment,' he said.

'You could call the estate,' Jolliffe replied.

'Do you have their number?'

'I'm sure I could find it for you, although an introduction might be more suitable.'

'Do you know the family?' Tayte asked.

'Not well,' Jolliffe said. 'But Lady Fairborne pops in from time to time. She's involved with various charities in the community.'

'Do you think you could get her to see me?'

'I can't promise anything, of course,' the reverend said. He touched his fingers together as an amused expression danced across his face. 'Have I acquainted you with our collection box yet, Mr Tayte?'

Tayte smiled. 'No, but I think you're about to.' He was used to paying for information. Everyone had an angle it seemed, even the church.

'All in a good cause,' the reverend called back as he scuttled away to the blue velvet curtain and returned a moment later with the collection box. 'It may take a while,' he said. He eyed the clock high up on the wall at the back of the church. 'Why don't you come back in a couple of hours? Perhaps a walk to Helford Passage? You could have an early lunch at the Ferry Boat Inn. They serve a fine local crab sandwich.'

Lunch sounded good. Tayte could already feel breakfast wearing off, which he all too readily put down to the fresh sea air. 'Thanks,' he said. 'I'll do that.'

When he reached the coastal path, he turned right for Helford Passage and made his way along the well-worn ground above Parson's Beach, heading west towards Mawnan Shear and beyond through Porthallack and Durgan. It made sense to Tayte that the family were buried on their own estate, though perhaps not the Daniels. Still, Clara was James's sister; there was a chance he might find her grave there, too.

He considered that the Daniels could have moved away, and several further explanations as to why none of the family were buried in the grounds of the parish church came to mind. But wherever they were buried, it didn't account for why he had found no details of their deaths in the parish records or why there were no entries for them in the Births, Marriages, and Deaths index. Nor could he explain why James Fairborne had been free to marry again so soon after arriving in England.

———

It was a Saturday and not a pleasant one at that. It began with good enough intent, but by late morning on March 12, 1785, the sky over Falmouth Bay was stewing; by midday it had boiled over. High winds and heavy rain assaulted the exposed coastline and quickly drove the guests at Rosemullion Hall into the house after a very brief reception in the grounds when they arrived back from the church.

But James Fairborne could not be discouraged today. Those dark lonely days he had known barely more than a year ago were so far behind him now that it seemed they belonged to some other lifetime. He was jubilant and had good reason to be, though his euphoric state was perhaps not based on the same emotional triggers that delighted his new bride.

'Susan! There you are…' A portly man with ruddy cheeks came into the long gallery, cursing the stairs he'd just climbed to get there and still fussing and brushing at the rain on his indigo velvet jacket. To one side, he was supported by his wife, Eudora, to the other by a fat wooden cane. He made his way towards Susan as the other guests continued to pour in behind him. 'How about a kiss for your old father?' he said. 'I've been trying to get to you since we arrived!'

The long gallery on the first floor of the manor house ran the full length of the upper hall. The room was as bright as the weather would allow, lit by tall stone mullioned windows on three sides. The inner wall hosted fireplaces at intervals along its length. There were surprisingly few paintings and even fewer portraits.

Susan pulled James closer to the doorway to greet her parents. 'You're not old, Father,' she said.

'Well, I feel it. This confounded weather's not helping much, either, I can tell you. And what the blazes has happened to your brother and sister? I've not seen them since we left the church.'

Susan was almost laughing with her mother. 'Jane is no doubt surrounded by boys somewhere, wondering which one to dance with first, and Charles is undoubtedly trying to fight them all off!'

Susan's mother could not take her eyes off her daughter any more than she could rest the smile that told her what a picture she looked. The wedding gown was gold dupion silk with just a hint of pink that shone through like an aura. The fabric poured from the pleats at Susan's tiny waist, splashing to the floor like liquid gold. The boned bodice accentuated her proportions and was decorated with rosettes diminishing down the centre; full sleeves, just covering her shoulders, dropped to further gold pleats and white lace flounces. The top of her chest was bare, creating a frame for the black velvet choker that ringed her neck, studded with a single attention-grabbing diamond.

'Beautiful,' her mother said as she leant in and kissed Susan's cheek.

'I've never been more proud!' her father added. He took James's hand and pumped it vigorously, and his strong grip was well met.

James beckoned to a servant standing by the doorway, who instantly arrived with a light skip and an almost worried look on his face. James liberated four glasses of champagne from an engraved silver tray as another servant joined the first with a freshly loaded tray to take his place. Their guests continued to stream into the room, everyone gazing at the happy couple and adding their remarks to the cacophony of words that circled the room.

It seemed that James Fairborne had no family at the church to witness the union, and none now at the reception, but it was not a matter for remark or supposition. The guests were almost exclusively from Susan's side of the family, related in some way to the Devonshire Forbes, and word of James's situation soon circulated. Other guests were prominent figures of the local community, such as the church warden and the parish constable.

'Today I am made a happy man,' James said. He served the wide-rimmed, coupe glasses, spilling champagne over his hands in his eagerness. He laughed and raised his glass. 'And your daughter, sir…' He bowed his head to Howard Forbes. 'Your daughter has made me so!'

Glasses tinkled and the confusion of words circling the room fell silent to the ground. Everyone with a glass raised it to James and Susan Fairborne, and those without one quickly rushed to remedy the situation.

'To the happy couple!' someone shouted, and the room erupted with congratulations.

James put an arm around Susan's waist and gazed intently into her eyes. The strength of his voice was only for their group now. 'And before this year is out we shall be celebrating again,' he said. He looked back to Susan's parents and smiled. 'And we shall be the happier for it.'

'And so you deserve to be,' Howard said. 'Every man must have an heir.' He came closer to James and reached a fatherly hand up to his shoulder. 'You've not had it good of late.'

'No indeed,' James said. 'Not good at all.'

But it was getting better—much better. Now James Fairborne was breathing again, deeper breaths than he had ever taken, sucking it all in and enjoying every moment. His personal darkness was at last ended, and the light that replaced it was already far brighter than he had ever imagined.

Chapter Ten

Amy Fallon continued to stare at the clock above the mantle, watching each painful minute tick away until she drifted into a state of unsettled half-sleep. She knew the dream well enough by now, only this time she knew she was dreaming.

The first part she liked…

She could see Gabriel out on the river in his little red boat. It was a beautiful day and he looked so happy. Amy was home at the cottage, upstairs in their bedroom—no work for her today. She couldn't recall why. She waved to Gabriel and he waved back, smiling the kind of smile that made her want to hold him and pull him home to her, to the bed that was still warm.

Amy knew it was a dream because she was aware that Gabriel was too far away to be able to see him so clearly. But she didn't mind. She liked to see him again. She felt light on her toes as she stood at the window, watching. She felt comfortable again, and complete. But she knew all that was about to change.

It always did.

The first crack of thunder in the bright and vacant sky always heralded the onset. The house shook, rattling the window in its frame. She became suddenly panicked and knew she had to warn Gabriel that the storm was coming. She waved frantically and slapped at the glass panes, calling him, over and over. Gabriel kept smiling and just waved back, completely unaware.

She thought to run to him. She turned away, reaching for the door. The brass doorknob was ice cold in her palm, but she held on, turning and turning at the knob that just kept spinning round and round in her hand. She tried to pull the door open but it was stuck. She knew it would be.

Without thinking, she knew exactly what to do next. She would open the window and drop down; it wasn't that far to fall. Then she could run out to the edge of the river and warn him. There was still time. She turned back to the window, only now there was no latch and the window was suddenly barred. Her bedroom had become her asylum. She gripped the bars and pulled at them, shaking herself as another crash of thunder rocked the sky and stirring shadows reached in across the room.

Towards the mouth of the river a contusion of black and green clouds quickly stained the sky. They began to froth over themselves, rushing into the river mouth like a pyroclastic flow. Coming for him— coming for Gabriel. Amy shook at the bars again, screaming now for Gabriel to turn back to safety, back to her. But she knew it was too late. Trees began to bend in the gale outside, and the light had all but faded to blackness beneath a heavy sky that was now full and bleeding.

Gabriel was no longer smiling.

Amy watched as lightning ruptured the cloud around him and his little red boat began to pitch on the uneasy water, lit by strobing white flashes. She grabbed a chair from beside the window, thinking to smash the glass. Maybe she could squeeze through the bars once the glass had broken away. She rammed the chair legs between the bars as the wind howled at the house and the shutters slapped shut against the impact.

The glass would not break.

The shutters banged open again as she drew back for another go. She knew it was useless, knew that the shutters would close every time, but she had to keep trying. She made several pitiful attempts. Then she stopped.

Gabriel's boat was empty.

The dream was nearly over now and she was calm again, staring out through the bars towards the river, looking for Gabriel until guilt began to rise like poison from deep within her. *Why didn't I go with him?* The bars became soft to her touch, melting. *Why couldn't I save him?* The questions tormented her. Then the bars were gone and the storm cleared as suddenly as it had arrived.

When it left, Amy was her incomplete self again.

———————

As she sat now with her thoughts, looking out across the quiet water from her elevated position above the ferry pickup at Helford Point, the images of that dream remained fresh in her mind, constantly reminding her that she was so very alone. Soon she would take the ferry, not on its usual journey across to Helford Passage, but elsewhere, pausing to place her flowers as she had on this same day the previous year—the first time. She carried gladioli, *G. communis,* known locally as Whistling Jack, an explosion of vibrant magenta picked from their own garden as the last offerings of a warm summer. They were Gabriel's favourite.

Wrapped around the flower stems, clutched so tightly that her knuckles strained her skin, was a familiar newspaper cutting, the start of their journey. The cutting was from the *Western Morning News,* dated October 3. She'd kept it these past three years.

The title ran 'Rare Business Opportunity.' It invited offers for the ferry business and a number of river moorings, including pontoon ramps and beach kiosks, with an option to purchase associated items such as vessels and marine equipment. According to the Truro-based selling agents, it would secure the buyer a new way of life, suiting somebody looking for a lifestyle change.

Beneath the main advertisement was a brief history informing prospective buyers that the Helford Ferry, now a foot ferry primarily for tourists, had been in continuous service since the reign of King Canute in 1023, serving as a working horse ferry and a valuable link to Falmouth. It had seemed perfect—and it was perfect, if only for the briefest of times.

Amy's stare remained fixed somewhere out on the twinkling water; countless sail boats were little more than white blurs. Silently, she wished she could give everything back in exchange for the hurried lives they had once shared. The lengthy, often delayed commutes during hot and sweaty summer months, carriages over-burdened with like-minded commuters affording no time to one another, with no interest in their fellow passengers.

'Morning!' Two walkers approached along the path, hand in hand, bringing her immediate surroundings back into focus. 'Lovely day.' And it was. It might still have been August.

Amy made a fist, still sensing the memory of Gabriel's hand around hers, wrapping it, protecting and comforting. She longed just to hold his hand again, to feel his skin, his warm breath on her lips before a kiss. She smiled at the couple through choked eyes, making no contact, the corners of her mouth barely lifting.

The man waved a collapsible walking pole towards her in friendly gesture as they passed, and Amy turned away again, looking down to her watch, a Cartier Lanières, worn for the occasion. Twenty round-cut diamonds bordered the long hexagonal face, linked by a slim, three-row eighteen-carat gold bracelet. It was a present from Gabriel and a reminder of her past life. The black, sword-shaped hands told her it was nearly time.

She rose slowly from the bench. Then she sat down again, unable to face what she had gone there to do. *Where's Martin?* She would wait. As she sat, the sun caught the bright gold of her wedding ring, drawing her eye. They had been Gabriel's idea, matching Celtic bands depicting a circle of delicately engraved interlocking hearts, each inverted against the other. It meant so much to her. The tangible symbol of their love that she had toyed with constantly, affectionately, for the last twenty years. Now she flicked at it anxiously with the edge of her thumbnail and recalled how they had both been urged by their parents to wait. She was barely nineteen. They had been told they should give it another year or so, just to be certain. Amy had never been more certain of anything in her life, then or now. Without warning the tears came, as if it had only just happened.

———

Across the water at Helford Passage, a twenty-six foot glass-fibre catamaran was being untied from its moveable pontoon. The first of its kind, it was powered by two 25-horsepower engines and was designed to land passengers on the beaches of Trebah and Glendurgan via a bow access ramp. It allowed the ferry business to expand to include trips to the gardens, and its design could cope with rough weather and still operate at low tide.

The ferry was not operating just now, though. A crude, handmade sign with the words Not in Service confirmed the fact to anyone who tried to board. On the pontoon beside it, Martin Cole was about to cast off.

Martin was the skipper now. He'd looked after the ferry business for Amy during the last two years—since she could no longer face it. He was fast approaching forty and felt very average. His clothes came off the shelf in medium sizes. His hair was mid-length and brown, neither too tidy nor too unruly, and his build was neither fat nor thin. Average. He looked over at Simon, his assistant, sitting on his hands behind the wheel, looking like he wished he was somewhere else. The logo on his vivid royal blue t-shirt said Rip Curl, a suggestion of where that somewhere else might be. Since taking Simon on at the start of the season, Martin wished some of the younger man's twenty-something spirit would rub off on him.

He threw off the stern line and gave the catamaran's rear end a firm push with his Derry boot. 'You might have worn something appropriate,' he said, stepping aboard. Simon's three-quarter length baggy grey shorts, and the bright t-shirt fell far short of Martin's expectations for sombre attire.

Sensing his cue, like an automaton with a new coin, Simon animated himself to the wheel and threw the boat into reverse.

'Could have smartened yourself up a bit, too,' Martin added over the accelerated engine noise. He thought Simon's hair looked like hay pulled from a horse's feed bag.

Simon looked over his shoulder and shrugged. 'Don't have a black t-shirt. She don't pay me enough to buy one specially.'

Martin shook his head. He slipped a Leatherman multitool from a worn leather holster on his hip and dexterously flicked open one of blades with his thumb. 'You must have been able to find something less colourful than that!' he said as he sliced through the frayed end of the stern line and pulled a lighter from his shirt pocket.

'What can I say,' Simon said. 'I'm a colourful guy.'

Martin sealed the fibres, pressing the hot nylon between his thumb and forefinger. Though he couldn't see Simon's face, he knew the smirk that lived there. He lifted a seat lid and pulled out a heavy, navy blue marine performance jacket. 'Put this on!'

The jacket thumped into Simon's back and dropped behind him. When he realised what it was, he looked out at the clear late morning sky and protested, 'You're kidding, I'll fry!'

'Just put it on!' Martin pointed a warning finger. 'And when we get there, remember…No one else gets on.'

'I know.'

Martin had his doubts. He checked the time and realised they were later than planned, but they were okay. There was still thirty minutes to spare. He looked across to Helford Point, his gaze fixed. By halfway he could see a few people at the bottom of the steps near the pickup point, no doubt waiting to cross. Today, they would have to wait.

As they drew closer, Martin saw another figure descending the steps, a lone figure moving slowly and deliberately, head sunken, clutching her flowers. He felt for Amy, for what he knew she was going through. He thought of that well-coined phrase, 'Time is a great healer,' but he'd seen no change in her since it happened, no sign of letting go and moving on with her life. *Two years today… Where does the time go?*

The engine revs dropped. A quick shift into reverse jolted Martin back from his thoughts, memories of a morning nothing like this. The catamaran sidled up to the jetty. A glance at his watch again told him they had twenty minutes left. Perfect. The two walkers waiting to cross seemed to get the picture. Clearly, they had seen the signs, had seen Martin in his black shirt and black jeans and Amy with her flowers, also in black. She wore an ankle-length skirt and boots, with a black turtleneck sweater finished at her slim waist by a narrow black velvet belt. No words were exchanged. The walkers respectfully stood back.

Martin pulled the boat close to the jetty and his eyes fixed on Amy. He thought how good she looked despite everything. Her bright eyes—a palette of greens and blues that matched the colour of the river beneath the full sun—shone out through the glow of her earlier tears, and he wanted to comfort her. He felt suddenly ashamed at the inappropriateness of his thoughts. He wanted to say he was sorry again, as he'd said so many times before.

As Amy approached, he stepped up and offered his hand to steady her aboard. He smiled an understanding half-smile that mirrored hers exactly. Amy did not speak as she sat down, and Martin could feel her hand trembling in his, could see her white knuckles locked tight around the flower stems. At the wheel, Simon kept to his business. The engine revved up again and they were soon heading out towards the mouth of the river, weaving between anchored sailboats towards Durgan and beyond to Toll Point, where Gabriel's fishing boat had been found.

Toll Point…

Christ! Martin thought. *That was a dark day.*

——— ———

Reaching above the north bank of the Helford River, Toll Point was little more than a small shingle beach and a quiet place to anchor. If Rosemullion Head to the north and Nare Point to the south delineated the mouth of the Helford River, then between the headlands of The Gew and Toll Point was the river's sometimes gargling throat. In bad weather it could be a dangerous place for the ill-prepared.

But not today.

As Amy arrived at that fateful place, the water was as calm as the sky that sighed gently over it. A cormorant swooped past, low on the water. Then it rose and folded its wings before darting beneath the surface without making a splash. Not much was said on the way. What was there to say? Martin had offered his support as he always did. He had suggested, as he had the year before, that she needed to move on with her life. She knew he meant well, but she didn't want to hear it.

The boat was steady, with the engine shut off. A gentle sway now and then was all that gave away the river's presence. Amy felt cold despite the sun. She rose slowly from her seat as though frail with old age and leant out over the water. Martin came to her side and Simon approached, mimicking the older man, as if he didn't know what use to make of himself.

Amy reached out to place the flowers. Her hand dipped into the water, breaking the seal. It was cold. Her thoughts drifted, and she wondered, as she always did, what it must have been like, what Gabriel had gone through before peace finally found him. Her fingers were numb. She could not let the flowers go, and she only knew she had when she saw them float away, drifting like her thoughts. *Where is he? Where is Gabriel?*

She watched the newspaper cutting sink out of reach and wondered how her heart continued to beat. She swallowed, dry and painful, forcing back the lump that had risen in her throat. Then she turned away and collapsed onto the seat, burying her head into her lap, unable to quell the shiver than ran continually through her.

She felt Martin's hand on her shoulder; heard him sigh as he began to circle a palm across her back.

'It *will* get better,' he promised.

Amy doubted it.

Chapter Eleven

The Ferry Boat Inn had overlooked Helford Passage for more than three hundred years, and it was still as popular with local sailors and fisherman as it was with the thriving tourist trade. Inside, the inn reflected its piratical past and tales of smuggled contraband in the area, with its ship's lanterns and bells, ropes, and wheels. An old ship's mast stretched the length of the bar like a sturdy lintel.

Jefferson Tayte was outside, still smiling to himself after learning from two of the locals that the place was known as the FBI; hearing Tayte's accent, they had been keen to engage him in conversation seemingly just to impart this information. He took a slow step beyond the terrace, leaving the cool shelter of the faux ship's sail that canopied over it, lashed to imitation masts.

He was facing the river, comfortably fed and slouched with his hands in his pockets, jacket resting loosely through his arm. Before him, a short but lively beach ran to clear water that was turquoise under a strong sun barely past its zenith. Children played at the water's edge, monitored by their parents, and further out, the river was active with the mid-week sailing fraternity, with a melee of white sails gently aslant in a soft breeze. The sun felt hot on Tayte's face.

Although not a great walker by preference, he found the stroll to Helford Passage almost as good a tonic as his lunch. Along the way he'd passed the hamlet of Durgan, which consisted of a cluster of stone cottages surrounding an old school house at the edge of a small shingle beach by the river. He'd spent a few minutes looking up into the subtropical gardens of Glendurgan while he was there, but the scant time he'd had did not do justice to the exotic beauty that was two hundred years in the making; to the giant camellias and magnolias that were now resting in preparation for next year's show, when they would once again exhibit in all colours from white to deepest crimson.

Tayte strolled onto the beach towards a metal railed gangway that arched onto the river to a floating pontoon. An unusual catamaran approached, and to his right, at the top of the beach and level with the gangway, a sky blue kiosk advertised 'Ferry Boat Hire.' Tayte went closer. Shingle and sand stirred and sank, crunching beneath his loafers. He glanced at the operating times, taking nothing in. Then he proceeded towards the pontoon, which rocked as the catamaran arrived and moored up alongside it.

Tayte watched a cheery-looking couple dressed in matching forest green walking garb disembark, and he wondered what it must be like to feel that close to someone. As soon as they were on the pontoon, the pair extended their walking poles in perfect unison and linked arms before setting off towards him. The boathands' attire was oddly conflicting, he thought: one dressed in black, the other in a bright blue t-shirt.

The man in black called out to Tayte. 'You going across?'

Tayte waved a dismissive hand. 'No thanks. Maybe some other day.'

He watched the ferry operators tie off the craft, then they followed after the walkers. A lunchtime lull, Tayte supposed. He smiled politely as they passed, all heading for the inn. Then his gaze wandered back to the start of the coastal path, wondering as he set off towards it whether his donation to the church of St Mawnan had been money well spent.

When he arrived back at the church, Tayte got the impression that the Reverend Jolliffe had been standing there in the south doorway all this time, just admiring the view. He was exactly where Tayte had left him a little more than two hours ago. He was all smiles as Tayte approached along the path, and Tayte perceived the news to be good.

'Lady Fairborne has been very accommodating,' Jolliffe said, his face beaming. He moved out from the doorway to greet Tayte, who returned his smile.

'I was lucky enough to be able to speak with her in person,' he continued. 'Did you have a good lunch?'

'Yes, thanks,' Tayte said. 'I took your advice. Good call.'

Jolliffe stooped and pulled a tuft of grass out from the gravel. 'Lovely down there on a day like this.' He scanned the path for further unwanted intrusions. 'I'm overdue a visit myself,' he added absently.

Tayte tried to catch Jolliffe's eye, raising his brows expectantly, urging him to continue.

The reverend stood up again, still smiling. 'I *am* sorry,' he said. He dropped the offending tuft onto the grass beside the path, brushing dust from his hands. 'Down to business as it were.' He studied Tayte now with forced determination. 'I've told Lady Fairborne all about you and what you're up to here in our little part of Cornwall.'

Tayte would have liked it put better. He immediately felt as if he were up to no good.

'She was quite excited about the project.'

Tayte was waiting for the good news, and he wished the reverend would hurry up and get to it.

'She's very keen to see your work and expressed her interest in obtaining the finished result.' Jolliffe moved closer to Tayte and slowly whispered, 'It would guarantee her full co-operation.'

Everyone has an angle, Tayte thought. He twisted his lower jaw, considering. He was sure his client would go off the rails at the idea of a total stranger having a copy of the chart *he* was paying for; even if they were technically family. But it was an interesting proposition. 'I can't promise anything,' Tayte said, but he wanted this interview. 'We should be able to work something out.'

'Of course,' the reverend said. 'I do understand.'

'So when will she see me?'

The reverend threw his hands out. 'Right away!' he said, clearly very pleased with his accomplishment. 'Lady Fairborne is at home this afternoon until three o'clock and can see you any time before then.'

Tayte was surprised at his luck and relieved to find someone so enthusiastic about his work. He was expecting some complication, like she couldn't see him until next week. He checked his watch: 13:21. There was enough time if he left immediately.

The reverend placed a hand on Tayte's shoulder. 'I was concerned that our many distractions would enchant you and keep you away too long,' he said. He led Tayte back towards the lych-gate. 'You're to call at the side entrance in the northeast wing.' Jolliffe gestured with his hands as though drawing a schematic of the house and grounds. 'You'll have to go all the way around the headland to find the main gates first,' he added. 'And be sure to ask for Lady Fairborne if she's not there to greet you herself.'

Tayte took the reverend's hand and firmly shook it. 'Thanks again.' He turned to leave.

'Perhaps we'll see you at one of our services?' Jolliffe said.

'I'll see what I can do,' Tayte replied, but he doubted it.

Chapter Twelve

Amy Fallon was sitting alone on a red settee, staring into a cold inglenook fireplace. Like so much of their furniture, the settee was from the Victorian period, gathered over the years on weekends away or on specific antique-hunting trips when they were looking for something special. Each piece reminded her of Gabriel. She knew where they bought every item, and every item linked to other memories, often of romantic breaks together that began with a customary predinner bath, stimulated by champagne and the heady aromas of scented candles and fragrant oils.

The black lion on the heavy iron fireback returned Amy's stare from deep within the grate. It was early afternoon, still bright outside. She'd not long been back from the river and Martin had not long since left; just enough time to have a quick cup of tea to calm her nerves. Something stronger was suggested, but she knew she would find no answers at the bottom of a bottle—she'd already looked there.

As soon as Martin had left, she'd changed into her comfy clothes: a faded pair of jeans that were so old and torn they were beginning to look trendy again, and one of Gabriel's old shirts, pale blue with a faint herringbone weave that had also seen better days. She was stroking her shirt sleeves and thinking about what Gabriel had said that last night they shared together. The conversation was often on her mind. There was something he wanted to show her, but it could wait…

'I'll show you in the morning,' he'd said. 'It's late and we've an early start tomorrow.'

Amy remembered the fire being low in the grate. She was sitting where she was now, Gabriel beside her with an arm around her. She knew he was teasing her—he loved to tease. But this time she'd sensed an edge of seriousness in his tone.

'Show me now,' she'd said.

'In the morning…it's no big deal.'

Amy recalled giving Gabriel a playful dig in the ribs. 'So show me then.'

'I can't—really.'

'Why not?'

'Because it's a secret!'

Gabriel laughed then, and Amy remembered his strong hands grabbing her wrists and pulling her onto him. She remembered the mischief in his half-Irish eyes, letting her know that he would never show her until he was ready. When morning came, Gabriel went out early, leaving her at the cottage with a sleepy kiss on her forehead. She'd forgotten to ask what he'd wanted to show her, and he had forgotten to say—or maybe he'd planned to show her later.

But later never came.

———

Apart from Amy's bedroom, the sitting room was the only safe place in the house, the only place left to any peace since the decorators moved in at the start of the week. Two days of banging and scraping had done nothing for her nerves, but she *was* trying. A fresh look, someone had suggested. Clear out the old cobwebs—the ghosts. Though it tortured her, she still wanted the reminders around her; she still needed them. She thought she might leave the sitting room alone, to have some part of the house still left to her memories.

The house was called Ferryman Cottage. It was constructed from flint and stone and located at Treath, a tiny hamlet of just a few cottages half a mile along the river from Helford Village on the south bank. Set back from the water, it had its own quay and mooring directly opposite Helford Passage. Secured to the mooring was a teak motor launch,which had been their pride and joy. It was ideal for trips down the river when the tide was in or to follow the coastline in search of a secret cove when the sea was calm. The coastal path ran between the house and the river, which was often busy with walkers during the high season, but not to such an extent that it detracted from its charm.

A covenant existed tying the cottage to the Helford Ferry, which at one time ran from Treath. It ensured that whoever owned the business would have somewhere local to live. Neither could be sold without the other, so when Amy and Gabriel bought the business three years ago, they also bought Ferryman Cottage. The house retained most of its original features and, although smaller than they were used to, in many ways it was well suited to the quieter lives they sought—lives that had since proved to be anything but quiet.

Amy might have burst into tears again were it not for the ten-pound hammer thumping into the wall on the other side of the fireplace. The whole house shook. The decorators were back at the wall again, knocking through into a side annexe that was used to store things that had no obvious place to go. It was proving a difficult task, but they were nearly done. It would give the room more space, but more importantly, the view from the window in the annexe offered a lovely second aspect along the river, back towards Helford and across to the inlet that ran up to Porth Navas.

The real reason she was having it knocked through was because Gabriel had wanted it. Gabriel would have taken that wall down the day they moved in, but there were too many other things to think about back then, when they had owned and operated the ferry service themselves. Now Amy had Martin to run things, along with a string of hired assistants, who seemed to change with the tide.

The house shook again and Amy winced. Beyond the wall to the left of the fireplace, she could hear workmen working on the floorboards. They had taken up the carpet, and now the boards beneath were to be repaired and treated. The constant scraping was getting to her now more than the banging, and she wished she'd told the decorators to take the day off. She could deal with it better on any other day, but not today. She decided she had to get out of the house and take a walk into the village.

Then it suddenly fell quiet. A moment later, voices began to echo in the dining room, and there was a knock at the sitting room door.

'Mrs Fallon?'

Amy sat up as the door opened and a heavily bearded man entered wearing bright yellow overalls emblazoned with the decorating company's name, Harpington. He looked surprised, with just an edge of excitement about him. 'You'd better take a look at this.'

In the dining room, in an alcove to the right of a smaller inglenook fireplace, a man dressed in the same familiar work overalls was on his knees with a torch. He was looking down into a dark space where a floor-to-ceiling cupboard had once been. Beside him was a block of what appeared to be floorboards, only they were connected to each other with batons beneath them, holding them together like a gate or door that was about two feet wide by three feet long. It was barely smaller than the recess.

Amy went closer. Her eyes followed the torchlight down through the floorboards until she could just make out the start of a few dusty steps, each stone worn to a crescent through use.

———————

Within fifteen minutes of descending into what her torchlight had revealed to be a small damp room with a claustrophobically low ceiling, Amy had dismissed the workmen, tied her shirt in a knot about her waist, and was heading along the summer-baked lane towards Helford Village. Tucked beneath her arm, wrapped in a blue and white gingham tea towel, she carried the cause of her excitement.

It's a secret... She couldn't get those words out of her head. *That's what Gabriel said the night before he disappeared.* Now she had convinced herself that Gabriel had found those hidden steps and that what she now carried under her arm was in some way connected with his disappearance. Amy had found Gabriel's secret—she was sure of it—and her discovery charged her with renewed determination as she made her way towards the bridge at the top of the creek, knowing just who to see about it.

Chapter Thirteen

To be considered truly Cornish is to be able to trace your ancestry back to when the Cornish language, or *Kernewek,* was still the primary tongue, though some maintain that it is enough to have three generations buried in Cornish soil. Fail to meet either criterion and you are an incomer, and whether or not you will ever belong is a matter of how much of your past life you are prepared to sacrifice to Cornwall's embrace. You could live in Cornwall all your life, yet still be regarded as little more than a tourist by the Cornish people. To belong in Cornwall is to become a part of it—or you are no part at all.

Tomas Laity was a true Cornishman.

Amy could see his unmistakable form from the short wooden bridge as she crossed the creek at the top of Helford Village. The tide was out, and this far up, the creek bed was caked in wet river mud, giving the area by the bridge a particular nose at low water. She stepped across and made her way down the narrow lane beside the inlet, where small dinghies and launches rested at a tilt all the way to the river. Patriotic bunting lined the lane, like the whole village was stuck in the past, still celebrating a royal jubilee. Behind her, beyond the bridge and the few whitewashed, cob-walled cottages with their shiny slate tiled roofs, a tall woodland canopy rose out of the low valley.

Laity was unmistakable to Amy because she'd never seen him look any different. She was still more than a hundred metres away and hadn't yet passed the post office and village stores, but she could clearly see his white t-shirt and wondered what caption it would carry today. A seasoned white half-apron reached most of the way down his beige combat trousers, which were cut off below the knee, dangling rough threads during the day, then turned up a few pleats for the evening. His scuffed walking boots were as much a part of him as Cornwall itself.

Laity kept his light grey hair trimmed short, shaved down to a number 2 on the clipper scale because finally, after forty-eight years, it was starting to go. His overactive lifestyle and the exuberant outlook of a Cornish piskie kept him youthful, if a little gangly looking. He was on the cobbled patio area outside his shop, standing at one of the sun-greyed bench tables, laughing to himself as he often did for reasons only he knew, as he collected the remains of an afternoon tea of fresh baked fruit scones, Rhodda's crusty clotted cream, and an unusual summer-berry jam that his mother made.

Tomas Laity had lived his whole life on the Lizard Peninsula, an area known locally as the Lizard, which is almost cut off from mainland Cornwall by the Helford River. Following in the family tradition, his shop was appropriately known as Laity's, which in Cornish literally meant 'milk house.' Inside, black-and-white and sepia photographs decorated the walls, giving customers a peek into the family's past and leaving no doubt that the Laity dairy tradition had been upheld through the centuries, although the business had changed considerably since those early days, particularly during Tomas Laity's ownership. The dairy had evolved more into a supplier of other people's dairy produce, and the sign on the front wall of the long and low whitewashed building now read Laity's Deli, rather than Laity's Dairy.

He had to stoop as he went back into the shop carrying an overburdened tray; the doorway was unsuitable for his six-foot, three-inch frame, and the ceiling inside was little better, forcing an unnatural kink to develop in his neck that he never thought to straighten when he was outside. He hadn't noticed Amy arrive with her gingham parcel.

'I'll just be a mo, Mrs Peterson,' Laity called to the elderly lady at the till, one of his regulars, waiting to pay for a packet of Rich Tea biscuits and a half-loaf of bread.

Mrs Peterson looked around in time to read the words on the front of Laity's t-shirt: *Pinta korev marpleg*—'Pint of beer please.' Mrs Peterson knew enough old Cornish to understand it, and the pint of frothing beer on the back was a fair clue to anyone who didn't. The frown on her face was as fixed as ever as she watched Laity's old walking boots whisk him past the refrigerated counter and through into the kitchen.

Usually, Laity had a couple of local school-leavers or his old mum to help him out. This afternoon, however, he was working alone. There was a clatter from the kitchen. Then he came into the shop again, still laughing at unexpected moments, perhaps at the madness that was his everyday life. If anyone asked him why he always seemed so happy or why he was always laughing, he'd laugh there and then and invite them to look at some part of the scenery, saying, 'Wouldn't you if you had to live here and wake up to this *gorgeous* place every morning.' Unfortunately, none of his character was rubbing off on Mrs Peterson, who paid Laity in her usual brusque manner, complained about the price, and was still shaking her head as she left.

'See you again tomorrow, Mrs Peterson,' Laity called with a chuckle. Another family of four were seating themselves outside. Someone else was waiting for cheese and there were two more customers reading the labels from an assortment of condiment jars on a table beside the olive counter.

He closed the till with a metallic thump. 'Have you tried the chilli jam?' he said, smacking his lips. 'Gorgeous with a nice bit of monkfish or seared tuna.'

Two girls in their mid-twenties looked up and smiled. Then Laity was behind the refrigerated counter grinning at the cheese like he was anticipating a quick nibble. 'What can I get for you,' he said to the man waiting on the other side. The man was glowing, like he'd had too much sun, and before he could answer Laity's attention was drawn elsewhere.

Amy was standing in the doorway.

'Hel-lo,' Laity called over the cheese customer's shoulder.

The man with the sunburn turned to see who was there, smiling along with Laity.

'It's madness!' Laity said, breaking into a short, chirpy laugh. He turned his attention back to the glowing man. 'So what will it be?'

Amy came further into the shop. 'Hi, Tom. Sorry,' she added to the man waiting to order his cheese. Then to Laity, she said, 'Maybe I'd better come back?'

'No, it's okay,' Laity said. 'It won't get any quieter today. Have a seat and I'll bring you a cup of tea. Or coffee? Nice cafetière?' He gave her a big grin and his eyes twinkled.

For the first time all day, Amy smiled too; Tom Laity was that infectious. She considered the choice briefly then said, 'Coffee sounds great. Thanks.' She didn't usually drink coffee, but Laity managed to offer it in a way that made it seem irresistibly special.

She apologised again to the man waiting to order his cheese and went back outside to sit at one of the bench tables, setting her gingham parcel gently down. The tables were laid out in a line with a generous space between them, one end butting against a walled rockery burgeoning with red and pink fuchsias. In the centre, a Cornish palm shot up like a firework in mid burst.

Amy drew a long breath and followed a trace scent of smoked mackerel to a homemade smoke box that Laity had set going along the wall. It reminded her of the times Laity had taken her and Gabriel out fishing. It had been a regular event at one time, but now that too was something that belonged to her past life. Her gaze drifted with the smoke, across the narrow creek, absently following a scattering of white houses with their multitiered gardens and private moorings. She wondered what Tom would make of her find, and what advice he would give. She knew he would have some answers, or at least he would know someone who did.

Amy and Laity had become good friends over the past few years, although their approach to the friendship was a casual one, picking up wherever they left off regardless of how long it had been since they last saw each other. That had been enough for Amy—all she had to offer just now. And she had much to thank him for. His cheery demeanour had gone a long way towards helping her through those early months after Gabriel had been declared missing, presumed drowned, then through the shock of learning that it would be seven years before Gabriel could be pronounced legally dead—seven years before the law would allow her closure.

But Amy was in no hurry. If the law allowed for the fact that Gabriel could still be alive, then it was a possibility she desperately embraced. And yet it all seemed like a dream from which she knew one day she would wake, only to find that it was no dream at all. Then the pending verdict of death by misadventure would be passed, and she would have to face it all over again. To Amy, it seemed so utterly inadequate an end to the story of Gabriel's life.

When Laity came back out from his shop, he was carrying the promised cafetière, which he plonked down on Amy's table with a wink. 'There you go,' he said. 'Be back shortly.' Then he marched away to the family of four to take their order, returning several minutes later carrying two trays, heavy with the makings of yet another cream tea.

Laity laughed as he distributed the contents. 'There you go,' he said. 'See what you can do with that little lot!' He chinked the last tea cup and saucer down, barely finding room for it on the crowded table and laughed again. 'That's a proper job, that is!'

He was still laughing as he struggled to fit his size eleven boots through the gap between Amy's table and the seat. 'Mad!' he said as he sat down. 'It's been like this all day.' He shuffled along the seat and sat on his hands. 'Keeps me on me toes, though.' Another chuckle squirted out then he fixed on Amy and his eyes grew serious in a way that only those who knew him could tell. 'So how are you holding up?' he asked.

Amy sighed. 'Oh, I'm okay.' Her tone was unconvincing. She pointed to the smoke box. 'I see you've been out,' she said, changing the subject.

'Yesterday afternoon,' Laity replied. 'Caught some lovely sea bass, too.' He fidgeted and brought his hands up onto the table. 'D'you fancy it?' he asked. 'Pop out about half three, four o'clock one afternoon?'

'We'll see—maybe not just yet.'

'Course not,' Laity said. 'Well, you just say when.'

Amy gave him a kind smile and placed a hand on the gingham parcel. 'I've brought something to show you,' she said in brighter tones.

Laity chuckled. 'I was hoping you had.' He shifted forward and leaned in across the table. 'I was wondering what you had there.'

Chapter Fourteen

Sitting with Amy outside his delicatessen, Laity's eyes were fixed and smiling. 'Go on then,' he said. 'Let's have a look.'

Amy draped one half of the tea towel aside to reveal another layer of blue and white checks. 'It was at the house,' she said, lifting away the final layer to reveal something the size and shape of a shoebox. She knew she'd found something special, although it was marred by time and a degree of water damage that had left discolouring scars.

Laity edged closer and ran a finger over a proud oval of carved ivory set into the lid of an ornate wooden box, tracing the outline of a woman wearing a flowing gown, reclined on a chaise. He noted the pearlescent letters, D and F, in the lefthand corner.

'The decorators found some steps leading down from the dining room,' Amy continued. 'Beneath the floorboards.'

Laity's eyes widened. 'A hidden room, eh?' His features twisted, feigning an air of mystery.

Amy smiled at his childish exaggeration. 'There wasn't much else,' she said. 'A few small barrels and several crates of tea.' She tapped a finger on the lid. 'This box was in a trunk, wrapped in an old cloth bag.'

Laity picked up the box and checked it over. He rubbed a thumb across a dull and tacky film, and the lustre of red mahogany and tortoiseshell blushed through as intricate patterns of whale-tooth detail became bright again, flowing seamlessly between box and lid. 'Anything else in the trunk?' he asked.

'Nothing. Just the bag with this box inside.'

'What's the bag like?'

'Plain,' Amy said. 'Coarse material, biscuit coloured. Looks like sacking, and it's got a shoulder strap.'

Laity flashed his eyebrows. 'Sounds to me like you've found an old smugglers' den. Cornwall's supposed to be riddled with them.' He tipped the box and looked underneath. 'Ideal site where you live, right there on the water.'

Amy had figured as much, but the box seemed out of place. It was clearly not smuggled contraband hidden away from the watchful eyes of the revenue men.

'The barrels are most likely tubs of old brandy or some other liquor,' Laity said. He smacked his lips. 'Shouldn't think it's any good now, mind.'

Amy watched as Laity continued to study the box. He seemed fascinated by the patterns. 'I was hoping you could give me a few pointers,' she said. 'Someone hid this box down there, and I'd like to know why.'

'Probably stolen,' Laity offered.

Amy agreed. She turned to face the creek and the gulls that were gathering to feast on the ebbing tide. 'There's something else,' she said. She paused and began to chew her bottom lip. She found it difficult to translate her instinctive voice into words that didn't sound absurd. All she had was that Gabriel had told her he had a secret to share, and from that, the possibility that he may have found the room the night before he disappeared. She knew it wasn't much. She rushed the next line out like she hoped no one would hear it. 'I think it's got something to do with Gabriel.'

Laity looked up from the box. He looked straight at Amy and she could see his eyes already questioning her reason. She understood why. She knew exactly what he was thinking, that she tried to connect just about everything unusual with Gabriel and why should this time be any different. But this *was* different. It *felt* different. She knew Laity wanted to ask why, but he didn't.

Laity set the box down and opened the lid. Inside, he found two things. One was a sewn cloth heart, sitting in an oblong compartment to the rear. It had a separator to the right, forming another compartment, which was empty. The other item was a slip of discoloured paper folded in two. He was reaching into the box when a deliberate cough from inside the shop drew his attention. Someone was waiting at the cash register.

Laity looked like he didn't know whether to laugh or cry. Then he laughed. He shut the box, twisted his boots free from bench table as he rose, and said, 'Don't go away.'

Thursday, July 18, 1792, was a special day. James Fairborne had anticipated its arrival all year, and now that it was upon him, even as he stood outside the door to his daughter's bedroom, deliberating, he was still unsure. Finally he shook away the last of his reservations and went inside.

Lowenna was a picture in her new saffron yellow party dress. White lace fringed the edges and matching silk ribbons tied her straw blonde hair. She was kneeling by a tall bay window that was alight with the glow of a hot summer's afternoon, diffusing her features—although her smile was as sharp as ever when she saw her father appear in the doorway.

'Look what Nana gave me,' Lowenna said. She offered up a china doll that was midway through being dressed in one of the gowns she had received with it.

'You've been very fortunate,' James said. His smile lacked warmth; there was a trace of doubt in his mind over what he was about to do, even now. He continued into the room and sat at the end of a tester bed that was several times larger than Lowenna yet required. The bed covering, like the décor of the room and Lowenna's new dress, was yellow and white.

Lowenna rose, discarding the doll amidst a scattering of other presents that were in various states of unwrap. Her eyes focused on the object her father had set down on the bed. It was a parcel of shiny red silk tied with a pink bow.

'Sit with me, Lowenna. I have something for you.'

'More presents?' Lowenna's eyes remained fixed on the parcel. 'I like presents!'

'This is something very special,' her father said. 'It once belonged to another girl. Someone like you, perhaps.' James was suddenly distracted by his words. He thought about Katherine and compared her to Lowenna until his hands began to shake. 'Maybe it was given to her on *her* fifth birthday?' he added. Then the images of Katherine became too vivid for him to bear, a reminder that those dark days were all too real. He fought to shut them out.

'Where is Mother?' Lowenna asked. 'Is it a present from her, too?'

'No, child,' James replied. 'This is from me alone.' He stroked his daughter's hair and left his hand on her shoulder. 'It is something you give to someone you love very much.'

'Is that why you're giving it to me and not to Mother?'

James was surprised at how intuitive his daughter had already become, but then his bitterness towards Susan of late was perhaps not as covert as he imagined.

'It is a different kind of love,' he said. 'Your mother...' He faltered. 'Look, aren't you going to open it?' He grabbed the ribbon. 'Here,' he said. 'Pull hard!'

Lowenna's tiny hand took the ribbon from her father's and she pulled, smiling a toothy and excited smile. The bow seemed to liquefy as the ribbon ran off the parcel and the silk wrapping opened to reveal the gift inside. It seemed that she didn't know quite what to make of the box at first, but the raised carving of the lady reclined on a chaise renewed her smile as she traced the outline with a single milk white finger.

James flicked the wrapping aside. He lifted the box and admired the patterns in the tortoiseshell inlay and the bright whale-tooth tracery. 'A special box for a special little girl,' he said, opening the lid. Inside, the box was empty and Lowenna looked disappointed.

'You must keep this box,' James said. 'It is to stay here in your room where you can admire it.' His tone changed then and his features became heavier than he intended. 'Keep it to yourself!' he said. Then he saw Lowenna's face reflect his own anxiety, and he softened. 'Perhaps you could put some of your favourite things inside to keep them safe,' he added. 'If you're good, maybe I'll find you a jewel to keep in there.'

Lowenna's eyes lit up. She was smiling again as she took the box and thanked her father, though James could not be sure that her gesture was not on account of the half-promised jewel. Slowly, he stepped away, lost in her innocence as he watched her return to her presents. It was done. And James Fairborne knew it was the right thing to do. He was letting go of the one thing he'd kept so very close to him these past ten years. And although he felt a weight lift from him, he remained anxious over his decision to do so.

Chapter Fifteen

By the time Laity came out from the deli again, Amy had convinced herself that it was best not to talk about Gabriel and her latest suspicions. *Just find out what you need to know,* she told herself. It was just another hunch after all. A faltering instinct that was easily misguided. She heard the cash register jangle and watched Laity follow two girls out of the shop, passing an elderly man who was very slowly on his way in.

'Afternoon, Mr Trenwith,' Laity said, almost shouting. 'Be with you shortly.' He perched himself on the edge of the bench table opposite Amy. 'Now then,' he added. 'Where were we?'

Amy opened the box again. 'I'd like to know more about this,' she said. 'I suppose whoever hid it must have lived at the house, and if that's true, they must have owned the ferry business.'

'Or been tenants who worked on the ferry,' Laity said. The covenant that tied the ferry business to the cottage was common knowledge locally. 'You could find out who lived at the cottage before. Might be a start.'

Amy liked the idea. 'Where do you go for that?'

Laity shrugged. 'Solicitor, maybe?'

He removed the sewn heart from the box. It was quite plain, bold crimson in colour with a stitched edge that pronounced its shape; it showed no signs of wear or fading. 'Box has kept that well,' he said, scrutinising it. 'Looks like a nice bit of silk.' The stitching was uneven and the material was rough at the edges. 'Looks like someone knocked it up in a hurry,' he said. Then he added, 'Or wasn't much good with a needle.'

He set the heart down and took out the folded note; his eyes looked restless with anticipation. 'Though we cannot be together, you will always have my heart,' he read. The note was signed, 'Lowenna,' and a short postscript read, 'It's what is inside that counts.'

'Lowenna…' Laity said. 'That's a nice old Cornish name I haven't heard in a while. Means joy, if memory serves.'

'What do you make of that postscript?' Amy asked.

'Sounds like a standard sort of phrase. I suppose she just means that it's how she feels about him on the inside that matters. Even if they couldn't be together.'

A call from inside the shop caught everyone's attention. 'Shop!' It was Mr Trenwith, waving at Laity like the place was on fire.

Laity sighed. 'No peace for the wicked,' he said. 'Tell you what…' He stood up. 'Give me a few hours. One of my locals is bound to know how you go about finding out who lived at Ferryman Cottage.' He leant over the table and collected Amy's empty coffee cup and the half-empty cafetière. 'I'll ask around.'

'Thanks, Tom.'

'Not a problem.' Laity waved the cafetière. 'Fancy a fresh one?'

'No, I really couldn't.'

Laity walked backwards to the door. 'If you're this way later on,' he said. 'I'll either still be here…' He rolled his eyes like he fully expected to be. 'Or with a bit of luck, I'll be down at the boat. Of course, if I'm neither, then I'm already out fishing!'

He was laughing as he disappeared into the shop to attend to Mr Trenwith. Amy watched him go, turning the note in her hands. She read it again, thinking about Gabriel and herself, and about Lowenna and her lover. She wondered what circumstance had forced *them* apart and how this box that once tied them together came to Ferryman Cottage all those years ago.

———— ————

They met every Tuesday as the afternoon began to fade and whenever chance allowed. But on this particular wet and chilly Tuesday afternoon, late in the spring of 1803, it was to be for the last time. Lowenna's father had made that very clear.

The caller at Rosemullion Hall left quickly again with James Fairborne's thanks and a shilling for his trouble. The news he imparted left its receiver with a cold sense of failure. James Fairborne was distraught, unable to fathom where he'd gone wrong.

'Have I not given you everything you could wish for?' he asked, searching his daughter's eyes for a glimpse of understanding. 'That you should set your mark so low!' He began to pace uneasily before the fire in his study. It felt suddenly cold to him. He looked angry now, disgusted. 'A farmer!' He spat the word out like it was a wasp lodged in his throat.

'He is a well-educated man, Father. A landowner, too.'

'Be silent, child!' James Fairborne fell heavily into a tall winged chair beside the fire and sank his head into his hands. 'And that you should be seen courting together!' His words were seething.

'But I love him, Father.' Lowenna reached out to touch his trembling hands. 'I am past sixteen years. I want to—'

'You are too young to know this kind of love!' her father snapped, slapping her soft hands away. 'And this *fool* is too far beneath you to deserve it.' His face boiled. Veins throbbed at his temples and spittle glistened in the corners of his mouth. 'You will *not* see him again!'

———— ————

Her lover was waiting for her at the usual place. The broad oak gave him shelter from the spattering rain, and the girth of its trunk afforded them privacy. His cart, sage green, riding on red wheels and undercarriage, looked weathered beside the muddy track that brought him to this side of the Helford River every Tuesday—market day. His Shire mare, Ebryl, named after the Cornish for the month of April in which she was born, was happily eating her reward from the morral looped around her neck.

The Falmouth market run was a routine he'd enjoyed with his father for as long as he could remember, until his father was taken by illness three years ago. He was eighteen then, and suddenly overwhelmed with responsibilities many thought beyond his years. But he'd since proven his doubters wrong.

The farmer's eyes settled on the track that wound away to his left, leading down to Helford Passage. She was late. He had been there nearly thirty minutes. *Maybe the weather.* He grew anxious, his heartbeat quickening. Then at last he saw her and a cool breath filled his lungs.

She moved as though gliding to some delicate score only she could hear. And although he had not yet had the good fortune to see her anywhere other than by the river or on this often muddy track, he knew that her gift was enough to stop all conversation as she entered a room, drawing all eyes to her. And he knew that when she left again, that room was left a dull place and that every man's heart therein suffered an unfulfilled longing. Lowenna…his Lowenna. She flowed towards him in her bright yellow silk dress, unprotected by the small matching parasol she was carrying. And although wet through and dishevelled, she seemed to care nothing for her state.

As she drew closer, the farmer heard her cry his name. He rushed to meet her and knew that all was not well. Her jade eyes looked troubled. His excitement faltered, giving way to trepidation. This was not the Lowenna who had come to meet him on so many other happy occasions. His concern stopped him, and Lowenna slowed as she approached. He could see her tears now, and he reached for her, holding her to him.

Lowenna did not speak.

She pulled away, but his strong hands held firm. Then she reached into a bag that had gone unnoticed over her slender arm and took out an ornate box. She pushed it towards him, and he took it without awareness, all the while looking into her eyes—eyes that spoke for her. He shook his head in denial of what those eyes were saying, what he already knew to be true. He thought she tried to smile through her tears, but only pain showed on her face. Then the space between them grew and their hands fell apart, leaving the farmer lost and numb as he watched Lowenna turn and run.

Chapter Sixteen

Lady Celia Fairborne was in the sun-washed drawing room at Rosemullion Hall, failing to distract herself with a few fashion magazines. Behind the glossy images of ever-diminishing models parading in the latest designs, she was contemplating her recent phone call from Reverend Jolliffe and this American genealogist who was coming to see her. She slapped the magazine shut and threw it hard into the armrest at the far end of the settee. At any other time she would have been excited to talk to Mr Tayte and to learn more about the family; that had been her reaction when the Reverend had phoned earlier. But a timely call from her husband soon afterwards had changed all that in an instant.

Six double-height, leaded windows were alight with the blaze of a full afternoon sun. They looked out unhindered across a perfectly manicured lawn to the south that was randomly scattered with topiary chess pieces, each standing some five feet in height. The view led the eye down and through the estate gardens to a deep perimeter of dense shrubs and prickly gorse, delineating the fringe of the estate, to the coastal path and the sea beyond Rosemullion Head. The room itself was half oak-panelled and decorated in soft neutral tones behind an array of family portraits.

Celia Fairborne was waiting for her son to join her for a much-needed chat. She'd called for Warwick immediately after receiving her husband's phone call, and she had not expected him to come promptly; Warwick seemed far too distracted of late.

Where is the boy?

She went to the window, taking in nothing of the view, hands clasped in an anxious knot behind her, aware that time was ticking away.

Everything about Celia Fairborne belied her fifty-eight years. She was stylishly dressed in a close-fitted, abstract floral print dress that hugged her regularly exercised frame. Her shoes were raspberry suede and had a slight heel to them, and her hair was artificially ash blonde and short in length, cut into the sides and feathered in a style that cost a fortune. Money had taken at least ten years off her. A rose cashmere cardigan rested across the arm of one of a pair of pale yellow settees that mirrored one another across an Aubusson rug before the fireplace. She was about to go and look for Warwick herself when he walked in.

Warwick's casual attire was as contentious as ever. He wore pale threadbare jeans and a navy merino sweater that he practically lived in. As he crossed the room, his expression was neutral, bordering resentment, like concentration interrupted. He slipped across the arm of the first settee he came to and left a worn-out tan leather deck shoe hanging from a bare foot.

His mother sat opposite him and shot him a disdainful glare. 'If you're going to sit down, Wicky dear, sit properly, will you.' Celia's urge was to go across and flick his leg around for him, and to put a comb through his unkempt almond hair while she was at it, but what was the point? After thirty years of trying, she had finally conceded that it was too late to effect any lasting change.

The deck shoe slid into place beside its twin and Warwick's knees fell apart as though in argument. He appeared relaxed, but Celia sensed an undercurrent of tension in the way his lower lip hung without purpose, and how his cyan eyes bored into her.

'Look, what is it, mother? I'm in the middle of something.'

Celia's face silently mocked him. 'Another girl?'

'Not before lunch,' Warwick said through the hint of a smile at last. 'So what's up?'

'I've had a call from your father.'

Warwick's smiled dropped. 'Where is the old man? I've hardly seen him all week.'

'He's in London, Warwick. You know very well where he is. He'll be back on Friday.'

'Yes, of course. He's there so often lately, his poor constituents must think he's deserted them.'

'It's an important week for him, Wicky.'

'That's right. It's a life peerage this time, isn't it?' Warwick scoffed. 'Old Dicky really is doing well for himself, isn't he?'

'Don't call him that, Warwick. You know he doesn't like it, and neither do I.'

Warwick crossed his arms then unfolded them again and started tapping the cushions. 'Well, you'd think any man would be content with inheriting a baronetcy, but not *my* father. He has to earn his own. First he gets an OBE for sticking with it and milking the last drop of tin out of a collapsing mining industry. Then when most people would be happy to retire with their lolly and take it easy under a palm tree somewhere, my father starts a career in politics. Twenty years later he's still not had enough!'

Celia heaved a frustrated sigh. She could guess well enough where all this bitterness was coming from. She'd seen it too many times before. His latest venture was in trouble.

'I thought the Internet was going to be your golden ticket.'

'I don't want to talk about it.'

'You know your father can help you, Wicky.'

Warwick scoffed again. 'Can he give me another loan? That's the only kind of help I need.'

'You know how he feels about that,' Celia said. 'I meant that he can help you in other ways. He knows how hard you try, even if he doesn't show it. He can still find you a position. You only have to ask.'

'Only!' Warwick said. He turned away, squinting from the glare at the windows. 'I'll open my own doors, thanks.'

'Headstrong as a mule,' Celia said with a dismissive shake of her head. 'At least you have that much in common.' She could see this coming between her plans for the weekend: the investiture at Buckingham Palace and the after party she'd put so much effort into. 'Just tell me that these latest problems of yours won't keep you from your obligations on Saturday.'

An edgy smile preceded Warwick's sharp snort. 'I'll be there,' he said. He looked like a man whose problems had taken him beyond worry into a protective cocoon of denial. His smile hung in contradiction on his face. 'So what did you want to see me about?'

Celia Fairborne sat forward on the settee and clasped her hands together. 'Something far more important than any of this,' she said. 'I need a favour.'

Chapter Seventeen

It was two in the afternoon when Jefferson Tayte arrived at Rose-mullion Hall, cursing the inadequate loafers on his already sore feet. After leaving Mawnan, he'd come through a small woodland called Mawnan Glebe, which he thought was like something out of a fairy tale. Chunky granite steps led down into the wood through a tangle of ivy. Then a pathway of earth and exposed roots wound through the steep terrain like a helter-skelter to the river's edge. Restless swatches of sunlight dappled the wood, shifting to the whispered tune of a gentle breeze. Beyond, Tayte walked beside fields of wild grasses to his left and the sea below the headland cliffs to his right, towards the gorse and grassy hummocks of Rosemullion Head.

He was standing between open gates now, looking up at the house along a blue-grey slate driveway, worn smooth with use; it looked wet in the shimmering heat haze. He dabbed his forehead with a white handkerchief, then drew it slowly across the back of his neck, glad of the strengthening breeze that had been with him since reaching the headland. He looked for an intercom and found none, so he followed the drive towards the house.

Rosemullion Hall had been built during the latter half of the sixteenth century. The manor house conformed well to the characteristic architectural design of the Elizabethan period, forming a decisive letter E in shape. It was constructed from red brick with stone facings and tall mullioned windows. The gables exhibited subtle

Dutch design influences, and the pitched roof was scattered with several clusters of tall chimney stacks, forming classical square columns. The main entrance was central to the building, facing away from the sea; it was typically ostentatious with oversized gilt-dressed doors set between highly decorated pillars.

Tayte could already see the door to which he'd been directed by Reverend Jolliffe, clearly a tradesman's entrance by its relative simplicity. He straightened his suit as best he could and knocked, bringing the heavy brass scroll in the middle of the door down with a thud. He glanced around, casually waiting, and then he knocked again. A moment later he heard a catch rattle on the other side, and the door opened just enough to accommodate the middle-aged man who stood in the gap. He wore a starched, light brown apron that put the creases in Tayte's suit to shame. The man was clean shaven, dressed in a white shirt with black trousers and polished black shoes. His hair was a distinguished shade of silver grey.

'Good afternoon, sir,' the man said with perfect diction.

Tayte gave a smile. 'Hi, I have an appointment with the lady of the house. Lady Fairborne?'

Tayte heard quick footsteps approaching from inside and before he got a reply, another voice cut in. 'It's all right, Manning. I'll handle it.'

The door opened a little further and another, much younger man replaced Manning. Tayte thought he too looked like hired help; a gardener perhaps, in a scruffy old pair of jeans and a casual sweater. He had the build of a man who might have held a manual position: lean and muscular such that his torso cut sculpted lines through the fabric of his clothing. But there was that Oxbridge accent and the air of authority.

'Mr Tayte, is it?'

'That's right.' Tayte thrust out a super-sized hand that competed only with the size of the smile on his face. 'Jefferson Theodore Tayte,' he announced a little too eagerly, wondering why he was suddenly using the overblown naming convention that was otherwise the reserved right of his former college tutors—and then only when he was in trouble.

Tayte's unmistakable American twang must have stood out like a jet screeching across an early Sunday morning sky. The man at the door recoiled from the shockwave. 'Yes…well…Warwick Fairborne,' he said. 'I'm afraid Mother's been called away.' He remained in the doorway, blocking any view Tayte might otherwise have had beyond. 'Sorry you've come all the way up here, but there was no way to contact you.'

The news knocked Tayte back. 'Did she say when she could see me?'

Warwick drew a sharp breath through his teeth. 'Afraid not,' he said. 'But it won't be for a while. Family affairs in London. Could keep her there for the rest of the week, I really couldn't say.'

'That's too bad,' Tayte said.

'Do you have a contact number?'

'Sure.' It was some hope at least. Plans change. Tayte reached inside his jacket and pulled out a small black pad and pencil. He wrote his name and number down, tore out the sheet, and then handed it over, thinking he should get some more cards printed.

'I'm only here until the weekend,' Tayte said. He slipped the pad back inside his jacket. 'If there *is* any way she can see me before then, I'd be grateful.'

Warwick Fairborne studied the slip of paper briefly, then carefully folded it. 'I'll see she gets it.'

Tayte found himself looking for an angle; a way to salvage something from the setback. 'Lady Fairborne expressed some interest in my work,' he said. 'Perhaps you could tell her I'm sure we can come to some agreement about getting a copy. She'll know what you mean.'

Warwick nodded. The door was closing. Tayte wanted to see the family crypt, and he knew the answers to some of his riddles at least had to be less than a few hundred metres from him right now. But he couldn't do it. He couldn't just turn up and ask to take a look. He knew more tact was required, and he didn't want to blow his chances with Lady Fairborne if she did get back in time to see him. They had his number. He'd have to leave it at that.

The door clicked shut.

Chapter Eighteen

The security room at Rosemullion Hall was located off the main hall-way, adjacent to the entrance. Lady Celia Fairborne's heels clicked double-time across the marble floor as she walked up to the security room door, pressed a few buttons on the bulky keypad, and entered; she was keen to get a look at this American. Warwick was already wait-ing for her, eyeing a row of flat-panel monitors that displayed multiple images of the house and grounds from the CCTV system. He was rocking back and forth on a brown leather swivel chair in the softly lit room. Intrigue seemed to have overtaken his own problems for now.

'So, are you going to tell me what's going on?' He flicked at the slip of paper in his hand, drawing attention to Jefferson Tayte's phone number.

Celia took it and sat in a matching chair before the security console. She pressed a few buttons and the recorded images from the driveway and the camera covering the door in the northeast wing started to play back from the selected time point. Together, their eyes followed images of the American walking along the drive towards the house, and then to the image of the door as the Ameri-can reached it. He waited, looked around, and then seemed to stare straight at the camera. Celia pressed the hard-copy button and the image froze as a printer at the end of the console began to whir. She studied the still frame for the three seconds it was on screen, then slid her chair across and collected the copy.

Perfect!

She looked Warwick in the eyes. 'This must be our secret,' she said. 'Not a word to anyone else. Do you understand?'

'Of course. What is it?'

Celia slid her chair closer. 'The call I had from your father this morning,' she said. She paused, thinking about her husband's troubled words again as she glared at the printout of Jefferson Tayte's portrait on the console. 'He warned me about this American—told me not to see him.'

'Does father know him then?' Warwick asked.

'No, I don't believe so,' Celia said. 'But he knew he'd be calling. Someone contacted him this morning.' She sat back, considering how much to tell—how much she knew. 'I've never heard your father sound so worried. We're being blackmailed.' Celia watched the muscles beneath Warwick's sweater tense and lock, straightening his spine like an arrow shaft.

'Blackmailed?' Warwick said. 'Over what?'

'I genuinely don't know. Your father wouldn't tell me over the telephone.'

'Any idea who the blackmailer is?'

Celia shook her head. 'The call was anonymous.'

'Of course. It would be.'

'Warwick?' Celia reached across and held his hand, squeezing it. 'Your father said that if what this caller claims is true, it could destroy us. The implications are that serious.'

Warwick Fairborne pulled away, slowly shaking his head. 'We've got nothing to hide from anyone, have we?'

'I didn't think so.'

'Did he have any proof?'

'Apparently he does.'

'So what can it be about?'

'I really don't know.'

'Something to do with this American, though?'

'So it seems. Your father warned me that the man was a threat when he told me not to see him.'

Celia stood up. 'Look, he said not to worry. Said he'd take care of it. He's a powerful man, Wicky, with a lot of important friends. He said he'd know more on Friday. He's expecting another call then, along with the proof.'

Warwick threw his head back into the headrest. 'So we just carry on like nothing's happened?'

'Don't worry, dear. If it's about money, I'm sure we can sort it out.'

Celia reached across to the console and switched off the image playback. 'Your father won't let this get out of hand any more than I will,' she said. She opened the door. The light in the main hallway seemed bright after the dimly lit security room. 'There's nothing more we can do until we see him.'

Chapter Nineteen

Jefferson Tayte's return journey from Rosemullion Head was slow and thoughtful. He took in little of his surroundings, barely noticing the pair of grey seals showing off at the mouth of the Helford River as he passed through the ferns towards Mawnan Glebe. He sensed the afternoon was fading, and it would be gone altogether by the time he got back to his accommodation and his neglected luggage. That pissed him off, but he knew there were other avenues. There were always other avenues.

As he entered beneath the woodland's piebald shade, along a trail of stepping stones that led through a narrow, winding passage of rock walls and vegetation, his right trouser pocket buzzed. It gave him a start. He fumbled for his phone, then stabbed at the green call-answer button.

'JT,' he said. His voice sounded chirpier than he felt, but he wasn't prepared for the energetic voice at the other end.

'Jeff!'

The voice buzzed the phone's plastic casing, and Tayte ripped it away from his ear as the tangle of branch and leaf under Mawnan Glebe came into sharp focus. Only one person ever called him Jeff. He was struck momentarily dumb.

The voice came again, distant now at the end of Tayte's outstretched arm. 'Jeff? Hey, big guy…you there?'

Tayte almost hung up. Almost. He took a deep breath, drawing the phone tentatively closer. This was all he needed.

'Come on Jeff, I know you're there,' the voice teased. 'I can hear you panting.'

Tayte gritted his teeth. 'Schofield,' he said coldly, without a grain of pretence, as Peter Schofield's toothpaste-commercial grin filled his head like some overt billboard advertisement. 'What do *you* want?'

'Oh, come on Jeff. Don't be like that! And really, you can call me Peter.'

Tayte *really* couldn't.

'So how's England?' Schofield asked.

Tayte felt his throat tighten. He sensed the sudden quickening of his heartbeat. *How does he know where I am?* Before he could ask—as if the phone was a conduit into his mind, allowing Schofield into his thoughts—the answer came.

'I got a call from Sloane!' Schofield said.

Tayte swallowed hard. Why was his client calling Schofield? He recalled the brief remark from Walter Sloane about Schofield back in Boston. He'd said nothing about actually involving him.

'Old Wally thought you could do with some help.'

'Say that again,' Tayte choked.

'Well, okay, he hasn't actually asked me to help out just yet— not officially anyway.'

Tayte didn't like the intonation there.

'He's put me on standby, though,' Schofield continued. 'That's really something.'

'Oh, that's terrific.' Tayte mumbled the words through clenched teeth.

'What was that?'

Tayte was silent.

'The man seems pretty serious about getting the job done by the weekend,' Schofield added. 'I don't know what you said to him before you left, but you sure gave him the jitters.'

Tayte heard Schofield laugh down the phone. *Like any of this was funny.* He reflected on that last meeting with his client. His uncertainty over what happened to the Fairbornes when they left America must have made Sloane wonder if he really could pull it off in time.

'It's just some misunderstanding,' Tayte said. 'I'll call Mr Sloane and straighten things out.'

'Well you'd better have some good news for him. He told me to expect his call anytime now. Hell, I don't even think it'll matter what you tell him. He sounded pretty keen to get me on board.'

'Look, after Walter Sloane hears my report,' Tayte said, 'you won't be hearing from him again.' Tayte's hackles were up. 'I'm making great progress over here.' A cold lie. 'Don't need any help, thanks.'

'Well that's good,' Schofield said. 'So what do you think about that claim against the family back in 1829?'

Tayte tripped on his tongue. He was stumped.

'You know all about that, right? Made headline news.'

'Sure,' Tayte lied again. 'Basic stuff.'

'Yeah, easy enough to find, I guess. You know, there might even be some truth to it. No smoke without fire in this game!'

Listen to this kid, Tayte thought. *He's probably still living with his parents and he's talking like he's been in the business longer than I have.* Tayte suddenly wondered why Schofield was already looking into the assignment—*his* assignment. 'I thought you said you were only on standby?'

'Yeah, that's right. But after I got the call I just couldn't sit still. Thought I'd get a head start, you know—make a good impression.'

Tayte began to climb the granite steps that led out of the woodland. His right hand gripped the rail for some much-needed support, the other continued to press his phone to his ear. He was panting as he left the wood, emerging to snatched views through nature's windows of white sails and a peaceful community further into the river.

'Old Wally's paying good money,' Schofield continued. 'I'll just backdate my expenses when the call comes in.'

Tayte shook his head. He couldn't believe how cocky this kid was. He was sure Tayte was going to fail. To Schofield, the expected call from Sloane was nothing more than a formality. 'Look, thanks for your interest,' Tayte said. He quickened his step. 'But you're wasting your time.'

'Hey, we'll see. Maybe we can meet up. I'm flying over in the morning.'

Tayte stopped in his tracks. He felt numb. His left arm went limp, falling sharply to his side. Then he rolled the phone over in his palm and calmly but firmly pressed the red end-call button. He slid his thumb across the phone and brought up his contact list, then scrolled through the names looking for Walter Sloane's number.

He didn't reach it.

Tayte felt a searing pain shoot across his skull, terminating right behind his eyes as they closed.

Chapter Twenty

After he felt the initial blow and the pain that exploded across the back of his head, Tayte felt nothing more for several minutes. His eyes opened slowly at first. His vision was hazy, like he was looking through a thin sheet that someone had thrown over him. It was bright. He closed his eyes again and blinked several times until they began to focus. Then the sheet seemed to flap away as if caught in a strong updraught, and the sky expanded like a camera lens zooming out from a close-up. He felt the pain in his head first, throbbing to the beat of his heart and the kick of his pulse.

The blow had come from directly behind him; he could feel the swollen lump it left at the base of his skull, just above his neck. There was no blood on his hand as he drew it away, and it was only when he sat up that he felt a stinging pain in his chest. It drew his eyes to a note that was pinned through his shirt into his flesh. He could see the yellow plastic pin stump sitting in the small pool of blood it had drawn. He winced as he pulled it away.

'Fuck off home!' was written on what looked like a torn-off piece of brown envelope.

Very succinct, he thought.

He got up and his head thumped with renewed enthusiasm, prompting him to crumple the note into an angry ball and throw it as far away as he could. He brushed the dust off his suit and checked his pockets. His pad was still there inside his jacket. His wallet was in his trouser pocket. His phone…He patted himself down then checked his pockets again. He didn't have his phone.

He remembered that he'd been about to call his client. He thought he must have dropped the phone when he was attacked, but he couldn't see it on the path. He kicked at the grass where he'd fallen, saw the phone, and stooped to pick it up. Halfway down he thought he'd been hit again. His head pounded and felt so full that he thought it might go off any minute like a grenade. He was grinding his teeth as he read the phone's display. There was a new text message. The sender's number had been withheld, but Tayte was in no doubt that this was another note from his attacker—someone who clearly had his number. This one read 'Next time the pin will be eight inches long.'

By the time Amy Fallon returned to Helford to catch up with Tom Laity, the September air had cooled considerably. She had tucked Gabriel's old shirt into her jeans for the walk and put on a cream zip-neck fleece for extra warmth. She had passed Laity's Deli a while back. The sun parasols were in, the lights were off, and the door was locked. There was no sign of Tom.

The sun was behind the Helford River now, low in the sky over Helston and Porthleven to the west. Cool shadows fell from furled sail masts towards the mouth of a river that was as calm as Amy had ever seen it. The late sun gave the water a metallic quality, like mercury reflecting a burnt orange glow.

Laity would certainly go fishing; Amy had no doubt of that. She hoped she hadn't left it too late. He usually tied his boat off near the river, barely into the creek at all. She was nearly there. She came out past the Shipwrights Arms, a centuries-old thatched pub near the bottom of the creek, following the path along the edge of the water.

Then she saw him.

Laity looked up from his fishing boat as Amy arrived. 'Ahoy, mate,' he said, laughing as usual. 'Just finishing off some repairs to this mackerel line. You sure you won't come out? Lovely weather for it.'

Amy took in all sixteen feet of Laity's white fishing boat, which stirred memories of some of the good times with Gabriel, huddled together from a shower beneath the walk-in canopy while Laity tended the lines. Part of her was tempted, but she couldn't do it—not today. Her eyes wandered into the boat; two planks for seats that were always home to nearly invisible fish scales that attached themselves to any clothing they came into contact with, clinging like wet sequins. She remembered her clothes always smelled of fish whenever she and Gabriel went out with Laity, but they were fond memories—and it *was* a fishing boat. What had she expected?

'I'm not really dressed for it,' she said. She knew it was a lame excuse.

'Well, I'll see if I can catch you something nice for your tea instead then,' he said. Then he dropped the heavy-gauge orange fishing line, climbed out of the boat, and sat with Amy on the low wall.

'Did you manage to find anything out?' Amy asked.

'I did,' Laity said. He flashed his eyes. 'I must have asked everyone who came into the shop after you left.'

'Sorry to be a pain. I know you're busy.'

Laity smiled. 'Never too busy for you.' He chuckled and sat rocking on his hands like a shy schoolboy. 'There's a records office in Truro,' he added. 'Old County Hall off Station Road. They keep all that stuff there apparently.'

A familiar sail tacked into the creek, and Laity gave it a high wave. 'Got a nice old dear to thank for that snippet,' he added. 'Mrs Menwynick from Orchard Lane. She said you need to ask for a house history search.'

Amy leant in and kissed his cheek. 'Thanks, Tom,' she said, and she sat on the low wall until Laity was gone, and his fishing boat appeared as nothing more than a gull at rest on the evening calm. Her thoughts were of the box and of Gabriel, and of the journey that now lay ahead of her as she strove to understand the connections she was so desperate to make.

Chapter Twenty-One

Jefferson Tayte was sitting up on his bed at St Maunanus House, settled in for an early night with a freezer block to soothe his head and no appetite for his host's recommendations on where to eat. His attention strayed from the laptop screen in front of him, across a powder blue room to a sash window that was raised several inches, inviting a soft breeze to play at the edges of sail white curtains. The window framed a landscape of late harvest farmland and a swathe of indistinct trees that appeared to reach up from the Helford River towards Mawnan Smith. Above them, scarlet ribbons underlined a fading sky.

Tayte thought he was getting a little too settled, like jet lag was calling his number. He swung his legs off the bed, thinking he should call the police and let them know he'd been attacked, but he reconsidered; the process would waste precious time he didn't have, and he could give them nothing to go on. His interest in the Fairborne family history had pissed someone off, that's for sure. But who and why? The questions just made him all the more determined to find the answers.

He removed his jacket and went through the pockets, turning everything out onto the bed: Judith's pamphlets, his notebook, a cheap pen, and an empty crisp packet from Heathrow Airport that was tangled with several miniature Hershey bar wrappers. The last thing he came to was Julia Kapowski's calling card. He'd forgotten about that. He read it for the first time: Julia Kapowski, Valuations. Skinner, Inc., Auctioneers and Appraisers of Antiques and Fine Art. Boston, MA.

Tayte smiled as he recalled the injections she'd given him with her fingernail to wake him up after he'd finally fallen asleep on the plane. He could laugh about it now. He dropped her card and the empty crisp packet into a wastebin that was recessed into the grate of a disused fireplace beside the bed and returned to his laptop, dragging his thoughts back to the call from Schofield and what promised to be an interesting lead. *1829…Made headline news,* he thought. Then like an archaeologist with a new bone, he began to dig deeper to see what else was there.

He brought up his preferred newspaper archive, a website that boasted access to twenty-nine million newspaper pages dating back to the late eighteenth century. He punched *Fairborne* into the search field and it came back with almost two hundred thousand matches. He narrowed the search: *Fairborne* plus *1829*. Better, but still nearly three thousand results. Then he added *scandal* and only five results came back. Two were for Scottish publications. He dismissed them. The rest were for *The Times,* the oldest of which was for Monday, June 15, 1829. Midway down the second column, the section heading read 'Fairborne Scandal—Unknown Heir?' The article described how twenty-six-year-old Mathew Parfitt from Plymouth was challenging the right of succession to the wealthy businessman, the late Sir James Fairborne, and all his estate and titles.

Tayte paused as he read the name Parfitt. It was familiar, but like a childhood tune he couldn't place. He opened the next file, an unrelated article about a protest in the north of England, prompting him to move on to the last of the pages from *The Times.* It was dated Wednesday, June 24, 1829—nine days after the first. The heading read 'Fairborne Claim Dropped.' The article was short, stating that Mathew Parfitt had withdrawn his claim. It gave no reason, and the obvious conclusion left to the reader was that it had been nothing more than a hoax. He scribbled himself a reminder to call the Cornwall Record Office for a copy of James Fairborne's last will and testament, then he wrote, *Mathew Parfitt – born 1803*, the date of the publication minus Parfitt's age at the time.

'No smoke without fire,' Tayte mused as he considered who this man was.

He accessed the online census and was soon looking at the heading '1851, England Census Record—About Mathew Parfitt.' He read that Mathew was forty-eight when the census was taken and that his relationship to the head of the household was 'son.' It showed where Mathew was born, in which parish, his address at the time, and his occupation. Tayte clicked the hyperlink next to the Household entry, and the screen displayed a list of people who lived under the same roof as Mathew Parfitt in 1851. It was a very short list.

The head of the household was Jane Parfitt, Mathew's mother, and reading her name gave Tayte a déjà vu feeling, but like before, he couldn't place it. No father was listed at the address, and there were no entries for a daughter-in-law to Jane Parfitt or for any grandchildren. In 1851, Mathew Parfitt lived alone with his mother. If he'd married and had any children, they either lived elsewhere or they had died.

No father listed, Tayte thought, considering that Mathew's birth record would tidy up that loose end. He grabbed a shortbread biscuit from the tray on the bedside table, tore the tartan wrapper open with his teeth, and bit the contents in two. His eyes remained fixed on the screen as another website came up—the International Genealogical Index. Tayte knew the information held on Family Search was rarely as full as the original documents, and that it was prudent to verify the information you found with other sources, but he also understood that it was a valuable resource nonetheless.

He punched in all the pertinent information from Mathew Parfitt's census report and selected to view all events from birth to death. A few entries appeared, but only one matched the civil parish listed on the census. He clicked the entry. No birth details were available, and he wondered why as he stuffed the rest of the shortbread biscuit into his mouth. Then an entry against Christening drew him on.

According to the IGI, Mathew Parfitt was christened on November 23, 1803. That tallied with Tayte's birth year calculations, giving him confidence that he was looking at the right record. He wrote the details in his notebook and then read the names in the Parents section. The name of Mathew's father, Lavender Parfitt, held his eyes as his earlier déjà vu episode rushed back at him. He almost choked on his biscuit. He knew he'd found something important, and he had the document to prove it.

He lunged across the bed for his briefcase, flipping his laptop onto the quilt. So many names lived inside Tayte's head, he could forgive himself for not recalling plain Jane Parfitt. But a man called Lavender...*What were his parents thinking?* To Tayte, names were like keys, each unlocking a door to another name, another story. Most of those stories were now long forgotten, trapped in another era like glitter in a snow shaker, but there were others still waiting to be told, and Tayte instinctively felt like he had hold of one of those keys now—and he could feel it starting to turn.

He pulled a bulging manila folder from his briefcase and rifled through the contents until he found what he was looking for, a marriage record transcript. He read the poignant words to confirm what he now already knew. 'Name and surname—Lavender Parfitt.' Beneath that was the bride's maiden name.

'Jane Forbes,' Tayte read aloud, smiling. 'Father's name and surname—Howard Forbes.' Tayte had finished his research on the Forbes, and he was smiling because that surname also belonged to James Fairborne's second wife, Susan. She and Jane Parfitt were sisters.

Tayte flopped back on the bed and pinched the sleep from his eyes; he could feel it creeping up on him like the evening was creeping up to the bedroom window. *Jane Parfitt and Susan Fairborne were sisters.* It was a good connection, two families bound together through Mathew Parfitt, who had claimed to be his uncle's rightful heir. He wished it was earlier in the day, wished he could call the record office in Truro right now about James Fairborne's will, but it would have to wait.

He started to pack the documents back into the manila folder, removing the section on the Parfitts so he could slot the marriage record back in its proper place. It was a small section. Jane and Lavender Parfitt's dependants' report stood out clearly, drawing his eye. He recalled their misfortune as far as children were concerned. He'd found records for the births of two dependants and two more records for their deaths the same day: two babies whose lives were over almost before they began. Nothing before now had suggested a son called Mathew Parfitt.

So why did Mathew have a christening record and an entry on the 1851 census showing him as Jane's son?

The census was good at finding people—especially if they had no reason to hide. He studied the details he had for the two ill-fated babies. Nothing unusual, although the birth dates were barely more than a year apart, suggesting they hadn't delayed in trying for another child after losing the first. That was in October 1802. The second was in January 1804, leaving just one year in between—1803. The year Mathew was born.

Then it hit him. Jane Parfitt could not have been Mathew's mother. It was a biological impossibility. There wasn't enough time to conceive and give birth to Mathew between her two failed pregnancies.

'So who were his *real* parents?'

Tayte mocked himself. It was a question he felt unqualified to answer. He stared over at the photograph on the bedside table, at the black-and-white image of his mother that was taken sometime in the sixties, he supposed, maybe earlier. She was standing alone between two stone lions in the doorway of a building that, from the partial lettering at the top of the image, Tayte figured was a hotel somewhere. Her hair was styled in a short bob, and he thought it must have been cold when the picture was taken; she was wearing a three-quarter length coat that kicked out at the hem, and her hands and knees were locked together, rigid as a sentry. Her smile always looked apologetic to him somehow.

Who are you?

Tayte heaved a familiar sigh and forced his thoughts back to the articles from *The Times* and the connection he'd made to Susan Fairborne. What if Mathew *was* a Fairborne? An unwanted child from another family member perhaps, given to Jane Parfitt to conceal an indiscretion. Had Susan had an affair? An unwanted pregnancy? Did she give her unwanted child to her sister? Tayte had no idea at this point, but even if Mathew was a Fairborne, he wondered how he could claim to be James Fairborne's rightful heir in place of any of his five legitimate children, all of whom were born long before Mathew Parfitt.

A coincidence suddenly struck Tayte. It was something that had been right under his nose, perhaps too close to see. *James Fairborne's five children...* He could find no marriage or death records for any of them, and he didn't care much for coincidences. A thought that he could barely entertain reached into his mind like a claw. *Unless the five legitimate children were all dead by 1829.* Someone had clearly gone out of their way to hide something from the Fairborne past, and Tayte knew it had to involve *all* the Fairborne children in some way. This was no longer just about Eleanor and her children. As far as Tayte was concerned, all their lives, and perhaps even their deaths, were inextricably linked.

His eyes began to sting. He yawned as he shuffled down the bed to rest his head on a pillow that felt so soft it was barely there. His mind was a confusion of possibilities, but two things remained clear: he needed to see James Fairborne's will, and he had to pay a visit to the current Forbes family. It was his first rule of genealogy: talk to the family. And there were always two sides.

Across the road, just beyond the shadow of a street lamp at the front of St Maunanus House, a man wearing a three-quarter length black leather jacket was partially hisdden behind an open broadsheet newspaper, like he was waiting for a bus—only there was no bus stop there. His head was bowed into the pages, but his eyes were raised well above them, looking at the house, taking in the name of Tayte's accommodation from the sign at the end of the driveway.

His eyes drifted to the silver car parked there, a Ford Focus with a conspicuous hire company logo on the boot hatch. He paused on the registration number while he committed it to memory, and when he was satisfied, he folded the newspaper and tucked it under his arm. His free hand reached over his chest, and through his clothing he felt the outline of a silver crucifix, hanging by a thick leather cord that was almost brittle with age.

Chapter Twenty-Two

Thursday.

It was just after one in the afternoon, and having lost more time than he cared to at the record office in Truro, Jefferson Tayte was in Devon, driving through Dartmoor at the end of an eighty-mile journey in search of the Forbes family, the descendants of James Fairborne's second wife, Susan. Apart from meeting Penny Wilson—the face behind the voice he'd spoken to so many times from back home in the States—his visit to Truro had been a disappointment. James Fairborne's last will and testament should have been there according to the indexes, but like so many other Fairborne records, the original and all copies were missing. Penny already had his number and she was looking into it, but he wasn't holding his breath.

Tayte's hopes were higher for the afternoon, although he was looking for an address he now realised he had little hope of finding unaided. The map that his bed and breakfast host Judith had given him before he left mainly concerned itself with trunk roads, showing little of the area he now found himself in. He'd driven through Buckland-in-the-Moor, skirting Dartmoor Forest for a while before plunging in. Now he was on the other side of the forest and none the wiser about how to find his destination.

In the distance he could see the moorland tors and cairns rising from the landscape like swollen bruises, and though not yet raining, the clouds that appeared with his arrival were gathering over

Dartmoor. He was looking for a place called Dunworthy. The 1901 census confirmed that the Forbes address at that time was the same address that appeared on all earlier census reports back to 1841. He was taking a chance that the house still belonged to the family a hundred years on, but even if they had moved on, he supposed that whoever lived there now might be able to point him in the right direction—if only he could find Dunworthy.

Tayte slowed the car, looking for clues. In the background a jazzy tune was spilling from the *Chicago* soundtrack CD he'd picked up at a petrol station on the way there, keeping him focused. A cyclist approached over the horizon in bright yellow-and-blue spandex, prompting Tayte to pull over. He got out and waved, hoping to stop him for directions. Then he saw another cyclist, this one in lime green, closing on the first until the pair sped past and a whole bunch of them rose up on the brow of the hill.

Tayte leant back against the car and watched the chasing pack arrive. 'Dunworthy?' he called. Most had their heads down and no one seemed to hear him over the whir of racing spokes. 'Can you tell me where Dunworthy is?'

The last cyclist in the group sat up, resting his hands on his thighs, panting. He was pointing back the way Tayte had come. 'Take a right down there and follow the lane!'

'Thanks!' Tayte called after him, though his gratitude was wasted on the backside that waggled back at him as the cyclist rose above a razor-sharp saddle and began to work the pedals.

———

The Forbes residence was well known in Dunworthy. It was an imposing thatched house on the edge of the village, and the gaggle of old dears Tayte had spoken to outside the post office had fought over themselves to rush out directions. The sitting room in which Tayte now found himself was decorated in dusty rose pink between light oak beams, and the entire ground floor had been lowered at some time, adding height so you didn't have to duck everywhere you went. He was sitting on a William Morris–style sofa that matched the curtains, waiting for a pot of tea to brew. Opposite were his hosts, David and Helen Forbes.

Helen sat back in a button-up blue denim dress, flicking out a mint green espadrille as she crossed her legs. Tayte thought her spiky hair, which was all the colours of autumn, gave her a funky look that conflicted with the floral surroundings. She looked like she was rebelling against something—age perhaps. David's hair appeared to be in a race with itself to go grey before it fell out. He looked casual in taupe corduroy trousers and a forest green shirt. They were sitting perpendicular to a vista of endless landscaped gardens, which they had been nurturing when Tayte arrived.

Helen poured the tea from a Royal Copenhagen teapot. 'Do you take sugar, Mr Tayte?'

Tayte edged forward. 'Two, please.' He patted his stomach and grinned. 'I know I shouldn't.'

Helen just smiled politely. 'This is all rather exciting,' she said. 'So what do we do?'

Tayte settled back with his tea. 'Well, there's no real formula, Mrs Forbes. I'm working on an assignment that's led me to a relationship between your family and the people I'm working for. I've some loose ends I was hoping you could help with.'

'I'm sure we can,' Helen said before she even knew what Tayte wanted to know.

David finished stirring his tea. 'I've a golf game booked at two. Do you play, Mr Tayte? We're looking for a fourth.'

'I don't. Often thought I'd like to, but I never seem to get around to it.' Tayte checked his watch.

'There's plenty of time,' Helen said, frowning.

Tayte set his cup and saucer down on the table and opened his briefcase. He pulled out the chart, unfolding a section on the table as Helen edged closer, clearing the contents of the table out to the edges to give him more room.

'This is the family tree I'm working on,' Tayte said. He had the names facing them. 'It's for a client back home in the States. Their family settled there in the early 1700s, and just after the Revolutionary War—the American War of Independence, that is—most of the family moved back to England. Did you know that around 70 percent of Americans alive today can trace their ancestry back to Great Britain or Ireland?'

Eyebrows rose at hearing the statistic. 'That's a lot of people,' David said.

Helen agreed.

Tayte craned his neck around the chart. 'You can see here that James Fairborne married Susan Forbes. That was shortly after he arrived in England.' He moved his finger up the chart. 'And Susan's parents, Howard and Eudora Forbes, had two other children. One was Jane Forbes and the other was Charles.' He could see that David's eyes were buried in the chart. 'You, Mr Forbes, are descended from Charles Forbes here.'

David appeared to have forgotten all about golf. Tayte could see he had them both hooked and he loved it. He watched Helen's quizzical eyes follow her finger over the dependant entries below Jane Forbes and Lavender Parfitt.

'You've got the same dates written against these two,' Helen said, meaning the dates of birth and death for the two children were the same. 'Is that a mistake?'

'Sadly not,' Tayte said.

Helen put a hand to her mouth. 'The poor things.'

Tayte drew their attention to the pencilled question mark beside Mathew Parfitt. 'This is my loose end,' he said, tapping the chart over Mathew's name. 'This is what I'm really hoping you can shed some light on. You see, Mathew shows up as being Jane Forbes's son, but because of the timing of her other two children, that's just not possible.'

Tayte finished his tea and returned it to the saucer with a musical tinkle. 'What I need to know is where Mathew really came from. My hunch is that the child belonged to one of these people.' He circled a finger around Susan Fairborne and her daughter, Lowenna.

'I know it was a long time ago,' Tayte said, eyeing the display of chocolate macaroons in the centre of the table. 'Two hundred years and several generations,' he added, taking the biscuit closest to him. 'Do you know anything about Susan or her children? Any history handed down?'

David shook his head and Tayte was getting ready for another disappointment when Helen began to smile.

'Not Susan, so much,' she said. 'But Lowenna…that's a name I've heard.'

David looked at his wife like she'd been leading another life.

'You know something about Lowenna Fairborne?' Tayte asked.

'Only a little,' Helen said. She looked at her husband, her eyes asking questions only David could hear. 'But I know someone who can tell you a great deal more.'

David suddenly twigged.

'If that's alright with you, dear,' Helen said.

'Of course,' David replied. His face collapsed into a frown. 'If you think you can get any sense out of her.'

'His mother loves to reminisce,' Helen said. 'She rambles a little, but I'm convinced her memory's better than mine.'

David eyed his watch. 'Look, I'd better get changed.' He rose. 'Do excuse me, Mr Tayte.'

Tayte got up with him. 'Of course,' he said. 'Thanks again for seeing me.'

'Helen can take you in to see Mother,' David said. Then to Helen, he added, 'Try not to get her too excited.'

Chapter Twenty-Three

The room exuded a subtle fragrance of violets and Yardley English Lavender soap. It was a bright room of white furnishings with accessories in shades of colours that matched the scent. Net curtains glowed at the window despite the changeable Dartmoor weather, which was beginning to turn. The woman Tayte had been brought to see was sitting up in bed as they arrived. Her hair was pure white like the nets at the window, brushed back high off her brow. She looked old in almost every way save for her eyes and her smile, and her smile softly spoke of a lifetime of kindness. Her skin was like rice paper, with the sheen of pearl pink silk.

Helen Forbes sat on the bed beside her and held her hand. 'I've brought someone to see you, Mother,' she said. 'His name's Mr Tayte. He wants to talk to you about Lowenna Fairborne—the girl you've told me about.' She looked back at Tayte, who was still standing in the doorway, and drew him in with a flick of her head. 'Mr Tayte, this is Emily, David's mother.'

Tayte approached the bed and stood opposite Helen.

'You won't be very comfortable standing up, dear,' Emily said. 'Sit down and let me see you.'

Tayte smiled and sat on the bed, sinking into a sea of goose down and feathers.

'Mother's eyes aren't so good,' Helen said in a low voice, as though expecting Emily wouldn't hear her.

'Nonsense, dear,' Emily said. 'It's just my legs that don't seem to work anymore.' Her eyes were fixed on Tayte. 'Closer,' she said. 'If I'm going to share a secret with a stranger, I should like to feel better acquainted.'

Tayte shuffled further along the bed, all the while looking back into Emily's eyes as she seemed to measure him, as though what she saw in his own eyes would determine whether or not she would share what she knew. Without warning her entire face began to smile, and although he couldn't explain it, Jefferson Tayte never felt more welcome anywhere in his life.

Emily broke the connection between them, looking away to Helen. 'Fetch my album would you, dear?' She reached a frail hand onto Tayte's, and he edged closer until he was within comfortable reach.

'You have cold hands, Mr Tayte,' Emily said.

Tayte hadn't really thought about it, but the hand resting on the back of his certainly felt warm. 'Not really, ma'am.'

Emily raised her eyebrows to him. 'Cold hands—warm heart,' she said.

'I'm afraid I don't know much about matters of the heart,' Tayte said, honestly.

Emily looked sad for him. 'No love in your life, Mr Tayte? No *passion?*' Her eyes sparkled.

'Only my work,' Tayte offered. 'I get so involved. Never seem to stay in one place long enough for romance.'

'Or perhaps you're running from something?'

Tayte was lost for words. It had always felt like he was chasing, not running away; chasing his identity. The vivid image of Sandra Greenaway, the last girl he'd found the nerve to ask out, pulled her sour face at him again, reminding him of that prom night rebuff he'd never really recovered from. Was that it? Rejection. Was he running from what he supposed must be every adoptive child's ghost, the fear of facing up to his own mother's rejection?

'I really don't think I'm the loving kind,' Tayte said, moving on.

'But you are,' Emily said. 'I can tell.'

Tayte felt a blush rise and break across his face.

Helen saved him as she returned to the bedside. 'Here you are,' she said. She placed a heavy brown vinyl folder on the bedcover next to Emily and opened it at random.

'Thank you, dear,' Emily said. She caressed the edge of one of the photographs like she was remembering the scene. Then she began to turn the pages back. 'Lowenna Fairborne knew about love,' Emily said. 'For a short while, at least.'

Tayte watched Emily's features change with every page she turned, as she seemed to relive every captured moment. The photographs were no longer in colour now, and soon they had gone back beyond even Emily's long lifetime.

'I never knew Lowenna Fairborne, of course,' Emily said. 'That was too long ago even for me. But hers was quite a story. Though not a happy one, I'm afraid.'

Emily kept turning the pages, pausing over the images as she went. 'But stories like hers, Mr Tayte, find their own way of being told. My mother-in-law told it to me, as her mother-in-law told it before that. I'm afraid my son has no interest.' Emily looked around the room. 'Where *is* David?' she asked.

'He has a golf game, Mother,' Helen said.

Emily smiled to herself. 'It's going to rain. You'd better tell him to take a brolly.' She turned another page, close to the start of the album now. 'Ah, there she is.'

The image was small, no bigger than a playing card, fixed to a slightly larger mount to stop the edges curling. 'This was made in the 1820s,' Emily said. 'Somewhere in London. She was brave to make the trip at her age, but I suppose the artist must have been in demand by those who could afford him.'

Tayte leant closer. The image was a miniature portrait painting of an elderly lady dressed in mainly dark clothing that was poorly defined. She wore a green bonnet and a very serious expression.

'This is Lowenna's mother, Susan,' Emily said. 'I suppose she would have been in her late fifties or early sixties when this was painted. I don't have many portraits of the family from that time.'

Tayte looked up from the album to Emily, whose eyes were still fixed on the painting. 'Have you ever heard the name Mathew Parfitt?' he asked.

Emily shook her head. 'No,' she said, taking no time to think about it.

'How about Jane? Parfitt or Forbes?'

Emily looked highly amused. 'I don't believe so.'

Tayte was trying to think of another question to ask her when Emily began to laugh.

'Do you want me to tell you about Lowenna Fairborne, Mr Tayte? Or do you want to go on fishing?'

'I'm sorry,' Tayte said, smiling with her. 'Please go on.'

Emily closed her eyes for what seemed to Tayte like an eternity. He felt like he was part of some captive audience waiting for the curtain to open.

'Lowenna Fairborne,' Emily began at last, 'was just sixteen years old when she was sent to live for a time with Susan's parents—sent to this very house. That was in 1803.'

Tayte heard the year and felt goose bumps tingle on the backs of his arms. *The year Mathew Parfitt was born.*

'There was some trouble with her father,' Emily continued. 'It was serious enough for her to be sent here without notice, which came as a shock to the family because Lowenna and her father had always been close—like two peas.' Emily closed the album and pushed it towards Helen. 'Lowenna arrived alone by carriage late in the night with very few personal effects, not even the maid she'd grown up with. Maybe it was just to cool Lowenna's heart, but everyone knew there was more to the matter than that. Lowenna brought many secrets to this house with her that night.'

'Cool her heart?' Tayte said. 'So she had a lover? Someone her father disapproved of?'

'Oh yes, Mr Tayte. A farmer, I believe. And not long after Lowenna arrived, our side of the family knew just how far their relationship had gone. Her father knew all about it, of course, and he had his plans carefully worked out for her. But something else had been troubling that one. Something that meant more to him than his own daughter, it seems.'

The gathering clouds outside brought with them a stiffening breeze off the moor. It started the trees in Dartmoor Forest whispering and aggravated the net curtain at the window, prompting Helen to go over and close it.

'Lowenna was inconsolable for weeks when she first arrived,' Emily said. 'You see, the love she had known, even at her tender age, was strong enough to break her heart when that love was snatched away from her. Carrying his child made it all the more unbearable.'

Tayte let out the breath he'd been holding. The Washington Redskins had just scored a touchdown right there in Emily Forbes's bedroom. An illegitimate pregnancy and a childless aunt and uncle who desperately wanted a child—Jane and Lavender Parfitt were ideally placed to take the child as their own. Tayte felt like a million fizzy bubbles had just risen through him, rendering him momentarily weightless.

'Lowenna tried to run away twice during her first week here,' Emily said. 'She must have wanted to leave very badly, but where could she go, poor thing? Dartmoor was her guard and her keeper, and very effective it was in those days. She almost caught her death the second time, when they found her wandering out on the moor. It's a wonder the baby survived. I think that's what stopped her trying again.'

Emily turned to Helen. 'Pass me that glass of water would you, dear?' She took a sip, then said, 'It was quite a few months later, sometime after her seventeenth birthday and not long before the baby was due, that Lowenna heard the terrible news that her farmer was dead. They said he'd been murdered, and it very nearly killed the poor child where she stood—and the baby growing inside her.' Emily took another sip of water and paused, like she was reflecting on what else she knew. 'It might have been better for the poor girl if she had died there and then.'

'What happened to her?' Tayte asked.

'Patience, Mr Tayte. I'm coming to that. You see, the family tried to protect Lowenna from the news for as long as anyone could. But it was all very public, with a hanging soon afterwards. Even so, by the time she found out, the murder was old news in Helford, where it happened. When Lowenna heard the date of the murder… well, she also knew that that was the very last day she'd seen him.'

'Do you know what that date was?' Tayte asked.

Emily smiled. 'It was all a very long time ago now, Mr Tayte. I don't recall ever hearing it, but I know it all happened in 1803. It was a busy year for the family, that much I do know.'

The bedroom door opened and David Forbes poked his head in. 'I'm just off then,' he said. 'Everything okay here?'

'Come and sit down, David,' Helen said. 'We're having a nice chat aren't we, Mother?'

David tapped his watch. 'Look, I really can't. We're teeing off in fifteen minutes. I'll be lucky to make it as it is.' He blew a kiss into the room. 'I'll pop in and see you when I get back, Mother—tell you all about it.' Then he was gone again.

Tayte heard Emily sigh, though from her face he supposed that she meant to hide her disappointment.

'Always in a rush to be somewhere else, that's my David,' Emily said. 'But he'll miss me when I'm gone.'

'Mother!'

Tayte caught Emily's wink and returned a sympathetic smile. 'So do you know what happened to the child Lowenna was carrying?' he asked.

'Oh, yes,' Emily said. 'About a fortnight before the child was due, Lowenna's father came to take her home, and he made it quite clear that she could not keep the child. It was for her own good, of course, that's what they told her. And it was for the good of the family. But she didn't understand, poor thing. How could she?'

Emily took another sip of water and handed the glass back to Helen. 'She was to have nothing to do with the child,' Emily continued. 'She wasn't even to be told what was to become of it, but I suspect she knew. Her mother, Susan, was a kind woman. How could she bear to keep it from her?'

Tayte knew, too. The child had to be Mathew Parfitt.

'She must have felt so helpless,' Helen said.

Emily nodded. 'Desperately helpless. Her lover was dead and their child was to be taken from her the instant the poor thing was born.' Her eyes began to glisten, like wet marbles. 'Yes,' she said. '1803 was a desperate year for Lowenna Fairborne.'

—— ——

It was late in October 1803. An early frost smothered the night, and to Lowenna Fairborne it was like a cold white pillow hovering over her face, ready to suffocate her. Rosemullion Hall and its grounds were still and crystalline beneath a near full moon that stole all colour from the world, replacing it with its own inimitable palette.

Behind a tall window on the third floor, set high into the southwest roof gable at the front of the manor house, Lowenna pretended to sleep. The room was not her own. It was seldom used at any time and had now been made barely accommodating for the solitary purpose of removing the baby from her womb as discreetly as possible. She had feigned sleep soon after the ordeal, and the nurse had left quickly, only calling in occasionally to check on her throughout the evening. But it was late now. The nurse had not returned for some time, and it seemed at last that she would not come again until morning. The exposed floorboards should have felt cold against the bare soles of Lowenna's feet as she lowered her legs out of the bed and slowly stood up. She felt nothing.

Lowenna knew what pain was. She knew pain in every way a person can know pain. It began in the rain that May afternoon, the last time she saw her love, and it spread through her like a vile disease when she learnt of his murder. She knew why he was dead, just as she knew who was responsible. And although the box her father had given her on her fifth birthday had come to mean so much to her, she wished now that it never existed.

But she felt that pain no more.

All the pain she knew was taken from her with the child she would never see or hold—would never know. She understood that now. When her pain left her, the chasm that remained was replaced by a singular determination that saw nothing else and felt nothing else beyond its own focused purpose.

Lowenna's bed gown glowed as she came to the window. She looked ghostly in the moonlight, gaunt and drawn, with her long and colourless hair still clinging to her face here and there by the sweat of her labour. Dark patches on the lower half of her bed gown were still damp from complications during the birth, but she was insensible to it. She stood there, staring absently into the silver night. Then she opened the window and the bitter air sunk its teeth deep into her pale, bluing skin. But Lowenna did not flinch.

She climbed onto the sill, grazing her knees on the rough stone. Then with the last of her strength, she raised herself into the open frame, leaning forward like a ship's proud figurehead, determined. There was no breeze. Not even the slightest sound. Her gown draped heavily from her body, weighted by her own blood. Three floors below, dark slate shimmered beneath the moon like a black sea that she knew would wash her and purify her, ridding her of that vile disease, and in doing so make everything better again.

Chapter Twenty-Four

The Dartmoor rain was heavy on Tayte's back as he climbed into his hire car. Peter Schofield was on his mind again. He could still hear his parting words on the phone yesterday: *Maybe we can meet up. I'm flying over in the morning.* If Schofield took an early flight, as Tayte was sure he would, then with the time difference he'd be in London sometime that evening. *He's up there right now,* Tayte thought. *Somewhere over the Atlantic.* He pulled out his phone, thinking it was time he called his client. The call rang twice before it was picked up.

Sloane's deep bass voice vibrated the earpiece. 'Shoot!' That was Walter Sloane. He was the only man Tayte knew who could make him nervous with a single word.

Tayte turned the volume down. 'Hi, Mr Sloane. It's Jefferson Tayte.'

'I know that, Tayte. I can see your name on the display. It's called technology. Now what have you got for me? I've another call waiting.'

Tayte updated his client—just the highlights, all upbeat and positive. 'And I'm just about to find out who his father is,' he continued, referring to the discovery of the illegitimate Mathew Parfitt and his connection to the Fairborne family.

'That's a nice touch, Tayte. But what about this James fella and the family he took over there?'

'Well, whoever was playing with the records back then missed this one,' Tayte said. 'Maybe they thought no one could make the connection; in 1803, I doubt they could. But with all the advances we've made since then…Parfitt's my way in, I'm sure of it. I'll have more for you tomorrow.'

'Okay, Tayte, tomorrow then.'

Tayte sensed his client was about to hang up. 'Mr Sloane,' he said. 'I had a call from Peter Schofield yesterday. He said you'd called him.'

Tayte heard a gritty, humourless laugh. 'Look, Tayte. I don't know what the problem is between you two, and I don't much care. I'm paying the bills here and time's running out. If Schofield's taken the initiative, then I say two heads are better than one.'

If Tayte had been wearing a tie, he would have loosened it. 'It's just that I always work alone,' he said. 'Never been much good in a team and I'm sure I'll—'

'I don't care how you do it, Tayte,' Sloane cut in, buzzing Tayte's phone again. 'Work with Schofield or use him however you see fit. Just keep it professional and get the job done. He's not taking a cut of your fee, for Christ's sake!'

The sudden silence in Tayte's ear told him that Walter Sloane had terminated the call. He closed his eyes and sank his head over the steering wheel, knowing that Sloane was right. This was his profession, and he was letting personal feelings get in the way. By the time he sat up again, he was considering that the idea of Schofield working *for* him rather than *with* him might not be so bad. Now he just had to think of some way to keep the kid out of his hair.

Tayte started the engine and left the drive, heading back along the lane towards the main road. Before he reached it, his thoughts forced him to pull over and kill the engine again. If Lowenna's lover was murdered and there had been a public hanging as Emily Forbes had said, he should be able to find some record of it. He didn't have the victim's name, just the year of the murder and the location, but he figured hangings were as much a morbid curiosity today as they ever were. It was worth a look.

Tayte climbed across into the passenger seat where he'd have more room and slid his laptop out from his briefcase. *Bodmin assizes,* he thought as he brought up a Google browser and typed *Bodmin executions* into the search field. The first result was a list of executions at Bodmin. He clicked the link and the screen displayed a chronologically ordered list of all executions at Bodmin Jail. As he scrolled through, he was distracted by the range of crimes a person could be hanged for back then, crimes considered petty offences today, like housebreaking and the theft of wheat and livestock. Only one entry appeared for 1803. The date of the hanging was May 25. Tayte read the details in the offence column: Murder of farmer, Mawgan Hendry of Helford.

'Touchdown!' Tayte closed his laptop and slid back across the gearshift into the driver's seat. 'Just follow the clues, JT,' he told himself. 'See where they take you.'

Now he had another name to focus on, another key that was beginning to turn, ready to open another door. And this one led to murder.

───────

It was four-fifteen when Jefferson Tayte pulled into a lay-by two miles outside Bodmin. The rain had been heavy all the way from Dartmoor, and it continued to drum on the roof as he called the record office in Truro. He'd made good time despite the weather, but office hours were nearly over; he needed a quick result on the location of Mawgan Hendry's murder trial records. His call rang too many times before being answered, and Tayte was disappointed to hear a man's static tones.

'Hi, can I speak to Penny Wilson?' Tayte said after listening to the least sincere introduction he'd ever heard.

'She's not available,' the man said.

'Do you know when she'll be free?'

'No, I'm sorry. Can I help?'

Tayte doubted it, but he didn't have time to wait. 'Maybe you can,' he said. 'I need to know where the court proceedings are kept for a murder trial back in 1803. It came under Bodmin assizes. The date I'm looking for is—'

'You'll have to call in person tomorrow,' the man cut in. 'We don't have the resources to handle enquiries over the phone.'

'If I had the time to call in, I would,' Tayte said.

'I'm sorry, sir, but—'

It was Tayte's turn to cut in. 'Look, please tell Penny I need to speak to her. I don't have much time. Just tell her it's JT. She knows me.'

'I think I already said that Penny's not available.' The man's tone carried an edge of sarcasm now.

Tayte sighed. This conversation was going nowhere. He was about to let rip, knowing before he spoke that it would get him nothing more than a short burst of self-satisfaction, when he heard a mild commotion in the background, quickly followed by a familiar voice that could not have been more welcome.

'Hello, can I help you?'

'Penny! It's JT. Who was that!?'

Penny's reply was muffled, like she was whispering into the mouthpiece through a cupped hand. 'He's part time,' she said. 'Only works Thursdays. He's nice enough really.'

Tayte thought that explained things.

'I heard my name and came over,' Penny continued.

'And I'm glad you did. Look, Penny, I know I'm pushing my luck, but I need a big favour and I don't have much time.'

'Is it about that probate record? I'm afraid nothing's turned up yet.'

'No, this is something else.'

Tayte told Penny where he was and gave her the details of the murder case he needed to see. 'The victim was a farmer from Helford,' he added. 'Mawgan Hendry.'

'We keep records here for cases that far back,' Penny said.

Good, Tayte thought. *Nice and easy.*

'Only, I know for a fact that the details of that particular case aren't here.'

Tayte couldn't believe it. He dropped his phone away from his ear and stared at the rain streaking down his windscreen. Then he wondered how Penny knew that without even looking. There had to be more to it. He could still hear her voice, tinny and distant.

'Sorry, Penny?' he said.

'I was just saying…I know the case details aren't here because someone else called in earlier to look at the same file. I had to tell them the same thing. What are the odds?'

Slim, Tayte thought.

'It was a few hours ago,' Penny added. 'Same year, same place. Then when you said he was a farmer…'

'Can you tell me who was asking about it?'

'I really can't, JT. We're not allowed to.'

'Sure, I understand. So where *are* the case details? Do you know?'

'I do. They're on loan to an exhibition. And by the sound of it, you're not far from them.'

When his call with Penny ended, Tayte knew exactly where he was going, though he was a little surprised. As he pulled the car back out onto the A38, heading into Bodmin, he wondered what made this case so special that it justified entry into an exhibition of crime and punishment.

⁘

Jefferson Tayte's hire car was not the only car heading for the exhibition at Bodmin. The driver of the beat-up electric blue Mazda was suddenly in a hurry to get there, although he hadn't anticipated returning so soon. He clutched at the silver crucifix that hung around his neck and made sure it was well concealed.

So the American is going to Bodmin...

The man was impressed with Tayte's ingenuity. It was clear that Tayte was good at his job, and at first that fact rattled him. His mind raced ahead, trying to work out if Tayte had any chance of getting to the truth. He couldn't allow that—that would spoil everything.

Not without the records, he concluded.

He was confident that Tayte had no hope of succeeding without them. Yet, as he reflected on the American's demonstrated ability, a shadow of concern darkened his thoughts. A moment later he smiled to himself. 'Who cares!' he said. 'If he gets too close...' He reached across to the glove box and popped it open. The four-inch barrel of his grandfather's old Webley .38 service revolver winked back at him as cold steel caught the daylight. It wasn't his tool of choice—far too noisy. But he considered that it might yet see further active service.

Chapter Twenty-Five

Bodmin Jail was built around 1778 from twenty thousand tons of local granite. During its working life, it had seen fifty-seven executions by hanging, fifty-three of which were public, drawing crowds of up to twenty-five thousand people. The last public hanging was in 1862, after which four further executions took place behind the prison walls. The jail closed in the 1920s.

Standing beneath the gatehouse archway, sheltering from the weather while he got his bearings, Tayte could smell the rain in the air and in the granite walls around him. The archway was set between two circular turrets joined overhead by a steep pitched roof that was topped with a central spire. The gatehouse itself had few windows, and most were no more than narrow slits, like archers' windows. The few that were wide enough to crawl through were heavily barred.

The weather and the late hour served well to keep the tourists away; the place looked deserted. Tayte peered out through an endless curtain of rain, watching it explode and hiss off the courtyard like thousands of tiny fireworks. The entire place looked as disconsolate and oppressive as the weather. He was looking for the jail museum. That was where Penny had told him to go. She'd said he would find what he was looking for there.

An open doorway across the courtyard looked inviting, and the scattering of blue signs that crowded it looked promising. He made a dash for the steps, and by the time he was halfway there, he was soaked. He burst through the doorway, almost knocking over the woman who was standing just inside.

'Excuse me!' Tayte said, reaching out to steady her.

The woman laughed it off and Tayte joined her. She looked a little older than Tayte, dressed casually in jeans and a mint green cardigan.

'Is this the museum?' Tayte asked. He'd been going too fast to take in any of the signs.

'That's right.' She was behind her desk now.

'How much is it?'

The woman handed Tayte a leaflet explaining some of the visitor attractions. 'That's £3.50, please.' Her smile froze on her face while Tayte rummaged through his pockets for change.

'Can I get a receipt for that?'

From the leaflet, Tayte learnt that the month-long attraction, now in its last week, brought together the cases of twenty of the most notable executions from the prison's grisly history. He stopped reading as he entered the exhibition, taking in the high ceiling and the arched windows that were set into the exposed brickwork. The floor was also brick, uneven and waxed over the years to a burnt red hue. Display boards divided the room, lit by halogen spotlights, guiding visitors from the first hanging to the last.

The first display Tayte came to was for a twenty-one year old man called Philip Randal, executed on Bodmin Moor on March 7, 1785. His crime was burglary. The display showed the original case records beneath a Perspex cover, so you could look but not touch. He moved further in and noticed that some exhibits featured items of evidence, including the murder weapons. In the case of Sarah Polgreen, a vial of poison was displayed inside a Perspex case. Some items looked original and others were clearly reproduced to help the exhibition come alive, along with simplified prints that depicted scenes of the associated crimes and hangings, adding a touch of the macabre.

Tayte had the exhibition to himself, and if he'd had more time he would have enjoyed reading every case. As it was he quickly moved on, checking the dates as he went, drawing closer to what he was looking for. He turned a corner and came to a case that was dated August 25, 1802. He was almost there.

Then he realised he was not quite alone.

Further ahead, a seated figure in a charcoal raincoat was huddled over the case notes at the next display along. Tayte approached. The bold typeface date stood out on the display board—May 25, 1803—the case he'd come to see. He continued apprehensively, supposing this was the same person who had enquired about the case with Penny at the record office earlier.

As he arrived he saw that the exhibit was not complete; the Perspex cases were broken and empty. He stopped beside the display and the seated figure looked up and smiled at him briefly before going back to the notepad she was scribbling into. Her coat, which revealed only the white ruffles of her shirt collar and cuffs and the hem of her claret and tan skirt, was dry, and with the obvious absence of an umbrella, Tayte supposed she must have been there a while. He thought the low-heeled black boots that filled the gap between her coat and the floor were a sensible option on a day like this.

'Gruesome place,' Tayte said, looking back at the mock gallows he'd just passed, erected for effect halfway into the exhibition.

The woman half-smiled this time and nodded. Then she carried on writing like she couldn't get the words down fast enough.

Tayte's eyes strayed to the display board. They were the only people there and he suddenly felt awkward—predatory—as if he were lingering with some nefarious intent, rather than simply looking for information. He knew it wouldn't be long before he made her feel uncomfortable, but he had to stay and he supposed the exhibition would be closing soon. He felt an explanation was in order.

'I'm a genealogist,' Tayte announced when the scratch of the woman's pen finally paused.

She looked up.

'Family history, you know...I've a special interest in this case.' He indicated the pen that was still poised over her notepad. 'So do you, it seems.'

'Oh, the notes,' she said, flicking the pen between her fingers like a metronome keeping an allegrissimo tempo. 'Yes, you could say that.'

'If you don't mind me asking,' Tayte said. 'When I called the record office in Truro earlier, they said someone else had enquired about this trial today.'

The woman looked interested, if a little confused. 'I was there earlier, yes.'

Tayte rushed a hand out and cheesy smile followed it. 'Name's JT,' he said. 'Seems we have a common interest here.'

'Amy Fallon,' the woman said.

Tayte turned back to the display and the magnified text that was there to give the passing speed-reader a general outline. 'I'm interested in the victim,' he said. 'He was the lover of a young woman called Lowenna Fairborne.'

'Lowenna?'

'That's right,' Tayte said, registering Amy's obvious recognition. 'I'm hoping her lover's going to lead me to the family I'm looking for. Connections,' he added. 'I'm always looking for connections.'

'Sounds interesting work,' Amy said. She sounded distracted, like her words as she spoke them were wrapped in thought.

'Most of the time it is,' Tayte said. 'Though it can be frustrating as hell. So what brought *you* here? Perp or victim?'

Amy smiled to herself. 'Perp,' she mimicked. 'Turns out my house once harboured a murderer or two.'

Tayte looked impressed.

'I'm here,' Amy added, 'because of a box I found at my house yesterday. I wanted to know more about it, so I went to Truro this morning to find out who'd lived there before.'

'And it led you to this old murder case?'

'Not straightaway. A friend recognised two of the names on the list. He told me about a verse the National Trust had published—it's all over Cornwall, apparently.'

'A verse?'

Amy pointed up at the display board. 'It was written by a local farmer about two drunken ferrymen,' she said. 'The National Trust people were very helpful. I found out that the farmer had been murdered the night he wrote it, which took me back to Truro looking for the trial details.'

'Two different routes to the same place,' Tayte said.

Amy nodded. 'So who's Lowenna Fairborne?'

'Daughter of James Fairborne,' Tayte said. 'A wealthy family then and now. They have an estate by the Helford River.'

'I know it,' Amy said. 'I run the ferry service at Helford.' She paused. Then in a manner that seemed to answer her own question she said, 'Lowenna would have had a maid then?'

'Sure.' Tayte thought the conversation seemed suddenly disjointed, but he could see it made perfect sense to Amy.

'I need to be getting back,' she said, sliding her chair away from the display.

'Hey, don't leave on my account.' Amy's explanation of how she came to be there had raised the possibility of other connections he didn't want to lose. 'This old place is already giving me the creeps.'

Amy seemed to settle briefly, and Tayte was close to asking her about the box she'd mentioned, when she got up. She collected her notepad and a spotlight caught the bright gold on her ring finger.

'Interesting ring,' Tayte said, trying to keep the conversation alive.

'It's Celtic.' She flashed it and Tayte caught the inverted pattern of interlocking hearts. 'Look, I really need to get back,' she said. 'Business calls.' She slipped her bag over her shoulder. 'Good luck,' she added. 'Nice meeting you.'

Tayte watched her leave, one foot slotting in front of the other like an experienced catwalk model until she turned beyond the far display board towards the exit. The room fell instantly silent. Then Tayte heard the rain again, rapping at the windows. He sat down, took out his notebook, and stared up at the story outline in front of him. The victim's name stared back, along with the verse Amy had spoken of.

On Tuesday, May 17, 1803, Mawgan Hendry stood silent in the late afternoon rain and watched Lowenna run from him. He felt light headed and detached from the scene, as though looking in on the life of some other unfortunate soul, standing beneath the shelter of that broad oak tree, watching *his* life run away with her, feeling *his* blood drain from him like it were washing along a fast gutter with the rain.

She had been gone several minutes before any feeling came back to him. Only then did his dull senses tell him that he was holding something. He recalled Lowenna giving it to him, but the memory of it was as stale as an old dream. He looked down, bringing an ornate box up to meet his faraway gaze.

When he could bring himself to open it, the note beneath the silk heart inside confirmed what he already knew. It was over. And he could guess well enough at the reason. He had always known the day would come. His mother, Tegan, had told him enough times— told him that one day Lowenna would have no choice but to break his heart, that their love would ultimately be denied. Yet in his heart a bright cinder of hope had lived, ignited like a phoenix rising every time they met.

By the time Mawgan reached Helford Passage, he was not the same man who had crossed the river that Tuesday morning bound for Falmouth market. As he pulled his cart up beneath a dark and crowded sky, the hard rain was relentless on his back, bonding his clothes to him like a second skin, flowing with the contours of his muscles. But it was no match for the unbearable weight that somehow managed to keep beating inside his chest. Mawgan Hendry did not want to be delayed by the ferrymen tonight. He wished only to get home now, and quickly. But he had no choice. He had been there nearly two hours already.

If Mawgan could feel any emotion, it would be anger. He jumped from the cart, mud splashing from his boots as he landed. Ebryl's hind legs stamped the ground and Mawgan stroked a firm hand along her mane as he passed, soothing her. He paced out onto the wooden pontoon at the edge of the water with purposeful strides, and the pontoon swayed beneath him. He was oblivious to the distant revelry inside the Ferry Boat Inn behind him.

The river was black and restless as the sky. Mawgan looked out across the darkness, barely able to determine the indistinct shapes of the vessels at uneasy anchor; there was still no sign of the ferry. The wind cut into the mouth of the river and blew cold at his wet shirt, but he was numb even to that. He sat down on the pontoon and took out a leather-bound book, then flicked through the pages, not caring that they were getting wet. He passed all his old passages of poetry and verse until he came to the next blank sheet. Then he began to write.

The wind howled through the boats on the river, flapping loose rigging and sailcloth into a violent dance, married to the beat of creaking timbers. When his verse was written, Mawgan stood at the edge of the pontoon and shouted his words across the water, fighting to be heard over the wind and the lashing rain.

> *Of all the mortals here below*
> *Your drunken boatmen are the worst I know;*
> *I'm here detained, tho' sore against my will,*

While these sad fellows sit and drink their fill.
Oh Jove, to my request let this be given,
That these same brethren ne'er see hell nor heaven;
But with old Charon ever tug the oar,
And neither taste nor swallow one drop more.

Mawgan's last words barely had a chance to leave his rain-soaked lips. He was not alone.

Chapter Twenty-Six

Tayte rocked back on his chair inside the museum at Bodmin Jail. He was looking up at the verse on the display board that forced him now to recall what he knew about Greek mythology. *But with old Charon ever tug the oar.* They were damning words, more a curse in many ways, and Mawgan Hendry had died the very day he wrote it, as if a pact had been made that night in 1803 and it had been sealed with his life.

Tayte thought back to his scholarly years. He'd covered Homer's *Iliad* and Virgil's *Aeneid* and had studied all three canticas of Dante Alighieri's *Divine Comedy*. Charon was the ferryman of the dead, an appropriate subject then for Mawgan Hendry's verse about drunken ferrymen. He was condemning the ferrymen to pull oars with Charon for all eternity on the River Acheron, the river of woe, ferrying the shades of the dead to Hades—the underworld. Tayte smiled to himself, remembering some of the heated discussions he'd been involved in back at university. Was it the River Acheron or the River Styx where Charon plied his trade? It was a topical question then, and he thought it probably still was today.

He pulled his chair closer to the Perspex sheet that protected the original murder trial documents and eyed the broken display cases again, wondering what they had contained. Perhaps the case notes would tell him? He leaned in on his elbows and began to read.

In May 1803, the unseen figure who watched Mawgan Hendry arrive with his cart at Helford Passage knew he would be there. He'd seen Mawgan go out onto the pontoon and sit in the rain; he'd listened as the farmer bellowed his verse across the river. And now, as though materialising out of the night from the wind and the rain itself, his brutish form reared up behind Mawgan with such improbable stealth for his size that his victim remained unaware of death's cold presence until it was too late to prevent it.

The man circled a cord around Mawgan's neck with well-practised precision. Then with a violent jerk he drew the cord tight and braced himself. He felt his victim begin to thrash, clenched fists striking out. He watched the book Mawgan had been reading from tumble to the pontoon. He tightened his grip and the cord held as his victim began to claw at his own neck, tearing his flesh.

Then he was still.

Rain lashed in off the river in gusts. At last his victim crashed to his knees, and the man dropped with him, pressing his face close to Mawgan's ear. 'You know what I've come for.' A weak shake of his victim's head was all the response he received, but he was satisfied with the reply. He smiled, wryly. 'No matter.'

He adjusted his grip on the stubby handles at either end of the cord. He was calm now and unrushed. There was no fight left in his victim, no struggle. He listened closely at Mawgan's neck as he tightened the cord further, slowly and purposefully. The anticipation of what he was listening for was almost unbearable to him. Then he felt it as much as he heard it, and when that delicate moment came to him, when Mawgan's hyoid bone fractured with the *snap* he'd been waiting for, his lips quivered and murmured a gentle, pleasurable sigh.

But something on the river disturbed him, destroying the moment. He looked up with hatred in his eyes, but he could see nothing in the darkness. His victim's body became suddenly heavy, forcing his attention back to his business as the body slumped forward, twitching and convulsing. He caught the deadweight by the ligature around Mawgan's neck, easing the body lower as he rose and pressed a muddy boot between Mawgan's shoulder blades. He gave the cord a final lingering tug to be sure. Then a light on the black river caught his eye, and he let the body collapse onto the pontoon before pulling it into the water after him.

On that same cold and wet evening in May 1803, Jowan Penhale and Davy Fenton were enjoying another tankard of ale in the Shipwrights Arms across the river. Their backs were to the fireplace, which cracked and spat beneath a blackened beam. Their eyes were fixed as usual on Jenna Fox, the barmaid, as she went about her business.

It was a busy evening; the weather had seen to that. It had invited patrons in and gave them little reason to leave. An erratic wind song filled the chimney, whispering to the flames in the fireplace, exciting their dance. Outside, it had become dark before its time, but the mood within was fighting a good battle against the elements. A song had struck up in one corner, a popular ditty that had everyone joining in. The thump of the coarse Cornish jig filled the inn, and hard heels beat the floorboards.

'We should get along, Jowan,' Davy said. He sounded serious for the first time that evening, despite the view he had of Jenna Fox, leaning this way and that, her chest bouncing with her laughter.

'Conscience got the best of you?' Jowan said. He turned away from Jenna then too, looking at Davy like he didn't believe a word of it. 'Who'll be out there tonight?'

'You never know.'

'Only fools, that's who,' Jowan continued, 'and they can wait.' He tried in vain to straighten his hair in case Jenna looked over: a thick black crop that had never been the same since he'd let Davy cut it.

'Let's take a look at least,' Davy said, scratching at his rough shirt fibres with blackened fingernails.

'I've a better plan,' Jowan said. 'Let's have another ale!' His voice rose to the level of the song that was getting into his head.

'A look after, then?'

Jowan shook his head, smiling. 'Who's possessed you tonight, Davy Fenton?' He sighed at Jenna. 'If it'll stop your worrying, then after it is.' He drained his tankard. 'Jenna, my love,' he called. His voice was as high as his spirits. He pulled a coin from his leather waistcoat pocket and slapped it down beside his tankard. 'Two more of your fine ales, if you please.' He could see Jenna was already serving someone else.

'You'll wait your turn, Jowan Penhale.'

Jowan and Davy looked at one another with mischief in their eyes.

'I love her most when she's feisty, Davy.'

'Me, too,' Davy said.

When they reached Helford Point, the ferry pontoon was empty, as Jowan had supposed. The river was black and the wind was shrill in his ears, driving the rain to such an extent that it stung his face. He let Davy out from under his arm and Davy staggered towards the ferry raft.

'Can't see a bloody thing,' Jowan said, squinting into the night. 'Sod it. Might as well go across, now we're here.'

Davy was already ahead of him. He was on the raft, loosening the ropes. 'We can get another ale when we get across,' he said.

Jowan smiled to himself as he jumped onto the ferry and lit the lantern. 'Good idea,' he said. 'Are you *sure* you're not my brother?'

Davy shrugged his shoulders. 'Who knows!' he said, and they were still laughing halfway across the river.

'Look, Jowan!'

'What is it, Davy?'

'I thought I saw someone.'

Jowan peered across to the ferry landing. The lights from the Ferry Boat Inn were clear enough, but he could make out little else. Beneath him the raft swayed on unsteady waters. 'I still can't see a thing,' he said.

'It's gone now. I thought I saw something on the pontoon.'

Jowan pointed ahead to a shape he was beginning to make out. 'What's that?' he said. It became clearer as they approached.

'Looks like a horse,' Davy said.

'It is. And there's a cart too.'

'Not a bad end to a bad day then, Davy. A horse and cart. That'll go well towards the beer.'

Davy raised a pole and pushed it out to buffer the raft against the pontoon as a heavy swell brought them crashing in. The raft tipped and the pole slipped away, catching Davy off guard. He stumbled onto his hands as Jowan caught a line on the pontoon and pulled them closer.

Both Jowan and Davy missed the small leather-bound book, discarded and wet on the pontoon boards, as they tied off the raft and made their way onto land. Their attention was on the Shire horse at the head of the green and red cart set back on the muddy track.

'No one there,' Davy offered.

'Probably inside having a drink,' Jowan said.'

Davy looked towards the inn. 'Sounds busy.'

They exchanged grins. Then Davy went to find the cart's owner as Jowan remained beside it, more interested in what the cart carried. To his disappointment, it was near empty: just a few spoiled vegetables. But something caught his eye. 'Hold up, Davy.'

Davy stopped in his tracks, looking at his friend one minute and then back at the inn the next. 'What you doing?' he whispered.

Jowan climbed up onto the cart and sat down. He pulled a haversack onto his lap and began to rummage. 'Would you look at this!' he said a moment later. He held up a heavy felt purse, whistling as he swung it. Then his eyes were back inside the bag.

'Leave it, Jowan. We'll get caught.'

Davy's eyes were fixed on the inn now, and Jowan seemed to wake to the possibility. He shoved the purse into his pocket and closed the bag. 'Come on, then. Let's get back.' He jumped down from the cart, splashing the mud.

'You're not taking it?' Davy said.

Jowan strolled back to the pontoon. 'Why not?'

Davy gave no answer. He stood there like he was trying to think of a reason, but none came.

'No one saw us arrive,' Jowan said when Davy caught up with him. 'And no one will see us leave—unless you count that horse.' He opened the ferry lantern and the wind blew the flame out before he had chance to. 'It's perfect. Like we were never here at all.' He jumped onto the raft and untied the rope, eager to get back into the gloom on the river.

Davy pushed off, beaming like a fool. 'Easy money, then,' he said. 'Easy money...'

———

Lying quietly at the waterline, a black shadow rested like a rock. He'd seen everything, watching as Jowan took the haversack from the cart, cursing them under his breath. The one thing he'd gone there for had slipped away from him. As the raft left the pontoon, the dark figure rolled quietly away from the lifeless body beneath him and loosened the ligature from his victim's neck. The noise from the inn grew louder as a door opened, and a silver crucifix that hung around Mawgan's neck reflected the light that spilled from the door. The dark figure grabbed the crucifix, extinguishing the reflection as easily as he'd extinguished Mawgan's life. Then he was still again—a rock once more.

———⁓———

Jowan and Davy were quick to tie off the ferry for the night when they got back across the river to Helford Point. It hadn't occurred to either of them until they pulled up alongside the pontoon that they might be seen bringing the ferry back; then someone would know that they had crossed. But the weather had not let up. The wind was just as strong, the sky as dark, and the rain as hard as it had been when they first crossed to Helford Passage. No one was out by the river when they landed.

Long strides took Davy away from the ferry and off the pontoon, and he didn't slow until he was up on the village path. 'We'll be needing another drink then, Jowan?'

'We will, Davy. A big one.'

Jowan felt the bulging purse through his shabby trouser pocket and quickened his pace as the Shipwrights Arms came into view beside the creek. It sounded as lively as ever, and before they entered, he took off his coat and wrapped it around the haversack to conceal it. The bundle was hard edged, but it looked like an armful of wet rags by the time he'd finished.

Jenna Fox looked surprised to see them back so soon. She stood behind the bar with her hands on her hips, waving her chest at them as they approached. 'Can't get enough of me, eh boys?'

'Never for a minute,' Jowan said, leaning in across the bar at their usual place by the fire. 'Not even if I was stuck in this very moment for the rest of my sorry days.'

Jenna laughed. Then she must have caught Davy eyeing her cleavage. She reached across and shook his cheek, pulling his face closer until his nose sunk into her bosom.

Davy was blushing when he came out again.

'The usual?' Jenna said, reaching for their tankards.

'And the smoothest rum in the house to chase it down,' Jowan replied.

Jenna winked at him. 'I like a man who can take his drink,' she teased.

Jowan grinned. 'One for yourself, then?'

To their left sat a man Jowan and Davy knew from the village. 'Jago, can I get you a drink while I'm about it?'

At the sound of his name the man looked up from his pipe. He looked grim as the weather. 'What's the occasion?'

Jowan and Davy stared at one another while they tried to think of one. 'It's my birthday!' Jowan lied, and they both laughed.

'No trade then?' Jenna asked when she returned with their ale. She set them down and poured out three measures of rum.

Davy was quick to answer. 'There was no one out there,' he said.

Jenna laughed. 'I'm not surprised!'

'That's right,' Jowan added. 'Not a soul on this foul night, so we waited a while then came running back to you.' He flashed his eyes playfully, studying her mouth as she teased a sip of rum through her cherry red lips.

'We didn't even go across,' Davy said. He picked up his tankard and his ale was half finished before he put it down again.

Jowan knew he needed to change the subject. 'Sorry, Jago,' he said. He turned to Jenna. 'Get this fine man whatever he's drinking would you, my love.'

Chapter Twenty-Seven

Voices at the entrance to the exhibition distracted Tayte. The display stands blocked his view, but he recognised the voice of the woman who had sold him his admission ticket. The other was a man; another customer he supposed. *Late, though...* He checked his watch: 16:50. He hadn't noticed what time the exhibition closed, but he thought it must be soon.

The talking stopped. Then Tayte heard quick steps beyond the displays, hurrying through the exhibition. His curiosity followed the sound until it ended abruptly and the room fell silent again. He thought the visitor must have come to view something specific, as he had. Maybe this new arrival knew there wasn't much time before the museum closed and was in a hurry to get around the exhibits.

He went back to the case notes, reading an account from Mawgan Hendry's mother, Tegan, about the items her son had with him the day he was murdered, items that were missing from his cart, presumed stolen: his haversack and the day's takings from market. His verse book had been recovered, and Tayte wondered if that was one of the items missing from the display cases. As he read on, he learnt of other items described by Tegan Hendry that had belonged to Mawgan—items that had later proven crucial to the prosecution.

On Wednesday, May 18, 1803, the morning after Mawgan Hendry was murdered, a crowd had gathered by the ferry pontoon at Helford Point. Jowan and Davy were late, which was nothing unusual. They drank hard the night before, even by their measure, almost emptying their ill-gotten purse. And they had slept hard. What *was* unusual that morning was the size of the crowd and the gossip that was spreading fast.

Jowan's head thumped to the beat of his footsteps as he marched ahead of Davy down the lane to the ferry. The ground was sodden from yesterday's storm, and although the sky was lighter, it remained grey, like collared-dove feathers. The rain had lessened to a soaking mist that veiled the entrance to the Helford River.

Jowan knew they were pushing their luck. He could hear the hum of the crowd long before he could see it, but when they arrived, their appearance went strangely unnoticed. There were a few glances, but there was none of the usual angry discourse that followed whenever the ferrymen were late. The crowd seemed too excited and too busy with their own conversations to pay them any interest as they pushed through towards the pontoon, snatching words from one conversation and then another.

'They found him caught up on the rocks last night,' one voice said.

'Did you know him?' a woman asked.

Davy didn't seem to have twigged, but Jowan's concern was growing.

'Shocking!' someone said. 'His poor mother…'

'They started the search after the inn turned out,' one man said. 'Saw the empty cart on the track. Well, it didn't belong to anyone there, so it was clear something was amiss.'

'And what a night for it,' another man said.

Jowan heard 'cart,' and his stomach knotted. The next thing he heard left him in no doubt.

'Been robbed and strangled, they said. Horrible marks cut into his neck.'

'Nearly took his head off! That's what I heard.'

Jowan stopped short of the pontoon at the edge of the crowd. He was thinking fast now. He caught hold of Davy and pulled him close.

'Davy?' he whispered.

Davy looked distant, like he hadn't heard a word of the circulating gossip.

Jowan shook him. 'Listen. There's trouble, Davy.'

'What trouble?'

'Be quiet, Davy.' Jowan edged his friend out from the crowd and stared into his eyes. 'Get back to the house.' His voice was barely audible. 'You must hide the bag…from last night!'

Davy looked confused.

'I'll explain later,' Jowan said. 'Just go.' He spun Davy around and whispered in his ear, 'You know where to put it.'

The words 'trouble' and 'bag' seemed to register at last, and Davy nodded, wide-eyed, as Jowan pushed him back into the crowd.

Later that evening, two men were talking in low voices in the muted corner of a poorly lit room that was damp and heavy with the decayed odour of rotting leaves. Their shadows were cast on the wall, one larger than the other, yet both shared a similar, brutish form. The lantern on the floor in the centre of the room was blackened on all sides, and what light it gave from its opening was directed into the room, away from an entrance overgrown with ivy and rose thorns.

The soft glow revealed hard stone edges and a dusty, bug-infested floor that ran to a wall of recessed chambers. An angel looked down on the room from those chambers, her features uncharacteristically malevolent in the dim light. To the side walls, grey headstones that were just visible stabbed out from the ground like dagger points, bearing obscured inscriptions that were impossible to read.

'It was not there,' the larger of the two men said. He spoke firmly, slowly, reiterating what he had already said.

'It has to be,' said the other, unable to believe otherwise. 'You did not look hard enough!'

'You should have let me do it my own way,' the larger man said.

'Like the farmer!?'

'I would have made Davy Fenton talk first!'

The smaller of the two men became animated. 'A simple robbery. That's all you had to do. Just enough to get the box back. Now there will be an enquiry—imagine the attention that will bring!' He sank his head into his hands. When he looked up again, he said, 'And what of the crucifix?'

The larger man nodded.

'Good.' The other took a scroll of paper from his coat. 'Deliver this to the church warden. And make sure you are not seen.' He collected the lantern from the floor and extinguished it. The darkness was absolute. 'We must hope for now that the box remains hidden.' He reached for the door, and a bright bead of silver moonlight cracked at the edges. 'Once the note is delivered, we will have all the time we need to search Ferryman Cottage.'

——— ———

A troubled mind had kept Jowan Penhale awake that night. He and Davy had spent the entire evening huddled around a candle considering their predicament until Jowan had at last concluded that they were in the clear. He was sure no one had seen them the previous night when they came upon Hendry's cart, and he knew the stolen haversack was hidden as well as anything so incriminating could be hidden. Having left Davy downstairs in a state of rum-induced narcosis, he was finally starting to drift himself when the peace of the early morning was violated.

He heard several sounds at once, all combining to overpower the silence. Crows caw-cawed as wood splintered and glass fell crashing to a quarry-tiled floor. Then raised voices, angry voices that echoed beneath the floorboards, sent an unmistakable message to the occupants of Ferryman Cottage, contradicting Jowan's earlier conclusions.

His first thoughts were for Davy.

Before the last man had entered the cottage, Jowan was hurtling down the stairs thinking only that he must get to his friend. He crashed into the first man, who was on his way up. He thrust an elbow into the startled face of the intruder and sent him tumbling and falling back into the man who was following after him. Jowan jumped and cleared them both. He made it to the room where he'd left Davy and was confronted by a host of accusing faces. He looked at Davy, lying on the floor, blood in his hair and on his face, and then at the man standing over him, his tipstaff recoiled from a recent blow. Jowan barely had time to take the scene in before he felt himself falling. He crashed to his knees and slid face first against the rough floorboards.

When he came to, Jowan was sitting at the table opposite Davy as they were earlier that evening, only now they were both in handcuffs and from the look of Davy, both in pain. Davy was holding his dirty shirt tails to the gash that started on his forehead and ran unseen beyond his hairline. As their eyes locked, Jowan thought he'd never seen Davy look so scared. The air stank of rum-laced vomit.

'At last,' a high, thin voice said.

Jowan stared into the crowded room. There were several serious-looking men staring back. Some had lanterns; others carried crude but effective clubs. Then he caught the brassy glint of a short sword guard: a hanger, the blade still secured in its scabbard. He recognised the local parish constable at once. Everyone in the village knew him and few with respect.

The role of parish constable was newly appointed each year and ran for a term of twelve months. There were several to each parish, and they were supported by the night watchmen and people from the village if the arrest called for greater numbers. Becoming a parish constable was like being called for jury service; everyone was expected to take a turn. Most hated the position and some even tried to buy their way out, or employed the services of paid deputies. But not Peder Trevanion. He enjoyed the authority.

When at home, he displayed his tipstaff outside his house like a trophy so everyone in the village knew his status. The tipstaff was the forerunner to the policeman's truncheon, usually shorter, about twice the length of the handle and often with a crown at the tip. They were highly decorated in brass, bone, or wood, sometimes hollow to carry an arrest warrant. The idea was that the tipstaff would be tapped on the shoulder of the person being arrested—then the warrant was served.

Peder Trevanion's tipstaff was more like a mace. It was made of hardwood and was relatively plain. The business end was a square-edged block, painted black with a red crown and the date of appointment on the side. And Trevanion liked to use it. He regarded the customary shoulder tap as an act that served no other purpose than to lose him the advantage of surprise. When Trevanion arrested you, the tap came much later, and the petite, almost feminine Trevanion was never braver than when he had an overpowering number of men at his command and the law on his side.

'I was beginning to think we'd be here all night,' he said as he approached the table. 'I could have killed you both for resisting.' He leant on the table. 'But we don't want to deny the public their sport, do we?'

'What are we supposed to have done?' Jowan asked.

'Oh, I think you know.'

Jowan feigned a blank look and Davy began to shake.

Trevanion snapped his fingers. 'Quickly!' he said.

A man with a lantern stepped forward and handed something to Trevanion who manipulated the item in his hand then let it fall. The item caught at the end of a leather strap and a bright silver crucifix lit up.

'So you wouldn't know who this belonged to or why it just happened to be at your house?'

'It's not our house!' Davy said, unable to stop himself.

Trevanion thumped his tipstaff hard onto the table, splintering the surface. 'You think I don't know this isn't your own house, you flea-host!' He raised the tipstaff to Davy and Davy nearly fell back off his chair.

Trevanion laughed. Then he pushed the crucifix in front of Jowan's face. 'You're both in a lot of trouble. You'd do well to cooperate.'

'I've never seen it before,' Jowan said. 'That's the truth!'

Trevanion slipped the crucifix into his waistcoat pocket and smiled. 'So tell me…' He turned to his men, looking amused with himself. 'How did such a thing come to slip from the neck of a dead man and land in a jug on the mantle in the next room?' A sarcastic laugh broke from his thin lips as he turned back to Jowan. 'I'm sure we'd all like to hear that one.'

The men with him were silent, their faces unemotional. None of them seemed to share Trevanion's sadistic disposition.

Jowan thought hard. They had been so drunk, yet he was sure he would have remembered finding a silver crucifix, and he was certain that if he had, he would have hidden it better than that. He had no explanation, but he understood the implications well enough.

Trevanion sighed. 'Why don't you confess to me now, eh? Get it over with. You'll save everyone a lot of bother.' He turned his needle eyes to Davy. 'What about you? You don't want to waste the magistrate's time, do you?'

Davy shook his head and Jowan sat up with a jolt.

'Leave off him!'

Trevanion pushed his tipstaff hard into Jowan's neck and left it there, forcing him down into his seat. Then his eyes returned to Davy, who looked like he was about to be sick again.

'Come on, lad,' Trevanion said. 'Do the decent thing.'

'Keep your mouth shut, Davy Fenton!'

A blow from one of the men in the room saved Trevanion the bother, or denied him the pleasure. Jowan slumped and rolled heavily to the floor.

Davy sprang up then, sending his chair flying back across the room. 'We didn't kill anyone!' he shouted. He backed against the wall holding his cuffed hands uselessly out in front of him as the constable's men closed in.

Trevanion shook his head at Davy. 'Too much to expect a little honesty from the likes of you,' he said. 'But I'll see you both swing. You mark me!' A cruel smirk cut across his face. He holstered his tipstaff and made for the door. 'Bring them along,' he said. They'll answer to the magistrate.'

Chapter Twenty-Eight

The man who had entered the exhibition at Bodmin Jail, distracting Tayte earlier, was on the move again on the other side of the display boards. The sudden and only sound in the otherwise lonely museum drew Tayte's attention again, pulling him away from a passage he was reading, which told him that Mawgan Hendry's bag—a coarse woven haversack containing his money purse—had never been recovered.

Tayte craned his neck, following the footsteps to the spot where he knew the man had to appear. He was more than curious now. Yesterday's warnings had left him on his guard, and his sore head still served as a reminder that someone out there wanted him out of the way. But just as Tayte expected the man to walk into view, the room fell silent again. Goose bumps tingled on the back of his neck, and as ridiculous as he suddenly found the situation, he could not look away. He knew the man had to come this way. He listened, but all he could hear was the rain outside, though lighter now, like radio static hissing in his focused mind.

A door banged over by the entrance. It startled Tayte, and he coiled instinctively towards the sound. Then he heard what he thought to be a heavy bolt grate against its iron guides. The footsteps started again. He spun around, expecting to see the man at last, but Tayte was alone. The late visitor was going back the way he'd come.

Tayte wanted to get up and cut him off at the door—to find out who he was. Instead, he scoffed at himself, surprised at the fragility of his nerves. It was ridiculous to think that anyone would have followed him there. He listened as the fast footsteps continued without stopping all the way back to the entrance. He heard a brief exchange of words that were too low to make out, and then it was silent again. He supposed that one of the doors at the entrance must have still been open, allowing the visitor to slip out, but the sound of the grating bolt earlier suggested that the place was closing up. He turned back to the case notes, now reading the secular court proceedings of the trial of Jowan Penhale and Davy Fenton, accused of the felonious killing of Mawgan Hendry and the theft of his belongings, to which they had entered a plea of not guilty.

———

Having found the crucifix and assumed murder weapon at Ferryman Cottage, Peder Trevanion's sworn testimony proved strong evidence against the accused, who were summarily interned at Bodmin Jail pending their trial. The witness accounts of Jenna Fox and two regulars at the Shipwrights Arms, who were there drinking the night Mawgan Hendry's body was pulled from the river, gave testimony to the fact that they had seen the accused leave the tavern that evening and shortly afterwards return in good spirits and with uncharacteristic generosity. The actions of Jowan and Davy that night were described to the court as 'carrying on like they'd come into money,' to which the prosecution had proposed that the ferrymen had stolen Mawgan Hendry's purse after they killed him, and then had squandered the money at the Shipwrights Arms immediately afterwards, hinting at their cold-hearted and insensate behaviour.

Tayte read how Mawgan's mother had identified the silver crucifix that had been found at Ferryman Cottage early on the morning of the arrest, stating that she had given it to Mawgan on his eighteenth birthday. She had broken down in the dock when asked to examine the crucifix, hearing for the first time that the gift which was intended to deliver her son from evil was alleged to be the very tool used to end his life.

Jowan and Davy's defence appeared little more than a formality. Only one noteworthy challenge was made at the end of the witness cross-examination, which concerned the information that led to the discovery of the crucifix. The defence had asked the court to identify the source of the information and questioned its validity as lawful evidence under the circumstances. But the challenge had been quashed with the production of an unsigned letter stating that, while the writer of the letter felt obliged to do his duty such that proper justice might be served, he wished to remain anonymous out of fear of reprisal. The letter had been deemed admissible as evidence as the account matched the specific nature of the crime so well, detailing facts that could only have been known by someone who had witnessed the heinous act for themselves.

A hand on Tayte's shoulder gave him a start.

'We'll be closing shortly.' It was the woman in the mint green cardigan. 'Sorry,' she added, 'I thought you'd seen me.'

Tayte gave a nervous laugh. 'That's okay. I was miles away there. I'll just be a few minutes, if that's okay.'

'Of course.' The woman was studying the broken display cases. 'Mindless,' she said. 'Can't have been valuable.'

'What was in them?' Tayte could guess at the answer.

'We had a leather-bound book in this one.' The woman pointed to the larger of the two cases. 'It showed the verse that's been reproduced here.' She pointed up at the display board. 'It was left to the museum by a relative of the victim,' she added. 'Such a shame. I don't suppose we'll ever get it back.'

'And the other case?'

'The smaller one contained the murder weapon. A silver cross on a leather cord. The real thing, I believe. I suppose that would have had some value.'

'Was anything else taken?'

She seemed to think about it. Then she shook her head. 'This display was the only one damaged,' she said. 'Nothing else was taken at all, come to think of it. Very odd.'

Tayte agreed. Someone appeared to have targeted this display—this particular murder trial. He felt the lump on the back of his head and wondered whether it was the work of the same person. Either way, he knew he had to be looking in the right place. He began to wonder at the identity of the thief, and that led him to consider whether Mathew Parfitt had had any children of his own.

'I'll leave you to finish up,' the woman said. Then she left as quietly as she'd arrived on flat suede shoes.

Tayte went back to the trial proceedings and read that in summing up, the prosecution had painted a verbal picture for the court of Jowan and Davy arriving with the ferry at Helford Passage that night, late and drunk, as character witnesses had stated they often were. It was proposed that the two ferrymen had encountered the farmer waiting to cross the river and had learned of the verse he'd written about them. The prosecution had then put it to the jury that an argument broke out, and that together, Jowan and Davy had wilfully murdered Mawgan Hendry.

Tayte came now to the verdict and read how the jury had taken no time in their deliberations, retiring only to huddle in the corner of the courtroom briefly before returning their verdict of guilty as charged. Tayte pictured Jowan and Davy standing before the judge to receive their sentence, their wrists and ankles bound in chains. In his mind he saw the judge place a nine-inch square of black silk on his head: the black cap. The court would then all rise, and the judge presiding would pronounce the sentence. The text was reproduced in full as it was spoken:

Jowan Penhale and Davy Fenton, you stand convicted of the horrid and unnatural crime of murdering Mawgan Hendry. This Court doth adjudge that you be taken back to the place from whence you came and there to be fed on bread and water till Wednesday next, when you are to be taken to the common place of execution and there hanged by the neck until you are dead; after which your body is to be publicly dissected and anatomised, agreeable to an Act of Parliament in that case made and provided; and may God almighty have mercy on your souls.

The forced cough Tayte heard at the entrance told him it was time to go. He stretched as he stepped away from the display. Then as he collected his notebook, he noticed the further reading that was hidden beneath it. The passage heading read 'Beyond reasonable doubt?' The question mark at the end drew him in.

Three days after Jowan Penhale and Davy Fenton were hanged for the murder of Mawgan Hendry, a woman came forward proclaiming their innocence. Tamsyn Brown, a lady's maid from Maenporth, further claimed that she had been sent to Helford Passage on the evening of Mawgan Hendry's murder by her mistress to recover a box that her mistress had given to Mawgan Hendry earlier that day. She had said that her mistress was detained, and that she had beseeched her to tell Mr Hendry that he was in danger.

When asked why she had not come forward sooner, either before or during the trial, when her testimony might have made a difference to the outcome, she had said that her cowardly silence was out of fear for her own life, until her great shame and guilt had become too heavy a burden to bear. A posttrial hearing of her evidence was scheduled for the following day, but the woman failed to appear. As no account was

given during the trial to suggest that Mawgan Hendry was
carrying any such box, and as no accusation or evidence had
been formerly presented, the matter was dismissed. Justice had
rightly been served.

Or had it?

There was that question mark again. It left Tayte wondering, as it was supposed to, but it would have to wait. This time he clearly saw the woman in the mint green cardigan approaching. He was on his feet before she arrived, already aware that he'd outstayed his welcome.

'I really do need to close up now,' she said.

There was a smile there somewhere, but Tayte had to look for it. 'Sure,' he offered. 'I'm just leaving. Thanks for your patience.'

Chapter Twenty-Nine

Outside, the sky was leaden. Tayte was pleased to see that the rain had stopped as he made his way across the courtyard in the shadow of the towering granite jail. His thoughts returned to the anecdote he'd just read. It excited him to think that the box that had brought Amy Fallon to Bodmin might be the same box he'd just read about; the box Tamsyn Brown had been sent to recover from Mawgan Hendry the night he was murdered. It could corroborate the maid's story.

Tayte knew he had to see Amy again. She'd mentioned that she ran the Helford ferry service, so he figured he could ask around in the village tomorrow to find out where she lived. He passed beneath the gatehouse archway and out into the car park. There was just one other car there now, a cream Volkswagen Beetle next to his, which he supposed belonged to the woman in the museum. It wasn't until he was in his car and the engine was running that he noticed the folded slip of paper beneath his wiper blade. He killed the engine and retrieved what he supposed was an advertisement. Opening it, he knew at once that it was not. The paper was dry; it couldn't have been there long. He pushed his door open again and launched himself from his seat, standing with one foot in the car and an elbow on the roof. He looked around, hoping to see who had left it, but it was quiet. A young couple with a dog passed by on the path next to the car park. They looked over at him, and then back to the path in front of them. A few cars drove anonymously past. Whoever had left the slip of paper hadn't waited around for him to find it. He looked at it more closely. It was a photocopy of an old newspaper page. A section, circled in green highlighter pen, carried the heading, 'Horrid murder! Missing woman found.'

> *The body of Tamsyn Brown of Maenporth was yesterday discovered in woods near the village of Constantine. The coroner's report so declared that the deceased, a maid formerly in service at Rosemullion Hall, died at the hands of some inhuman monster after suffering repeated and barbarous attacks to her person, causing massive haemorrhaging of her internal organs. The deceased's neck was also found to have been crushed post mortem.*

Tayte checked the date at the top of the article—Thursday, June 9, 1803—little more than two weeks after the hanging. He was puzzled as to why the note had been put on his windscreen, and by whom. The lump on the back of his head told him he had few friends where this assignment was concerned. He thought about the late arrival at the museum and easily convinced himself that the visitor's behaviour was odd. Whoever left this was clearly dropping him a lead, though, a firm connection to the Fairborne family through this maid, Tamsyn Brown, who worked at Rosemullion Hall. Someone out there seemed to believe, or know, that the maid's story was true.

Lowenna's maid...

It fitted well enough. He recalled Emily Forbes's story about Lowenna and remembered that she'd said Lowenna had arrived without her maid. Back then, a lady travelling without one was unusual and, according to Emily, the maid Lowenna had grown up with hadn't followed on later to be with her mistress at the Forbes household—she hadn't arrived at all. But then, if Lowenna's maid was Tamsyn Brown, how could she? She was dead.

And if the maid's story was true, Tayte considered, then the box Amy found had to be the same box that Tamsyn Brown was sent to recover; no other box could have led her to Mawgan Hendry. *Lowenna's box,* Tayte thought. *Another connection to the Fairbornes.* And this was a connection that people were prepared to kill for. He felt the back of his head again and reminded himself of the death threat that had been sent to his phone after he'd been attacked. He considered then that if Amy was looking in the same places he was, then she was in harm's way too. This could no longer wait until morning. He had to find Amy and warn her.

On the A39, south of Truro, an electric blue Mazda 323 was being pushed to its limits. The driver was in a hurry to be somewhere and he gave little consideration to the rush hour traffic that was building around him. As he swerved off the A39, heading for Helston, his excitement grew. He knew who Amy Fallon was. He'd been watching her long enough now, knowing all along how important Ferryman Cottage was to his final goal. He knew the box had to be there at the cottage somewhere.

He cursed himself again for not managing to secure the purchase of the Helford ferry business when it came onto the market. If he had, then it would all have been so much easier. He could have turned Ferryman Cottage inside out and no one would have been any the wiser. He would have found the box a long time ago, well before the American took an interest in the Fairbornes.

*Fairborne…*He couldn't help but smile to himself. He knew he had more right to that name than any of them. *I must find that box!* He was confident that it had surfaced at last. Amy turning up at the record office looking for a house history search had excited him.

And the American…If the box *had* been found, then he was sure he'd given him enough information to lead him to it and hopefully bring it into the open.

But he knew he had to be careful. He had to watch and wait just a while longer. He didn't mind. He liked to watch Amy; he liked to see what she was wearing and what book she was into. He thought she looked so peaceful when she was reading—like an angel, with her head gently bowed in prayer. He was looking forward to seeing her again tonight.

Chapter Thirty

Tayte made good time getting to Helford Passage. He'd parked along from the Ferry Boat Inn and was standing on the shingle beach beside the ferry pontoon, wondering what to do next. The empty ferry boat beside the pontoon looked tied off for the day. He checked the time; it was twenty past six. The notice board in front of him told him he'd missed the last ferry by almost an hour and a half. There was no one around.

His briefcase began to feel heavy. He stepped away from the water and looked back at the Ferry Boat Inn. It was quiet, but there were several cars nearby. Someone inside might know Amy. He was about to head across the shingle and go inside when a last glance at the river stopped him. He was looking at the ferry boat. Beyond the canopy at the bow, a scattered plume of smoke drifted like chalk dust into the grey backdrop of low cloud. Tayte was up onto the pontoon in a second, looking down into the boat at someone he supposed was in his mid-twenties.

The kid was lying on the moulded seats on the opposite side of the boat, nodding his head to whatever he was listening to on the iPod resting on his chest. He wore blue and white shorts detailed with a swirling sea foam pattern and a navy sweatshirt that had Southwest Airborne printed on the front in mixed fluorescent colours. Beneath the logo was an arty wire-line drawing of a hang glider. It made Tayte cringe just looking at it. The smoke was coming from something the kid no doubt knew he shouldn't be smoking, which Tayte supposed was why he was hiding out where he thought no one could see him. His eyes were shut tight, away with his tunes in whatever place the substance he was smoking had taken him.

Tayte put a foot on the boat and started rocking it to get his attention, but it only seemed to mimic the swell on the river. He slapped a hand on the canopy over the wheel. 'Excuse me,' he called. He slapped the canopy again, a little harder. 'Hey!' Nothing.

Tayte stepped into the boat and it tipped under his weight, upsetting his balance, causing him to slip and fall the rest of the way, dropping his briefcase as his hands threw out to break his fall. Fortunately for Tayte, the kid took most of his weight. He shoved Tayte away as he sprang up, looking confused and acting defensive. His iPod was swinging from the strap around his neck, his in-ear headphones were out and dangling, and his spliff was floating in the river.

'Eh, what's your game, pal? The ferry's closed.'

Tayte got up and raised his hands in the air like he'd just been arrested. 'Sorry. I slipped,' he said. 'I was just trying to get your attention.'

'Well you've got it all right. Jesus!'

Tayte sat down. 'I didn't mean to startle you.' He took out his handkerchief and wiped the damp grit from his hands.

'What do you want?' the kid asked. 'I already told you the ferry's not running.'

'I know. I just need some information.'

The kid in the navy sweatshirt looked suspiciously at Tayte. 'What sort of information?'

'I met this woman today. Her name's Amy Fallon and she said she had something to do with the ferry business.'

'Amy? Yeah, I know her. She owns it.'

'Well, I need to know where she lives,' Tayte said.

The kid laughed. 'And you expect me to tell you? Just like that? I don't even know who you are.'

'It's very important,' Tayte said. He took out his wallet and pulled the largest bill he could find. 'It's worth a twenty.'

The kid laughed again. 'This might only be a summer job, but it's worth more to me than that.'

Tayte took out another twenty and he could see the kid was starting to look interested.

'What do you want to see her for?'

'This might sound a little crazy,' Tayte said. 'But I think she's in danger.'

The kid came closer. He eyed Tayte up and down like he was about to measure him for new suit. 'S'pose you look harmless enough for a foreigner,' he said. 'Tell you what. Double what's in your hand and I'll take you to her.'

Tayte smiled. He liked the kid's eye for business, but he was no match. 'Take me to her for forty,' he said. 'And I won't tell her what you do on her boat after hours.'

The kid looked beat. 'Deal,' he said. He extended his hand and Tayte shook it, folding two twenties into his palm.

'I'm Simon,' the kid said. He slipped past Tayte and untied the boat. 'You'd better be on the level.'

As they moved off, Simon handed Tayte a pole with a net attached to one end. 'Hook my smoke out of there when we pass it, will you? That shit's expensive.'

Simon rammed the ferry boat into the shoreline at Treath like he was landing an amphibious assault craft on a beach under heavy fire. Tayte steadied himself as the catamaran's hulls cut into the shingle and lurched to a full stop.

Simon dropped the bow access ramp. 'It's that house there,' he said, pointing to the only house Tayte could see. There was a light on downstairs, repelling the onset of dusk.

Tayte disembarked, jumping to clear the water, sinking his loafers into the damp shingle beyond a thin tide line of river silt and vegetation debris. 'Thanks,' he said. He slipped the kid another tenner. The fare seemed reasonable under the circumstances.

Simon smiled as he stuffed the cash into his pocket with the rest. 'How you getting back? I could wait.'

Tayte could see the pound signs glinting in Simon's eyes. 'That's okay,' he said. 'I've no idea how long I'll be. I'll get a cab.'

He started off, admiring the teak motor launch moored up at the bottom of the garden. Behind him, he heard the catamaran's access ramp rattle.

'I'd rather the boss didn't know about this,' Simon called. 'Or about…well, you know.'

Tayte threw him a grin. 'Don't worry. Your secret's safe.'

Tayte felt uneasy as he pushed the gate open. He stepped through beneath a full rose arbour that came alive in a breeze that had arrived without introduction. *She'll think I'm stalking her*, he thought, but he knew there was no other way to handle this. He had to tell her what he knew. He followed the curve of the stone pathway that ran up to Amy's front door and flicked at the letter box a couple of times; there was no bell push or knocker. His palms began to slip on the handle of his briefcase.

The smile that greeted Tayte when the door opened put him back at ease, though Amy's eyes were inquisitive. Settled into her faded jeans, oversized shirt, and a pair of loose-fitting grey marl socks that could keep a fisherman warm on a rough night, she looked very different from when Tayte last saw her.

'Hi,' he said. 'Remember me?'

Amy's puzzled expression asked all kinds of questions. 'Of course,' she said.

Where to start? Tayte thought, but there was no easy way to say it, so he just rushed it out. 'Look, I know this might be hard to believe, but I think you're in danger.'

Chapter Thirty-One

On a wide mahogany stool in front of a cold inglenook fireplace, a book rested on an oval wooden tray. The book was open, face down to keep the page, and beside it a glass of red wine waited. Amy settled back into the settee and tucked her legs up beneath her, wrapping a cushion in her arms as Tayte sat in the wing chair to the left of the fireplace. His briefcase was on the floor beside him.

'Did you read the maid's tale at the end?' Tayte asked.

'I did.'

Tayte reached into his jacket pocket and took out a folded slip of paper. 'Someone left this for me,' he said, passing it to Amy. 'It was pinned under my wiper blade.'

Amy scanned the article. 'Horrid murder! Missing woman found,' she said. She was nodding thoughtfully as she read the rest of the article, as though confirming some previous supposition. When she looked up again, Tayte could see that it troubled her.

'My husband, Gabriel, disappeared during a storm on the river two years ago,' Amy said. 'He told me he'd found something—said it was a secret and that he'd show me in the morning. He went out early that day and never came back. I think his secret was that he'd already found the box.'

A gust of wind rattled the windows, and Tayte followed the sound, looking past Amy to a grey and dusky vista. His eyes were distant, somewhere on the river. 'Secrets...' he said as the first spray of rain streaked the glass.

Turning back to Amy, he said, 'You should know that I was attacked yesterday. Whoever it was left a note telling me to go home. Another message threatened my life if I didn't. Then I get this newspaper article pinned to my car, like someone's trying to help. If you're looking under the same rocks as me, you need to be careful. That's largely why I came over.'

He turned the conversation to the other reason he was there. 'I don't mean to be pushy,' he said. 'But I'd really like to see that box?'

'The box, of course,' Amy said. She got up and went to the back of the room, and Tayte watched with barely controlled anticipation as she opened the drawer beneath a tall display cabinet. He felt himself rising out of his seat to get an early peek as Amy lifted something out and pushed the drawer back with her socked foot.

'It's in good condition, considering,' Amy said. She sat on the settee with the box on her knees.

'Touchdown!'

'Sorry?'

'Oh, you know. A defining moment, like wow—there it is!'

Amy looked sympathetic.

'It's bigger than I'd imagined,' Tayte said, moving on. He sat next to Amy and she slid the box across. He read the initials and wondered whose name they belonged to.

'Open it,' Amy said. 'There's a note inside.'

Tayte finished admiring the carving on the lid and lifted it open to reveal the silk heart and the note beneath.

'See what you make of it,' Amy said.

Tayte unfolded the note and read it aloud. 'Though we cannot be together, you will always have my heart.' He read Lowenna's signature and smiled. 'So this *was* Lowenna's box.' All the pieces fell into place. 'And her maid saw the real killer at work and was silenced for it. I never did like the convenience of the anonymous tip off that led to the ferrymen's arrest. It was an easy framing tool.'

'And the real killer got away with it,' Amy said like it was personal.

Tayte nodded. He supposed she felt a connection through her association with the Helford Ferry. 'And whoever did kill Mawgan Hendry was smart enough to stay out of the picture. It looked like an open and shut case. A robbery gone wrong and justice served. There was nothing to implicate anyone else.'

'Apart from the box,' Amy said.

Tayte agreed. 'Hendry's murder wasn't the result of some chance robbery gone wrong. I've no doubt now that his killer was after this.' He tapped the box and fixed on Amy with an uneasy stare. 'Does anyone else know about it?'

'Just a friend in the village,' Amy said. 'Tom Laity. He owns the deli.'

'Do you trust him?'

'I guess. I've known him pretty much since we moved down here. He's been a good friend since Gabriel...' Amy spun away, staring at the window. When she turned back she was tight-lipped and determined. 'Since Gabriel died,' she continued, adding, 'I'm sorry. It's the first time I've really thought about him like that.'

'Hey, nothing to be sorry for. And I'm sure Tom Laity's fine. I just wondered if you'd made a big fuss about it.'

'No.'

'Good. I suggest we keep it that way.'

Tayte went back to Lowenna's note, mulling over the short postscript. 'It's what is inside that counts.'

'Say that again,' Amy said.

'It's what is inside that counts.'

Amy took the note and looked it over. 'Maybe it's your accent, but there seems to be an emphasis here I didn't get before. *Inside...*'

she added thoughtfully. 'Inside the box? But there was just this note and the silk heart.'

'Or inside Lowenna. I found out today that she was pregnant when Mawgan Hendry was murdered.'

Amy's face dropped.

'It gets worse. Seems she killed herself the night the child was born.'

Amy put both hands to mouth. 'That's terrible,' she said. 'So you think Lowenna was referring to their child. She was telling Mawgan that the child was what really mattered and that she would always love him, despite their circumstances.'

'Sure looks that way,' Tayte said, 'but why did she send her maid to get the box back? There has to be more to it. What changed after she gave it to him?'

'Maybe her father had him killed. She says in her note that they couldn't be together. Perhaps he was making sure.'

Tayte shook his head. 'The box seems to be the focus here, not Hendry. I think he was just in the way. But of what?'

Amy scooped up her wine from the stool in front of the inglenook. 'Can I get you a glass?' she asked.

'Sure, why not?'

As Amy poured, Tayte turned the box in his hands, admiring the bright detail. The inlaid mother-of-pearl initials drew his eye again. He knew the box belonged to Lowenna—the 'F' then stood for 'Fairborne', but it was not Lowenna's to begin with.

'There you go,' Amy said, handing Tayte his wine.

'Thanks.' He raised his glass. 'Bottoms up,' he said, smirking playfully. 'That's how you say it here, right?'

A slow smile crossed Amy's face. 'Not unless you want to leave.'

'Cheers it is then.' Tayte took a mouthful and set the glass down on the stool.

'So how did you get into genealogy?' Amy asked. 'Seems like an unusual profession.'

'I guess it is,' Tayte said, 'and I sure wish it paid better.' He sat back. 'Truth is I had to. When my parents died—my adoptive parents that is—I was still going through college, trying to find myself, you know—discovering my purpose in life. I had no idea I was adopted until I read the letter they left explaining things. Then it was all so clear. Not knowing who you are just eats away at you, like a hunger you can never satisfy.'

'Until you find out,' Amy said.

Tayte nodded. 'I sure hope so, although I've not tried in a while now.'

'Why's that?'

'Oh, I dunno…' Tayte took another slow sip from his wine glass and thought that he knew only too well. He recalled how low he'd sunk the last time; how it had almost been his very last time. 'I guess I just don't feel quite ready yet,' he added. 'Meanwhile, assignments like this keep me going. They feed the hunger, so to speak. I figure if I can stay on top of my game—keep finding the connections for other people—then I must be good enough to find my own someday.'

'Sound logic,' Amy said. 'But what if you don't find this family?'

Tayte took a deep breath and slowly released it. He couldn't think of a single answer that didn't scare him. 'I *have* to find them,' he said. He stared at the box and his thoughts returned to it. 'I've been wondering about these initials.' He fetched an A4 notepad from his briefcase—an indexed listing of the Fairborne family tree—and began to thumb through the pages. 'Somewhere in here there should be a match.' A moment later, he added, 'How about Daniel Fairborne?'

They both looked at each other, shaking their heads.

'Here we go,' Tayte said. 'Dorothea: Born, 1683. Died, 1744. It's the only other name that fits.'

James Fairborne's grandmother, he thought. His connection had arrived. 'So the box was handed down,' he said. 'It must have come to England with the family I'm looking for and somehow it found its way into Lowenna's care.' He paused that thought. 'But it shouldn't have passed to Lowenna,' he added. 'It should have been Katherine's, the eldest. Then Katherine would have given it to *her* daughter and so on.' Tayte scoffed. 'No way would she give it to a half sister.'

'Maybe something happened to Katherine,' Amy said.

Tayte was already thinking the same thing; he'd been thinking it since Boston. 'It all comes back to this box,' he said. He continued to study it, wondering again why someone in 1803 wanted it so badly they were prepared to kill for it. He considered that the reason could be the very answer he was looking for. 'I'd sure like to know more about it,' he added.

'How about an antiques dealer?' Amy said. 'I used to know a few, but—'

'Kapowski!' Tayte blurted.

Amy looked concerned.

'Julia Kapowski! She's a little wired, but she might be able to help. I met her on the plane coming over. She told me she worked in valuations, pricing up antiques for auction.'

Chapter Thirty-Two

'Damn!' Tayte said. 'I threw her card away.' He took a big slug from his wine glass and sat back with it, nestling into the wing chair by the inglenook. 'Julia Kapowski works for a firm of auctioneers back in Boston,' he added. 'They must operate in London, too.'

'Could you call the company she works for?' Amy said.

Tayte thought about it, but he couldn't recall the name; he'd given it little consideration.

Amy got up and went back to the bureau. She dropped the flap and a moment later she returned with a laptop. 'What did you say her name was?'

'Kapowski,' Tayte said. 'Julia Kapowski.'

'She might be listed under the company's website. With a name like that it shouldn't take long to find out.'

As Amy worked the keyboard, Tayte's eyes drifted to the window and the shapeless nightscape, punctuated by the lights on the other side of a river he could now barely distinguish. When he looked back at Amy she was practically laughing to herself. She spun the laptop around on her knees and Tayte found himself looking at a glamorous gallery-style portrait of Julia Kapowski. He had to concede that he thought she scrubbed up well.

'That's her,' he said. 'That's the woman from the plane.' He couldn't believe she had her own website.

'It's a blog,' Amy said. 'Nothing came back under any auctioneers. In fact, nothing much came back at all. This jumped straight out at me.'

Tayte read the heading on the screen: Looking for Larry.

'Kapowski's blog,' Amy said, 'seems to follow her attempts to find the love of her life.' She pulled a cute face and fluttered her eyelashes. Then she laughed and scrolled back through the blog to what she'd been reading while Tayte was staring out the window. 'She's had a string of husbands according to this. None of them lasted long.'

'Who's Larry?' Tayte asked.

'It doesn't say.'

Tayte caught the odd word on the screen as Amy continued to scroll back, reading snippets here and there.

'It's addictive reading,' Amy said.

Tayte saw something then about Kapowski's flight to London a few days back.

Amy stopped scrolling. 'Oh my God! That's you, isn't it?'

Tayte was blushing. 'It could be anyone,' he replied, trying to dismiss it.

'But it's not anyone, is it? It's you.' Amy was all smiles. 'Listen to this, *then* tell me it's not about you.' She forced herself to be serious for a minute, barely able to maintain the façade. 'He had the aisle seat and I was by the window,' she read. 'I don't know… there was something I liked about him the minute he sat down. It wasn't his tan suit or his manners, and he needed to lose a few pounds…'

Tayte heard Amy's stifled giggle through those last words. Then she put on a voice, exaggerating like some cheap actress playing a badly written love scene.

'But there was something in his eyes,' Amy continued. 'He had nice eyes, and I told him so…' She skipped to the end of the paragraph. 'I gave him my card. Maybe he'll call. Maybe he won't.'

Amy couldn't control herself any longer. Laughter erupted from the pit of her stomach and she rolled into the armrest to muffle the sound. 'I'm sorry,' she said once she'd recovered. She had tears in her eyes.

Tayte was trying to keep a straight face, but he was caught in the moment. He hid his smile in his wine glass.

'What was that about manners?' Amy asked.

'I don't like flying. I had a bad experience when I was a kid. I guess I was a little edgy on the flight over.' Tayte knew he was understating the truth. He was surprised Julia Kapowski had thought anything of him at all.

'There's a comments field,' Amy said.

Tayte knew what she was thinking. He wasn't sure he wanted to go public, but he knew it was their best shot. He reached for the laptop. 'May I?' he asked.

Tayte added his comment: *Hi Julia, it's JT. We met on the plane from Boston. Please call me as soon as you read this.* He added his phone number then saved his comment.

'She's been updating the site pretty frequently,' Amy said. 'We might get lucky.' She threw Tayte a cheeky smile. 'She wants you to call her. Should be easy to set up a date.'

Tayte rolled his eyes. 'If I *can* get to see her, I'm sure she'll be in London. We'd have to take the box to *her.*'

Amy went quiet, thoughtfully chewing at the edge of her lip like she was considering the best way to approach this. Then she opened the box, removed the silk heart and closed it again, leaving Lowenna's note inside. 'I'll keep hold of this,' she said, resting the heart beside her on the settee. 'You go by yourself.' She winked at him. 'You'll have a better chance and I wouldn't want to spoil your date!'

Tayte was reaching for his wine glass again when his phone stopped the conversation. He stared at Amy for a couple of long seconds. Then he picked up the call.

'JT.' His throat felt parched. He took a sip of wine and choked on it.

'Hello,' the caller said.

Tayte couldn't speak. He coughed.

'JT…you there, honey?'

Tayte coughed again. Then in a croaky voice he said, 'Julia! Sorry, I just took a sip of wine and it went down the wrong way. I wasn't expecting you to call so soon.'

'Oh, I was already hooked up,' Kapowski said. 'Saw your note there. It's great to hear from you. I really didn't think you'd get in touch.'

Tayte began to pace the room. 'Yeah, that was a bit of luck,' he said. 'I lost your card.'

'Hey, you gotta love the Web,' Kapowski said. 'So where are you? Anywhere near my hotel room?'

Tayte heard a giggle and snorted. 'Not really,' he said. He thought he heard ice and crystal clinking in the background.

'You know, the décor in my room reminded me of you the minute I opened the door,' Kapowski added. 'Lots of neutral colours, just like your suit. So exactly how far away is 'not really'?'

'Look, Julia,' Tayte said. 'I'd like to see you, but it's not what you think.'

'But you *do* want to see me, right?'

'Yes, I do, tomorrow if possible, but the truth is I need a favour.'

The call went quiet for a few seconds. Then Kapowski said, 'Okay, I'm still interested.'

'Great. I've something I'd like to show you.'

Tayte knew Kapowski wasn't about to let the conversation get all serious after a line like that, but it was out before he could stop himself.

'Easy there, fella,' she said. 'I don't know what you've heard about us Brooklyn girls…' She was laughing in Tayte's ear. 'But I'm sure it's all true.'

By the time the call finished, Tayte was blushing like an overripe tomato. He put his phone away and looked across the room to Amy, who had been watching him intently, grinning like a schoolgirl.

'Don't say a word,' Tayte said.

———————

Tayte was back in his room at St Maunanus House the next time his phone rang. He'd only been back ten minutes and the display told him it was almost nine o'clock. Peter Schofield's typically hyper greeting opened a floodgate of unpleasant memories along with the sudden realisation that it wasn't just a bad dream.

Schofield had landed.

Tayte's emotions sank with him onto the bed. He couldn't mask his disappointment. 'Oh, it's you,' he said. Everything about the man scraped at Tayte's nerves, like a screaming dentist's drill.

'Who were you expecting, big guy?' Schofield said. After a pause he added, 'Never mind. Main thing is, I'm here and I'm raring to go!'

Tayte wondered where Schofield got his energy. The only place Tayte wanted to go was to bed. 'Look, Schofield,' he said. 'Seems we're destined to work together on this. I can't pretend I'm happy about it, but there it is.'

'Yeah,' Schofield said. 'I had a message from Wally Sloane waiting for me when I cleared customs. I know the score. You're running the show.'

Tayte was happy *that* much was clear.

'And, hey,' Schofield said. 'I've got no problem with that. Just so you know.'

'Okay, then,' Tayte said. 'I've got something for you when you get down here tomorrow. I'll be away most of the day, so you'll have to go it alone 'til I get back. I'll fill you in then.'

'Whatever you say, Jeff.'

Tayte had already concocted the assignment he planned to give Schofield. Something that would keep him busy all day—keep him occupied and make him regret ever getting involved. 'I need all the churchyards in the area checked out,' he said. 'Start where you like. Cover the gravestones and check out any local church records you come across. I'll e-mail you with the names and dates we're looking for.'

'Already got 'em,' Schofield said.

Tayte wasn't surprised.

'I'm driving down first thing,' Schofield added. 'Got this cool car—very British.'

'You're staying in London tonight?'

'Yeah. Thought I'd check out the nightlife first. Few drinks, ya know...I'll get some rest before I set off.'

*Rest...*Tayte thought Schofield ran purely on adrenaline and annoying people.

'Don't worry,' Schofield said. 'I'll be there bright and early. I'll get straight to it.'

Chapter Thirty-Three

Friday.

The envelope had arrived at Rosemullion Hall looking as innocent as the rest of the morning post. It was addressed to Sir Richard Fairborne, and the phone call Manning was about to put through to him in his study prompted him to reach into the breast pocket of his navy suit and take it out for another look. He turned it in his hands then studied the Bodmin postmark for the umpteenth time, getting no further clue as to who the sender was.

Sir Richard Fairborne was the kind of man who did not lose. When the last tin mines closed in Cornwall in the early 1990s, he was already well into his second career. The tin market was all but over by 1985, and he'd seen it coming. He'd kept employment going for as long as he could, and he was there among the last to call it a day, but he'd been clever about it. He was able to turn a profit right to the end, however small. He'd kept things ticking over for a grateful community while he increasingly detached himself from the business. The key then was to have other irons in the fire. As one market dies, another emerges.

As a politician of retirement age, he'd put on a little weight and lost a little hair over the years, but those years had been good to him, and he was ever mindful of the people who made him who he was. He had never failed them, had always been fair and true to his word, and his intent was staunch once fixed—however much that intent might be skewed at times by well-meaning others. *Systems fail. Sir Richard Fairborne does not.*

It was now late morning, and Sir Richard was not long returned from London. His study was a small private room containing a desk to sit at and little else that was not used to store books or papers. It was the only place in the house where he could think and speak freely without fear of being overheard. The room was on the ground floor to the front of the house, looking out towards garages that had been converted from the old stable block some years ago. It was also the least distracting view in the house.

Sir Richard picked up the handset on his desk and pressed a button. 'Thank you, Manning,' he said. He heard a beep as Manning dropped out.

The caller wasted no time. 'Do you have the document I sent you?'

Richard Fairborne felt his hackles rise to attention. 'I have it,' he replied with a level of stoicism that surprised him. 'And I'm at a loss to understand how it's of any interest to me or my family. You said you'd be sending proof. Something I'd want to pay for.' He opened the envelope and pulled out the contents, unfolding a crisp sheet of A4 photocopy paper bearing a scanned image of the last will and testament of James Fairborne. He slapped it down on the desk. 'What you've sent me isn't worth a penny.'

The amused laughter Sir Richard heard in response unsettled him. Clearly there was more to it than was apparent.

The laughter stopped. 'You're right,' the caller said. 'By itself it's worthless. But look into James Fairborne's brother, William Fairborne, and you'll find that he never left America. His descendants still live there today. That's who this American, Tayte, is working for.'

Sir Richard eyed the document, paying particular attention to the words 'sole beneficiary' and 'William Fairborne.' He began to see the angle. Then his caller confirmed it.

'You're no Fairborne,' the caller said. 'Trace your ancestry back two hundred years and you'll find a liar who stole a baronetcy and a good man's fortune by pretending to be someone he wasn't.'

For the first time in Sir Richard Fairborne's life he had no immediate answer. His mind was busy working out the implications, forcing a silent pause. Instead of a defensive strike that negated the blackmailer's weapon, the best he could manage was, 'This is absurd!'

'Is it? I doubt the papers will think so. They just love a story like this. It'll do wonders for your political career—your *Lordship*. Not to mention how William Fairborne's real descendants will take the news. Just think about it. Can you really believe they'll just let it go? That's their house you're living in.'

Sir Richard's breath caught in his chest. He knew the caller was right. If what he claimed could be proven so easily, then he would be ruined. The family would be shamed and the hereditary peerage would be lost forever. And the press would carve him up; his political career would die a quick and ugly death. On top of all that, there would be a lawsuit to fight, and with so much at stake, it would be a costly battle with no certainty of a favourable outcome. It was not a path upon which he wanted to tread.

'So what do you plan to do with this knowledge?' he asked.

'I don't plan to do anything with it. You're going to pay me a considerable sum of money to ensure that I *don't* do anything with it.'

'And what about the American? He called here today.'

'I know. Don't worry about him. I have Mr Tayte on a leash.'

'I won't pay a penny until he's taken care of.'

Sir Richard bit his tongue. He couldn't bear to listen to himself, unable to believe what his own words were condoning, even bidding, this low-life to do. But Sir Richard Fairborne was a winner. Sir Richard Fairborne did not fail, and on this matter there was no other acceptable outcome. *At any cost...*

'If I'm to go through with this,' he added, 'then I need assurances. I can't have anyone else finding out.'

'He'll be taken care of before we conclude our business.'

'Does anyone else know about this?'

'No one. I'm a strictly *private* enterprise.'

'Don't call me again until it's done.'

Sir Richard hung up, suddenly feeling his age for the first time in his life. His hands were shaking as he pushed his chair away from his desk. He didn't dare try to get up yet. His only thought was that he could not fail. He would do whatever it took to beat this. The family had to come first. Lose now and he would lose everything. His entire life would have been in vain.

Sir Richard Fairborne was noticeably pale when he returned to the drawing room at Rosemullion Hall. Celia and Warwick were there, waiting. He approached slowly, his thoughts locked in repetition like an endless loop recording, playing back his limited options and the unthinkable deeds he'd just sanctioned.

A man's life to keep a secret...

Sir Richard arrived between the pair of yellow settees without making eye contact with anyone. He looked up from the rug in front of the fireplace, first to Celia, then to Warwick where his eyes paused. 'Leave us, would you.' It was not a question.

Warwick was about to go when Celia said, 'It's all right, Richard. He knows.'

Sir Richard sighed into the settee opposite them, too drained to argue the matter. The letter from the blackmailer was prominent in his hands, drawing their eyes. He slid it onto the coffee table. 'This arrived earlier,' he said. 'I'm afraid the call I received the other day was not without foundation.'

'What does it say?' Celia asked.

Warwick edged forward, his eyes fixed on the envelope.

'Not much. It looks just like any other last will and testament. But throw in a few other facts that are easily proven and it says more than enough.'

Sir Richard gave a full account of his conversation with the blackmailer—everything but his demand for Jefferson Tayte's removal. He dealt with Warwick's presence largely by ignoring him, and Warwick did well to keep quiet and listen.

Celia picked up the envelope, removed the contents, and read the salient words from the photocopied probate record she found inside. In light of what she'd just heard, she looked dumbstruck by the obvious implications. She let the papers fall into her lap. 'What are we to do, Richard?'

Sir Richard held her eyes. 'I'll deal with it,' he said.

Chapter Thirty-Four

Kensington Gardens covered some 275 acres of royal parkland between the City of Westminster and the Borough of Kensington and Chelsea to the west. Jefferson Tayte had arrived in plenty of time for his meeting with Julia Kapowski. He'd taken the first train from Truro, and the long journey afforded him time to reflect on his findings and update his notes. Now, as he stood looking into the park from Palace Gate where the cab had dropped him, all he needed to do was work out where the Peter Pan statue was. That's where Kapowski had said she'd meet him.

Tayte checked his watch again. He still had time to spare. Behind him, Kensington Road was busy with the constant grumble of traffic, and it was only through standing there between the green parkland and the contrasting grey city streets and shops that he realised how high his regard for Cornwall had become. He could taste the air, thick with fumes despite the expansive park that was like an overworked respirator, struggling to pump enough oxygen into an ailing patient.

He did not linger. He stepped through the park gates and turned right onto the Flower Walk, heading away from Kensington Palace towards the Albert Memorial; he could clearly see its gilt spires over the trees that lined the walkway as he made his way further in, shadowed by the ever-hungry grey squirrels that populated the area. In his left hand he carried his briefcase. On his back was a conspicuous orange and blue rucksack that Amy had lent him to carry the box in. Kapowski had given him limited instructions: just head for the lake, she'd told him. If he followed the lake path, then apparently Peter Pan would be impossible to miss.

Tayte saw her before he saw the statue. He recognised her raven hair and that close-fitted black trouser suit, this time with a lime-green silk scarf at the neck. As the path turned with the contours of the lake on his right and the foliage ahead cleared, he saw that she was standing by a low iron railing looking up at the sculpture of the boy who continued to play his pipes, never growing a day older. She was tapping her foot and every now and then fussing with her hair. She had someone with her—a man wearing grey trousers and a check sports jacket with a heavily knotted tie around his neck. His short grey hair was receding and he had a dense moustache which sat proudly on his face, balancing things out.

Tayte knew he must have been just as easy to recognise the moment Kapowski turned to face him.

'JT!' she called, waving as she came to meet him, leaving the other man behind.

'Julia, hi.' Tayte put on his best cheesy grin as she approached, and up close he thought she looked more like that portrait-style photograph from her website than the plain-faced businesswoman on the plane. She seemed taller too, and her lips were a little sultry looking for the daytime, he thought. But then again, he had to concede that she brushed up pretty well.

Kapowski offered a hand and Tayte leant in and gave her a peck on the cheek, surprising himself. It wasn't much, but he could tell by the sudden glow of her skin and the mischief in her smile that she considered it plenty to be going on with. He sampled the air as he pulled away and he wondered if she always wore expensive-smelling scent to work.

'Thanks for seeing me,' Tayte said. 'Before we go on, I really want to apologise for my manners on the plane. I had no idea at the time what a total jerk I must have seemed.'

'Hell, you were just *nervous*,' Kapowski said. 'Don't give it a thought.'

The man who had been standing with Kapowski when Tayte first saw her arrived beside them.

'This is Gerald,' Kapowski said. 'He's really into boxes.'

Gerald frowned. 'Gerald Braithwaite,' he announced like he already wanted to be somewhere else. 'And that's antique box specialist,' he added, throwing Kapowski a raised brow.

'Oh, don't mind him,' Kapowski said. 'He's just cranky because he's missing his lunch break.' She gave Gerald a playful pinch on the arm and his moustache became animated. 'Was there a smile somewhere in there?' she said.

Tayte pumped Gerald's hand. 'I'm happy to meet you,' he said. 'I appreciate your time.'

'Not at all,' Gerald said. 'Actually, I'm quite excited. I believe you have something to show me.'

Tayte could feel Kapowski's eyes burning into him as he lifted the rucksack off his shoulder and reached inside, sensing that she wasn't so interested in what he'd brought along. He lifted out the box and offered it to Gerald, who immediately reached into the breast pocket of his jacket and pulled out a pair of half-frame glasses. He began to scrutinise the box like a diamond grader checking for inclusions.

'This really is quite something, Mr Tayte. Exquisite workmanship.'

Kapowski grabbed her associate's arm. 'Gerald's taking the box back to the office, aren't you, Gerald?' She spun him around.

'Hmm?' Gerald peered at her over the rim of his glasses. 'Oh—yes, that's right.' He feigned a smile at Tayte. 'Better equipped there.'

'Well, I'm not sure…' Tayte began. He was uncomfortable with the idea of letting the box out of his sight.

Kapowski cut in. 'He'll take good care of it,' she said. 'Won't you, Gerald?'

Gerald returned an eager, rapid-fire nod.

Tayte thought about it. He'd called them, after all. Not the other way around. He held out the rucksack and Gerald slipped the box back inside. Then he was off.

'We'll be at the Orangery when you're done,' Kapowski called after him. 'Take your time. There's no rush.' She passed an arm through Tayte's and led him away. The move was deftly executed. Tayte had no time to counter.

'I know a place close by where we can get lunch,' Kapowski said as they walked beside the lake. 'You gotta be hungry after your journey.'

Tayte hadn't known quite what to expect from the meeting, but this wasn't it. *Meeting?* Who was he kidding? He was on a date whether he liked it or not.

The Orangery at Kensington Palace exuded eighteenth-century charm, with its Corinthian columns and white-panelled walls and wood carvings; Julia Kapowski had chosen the setting for her lunch date with Jefferson Tayte well. They were sitting at a corner table looking along a bright, neutral interior that stretched away beneath a high ceiling, past tall sash windows through which the afternoon splashed in. The place buzzed with relaxed efficiency.

When Gerald Braithwaite found them again, they were sipping coffee and amiably discussing their interests between homemade petit fours. Tayte watched Kapowski slump back into her chair as her associate appeared at the entrance and came pacing towards them like a man charged with purpose. He had the rucksack with him, and his face was alive with hope.

'You were right, Julia!' Gerald said as he arrived. 'I *have* had some fun.' He pulled out a chair and sat down, resting the rucksack on the floor beside him. 'Fascinating,' he said as he reached into the bag and produced the box, setting it onto the table in front of him. He looked pleased with himself. 'It's a writing box!' he announced. 'But there's more to it than that. This box harbours a secret.'

Tayte's interest piqued.

'Certainly made in India,' Gerald added. 'An early example—possibly seventeenth century. The inkwell is missing from its compartment, and it's rather crude on the inside by later standards.'

'A secret?' Tayte said, holding on to the words before Gerald got carried away.

'That's right. The first thing I do with any new box is take a few measurements. The internal dimensions of this box, specifically the height, are conspicuously less than the external size.'

'And that tells you it has something to hide?' Tayte said.

'Not entirely, but it does suggest that some further investigation is in order.' Gerald opened the box so the inside was facing them. 'Writing boxes with secret compartments are not that uncommon,' he said. 'Normally you press something here or there and a secret drawer pops out, but this is something else. Very clever.'

Tayte watched as Gerald gripped the carved ivory rose dial inside the lid and rotated it counterclockwise. He knew it spun around, but he hadn't thought anything of it. He heard a click, and Gerald turned it the other way, listening to it like he was cracking a safe. When a second click came, he looked up and his thick moustache began to twitch. He closed the lid again and pressed the initial D in the left corner. Then he slid a bright whale-tooth tab out from the lower left side.

'And you've found something?' Tayte said, grinning because he already knew the answer.

Gerald opened the box again. 'I have.' He reached inside with both hands, gripping the inner walls with his fingertips. Then slowly, he lifted out the main compartment containing Lowenna's note. He set everything down beside the box, and his hands were shaking as he tipped the box forward to reveal what he'd discovered.

The box reeled Tayte and Kapowski from their seats, drawing them in with irresistible purpose, like a pair of fish caught on a single line.

Tayte had forgotten all about his lunch and the obvious romantic play from his date sitting next to him. His eyes were fixed on the writing box and the contents of a previously hidden section beneath the main compartment.

'Amazing,' Tayte said. He reached in and withdrew a letter that had been hidden for over two centuries.

Gerald tipped his head by way of a bow for his efforts.

'Oh, you're good!' Kapowski added.

Gerald grinned and nodded his agreement. 'I've read it,' he said. 'Hope you don't mind.'

Tayte shook his head, not looking up from the letter.

'Interesting reading,' Gerald added. 'Might mean more to you than it did to me.'

Tayte noted that it was signed by Lowenna, and that it carried the date, Tuesday, May 17, 1803—the day Mawgan Hendry was murdered. Kapowski shifted her chair closer to Tayte until she could read the letter with him over his shoulder.

Mawgan, my love, firstly I must ask that you deny the sadness you are surely feeling, for however contrary things may appear, these are happy times and soon they will be happier still. That we cannot be together is a lie, forced upon me by my father. It is his wish alone and one that with all my heart I do not share. I cannot yet tell you the truth in person, and so for now this letter must suffice. We must maintain a pretence if my plans are to be realised. You have to believe that our love has ended today for the satisfaction of the man in my father's pay who will be watching to ensure that I do not deviate from my father's bidding.

My sincerest hope is that the postscript on the first note you will read shall bring your eyes with all speed to this letter, and that at reading it your sadness will quickly pass. It surely is what is inside *that counts, and this message that only you can fully understand has further meaning.*

Mawgan, my love, I carry our child inside me even as I write—though I regret to say that my father also knows of this and has made plans of his own. The child is to be taken from me as soon as it is born and given to my Aunt Jane to bring up as her own. I am not to see the child or to know anything of it. Such is their plan, but upon my life this cannot be.

For there is hope.

I have recently made a discovery so dark and unsettling that I would wish now with all my heart to remain innocent of it—and yet it may be turned to our favour. Very soon I shall leave Rosemullion Hall, never to return to that place I no longer know or to the father I only thought I knew. Then we shall be together again. Go about your routine as though you know nothing of this. I shall come to you again one happy day and our plans can be set. You must not come to the house! Stay far away from Rosemullion Hall.

There is one other thing I must ask of you, my love. At all cost you must keep the box safe. I cannot stress the importance of this enough. Keep it safe, knowing only for now that it will protect us. It is our only security.

'Well…' Kapowski said, drawing out the word softly in Tayte's ear. '*Does* it mean anything to you?'

Tayte considered that Mawgan Hendry may have died without knowing anything of Lowenna's plans, or anything about the child she carried. 'It means plenty,' he said. 'And I think it might come to mean a great deal more.'

He wondered what dark discovery Lowenna had made, and whether it had anything to do with what happened to Eleanor and her children. *Why did she feel she no longer knew her own father?* Maybe it was enough that he'd insisted Lowenna end her relationship with Mawgan and give up her child. Might that have been enough to brand him an unrecognisable monster in her eyes?

'Glad to have been of service,' Gerald said, getting to his feet. 'I have to get back,' he added. 'I've a jewel box to look at this afternoon. Probably Fabergé. Should fetch a fortune.'

Tayte stood up and shook Gerald's hand. 'You don't know how helpful you've been.'

'Not at all,' Gerald said. Then he turned to Kapowski. 'See you later.'

Tayte slipped the letter into his jacket and sat down, pulling the box closer. He slid the main compartment back inside and followed the reverse of what Gerald had just shown him, getting a good understanding of how it all worked so he could show Amy when he got back. *She won't believe it,* he thought. He felt like a kid with a new toy.

'So I guess this is it,' Kapowski said. 'The coffee's finished, the cheque's paid. Now it's back to reality?'

Tayte looked up from the box, spinning the rose dial to reset it. He closed the lid, knowing he hadn't been paying her enough attention since Gerald had reappeared. 'Sorry,' he said. 'Miles away there. Look, Julia, thanks for this, really. If there's anything I can do for you. Well, you've got my number.'

Kapowski's eyes sparkled, like she was imagining several things right there and then.

'I've got to ask,' Tayte said. 'Looking for Larry?'

Kapowski actually blushed. 'I'm not sure I can tell you.'

'Then I'm not sure I can call you and tell you what flight I'm catching back to Boston.' Tayte looked nonchalant. 'It's a shame,' he added. 'I'm already getting the shakes just thinking about it. You might have helped distract me from my phobia.'

'Larry Hagman,' Kapowski blurted.

Tayte's mouth twitched with amusement. 'Dallas?'

'That's the one. He was my Mr Right when I left college. After three bad marriages, I'm still looking.'

Tayte turned to the window for distraction.

Kapowski laughed at him. 'Don't look so worried,' she added. 'It's only our first date!'

Tayte laughed along with her, then he glanced at his watch and sighed. 'I guess it *is* that time.' He put the box away. 'Can I walk you back to your office?'

Chapter Thirty-Five

Jefferson Tayte passed through the ticket gate at Paddington Station and made his way along the platform, heading for the 17:03 to Truro amid a jostle of Friday commuters. Looking up, he admired Isambard Kingdom Brunel's collaborative creation with architect Matthew Digby Wyatt. The glowing central span arched like a decorative wrought iron rib cage a hundred feet above him. It was supported on red and white steel columns and ran some 500 feet in length to a bright fan of light at the opening. He wondered how many of the people rushing around him spared any time to look, how many stopped to read about its history or knew anything about the place at all.

After he'd left Kapowski, taking a cab from outside her office building not far from the park where they'd met, he'd updated his client. Then he'd called Amy to share his news about the box. He'd been disappointed to get no reply, but he figured the good news would keep, and a large part of him wanted to see her face when he revealed what the box specialist had discovered.

He followed a grey suit into the vestibule area of the train carriage with another similarly attired man at his heels. The carriage was already busy as he went through, and the air immediately assaulted him with a mixture of new plastic and velour seat coverings fused with overheating bodies, sweaty from the office march and the London Underground. He hoped the air-conditioning worked.

He hadn't long found a seat when his phone rang. The train was still in the station, although the doors had closed, sealing everyone in for departure. He had his briefcase clamped between his feet and the rucksack was on his lap. His phone's simple ringtone amplified as he took it out of his pocket, drawing attention. The display gave him no clue as to the caller's identity.

'JT,' he announced. The woman in the seat opposite him looked up from her book, distracted by the obvious burst of something foreign. Beside her a young headphone-clad office worker remained oblivious.

'Mr Tayte?' the caller asked.

Tayte thought it sounded like a man's voice, but there was something odd about the tone and he couldn't be certain. 'Speaking,' he said.

'I have something for you, Mr Tayte.'

The voice sounded cartoon-like and unnatural, like whoever was speaking was breathing helium between sentences. 'Who is this?' Tayte asked.

'Who I am doesn't matter. You'll know soon enough.'

Tayte was intrigued. 'Did you leave that old newspaper copy under my wiper blade at Bodmin yesterday?' He was speaking louder than he meant to. The whole carriage seemed to go silent. He turned to the window and asked, 'How did you get my number?'

'Just listen, Mr Tayte. I didn't call you to pass the time. We need to meet. I can help you.'

Tayte felt the train jerk as it started to move. A late boarder wielding a laptop suddenly filled the empty seat beside him.

The voice in Tayte's ear continued. 'I don't have much time, Mr Tayte. When I've finished speaking, this call will end.'

The caller had Tayte's full attention.

'There is a place on the Lizard Peninsula,' the voice said. 'Not far from the inlet to the Helford River on the south bank— Nare Point. I will be inside the observation hut there tonight at seven-thirty. I have a copy of James Fairborne's last will and testament for you. It's something you need to see.'

Tayte was about to cut in and say he couldn't make it—that he was on a train and it wasn't due into Truro until after nine-thirty. He waited too long for a pause that never came and the sudden silence in his ear told him he'd missed the opportunity. The caller had cleared.

Tayte sighed, heavily. He wanted to see that probate record all the more now. It was a missing document, and there had to be a good reason. He wondered who was trying to help him and why they were in such a rush. The only obvious candidate was someone from the Cornwall Record Office. Penny Wilson had his number. *Someone must have found the document,* he thought. But he couldn't make the train go any faster. It was due to arrive two hours too late, and he'd be much later still by the time he'd found Nare Point.

Peter Schofield... The name that couldn't have been further from his thoughts all day suddenly popped into his head. The solution was obvious. Schofield could go in his place. Tayte thought he'd probably welcome the chance after prowling around graveyards all day. He reached for his phone again, wondering for the first time how Schofield had got on.

Peter Schofield answered the call with his usual business greeting. 'You've called Peter Schofield. Don't know where we're going, but I sure know where we've been.'

Tayte shook his head. 'Schofield, it's JT.'

'I knew that,' Schofield said, laughing. 'You won't believe the trip I've had today.'

Tayte could hear the unmistakable rasp of a V12 engine in the background, heightened by an intermittent rushing sound, which made him think that Schofield was driving a sporty roadster between narrow country lane hedgerows with the top down.

'Turn anything up?' Tayte asked. He wouldn't have put it past Schofield to turn a goose chase into a golden egg hunt.

'I sure have, buddy. And you're gonna love it.'

The conversation paused briefly while Tayte waited to hear what Schofield had to say, but Schofield remained silent.

'So let's have it, then,' Tayte said.

'Well now, that wouldn't be right. You're holding all your cards close to you chest until you get back. It's only fair I do the same. We can exchange information later over a drink.'

Tayte shuddered at the idea. He knew better than to expect anything straightforward from Peter Schofield.

'Yours had better be good,' Schofield added. 'It had better be really good, 'cause mine's the Elliot Ness of news!'

'Elliot Ness?'

'It's untouchable, man!' Schofield hooted and whooped down the phone. 'Tell me you've seen the movie.'

Tayte just shook his head and moved right on. 'Schofield,' he said. 'I need you to meet someone tonight at seven-thirty. It's important, so don't be late. They'll be waiting inside an observation hut at a place called Nare Point. Should be on the map. It's somewhere near the mouth of the Helford River. There's a document they want to give me, but I won't be back in time.'

'What is it?'

'A probate record. It won't mean much to you, and I'm not exactly sure yet what it'll mean to me, but I'll tell you what I know over that drink.'

'No problem, big guy.'

'And you'd better take a flashlight with you,' Tayte added. 'It gets dark over here about then.'

When the call ended, Tayte had something else to think about. What had Schofield turned up? What was he so wired about? As he relaxed into his seat, he knew the answer would have to wait. The writing box had raised new and more pressing questions. He felt its hard edges through the rucksack on his lap, wondering what 'dark discovery' Lowenna had made, and why the box was so important to her.

It was their security, he thought. But how could it protect them? *Protect them from what?* He shook his head and laughed to himself. *One question gets answered—another replaces it.*

He began to chew over what he knew about the box. He now had a good idea of where and when it was made. The initials suggested it had been in the Fairborne family a long time, handed down from one generation to the next until it passed to Lowenna. Lowenna's letter told him she had planned to run away with her lover and their child, believing that something about the box would protect them. If that was true—if the box really did have that kind of power—then it was clear to Tayte that it had more to say. He cocked an eyebrow. *Something dark,* he supposed.

Tayte scratched at his cheek, considering that Gerald had already found the secret compartment and there was nothing in there that Lowenna could have used against anyone in the way her letter suggested. He wanted to get the box out right there on the train and take another look, sure that Gerald must have overlooked something, but he resisted. He owed it to Amy to keep the box safe, and for all he knew, whoever wanted it now might have followed him onto the train, just as someone had followed him to Bodmin. He looked around. There were no obvious candidates. Everyone seemed wrapped up in their books, their laptops, or their dreams.

Tayte pushed his head into the headrest and closed his eyes, pulling the rucksack protectively close, linking his arms around it like he was cradling a child. His thoughts wandered back inside the box, to Lowenna's secret letter to Mawgan Hendry, pondering what it all meant. It was certainly conclusive proof that Mathew Parfitt was her son and that Mawgan Hendry was his father, and that he had been raised by Lowenna's aunt and uncle, Jane and Lavender Parfitt. But clearly that was not Lowenna's wish. According to her letter, she had made other plans for her child.

Drifting to the rhythm of the train, Tayte understood that the most promising thing about the box was that it must have come to

England with Eleanor Fairborne and her children when they left America. He opened an eye and fixed it on the rucksack, knowing that the answers he was looking for had to be right there in front of him.

Chapter Thirty-Six

In 1803, two weeks before Mawgan Hendry was murdered, and before James Fairborne knew that his daughter was in love with a farmer from Helford or that she carried his child, Lowenna chanced upon something that both confused and disturbed her so deeply that she refused to believe it, blocking it from her mind as best she could for several days. She'd convinced herself that it could not possibly be true. What she had discovered, however disturbing, made no sense. And yet her discovery left her with a recurring question that haunted her sleep.

It concerned the box her father had given her on her fifth birthday and the revelation that it concealed not one but two secret compartments. She remembered little of the day, but she recalled that her father had told her the box was very special. It followed then that he would be the best person to answer the question she knew she must ask—then her ghosts would be silenced. But she did not want to ask it, fearful that the answer might somehow confirm those dreadful words she'd read. Then her ghosts would become all too real.

Lowenna had suffocated her question for eleven days, and she might have buried it forever had her father not come to hear of Mawgan Hendry from that wretched brute of a man who was always drifting about the estate. She supposed he was the one. When James Fairborne forbade his daughter to see Mawgan Hendry and subsequently learnt of her condition—when he made clear his plans to deny her the love of her own child—only then was she resolved to ask that question of him.

They had been riding beneath a hazy sky all morning. Lowenna wore tan breeches and a green silk tunic, and she rode like a man as her father had taught her; sidesaddle in a pretty dress was purely for show when riding in company. This was a daily ritual, time shared together, father and daughter. But this morning's ride was no longer the same happy time for Lowenna. She saw her father now in a different light, and his plans to give her child away, even if it was to her aunt Jane, were as unthinkable to her as the dark discovery she'd made—more abhorrent even than those terrible words she had read.

The seed of Lowenna's plan to run away with Mawgan and have their child together had already begun to grow. Until she was fully ready, she would pretend to go along with her father's wishes, and today she would keep up appearances. They rode out seemingly in good company, talking idle talk about anything other than Mawgan Hendry or Lowenna's condition. She could see from his usual bright demeanour that this was still a happy time for him, regardless of what had passed between them.

'See the buzzards,' her father said, pointing across the neighbouring farmland towards a small copse of trees. 'They'll have rabbit for lunch.'

Lowenna simply nodded, willing the rabbits to make it safely back to the cover of their burrows.

'Speaking of which,' her father added, 'I've a hearty appetite myself.'

The morning ride always ended in a race back to the stable block, and it always began with a look from her father to ask if she was ready for the off. And there it was, just as on any other day, like nothing so bitter had passed between them. James Fairborne dug his heels in and his horse reared up.

'Come on!' he yelled.

Lowenna seldom won the race, and not once before she had turned fourteen. In those two years since that first victory, she could count her triumphs on one hand. But today Lowenna's resolve to beat her father could not have been stronger. Today she would not falter at the stream as she had so often in the past. She would jump it clean to spite him.

The head start her father always gave himself was closing. Beneath her, Lowenna could hear her old friend, Gwinear, panting over the thud and rumble of his hooves, and by the time they reached the stream they were level. Lowenna was out of her seat like a derby racer going for the finish line and she did not falter. Gwinear's front hooves thumped down first on the other side of the stream, and now the stables were in sight. She pushed on, not looking back. Then as the stables grew in her vision, her thoughts distracted her. She knew that when this race was over, she would ask her father the question that tormented her.

Katherine's name was suddenly spinning in her head. She grew uneasy, and Gwinear must have sensed the change. The horse slowed not two hundred yards from the stables and her father passed her like an unstoppable locomotive, gaining ground with every stride, lashing his whip and yelping for more speed.

When Lowenna reached the stables, she arrived to see her father handing his bridle to the stable boy. 'Maybe tomorrow?' he called to her as she arrived.

*Tomorrow...*Lowenna knew there would be no more races between them. As she approached, she did not dismount, but remained tall on her horse as her father took Gwinear's reins and held her steady. Her unease must have been all too apparent. Win or lose, this was always a happy moment between them: a cuddle and a kiss on his cheek by way of a prize for his win. But not today. She watched his head sink to the ground, and then slowly he looked up again, trying to make eye contact, but failing.

'I cannot expect you to understand my decision,' he said. 'You are too young to know what is for the best. But one day you will thank me for seeming so hard on you now.'

Lowenna did not want to have the argument again. Where was the sense in arguing over something she knew she could not win? The question she had to ask dominated all else. 'There is something I must ask you, Father,' she said. The words formed in her mind, but still she could not speak them.

'Pray, what is it, child? You know you can ask anything of me. Anything at all.'

Lowenna looked away, wondering how he could be the caring father she had loved so well, while inside him breathed the monster she had come to detest. When she turned back to him, her jaw had tightened, ready to force the question out, but she skirted. 'I have found something, Father.'

'Yes…'

'I am sure it is absurd. It really makes no sense.'

'Go on.'

Lowenna hesitated, dry-mouthed. She wanted to ride away even now, but she had to ask her question. She had to make sense of it all. She swallowed hard. 'Do you know who Katherine is?'

Her father stepped away, but he could not hide the dour expression that washed over him. 'Why do you ask?'

A column of silence rose between them. Knowing what she knew—what she had discovered—her father's sudden mood swing warned her to be cautious.

He came close to her again. 'Where have you heard that name?' he insisted. 'I must know.' His tone was sharp now. He gripped her boot until Lowenna could feel his fingers tight around her ankle, as if her leather riding boots were made from nothing more than rice paper.

'Do you know the name, then?' Lowenna asked, her small voice wavering.

James Fairborne stared at his own boots and Lowenna heard him sigh. 'I do,' he said. 'I know it well indeed.' They were solemn words.

'And may I ask *how* you come to know of her?'

The awkward pause returned. Her father shook his head as though denying his own thoughts, but his words betrayed him, although he could not yet know their significance to Lowenna. 'She was my daughter,' he said. 'By my first marriage.'

Lowenna felt light-headed. She looked pale despite the midday sun. It was an answer she could not have prepared herself for. It was the very last answer she wanted to hear, and until now she had not contemplated it or understood what it meant in light of what she had read. She swayed in her saddle. Her eyes fluttered. Then as her father reached out for her she fell.

Unconsciousness lasted only briefly. When Lowenna's eyes opened again, she was in her father's arms being carried towards the house. She looked up at him, recognising his features, yet the eyes that looked down at hers were the eyes of a man she no longer knew. Katherine was real. The contents of Katherine's journal pages were real. Her father's answer had confirmed everything—and so much more.

Lowenna felt sick.

She struggled to be free, kicking her legs until her father let her go. Then she ran from him, away into the house and up to her room, where she fell onto her bed, sobbing. Her whole world was crumbling around her. She knew she must leave Rosemullion Hall; knew she had to take control of what remained to her if there was to be any salvation. And she now knew that Katherine Fairborne's words, her few journal pages, could be used to protect her and her child if her father tried to stop her.

Three days later, on that fateful Tuesday in May 1803 when Lowenna went to meet her love at the usual place beneath the broad oak, she went to tell him that their love must end. Her father had allowed her this one grace upon her promise that she would not try to see Mawgan Hendry ever again. Her promise had been given readily enough, and now as she trod the path that led away from Rosemullion Hall, between lavender shoots that grew to meet their summer, she went to deliver that promise—or such was the illusion she would have her father believe.

Lowenna wore yellow, in part to spite the deepening grey of the afternoon and to brighten her spirits, but most of all she wore yellow to conceal the bag that hung from her shoulder, fashioned from identical silk. She passed through an iron gate at the end of the lavender path and breathed the fresh air that she could no longer find within the bounds of Rosemullion Hall. Her eyes scanned the periphery, knowing her father's man would be there, watching her, waiting to follow her down to the river and along to their meeting place where he would witness the scene she had rehearsed in her mind so many times. She was concerned at how Mawgan would react, but he had to suspect nothing. It must look real to the man who would later report back to her father. The letter hidden inside the box would explain everything, and she was confident Mawgan would find it; the secret compartment was no secret to him.

She thought herself clever that the clue she had placed in the box with the silk heart had further meaning. She caressed her midriff in a gentle circular motion, thinking fond thoughts of Mawgan. Then she wondered how she could have been so foolish as to let her father know. The baby inside her barely showed. She could have gone another month before nature would wield itself too obvious to conceal. Were it not for her anger at her father's insistence that she should see no more of Mawgan, things might have been easier. That anger rekindled when she recalled her father telling her how fortunate she was that he had *allowed* her to see the farmer this one last time.

The sea was dull and brooding as Lowenna came upon it, reflecting a moody sky that quickly began to spit down at her. As her pace quickened, following the path through flowering gorse that was yellow as her dress, the heavens heaved and opened. But she was not deterred. She had to see this through. As she took the box now to Mawgan, she knew it was her only hope. If she failed, she would lose both her child and her love, and she cared nothing for a life without them.

Chapter Thirty-Seven

When Jefferson Tayte awoke he had no idea where the train was. The display on his watch told him he'd been out almost two hours. He gazed through his reflection in the window, at the darkening countryside that sped past his eyes. In the distance there was a slow-moving landscape of fields and farmland, a faraway woodland, then a town unmindful of their passing. He gripped the edges of the rucksack on his lap, feeling the outline of the box again, just to know it was still there. It caused him to think of Amy. He tried her number again.

The call rang unanswered as before, and as he listened to the ringtone, he wondered why Amy hadn't tried to call him. Surely she would want to know how his trip to London had gone—would want to know that the box she was pinning so much hope on was on its way back to her. He couldn't quell the anxiety that began to take shape inside him, particularly when he reminded himself that they were not the only people interested in this family history and the box that was the key to unravelling it. A box that in 1803, some-one had been prepared to kill for.

When Lowenna arrived back in her room at Rosemullion Hall that Tuesday in 1803, the day she had feigned the end of her association with Mawgan Hendry, she was still crying. She had cried all the way back through the rain, and her tears were genuine enough, unable to bear Mawgan not knowing what was in her mind, unable to bear his obvious suffering at the notion that the love between them had ended so abruptly. But her tears had served her purpose well. The illusion could not have been more complete.

The man in her father's pay, whom she knew had witnessed everything, did not follow her into the house—he never did. He and her father would always meet elsewhere so their business could not be overheard. Whenever Lowenna asked about him, her father would say nothing other than to portray him as a man who did occasional work for him around the estate.

But Lowenna knew better.

As she lay on her bed, listening to the rain at the window, her tears gradually dried. She began to smile again as she pictured Mawgan opening the box and finding the silk heart she'd made for him; her heart, which belonged to him and was now returned for his safekeeping. Her clue would be plain enough to Mawgan. He would find her letter, understand her true intentions and be overjoyed, knowing that it *was* what is inside that counts.

He must know everything by now…

Lowenna went to the window and opened it, knowing that she could not remain at Rosemullion Hall one hour longer than she had to. The very idea left a taste in her mouth so bitter it made her retch. Rain gusted at her already soaked clothing until it rolled from her skin like glass beads. She looked out towards the river, towards Mawgan. The box was away now and in strong hands. It held the secret to their happiness, and very soon she would follow after it. And if her father came for her or tried to take her child, then she would use the contents of the box without compassion for the man she no longer knew.

Such were her plans.

But she was suddenly distracted from them. Lowenna turned away from the window and stared across the room as the door creaked slowly and deliberately open. There was no knock or announcement and she sensed that her caller would not be welcome. She had never seen her father look so utterly terrifying—or so terrified. He stood there, filling the doorway, his head bowed low to his chest, fists clenched to control the beast within as though knotted in a struggle to prevent it from lashing out. His eyes just glared at her.

'Where is the box?' her father demanded through gritted teeth that spat down onto his waistcoat. 'Do you think me so foolish that I cannot understand how you come to know of Katherine?' He lumbered into the room. The door splintered the frame behind him. 'The box is all that remains of my old life. There is no other way you *could* know of her!'

Lowenna cowered against the open window. The rain felt cold on her back. She shook her head as her father came closer, her eyes pleading that he retreat. But he did not. James Fairborne caught her wrists and held her, staring straight through her until she thought he would crush her bones.

'I do not have it!' Lowenna yelled.

Her father locked eyes with her then, holding her close to him. 'Then where is it? What secret has it shared?'

'You're hurting me!'

'You bring this all upon yourself.' His grip did not relent. 'What have you done with the box?'

Her wrists began to burn and the pain at last gave Lowenna the strength to defy him. 'You will not have it!' she said. The box was the only card she had to play against her father; she could not give it up. 'It is safely away from here and I will not hesitate to use it against you!'

Her father let her go. Lowenna continued her defiance, standing tall to him. The two were locked like battling stags, neither giving ground to the other. Then at last her father stepped away.

'So the box is not here?' he said a moment later.

Lowenna said nothing.

'Safely away, you say?' Her father suddenly looked pleased with himself. 'And I can guess only too well where you have taken it.'

Mawgan! Lowenna thought. *Was it so obvious?*

'You will remain in your room!'

'Father—no! I will get the box for you.'

'And take your little secret to the warden or the constable perhaps? No child, it is altogether too late for that. You will leave for your grandparents' house this very night and you will return again only when this—' He waved a dismissive hand at Lowenna's belly like he was flicking at a fly that was bothering him. 'When this bastard child is ready to show itself!'

Her father turned away from her then and Lowenna impulsively threw herself at him, stumbling to her knees. 'Where are you going, Father?' She was close to tears. She knew the answer.

Her father stared down at her, his eyes now bereft of emotion. 'Your door will remain locked until I come for you myself. Then a carriage will take you to Devon.' He pulled away from Lowenna and passed through the doorway.

'Father!' Lowenna could no longer control her emotions. She lay there, sprawled and wet through, openly sobbing.

James Fairborne paused a moment in the doorway. Then he turned back to Lowenna and drew a deep breath to calm himself.

Lowenna lifted her eyes to meet his. 'What will you do, Father?' Her eyes pleaded with him, but he made no attempt to answer.

'I will send your maid in with supper,' he said. 'And that is more than you deserve!'

The door slammed and a key rattled in the lock.

As Lowenna lay there, she could think of nothing other than Mawgan Hendry. She had not foreseen this. This was not part of her plan. Now, by giving the box to Mawgan, she had put her love in danger.

I must get word to him, she thought. *I must recover the box. Tamsyn…*

———

The pitiless rain fell as heavy as Lowenna's heart that evening when her father returned to her locked room and dragged her out by her wrists. He carried her to the waiting carriage, kicking and screaming, seemingly ignoring her pleading questions about Mawgan Hendry. As he lifted her into the carriage, she glimpsed the lumbering form of the man in her father's pay, waiting by the horses. It made her shiver all the more to think that he was the man charged with her delivery to her grandparents' house in Devon.

The carriage door slammed shut, shattering her already brittle nerves. Lowenna watched her father fix a bar across the door, sealing her in, making no eye contact with her as he turned and walked away. She draped herself against the window, hanging onto the rail by her fingertips in the vain hope of opening it. But it was useless. The iron nails she could see beyond the glass were driven deep to prevent the window from dropping. She slumped back onto the carriage seat and as she settled, she heard their conspiring voices. She heard mention of the box.

'Just tell me you have it!' her father said.

'I cannot.'

The exchange lifted Lowenna's spirits. If the box had not been recovered then she supposed Mawgan was safe, that her maid must have reached him in time. The conversation beyond the carriage came and went with the severity of the rain that continued to beat a sharp drum roll against the roof. But sitting close to the window, she was able to follow it in part.

'We must cover this up,' she heard her father say. 'And soon, such that the matter is quickly forgotten.'

Lowenna could still see her father through the window. He stopped pacing and the other man came close to him, like an overbearing shadow.

'The box must be returned to me,' he added. 'It must never be allowed to tell its secret.'

'There is a greater risk of that sitting in your carriage,' the other man said.

'She is my daughter! What would you have me do?'

Lowenna saw his answer. She recoiled from the window, startled as his eyes pierced hers. She receded into shadow, yet his eyes still managed to find her, holding her with such hatred as to suggest that he would have her father bid him kill her and be done with it.

She watched her father move away then, back towards the house. 'We shall conclude the matter upon your return,' he called.

Then he was gone, leaving Lowenna to the other's mercy.

thinking he'd try Amy again, this time to let her know he was on his way over. *She must be home now,* he thought. His phone rang before he had chance to dial. *Schofield,* he thought. *About time.*

He answered the call. 'Schofield! How'd it go?' He didn't recognise the voice that answered. The caller spoke slowly, almost mechanically, punctuating every few words with sharp precision.

'Is that Mr Tayte? Mr Jeff Tayte?'

Tayte was cautious. Only Schofield called him Jeff. 'Who wants to know?'

'Detective Chief Inspector Bastion, Mr Tayte. Devon and Cornwall Police. I am speaking to Mr Tayte then, am I?'

'That's right.'

'And *Jeff*? Short for Jeffrey, is it sir?'

'It's Jefferson actually. Look, where did you get my number and what's this all about?'

'Well that's just the thing, sir. I found your number in the call directory of Peter Schofield's mobile telephone. Are you related to Mr Schofield, sir?'

'No, I'm not.' Tayte gritted his teeth. 'We're...working together.' It was painful to say it. 'What's he been up to?' A few random thoughts scattered through Tayte's mind, reasons why Schofield might not have made the meeting he had lined up. He knew he'd be unreliable. 'Don't tell me,' Tayte said. 'He's had a couple of drinks too many, been a pain in the ass, and now you need someone to look after him.' *Well, not me,* he thought.

'I wish it was that simple, sir. I'm afraid Mr Schofield is dead.'

An eerie calm washed over Tayte, punctuating the silence.

'Sir?'

He wasn't sure how to react. That he didn't like Schofield was no secret—but dead! Peter Schofield! He'd always put him up there with the battery bunny when it came to staying power. He'd been a constant thorn in his side, an itch that would never go away. Only now it had, and it felt like it had taken something vital to him along with it.

Chapter Thirty-Eight

The man rocking Tayte's shoulder startled him.

'End of the line,' he said with an obvious Eastern European accent.

Tayte's head felt sore as he recoiled from his glass pillow to the almost musical twang of the nerves catching in his stiff neck as he straightened. The train was at a standstill. Through the window he recognised Truro train station. He blinked and rubbed at his neck.

'Thanks,' he said, but the man had already moved on to the next wastebin.

Tayte checked his watch; it was almost half past ten. That last snooze had taken him out cold for a few hours, rendering him oblivious to the fact that the train had lost some time and was overdue. He grabbed the rucksack and his briefcase, then struggled out of his seat, passing the cleaner as he left the otherwise empty carriage. He was surprised that a call from Schofield hadn't woken him before now with news of James Fairborne's last will and testament; the meeting with his mystery caller should have taken place almost three hours earlier. He checked his phone for missed calls—nothing.

What's Schofield playing at?

Tayte cleared the station concourse like he was running late for an interview. It was a cool night, pricked with stars and the slightest crescent moon. Floodlights over the car park shone circular pools onto the tarmac. As he reached his hire car, he pulled out his phone,

'Dead?' Tayte said. He was thinking about that cool British sports car Schofield had mentioned earlier. Had he pushed it too hard on Cornwall's tight country lanes? 'I spoke with him just this afternoon,' he added.

'I know, sir. Yours was the last number to call him. Are you in Cornwall by any chance?'

'Truro. I just got back from London.'

'That's very useful, sir. I'd be grateful if you could identify the body for us. Help speed things along.'

'Yes, of course.' Tayte had no idea how this sort of thing worked. 'When do you want to see me?'

'Right away, sir. If that's at all possible. We're still at the scene if you'd care to come down.'

'Scene?'

'That's right, sir. The crime scene. Peter Schofield was murdered.'

The unusually pitched voice of Tayte's earlier caller replayed in his head, setting up the meeting at Nare Point. *What have I done?* There was no other explanation. He stared out into the quiet car park and tried to convince himself that this was real, that he wasn't still on the train, asleep with his head against the window. He'd sent Schofield to his death tonight, and he wasn't sure if that upset him more than the realisation that it should have been his own life instead.

'I know it's a little irregular,' Bastion added. 'But we're about wrapped up here and I was hoping you could answer a few questions for me. Might take a couple of hours.'

'Sure, anything,' Tayte said, distracted.

'We're at a place called—'

Tayte cut in. 'Nare Point,' he said.

'Nare Point, sir?'

'Isn't that where you found him?'

'No, Mr Tayte. The body was found in Treath, down by the Helford River at a house called Ferryman Cottage.'

Chapter Thirty-Nine

Detective Chief Inspector Leonard Bastion was in his late forties. He wore navy suit trousers whenever he was on duty, but rarely the jacket, with a pressed white shirt and black cleated shoes that always looked like he'd just taken them out of the box they came in. He was a stocky man: barely five feet, eight inches tall, clean shaven with a thick crop of short silver grey hair that to his constant irritation would never stay down, spoiling an otherwise pristine appearance.

He was standing outside Ferryman Cottage, which was lit up by several crime scene floodlights. An ambulance was on standby alongside two police cars that continued to bathe the house in a lively blue and red glow. Beyond the lights, the lane and the woodland were in blackout, camouflaged by the night and the dark Helford River. Opposite Inspector Bastion stood the man who had discovered Peter Schofield's body.

'Sorry you've had to wait around so long, sir,' Bastion said. He flipped the cover of a small reporter style notepad. 'So you say Amy Fallon joined you every Friday?'

Martin Cole lit a roll-up cigarette and drew heavily on it, making the tip glow as it burned down the filter paper. 'That's right,' he said. 'Why are we going over this again? I've already explained why I was here.'

'Indulge me, sir,' Bastion said. 'If you don't mind.'

Martin snapped his lighter shut and slipped it into the side pocket of his jeans. 'When Amy didn't show,' he said. 'I walked up to the house to drag her down there.'

'To the Shipwrights Arms?'

Martin nodded. 'It's been a bad week for her. I thought maybe she needed some encouragement to come and have a drink with us.'

Bastion's pencil stopped twitching. '*Us* being?'

'Simon,' Martin said. 'Simon Phillips. He's the boathand who works with me. Amy always joined us at the Shipwrights on Fridays for a...well, a sort of social team brief, I suppose you'd call it. Just a couple of drinks and a chat.'

'And presumably Simon can vouch for that, can he, sir? And the staff at the Shipwrights?'

'Of course.'

'So you called Amy Fallon, and getting no answer you left Simon at the pub at twenty past eight and arrived at the house here approximately twenty minutes later? Seems a fair walk, sir. Just on the off chance?'

'I do a lot of walking. Most people around here do. It was nothing.'

'You said Amy was having a bad week, Mr Cole?'

Martin nodded, taking another drag on his cigarette. 'Her husband went missing two years ago this week. She's having a rough time of it.'

'I see. Well, who wouldn't?' Bastion put a hand on his head and flattened his hair across his forehead. It sprang straight up again. 'So you came to Ferryman Cottage,' he continued. 'And instead of finding Amy Fallon, you found the victim's body?'

Martin flicked the glowing stump of his cigarette away and watched it corkscrew into the night. As it hit the ground he took another from a brass case in the chest pocket of his green check over-shirt and fixed it loosely into the corner of his mouth. 'I knocked. There was no answer. No lights on. So I waited.'

'For how long?'

'Not sure....about five minutes, I guess. I sat and watched the river.'

'Not much to see, I shouldn't think?'

'No. Not much.' Martin reached for his lighter. 'Peaceful, though.'

'And then?'

'Then I went round the back of the house,' Martin said. 'Thought I'd take a look around before I left. I knocked on the back door and it swung open. I called out, got no reply, so I knocked harder and went inside.' He lit his cigarette and forced the smoke high above Bastion's head. 'The place was a mess,' he added. 'I know she'd had decorators in all week, but this wasn't home improvement mess.'

'That was about a quarter to nine, was it, sir?'

'Give or take.'

'And did you touch the body? Move anything?'

'No...well, not much. I went into the sitting room first. I turned on the light and saw him sitting there on the sofa, staring straight at me. I asked him who he was, got no response, so I went closer. That's when I saw the blood. It wasn't clear against his dark shirt, but I saw his trousers were spattered with it. I nudged his shoulder and then his head flopped back and his neck opened right up.' Martin pulled a sour face. 'I'll never forget it.'

'No, I'm sure,' Bastion said. 'What happened after that?'

'I called for Amy again, had a quick look around. She wasn't there.'

'So at precisely three minutes to nine you called the emergency services?'

'If you say so.'

'Thank you, Mr Cole. That's all I need for now.' Bastion licked his palm and tried to flatten the right side of his hair with a single smooth stroke. 'I'll send Sergeant Hayne over to take your details.

You'll be in the area for a while, will you? We'll need to take a formal statement at some point.'

'What about Amy? You're looking for her, right?'

'I'll have the immediate area checked, of course. Though technically she's not missing yet, and as you say, she's had a bad week. Maybe she took herself off somewhere to cheer herself up.'

Martin shook his head. 'It's not like her.'

'It is suspicious, sir, of course, and believe me, we're as anxious to talk to her as you are. But let's not jump to conclusions, eh?'

Bastion looked around for Sergeant Hayne. He saw him leaving the house with the coroner and raised a hand to get his attention. 'I'll let you know as soon as we make any progress, Mr Cole. Can I offer you a lift anywhere?'

'No, thanks. I'll take a walk back down to the Shipwrights. I could use another drink.'

Chapter Forty

Detective Sergeant Bill Hayne wore a light-grey suit over the standard-issue white shirt. At his neck, a plain navy tie was pushed too far up to be comfortable. At just twenty-seven he was young for the rank, but what he lost to youth and relative inexperience in the role, he made up for with a sharp intellect and his eagerness to get results.

Tayte had arrived at Ferryman Cottage out of breath and anxious. Sergeant Hayne had led him straight into the shell of Amy Fallon's dining room.

'He won't be a minute, sir,' Hayne said. 'Just finishing up in the sitting room.'

Tayte sat down on a lone Windsor chair by the window and pulled Amy's rucksack onto his lap. His briefcase was back in his hire car, hurriedly parked beyond the police barrier on the only lane that led in and out of Treath. He could hear a conversation in the hallway as two men were leaving.

'No cuts to his hands or arms,' one man said. 'Why is that unusual?'

'There was no struggle, sir,' the other man said. 'He couldn't have seen it coming.'

'Correct. Any other reason?'

'He was already unconscious? Drugged, maybe?'

'Well done, lad, but let's not get ahead of ourselves. Wait and see what the lab comes back with.'

Tayte stared up at a bare lightbulb hanging from the ceiling. It radiated a dim but harsh light against naked walls and floorboards, making the place feel like an interrogation room. He clutched subconsciously at the rucksack and watched the blue and red beams from the police lights outside sketch colourful horizons across the far wall, wondering where Amy was. He found himself considering that she might have been right: maybe her husband *had* found the box. Maybe now she was missing, too. *She knew I was bringing it back this evening,* he thought. *She would have tried to contact me by now. Why hasn't she answered her calls all day? Where is she?*

'Mr Tayte?'

The voice in the doorway startled him. Tayte rose as DCI Bastion entered the room with Sergeant Hayne in his shadow.

'Where's Amy?' Tayte asked. 'Is she all right?'

'We don't know at this time, sir,' Bastion said. 'There was no one else here when we arrived. Just Mr Schofield and the man who found him.'

Tayte nodded. Distracted.

'It was good of you to come so quickly,' Bastion said. 'The only address for any next of kin we could find on the victim is thousands of miles away in America.'

'Mother?' Tayte enquired.

'His wife, sir.' Bastion winced. 'Two small children as well, according to the photos we found on him.'

'Children?'

'That's right, sir. Always hits me hardest when I think of the little ones.'

'He didn't seem the type,' Tayte said, wondering if he'd completely misjudged the man, if there had been more to Peter Schofield behind that arrogant façade.

'You think you know people, eh, sir?'

'I know why he's dead,' Tayte said. He couldn't stop himself from saying it, however much it might implicate him.

'I was hoping as much, Mr Tayte, but we'll come to that. Let's make sure we have the right man first.'

Bastion put a firm hand on Tayte's shoulder and led him into the sitting room. It was nothing like Tayte remembered from last night; everything had been moved. The red settee drew his eye first. It was askew, pushed across the room away from the fireplace, facing the door. Then he saw the body outline and his eyes dropped to the body itself—to the white body bag laid out on a stretcher, ready for removal. Bastion knelt beside the bag and reached for the zip.

'If you're ready, sir.'

Tayte nodded and Bastion eased the zip down, being careful not to expose too much, sparing Tayte the images of the victim's fatal neck wound. Tayte could hear every click as the heavy-duty zip ticked down the bag like a clock running double time. Then Bastion pulled the zipper apart, and the image that met Tayte as he leaned in made him draw away again. The skin looked waxy and translucent, and he could no longer picture that toothpaste commercial grin on a face now drained of colour and emotion.

'That's him,' Tayte said. 'That's Peter Schofield.'

The zipper closed with a buzz, and DCI Bastion stood up again. Tayte continued to stare down at the top of the bag where Schofield's face had just been, like he could still see the ghostly image of it.

'We'll go outside, shall we?' Bastion said. Then he guided Tayte towards the door in baby steps, like he was helping an overprescribed psychiatric patient.

The air blowing in off the Helford River felt cool in Tayte's throat. He followed it, lit by the floodlights and the spinning glow of the police lights. He came right to the edge of the water before he stopped and his eyes wandered to Amy's teak motor launch, wondering again where she was. Bastion and Hayne were close behind him. Bastion took the lead.

'Do you know the owner of the house well, sir?'

Hayne checked his notepad. 'Amy Fallon,' he added.

Tayte shook his head. 'I met her just yesterday,' he said. 'I came to see her last night about something we had a common interest in.'

'And what was that, sir?'

Tayte sketched a brief outline of what he did for a living, the assignment he was working on, and why he'd come to England. He said nothing about the box or about the assault outside Mawnan Glebe two days ago. He knew these were the good guys, but a warning voice in his head told him not to complicate things. He couldn't risk losing the box.

'Amy was interested in who used to live at the house before her,' Tayte said. 'My assignment led me to the same people, so I came over to talk about it. I got here around six-thirty last night. We talked. Drank a glass of wine.'

Glass of wine…

The words triggered images of Amy's sitting room where he'd been standing just moments ago. Not everything in the room had been moved. He saw it again in his mind now as if for the first time. The wine glasses were still there on the low stool by the fireplace. The wine bottle was beside one of the table legs. He didn't need to ask if Bastion or Hayne knew where Amy was now. He'd confirmed his own thoughts.

'She would have cleared the glasses away by now,' he said.

Bastion scrunched his eyes. 'Excuse me?'

'The wine glasses are still there. Just as they were when I left last night.'

Bastion looked at Tayte like he was waiting for him to elaborate further.

Hayne seemed to understand. 'You think something happened to Amy last night? Before she had chance to clear the glasses away?'

Tayte nodded. 'She hasn't answered my calls today either.'

'You as well, eh?' Bastion said.

'As well as who?'

'The man who found the body, sir. Martin Cole. He was concerned for her too. She was supposed to meet him and his colleague for a drink this evening.'

Hayne's pen was poised. 'What time did you leave here last night, sir?'

Tayte thought about it. 'Must have been around eight o'clock.'

'So it looks like Amy's been missing more than twenty-four hours?' Hayne said, scribbling into his pad.

'You said you knew why the victim was dead,' Bastion said.

'I had a call this afternoon, not long after my train left London. Someone had information for me about the assignment I'm working on. I was supposed to meet him tonight, only I couldn't make it. I sent Peter Schofield instead.'

'And what time was the meeting arranged for, sir?'

'Seven-thirty.'

Hayne gave Bastion a nod. 'Fits the estimated time of death, sir.'

'Did you arrange to meet this man here?' Bastion asked.

'No,' Tayte said. 'Someplace called Nare Point.'

'Ah, yes,' Bastion said. 'Nare Point. You mentioned that earlier on the telephone.'

Hayne cut in. 'I've got a car on its way there now, sir.'

Bastion looked impressed. 'We know the murder didn't happen here,' he said to Tayte. 'Sorry to be so graphic, but there's not enough blood.' He brushed a palm down the back of his head. 'Though there's clearly been a struggle.'

'Looks more like someone was looking for something,' Hayne added. 'Any idea what that might be?'

Tayte stared at the lights across the river and shook his head, unable to lie so blatantly to their faces.

'Question is,' Bastion continued, 'why would anyone go to the bother of moving a body all the way here from Nare Point?'

Tayte turned away from the river and saw the expectant look on Bastion's face, like he hoped Tayte was about to furnish him with the answer. Tayte didn't have one.

'The killer's obviously making a statement,' Hayne said.

Tayte shrugged. 'I don't know. Whoever called me just said they had a document for me. A probate record. Something I needed that I hadn't been able to find.'

DS Hayne checked the knot in his tie. 'And you didn't think that odd, sir? Getting a call to meet a stranger at a place like Nare Point after dark?'

'I'd never heard of Nare Point until today. I was so focused on that document I just figured someone out there was trying to help.'

'Only their real motive was to kill you,' Bastion said.

Tayte nodded. 'So it seems.'

'Do you have any idea why that might be?' Bastion asked.

Tayte knew. Just like he knew he'd been played—the warning outside the woods at Mawnan and then the note under his wiper blade at Bodmin. Now he was supposed to be dead, and that could only mean one thing: Schofield's killer knew that Tayte had the box, and tonight at Nare Point he'd hoped to collect it off his corpse. And if he knew Tayte had the box, he also knew that Amy did not. Dumping Schofield's body at Amy's house was a clear signal to Tayte that the killer had Amy. The box was even more important now. It was currency.

'Can I see your train ticket, sir?' Bastion asked. 'Or a receipt. Usual formality. I just need to confirm your whereabouts this evening.'

Chapter Forty-One

By the time Tayte got back to his hire car, it was gone midnight. He climbed in and set the rucksack down onto the passenger seat. Seconds later he was following the glow of his headlights away from Treath. His mind raced with questions that all asked just one thing. *What the hell am I going to do now?* He arrived slowly at the top of the lane where it joined the main road, indicating left, away from Helford, back towards his accommodation, where he hoped he might be able to clear his head and come up with some answers. He paused at the junction, listening to the turn indicator tick-ticking as he watched the flashing green light in the dash. Waiting… Thinking…

His eyes wandered down to the passenger seat footwell. His briefcase was open, his assignment papers ruffled. He was confused momentarily. He knew he hadn't left it like that. Then as he reached across to retrieve it, the left side of his neck began to sting like a paper cut.

His hand never made it past the gear shift.

Jefferson Tayte felt his hair jerk violently back, pulling his head into the headrest, exposing his fleshy neck to the blade that was almost too sharp to feel at first. Then an unnaturally deep voice close to his ear sent a chill through him.

'Mr Tayte. At last. Now slowly reach across and pass me that rucksack.'

It was obvious to Tayte that the speaker was manipulating his voice to disguise it. It sounded throaty and strained. Tayte's heart was racing. He could feel the blade pressing at his throat now, threatening to break the skin. The sting on the left side of his neck where the knife had first slid into place began to burn. He thought of Schofield and the body bag, reminding himself what this man was capable of. Then he thought about Amy.

'You've got some balls!' he said, finding some of his own. 'The place is crawling with cops.'

Tayte felt the blade bite into his neck.

'Just do as you're told and you'll get through this.'

Tayte seriously doubted it. No immediate way out presented itself. He handed the rucksack over, trying to glimpse his attacker in the rearview mirror as he did so. But it was too dark back there, and his movements were restricted by the blade at his neck and the hand tugging at his hair.

'Now what?' Tayte said.

'Now drive! Go right.'

Helford, Tayte thought as he pulled out and turned the car down the hill. He went as slow as he dared. He needed time. It was too quiet here. No other cars around. No people. A canopy of trees shrouded the road.

'Where's Amy?' he said, but he got no reply.

A moment later he heard a line spoken softly as though in self-gratification. 'I knew they'd bring you here.'

Tayte felt the pressure on his scalp ease off a little. 'Why are you doing this?' he said.

The man continued to ignore him. 'At the bottom of the hill take a right into the car park.'

Tayte didn't like the sound of that. In his headlights he could already see the parking sign. It looked so dark down there with all those trees. The car arrived too soon at the turn off.

'Here,' the voice said.

Tayte turned in. To his right a small fire caught his eye. It was a good 200 metres away on the other side of an otherwise empty car park that was essentially a grass field in the woods.

'Take it down there on the left. Then shut off the engine.'

A dusty track circled the car park like a speedway circuit. Tayte took the clockwise route, crunching loose stones beneath the tyres. It led the car down towards the perimeter of trees. Through them he could just see the Helford River's dull highlights, shifting with the current beneath a hiding moon. He sensed he had little time to act now. If he was going to do anything, it had to be soon. A small voice in his head tried to tell him it would be okay, that the man with the knife to his throat had what he'd come for. As Tayte killed the engine, a far bigger voice in the sudden darkness told him otherwise.

'That note I pinned to your chest... You should have taken my warning more seriously, Mr Tayte. Before it became necessary for me to kill you!'

Before the man's words had faded, Tayte's head was back against the headrest, chin proud, like he was waiting for a shave. He winced as the man's hand knotted through his hair, straining his scalp as he brought the knife into position further around his neck, ready to slice it back again.

At that moment Jefferson Tayte knew his life was over. He was unprepared and constrained by his assailant's grip and a tight seat belt. He'd had no time to react, and although agnostic as far as religion was concerned, the only thing on his mind right now was the Lord's Prayer. He pictured the Gideon Bible he'd found in the bedside drawer back in his room at St Maunanus House, with the bright cross emblazoned on the cover. Then he remembered the broken display cases at Bodmin Jail.

'Why d'you steal that crucifix?' he blurted. He swallowed hard. His throat felt like blotting paper. 'And the verse book? Why did you steal them?'

Tayte felt an arm tighten around his shoulder as the man's muscles contracted. The knife pressed closer to his skin, but it was steady and Tayte knew that his questions had struck home.

The man scoffed in Tayte's ear. 'I didn't *steal* them,' he said. His voice rose then for the first time. 'They were mine to take!'

'They belonged to a man called Mawgan Hendry,' Tayte said, as assertively as he could manage. 'That was 200 years ago, so unless you've returned from the dead, I'd say you *stole* them!' Tayte knew he was playing a dangerous game, but what did he have to lose? He'd bought himself some time, that's all, and he had no idea how much. If he had any chance of getting out of this alive, he had to keep the man talking, keep him worked up until some opportunity presented itself. His eyes were all over the car, looking for something he could use.

'They should have been *given* to me,' the man said.

'But they weren't, were they? So you stole them.'

'They were stolen from Mawgan.'

'Stolen after he was murdered?' Tayte said. 'And you think the box will tell you who really killed him?'

'I already know who killed him.'

Tayte could feel the man's breath, hot on his sore neck. 'But you want to know why, right?' Tayte wanted to know why, *and* who, but now was not the time to ask. After ruling out trying to burn the man with the cigarette lighter because it needed to warm up first, he considered trying to stab him in the eye with the car key.

'And I suppose you already know why, do you, Mr Tayte?'

Tayte shook his head. It was a mistake.

'Then it's as I thought. You're no further use to me.'

Tayte felt the skin on his neck break and knew he was bleeding. It was like he was sitting next to himself watching a slow motion rerun that he was helpless to stop. He saw his own hands reaching for the knife in defence, but the man's hold on him was too strong, the knife, too close. Then a face at his window startled him. It was surreal.

A long-haired man in need of a wash and a good meal was staring at him through the window. Then behind him he heard a metallic, tapping sound. By the time he fully registered what was going on, the knife had suddenly pulled away, not across his throat, but away, catching his left hand as it went. Then he heard one of the rear doors open.

He unclipped his seat belt and spun around, aware now that he was losing a significant amount of blood from both his neck and his hand. The rear seats were empty. The man who'd come close to killing him—close to finishing what he'd set out to do at Nare Point—had fled, taking the rucksack and the box with him.

The tapping at the window drew Tayte's attention again. Then he saw why he was still alive. Another man, not unlike the first, had his face pressed to the rear window, staring in. The metallic tapping sound was coming from a can of Carlsberg Special Brew that he was clanking against the glass. Tayte realised then that the fire he'd seen when he'd first entered the car park had to be their campfire. They were unlikely saviours, but saviours nonetheless.

Tayte leapt from the car and the strangers backed away, observing Tayte as he looked frantically about. His right hand clutched the wound on his neck to stem the blood flow and his left hand hung loose, dripping. His suit was a complete mess. In the darkness there was little to see, no sign of his attacker. Then away beyond the trees, lost to the night, he heard a screech of tires and a distinctive engine note—a V12. He recalled hearing a similar sound recently, altered through his phone's speaker, but the sound was unmistakable to him. The last engine like that he'd heard was when he'd called Schofield on the train back from London. It was playing over Schofield's voice in background.

It forced him to recall the last conversation he'd had with Peter Schofield. He heard himself asking him to go to Nare Point in his place—to his death. He remembered how excited Schofield had been, how energised. Schofield had spent his last hours prowling graveyards at Tayte's behest and he'd come up with something big. Now he'd taken it with him to his grave.

The man with the beer can staggered closer, studying Tayte. 'You should see a doctor,' he said, slurring every word.

Chapter Forty-Two

Four hours after Jefferson Tayte had almost died, he was sitting in the passenger seat of a strange car, parked somewhere equally unfamiliar to him. He had no idea where he was, and the only light he allowed himself came from the glow of his laptop screen. Bastion and Hayne had been shocked to see him again in such a state, but the staff of the Royal Cornwall Hospital in Truro soon had him patched up. After he'd given a statement and was allowed to go, having refused the offer of any direct police protection beyond the usual point-of-contact phone number, he just got in the courtesy car that was waiting for him and drove, heading anywhere just to lose himself. As much as he needed a change of clothes, he knew he couldn't risk returning to St Maunanus House.

Tayte was sitting somewhere off a single lane track by a galvanized farm gate, punching names into database fields as fast as his bandaged hand would allow. He was glad he had a power supply he could run off the car; he knew it was going to be a long night.

Almost Saturday, he thought, knowing that he should have been close to wrapping this assignment up by now and heading home. But it had led him into a past that would not let go, and now he had Schofield's killer and Amy to add to the list of people he needed to find. People connected by one thread or another to the writing box Amy had entrusted to him. The box he no longer had.

And yet he knew that was not the last of it.

He stopped typing. The tangled thoughts spinning in his sub-conscious suddenly popped a clear fact into his head. He'd lost the box, but he had not lost everything. He patted his jacket pocket and heard paper crumple. *Lowenna's letter...* He hadn't put it back in the box. He smiled to himself, knowing that he still had a hand to play in this game. He also knew that he had a good chance of finding out who the man who wanted to kill him was. When he stole the crucifix and the verse book from the museum at Bodmin Jail, he'd made a big mistake—he'd made it personal.

Tayte had suspected as much and tonight he'd confirmed it. The man was related to Mawgan Hendry. Those few words exchanged at the edge of the killer's knife had left Tayte in no doubt. Now he figured that if he could find the names of Mawgan Hendry's living male descendants, he would have a strong list of suspects.

The idea was simple enough. He had the root name from which all other family members descended: Mathew Parfitt. Take that name and find out who his children were, then repeat the process for each child and their children until he came to those who were still alive. A quick-fire run-through, following dependants to their children, ruling out as many as possible by gender and age until he was left with just a few names—a few suspects.

In practice the process was not so simple. He knew he would have to cut corners, make guesses, and follow lines on unconfirmed data, which was not his style at all. It carried a high risk of error, but there was a chance that some of the names he reached would be correct, and a chance that one of them would be the man he was looking for. He had access to the family history of more than four billion names worldwide. Tonight, he just needed one.

Tayte had been absorbed by the information coming off his screen for over an hour now, dragging names and dates into a sepa-rate notes window to keep track of them. The 1911 census had made the first part relatively easy, but there was no access to cen-sus information for the last hundred years. He was using all the online resources at his disposal, and more than once he'd paused to think about Peter Schofield. This was right up his street—genealogy, Schofield-style. In spite of everything, he wished the kid was in the car with him now.

Somewhere in the first half of the twentieth century, Tayte pulled away from his laptop and pinched his eyes. He turned away from the screen and looked into the black night, thoughtfully stroking at the butterfly stitches on his neck. The stars were like he'd seldom seen them; there was no light pollution here. Whole galaxies presented themselves to him like silver dust flicked from a brush across a black canvas.

The hunt was going well. Two world wars had expedited the search, significantly reducing the number of dependants who had lived long enough to have children of their own; many had been taken prematurely by one war or the other. Yet the line continued along multiple branches of possibility, changing surnames where no male heir had been born to carry it. Mathew's branch of the Parfitt name had died out by the end of the 1800s, replaced by Miller through one daughter and Bakersfield through another. He still had a few hours until daybreak, and somehow he wasn't tired. He was too wrapped up in the chase, too mindful that he'd narrowly escaped death tonight and that Amy, if she was still alive, was somewhere in great need.

Before another hour passed, Tayte knew he was close. The dependants he was looking at now could still be alive, yet were too old to be considered. It was from their children that Tayte was sure he would get his man: the final layer.

Chapter Forty-Three

Saturday.

By the time Tayte realised the new day had broken, the sun was already bright in his sensitive eyes as they peeled open. His head was against the car window, his neck was sore, and his stitches itched. Two cows stared at him from beyond the galvanised gate he'd parked alongside; a third had its rump to him. He felt just like that last cow looked. The sound that woke him buzzed again in his trouser pocket with a ringtone he was fast growing to hate. He glanced bleary eyed at the clock in the unfamiliar dashboard and noted that it was a quarter past eight. His laptop lay open on the driver's seat, discarded at the end of his research, still sleeping after a good night's work. Tayte wished he was too. His phone buzzed again, denying him the chance.

'JT,' he said.

'I *do* hope I didn't wake you.'

Tayte was about to say that he needed a wake-up call anyway, but the caller continued.

'But then how could you sleep?' the caller said. 'I'd be grabbing all the life I could if I'd nearly lost mine last night.'

Tayte was suddenly wide awake.

'Why is everything so complicated, Mr Tayte?'

Tayte just listened.

'I've been looking for this box since I knew it existed. Now I have it, and yet I don't, do I? Don't have what I've been looking for.' There was a pause. Then the voice said, 'It's what is inside that counts…That's what the note I found in the box tells me. So what else was inside the box, Mr Tayte?'

Tayte played his card. 'If you want what was inside that box,' he said, 'let Amy go!' He heard mocking laughter. 'It's the only way you'll get what you're looking for.'

The laughter stopped. 'A stalemate then,' the caller said. 'I don't play chess, Mr Tayte. How about you let me have what was in the box or by this afternoon the police will be investigating another dead body!'

'No dice.' Tayte's response was sharp—stuff the chess, this called for hardball. If he just handed everything over he knew Amy would never make it through the day. 'It's an exchange or nothing,' he added. 'Amy for the contents of the box, or you can go to hell!'

The line went silent. Tayte hoped his caller was giving it some serious thought. After the silence turned uncomfortable he hoped he hadn't overcooked it. Then he knew he had. He heard a faint click and then static. He checked for the caller's number, but as he expected, it had been withheld.

'Shit!'

Tayte had to know who this man was and he had to know fast. He woke up his laptop and the results of his hurried research glared back at him—five names that meant nothing to him, five possible suspects, all male descendants of Mawgan Hendry and Lowenna Fairborne through their illegitimate son, Mathew Parfitt. He had the age and place of birth for each, which was sure to help.

But where are they now?

He reached into his jacket pocket and pulled out the calling card DCI Bastion had given him. Further investigation into the names he'd come up with would need police resources. He was half-way through punching in the number when the digits cleared and the screen changed, displaying an incoming call—no number. He picked it up at the first buzz and pressed the phone to his ear.

'An exchange then,' the caller said.

Tayte drew a deep breath and let it slowly out again. 'Where?'

'There are strict rules to the game, Mr Tayte. Like all good games, it will be played in two halves. First, you will go back to Amy's house—to Treath. Board the motor launch there and wait. I will call you again in precisely one hour.'

Tayte glanced at his watch; it was 08:30.

'If you are not in that boat in exactly one hour,' the caller said, 'then Amy dies. If you call the police or I suspect you have brought anyone with you—Amy dies. I'm giving you this one chance to save her. If you do not play by the rules, then you will learn just how strong my resolve can be. I will not be screwed with, Mr Tayte. Are we clear?'

Tayte's heart was already racing. 'Crystal,' he said, looking out the car windows at the single lane track and the tall hedgerows to either side of him. He wished he knew where the hell he was. An hour didn't seem long under the circumstances.

As the call ended, Tayte was already sliding across into the driver's seat, fighting his way across the gear shift and the power cable feeding his laptop. The key was already in the ignition. He turned it, thinking his call to DCI Bastion would have to wait. The rhythmic grating that came from the engine compartment froze his heart. It was a painful sound to hear at the best of times, but now…

Come on. This isn't happening!

The engine churned more than it turned, slowing and groaning more and more with every cycle. He unplugged the laptop power cable and tried again. This time the engine barely turned over at all. One last moan, then it died.

The car waiting on the drive outside Rosemullion Hall looked like it was going to a wedding; the 1937 black and cream Rolls Royce Phantom III lacked only the ribbons. It was a special car for a special occasion: the official investiture of Sir Richard Fairborne's life peerage. Sir Richard and Lady Fairborne were already seated in the back of the car, trying to relax on the bisque leather seats while they waited. A grey-liveried chauffeur stood outside, ready to open the door for the last of his charges before conveying them all to the VIP air taxi that was waiting for them.

'Well, what's keeping him?' Sir Richard said. 'Another minute and we're leaving.'

Celia was trying to remain calm, but she knew Warwick was cutting it fine. 'There's plenty of time,' she said. 'Stop fussing. He had a late night, that's all.'

'I don't know why you insisted he come.'

'He's coming because we're a family, Richard. And I want to remember what that feels like.'

Sir Richard scoffed, checking his watch again.

'Here he is,' Celia said.

They both looked out the window and saw Warwick pacing towards the car, smart for a change in a charcoal pinstripe suit. In one hand he waved a bright cerise tie. In the other he was closing the flip on his phone. One corner of his mouth was raised like he knew he'd kept them waiting.

Celia wound the car window down. 'Do come along, Wicky!'

Warwick raised a hand in apology. He stuffed his tie and his phone into his pockets and quickened his pace.

Beside the car, the chauffeur smiled and readied himself to open the door. His last passenger was nearly there. He reached for the handle.

The dance tune playing on Warwick's phone glued him to the spot. He checked the caller number and the colour drained from his cheeks, taking his grin with it.

'Is everything all right, Wicky?' his mother called.

'Business,' Warwick said. 'It's complicated, but I really need to take this.' He backed away.

'Driver!' Sir Richard called.

'I'll follow on, Mother,' Warwick said. 'Once I've sorted this out. Meet you at the heliport.'

Celia shook her head, rapping her perfect fingernails on the armrest. 'Things aren't going too well for him, Richard,' she said.

'I could have guessed,' Sir Richard said. 'What fool's funding him this time? No one we know, or I'd have heard about it.'

'He won't say, but he looks worried sick. Can't you do something for him?'

'The boy's old enough to sort his own problems out. For God's sake, he's had enough practice!'

Celia watched Warwick recede towards the house, his free hand gesticulating aggressively one minute then resting in defeat behind his head the next. As the car moved off, she knew in her heart that he would not be going with them to London after all.

Chapter Forty-Four

Jefferson Tayte was lost with a car that wouldn't start, and he now had less than an hour to get back to Treath or in the killer's own words, *Amy dies.* He kicked a tyre on the diminutive lemon yellow car he now knew to be a Citroen C2, cursing his stupidity, knowing now that his laptop must have drained the battery. Since returning to Cornwall yesterday his life had been turned on its head, and the new dawn promised no better.

There has to be a number to call.

He was heading back into the car when he stopped that thought in its tracks. How could he call for assistance if he didn't know where he was? Even if he did, he knew it would take too long. In both directions he could see nothing but a narrow winding track hemmed in by tall hedgerows. He doubted the road was used all that much; nothing had passed him. It was just him and the cows. They retreated as he approached the galvanised gate. Beyond, all he could see was a few more cows and an ever-deepening field. He knew the only chance he had was to get the car started, and that meant pushing. But he could also see that the road was too narrow. There was no room to run alongside it until he reached one of the wider passing places he'd seen. It would be tight. He would have to get the timing right.

He studied the road. It was relatively flat, running straight for a while until it dipped. It looked wider there. That's where he would have to get in quick and coast until he picked up speed. He made sure the car was in neutral and took off the handbrake. He closed the door and got around the back, and then he started to push, mindful of where the dip in the road came, knowing he would have to get in before the car ran away from him. He peered over the roof as he walked with it. It was hard to see where the dip began now. Then the car began to roll unaided.

With no one at the wheel to steer, the car veered left to right at random. The gap was too tight to get alongside yet, and even if he could squeeze in, he realised now that he would have no room to open the door. The car was picking up speed by the second. His walk became a jog. Then ahead, a few cars' length away on the apex of a tight bend, the road widened. It was his only chance.

The hedgerow continued to guide the car as it picked up speed, scraping the paintwork. By the time the road widened, he was jogging and out of breath. He ran for the door and opened it as the track narrowed again. Then he jumped for the seat head first. The pain echoing around his right ankle told him he hadn't quite made it. The door bounced off his ankle, back into the hedgerow, and then returned for an encore that brought tears to his eyes.

But Tayte had no time to indulge his pain. As he settled into the driver's seat, dipped the clutch, and engaged second gear, ready to bump start the car into life, the front end of a tractor turned the corner and came straight at him. He yanked at the hand brake and the car lurched to a stop, putting him back where he'd started. Only now he had even less time, and he was trapped in his car by the hedgerows, nursing an ankle that felt like it needed a plaster cast. Frustration arrived like a bullet. It hit him hard and he flopped lifeless over the steering wheel.

'What am I doing here?' he shouted. He forced himself back into the seat and cried, 'I'm a genealogist, for Christ's sake!'

Tayte's encounter with the tractor turned out to be something of a godsend: not only did the driver give him a push, but he told him exactly where he was and gave him directions. Tayte arrived at Treath with five minutes to spare.

As he came in sight of Ferryman Cottage, he could see that a police presence had been maintained. So as not to draw attention, he parked beyond the roundabout at the bottom of the lane, screening his arrival beyond a display of colourful vegetation. He alighted unseen from the Citroen, walked with a mild limp to the water's edge, and casually skimmed a stone onto the river, like a tourist taking a morning stroll. He kept his back to the house as he made his way along the shore, trying to conceal the blood stains on his suit and the bandages on his hand. He could see Amy's motor launch, moored up at the end of a garden that stretched down from the gated entrance and the rose arbour. He chanced a look at the house and saw a fresh-faced police officer standing by the front door like a sentry. He knew this wasn't going to be easy.

Before Tayte reached the boat, his phone rang. He checked the time: a few minutes to spare. He quickened his pace and answered the call.

'What in the name of Mary's going on over there, Tayte?'

Sloane... This is all I need!

'I've just been woken up in the middle of the night with the news,' Sloane said. 'Now I've seen it on the goddamned TV set, for Christ sakes! Tell me I'm still dreaming.'

'Look, I can't talk right now.' Tayte knew he had to get rid of his client and fast.

'What do you mean, you can't talk? I sent Schofield over there to help you out, now he's dead! Mistaken identity they're calling it. Mistaken for who?'

'He was mistaken for me,' Tayte said. 'Look, I need to go. I'll call you back when I get a chance.'

'Call me back! Get your ass back here, Tayte, that's what you need to do. I don't want another death on my conscience. It's just a freakin' birthday present!'

Tayte hung up the call. *Just a birthday present?* This assignment was way beyond that.

Tayte's phone rang again.

'I don't like to be kept waiting, Mr Tayte.'

'I had another call come in,' Tayte said. 'Took a while to get rid of them.' He had one foot in the motor launch. Over his right shoulder he could see the police officer at the house getting interested.

'I do hope you've not been discussing our business arrangement with anyone.'

'No,' Tayte said. 'It was just someone from back home.'

'Then sit down, Mr Tayte, and open the compartment to the right of the wheel. There's a key. Take it out and replace it with the contents of the box—and no games! I'll know if you're cheating.'

Tayte looked around. There were at least a hundred boats on the river. The man could have been watching from any number of places. Then his eyes fell back to the house. He could see the police officer coming over. He reached a hand inside his jacket and pulled out Lowenna's letter, holding it awkwardly in his bandaged hand with his phone while his free hand fumbled around the compartment for the key.

'That copper's looking very interested, Mr Tayte. Better hurry.'

The police officer was closing. 'Everything all right there?' His voice was an unwelcome jar to Tayte's already frayed nerves.

Tayte glanced over his shoulder. 'Fine,' he called. 'Just dropped my key.'

The officer kept coming, his pace a little quicker now, his expression suspicious.

'Get the key, Mr Tayte. Start the engine and pull out towards the mouth of the river. If you speak to him again, Amy dies.'

'Got it,' Tayte said at last. He glanced at the silver key in his palm then stuffed the letter into the compartment, closed the cover, and started the engine, half expecting it to sound like his car had earlier. It didn't. The inboard motor fired up first time and ticked over to a throaty drumbeat.

Tayte flicked a rope off the boat and pulled away behind a screen of white smoke. 'Okay,' he said. 'Now what?'

'Well done, Mr Tayte. Now keep the land to your right and you'll come to a headland—Dennis Head. Look out for the shallows. The rocks around here will send you straight to the bottom.'

Tayte looked back to see the police officer standing at the water's edge. He was on his radio. Tayte waved to him and watched as the officer retreated towards the house.

'Follow around the headland, Mr Tayte. Then continue inland. You'll be on your way into Gillan Harbour. Next stop will be St Anthony. When you see a church just off a small shingle beach to your right, stop and wait for my next call. I've allowed you forty minutes, less the time you've wasted getting the boat away. Better hurry—no time for detours. And remember, Mr Tayte. If you're not there at precisely ten minutes past ten—'

'Don't tell me,' Tayte cut in. 'Amy dies, right?'

'I'm glad you're paying attention, Mr Tayte.'

'Just make sure she's there,' Tayte said, but the call had already ended.

Tayte pushed on the revs and found the boat sprightlier than he'd imagined. He pulled back a little and settled into a steady run, barely breaking water. He kept the land to his right as instructed, cruising out towards the mouth of a tree-lined river that here and there revealed rocky outcrops and sand spits at low tide.

The scenery scrolled by and the tree line Tayte had been following soon thinned out, giving way to a rocky fringe. Further on, the headland Tayte supposed was Dennis Head rose from the landscape as a pronounced hump, like the head of some sleeping giant that time had long since fused into the land. He was aware now that the water had begun to chop at the sides of the boat, becoming unsettled as the river began to stir with the sea. Then over the low drumming of the engine, he began to hear another sound that grew rapidly louder.

He looked back to see another boat hurrying along behind him. It was a larger boat, white with a short canopied bow. Its single outboard motor made a distinctly higher-pitched sound as it strained to push it along at twice the knots Tayte was going. He watched it approach, thinking about the police officer back there on his radio and wondering if he'd sent someone after him. Or maybe it was his caller.

As the boat came closer, heading straight for him and showing no sign of slowing, Tayte knew it was not the police. It arrived like a torpedo, ramming broadside into the motor launch, knocking Tayte off his seat. He saw a hooked pole reach in and lock the vessels together. Then before he could recover, the launch tipped again and the hooked end of the pole was suddenly jabbing at his face.

Chapter Forty-Five

Tayte looked up from the pitching deck of Amy's teak motor launch and saw a gangly figure bearing down on him. He wore old walking boots and cutoff combat trousers, and his white t-shirt carried the words 'The Wetter the Better' above an arty graphic of a sailboat. Tayte had no interest in it. His attention was on the hooked pole the man was holding and the raw aggression in his eyes.

'Where's Amy! And what are you doing with her boat?'

Tayte steadied himself and went for the seat.

'Stay down!' the man warned. His posture was dynamic—ready.

The pole jabbed again, and Tayte did as he was told. He remained on his knees, hands held up in front of him. 'You're making a big mistake,' he said. 'I know Amy. I'm trying to help her.'

The man mocked him. 'You expect me to believe that, do you? I know Amy very well and she's never mentioned knowing any Yanks.'

Tayte wondered how he could prove it. This guy had clearly heard the news. He could understand how seeing a stranger on Amy's boat the next morning, looking bloody and bandaged as he did, might appear highly suspect. 'Her husband's called Gabriel,' he said. 'He went missing two years ago.'

The man with the pole advanced. 'Everyone in the village knows that,' he said. He stabbed the pole closer to Tayte's face.

'Look, I just met her two days ago in Bodmin. We had a common interest.'

'In what?'

Tayte thought about it. The fewer people who knew about the box, the better. 'Just some research we were into. I haven't seen Amy since the night before last.'

'The *night* before last?'

'That's right. I went to call on her with something I thought she'd be interested in. We talked, had a few drinks, you know…'

The man holding the pole relaxed a little. His expression was a portrait of disbelief, like what he was hearing couldn't possibly be true. 'I'm not so sure I do know,' he said. 'What sort of drinks?'

'Just wine,' Tayte said, bemused by the man's interest in what they were drinking. 'Does it matter?'

The man looked disappointed and a little distant. After a few seconds he came back from his thoughts, reasserting his command of the situation with another firm thrust of his pole. 'Did this research have anything to do with a box?'

The question hit Tayte like a demolition ball, leaving him in little doubt over who was interrogating him. 'Laity?' he said. 'Tom Laity?'

The pole stood at ease. Looks were exchanged and the bewilderment on Laity's face at hearing his own name from this stranger soon passed. 'She must have considered you a friend if she showed you that box,' he said. Then a moment later he smiled proudly and added, 'She told you about me then?'

Tayte nodded. 'You own the deli in the village.'

'That's right.' Laity laughed and offered Tayte his hand. 'Now then,' he said, pulling Tayte to his feet. 'What's happened to Amy and what are we going to do about it?'

———

It did not take Tayte long to convince Tom Laity that, for Amy's sake, he had to proceed alone and quickly. He'd given Laity a rushed summary of all the key points that led to Amy's disappearance, figuring that if Amy trusted him, then why shouldn't he? The plan now was that Laity would wait for him to return. If he wasn't back within thirty minutes, Laity would follow into Gillan Harbour.

Alone again in the teak motor launch, as he turned Dennis Head and made for Gillan Harbour, Tayte hoped that Tom Laity's outlandish introduction hadn't lost him too much time. His cheap digital watch, which he was surprised to find still worked after all the knocks they had shared in the last twelve hours, told him he had just fifteen minutes to spare. Looking back through the bright morning glare, he could still see Laity's boat in the mouth of the river—waiting.

Tayte had no idea what lay ahead, no clue as to what further instructions he might have to follow when the next call came. But Laity had assured him that there was no way out of Gillan Harbour by boat that he could miss from his vantage point. He was Tayte's backup. Yet Tayte still felt very much alone as the little boat carried him into the neck of a harbour that became narrower and shallower the further he went. He felt like a fish swimming in a net that was gradually closing around him.

To either side as he went, the banks of the inlet rose from granite foundations to a fringe of ancient oaks and other flora. Then higher up, beyond a scattering of nestled houses, green fields rolled away. He could soon see the harbour boats ahead, moored to buoy markers out on the water. He looked back for Laity's boat again, but could barely see it now. He tried to remember his instructions.

When I see a church on my right, stop and wait.

He looked along the bank; nothing yet. He checked his watch again. He still had five minutes left. He pushed the throttle forward and quickly arrived among the resting boats. Then easing back, he worked his way through until he came out into another stretch of clear water.

Further ahead he could see another group of boats, moored like the first, only they were fewer and generally smaller. He approached and to his right he saw a small shingle beach. There were a few buildings and a short makeshift jetty. Then as he cleared the bank, he saw it. The Norman tower of what he supposed must be the church he was looking for rose above the trees, dominating the scene.

He throttled back until the boat was barely moving and pulled out his phone in readiness, looking towards the beach. It was quiet; there was no one about. Then he saw a car arrive along a road to his left. It was a blue hatchback, old and shabby-looking. It continued into what he supposed was a car park further along and to the left of the church. Then a moment later he saw it come out again towards the same road it had arrived by. It crawled along a few metres and then stopped.

Tayte supposed the driver might be lost, or a sightseer, perhaps, not staying long. Then his phone rang and he nearly dropped it in his haste to take the call.

'Tayte,' he said, short and sharp.

'Congratulations, Mr Tayte.'

Tayte's eyes were still on the car. A door had opened. Someone got out. He wished he had some binoculars.

'Now,' the voice continued, 'look for a blue and yellow rowing boat. It's tied off to an orange marker buoy, number twenty-seven.'

Tayte was reluctant to take his eyes off the car. Someone else had got out. The two figures were standing close together now, both similarly dressed in light grey hooded sweatshirts and jeans. One was taller than the other and thicker set. Tayte looked for the row-boat. It was easy to spot, some twenty metres back. He looked to the shore. The two figures were walking onto the beach, joined at the hip like newlyweds. *It has to be them.* His eyes were fixed on the smaller of the two. *That must be Amy,* he thought.

'Tie the launch to the rowboat and turn off the engine, Mr Tayte. Leave the key in the ignition.'

Tayte blipped the throttle and spun the boat in the water, showing his back to the beach. He had no way of knowing now if that was Amy.

'Put her on,' he said, closing on the rowing boat. The next voice he heard was thankfully familiar.

'He said he'd let me go if he got what he wanted,' Amy said.

Tayte thought she sounded tired and unconvinced.

'Don't trust him!' she shouted.

Tayte heard her from the beach. He spun around to see one of the figures wrench away. A well-placed kick sent the other crumpling and she was free. Running.

Go on, Amy! Tayte willed her to get away and he could only watch as he saw the crumpled figure rise again, showing no urgency. Amy's movement looked awkward, like her legs were tied above the knees. The man was on her instantly and Tayte felt pathetic as he watched a two-handed blow beat her to the ground. Then she was yanked to her feet again.

Tayte pressed his phone hard to his ear. 'Amy! Are you okay?'

'I think that's enough talk, Mr Tayte. Now keep to our arrangement.'

Tayte could feel his anger rising. He wanted to head into the beach and take Amy back by force—a lot of force.

'You're thinking too hard, Mr Tayte. Just do it or I'll kill her here and now!'

Tayte caught the flash of a blade in the sunlight and his focus returned to the blue and yellow rowing boat. He bit his lip until it bled.

'Change boats, Mr Tayte. Then row ashore. When you're halfway, I will leave. Amy will remain.'

Tayte secured the launch to the buoy and climbed across into the rowing boat. He untied it and pushed himself away then began to row ashore. He saw no problem with the plan so far, not as long as he was between this man and what he wanted.

'That's it, Mr Tayte. This will soon be over.'

Tayte still had his back to the beach, and looking over his shoulder only upset his stroke when he tried, so he kept rowing. He was halfway to shore when he became aware of an inflatable orange dinghy powering straight for the launch. He stopped and looked back to the beach, where the hooded figures were now moving away. Then someone climbed across from the dinghy into Amy's motor launch, fired it up and left again at speed, chasing after the dinghy without a glance in his direction. On shore, Tayte saw Amy being forced into the back of the car.

'Hey!' he shouted into his phone, but the call was over.

Tayte suddenly felt like he was running in both directions and getting nowhere. He knew he couldn't get to Amy before the car drove off, and he knew he had no chance of catching the launch. He watched as the driver got into the car. Then he heard the distant thump of the door closing. Looking towards the harbour entrance, the launch was already gone.

Tayte stood up and steadied himself as the rowing boat tipped beneath him. He watched the car pull away and tried to make out the face he knew was looking back from the rear window. He wondered how he'd fallen for this simple deception, but he was confused. *Who took the launch?* He'd assumed the killer was working alone. All he knew for sure was that he'd lost the box, the letter, *and* Amy to the man who had killed Schofield and who, in his own words, wanted *him* dead.

In the back seat of the electric blue Mazda hatchback, Amy Fallon shrieked into the gag at her mouth. But her cry for help was useless. There was no one close enough in sleepy St Anthony to hear her. With bound hands she thumped at the car window as it pulled away from the shingle beach, all the while looking back across the water to the man who had come to help her. She saw Tayte stand up on the boat. She cried out again in vain desperation.

Then the car stopped. She could see Tayte clearly now. She quietened. Through her gag she tried to smile at him, for trying perhaps. Then she saw an intense flash and the blue and yellow rowing boat splintered apart. The sound of the explosion seemed to wait for her to comprehend what had happened. Then it came and there was no denying it. As the debris fell, Jefferson Tayte and the rowing boat were gone.

Several minutes later, somewhere on the road between St Anthony and Helford, the man driving the beat-up Mazda made a call.

'It's done,' he said.

There was a pause while he listened to the response. Then he turned his head towards the back seat where Amy was sitting huddled. She felt numb from the shock of what she had just witnessed. His eyes flashed on her briefly and she sensed he was talking about her.

'No,' the man said. 'I already told you. No one else knows.'

His voice lowered then, until Amy could just about hear it. 'Have the money ready,' he said. 'I'll call again with the time and place.'

Chapter Forty-Six

Waiting in the mouth of the Helford River off Dennis Head, Tom Laity was anxious. The early sun was like a floodlight behind him, flushing the shadows from the inlets to Gillan Harbour and the river, affording him an advantageous view. It had been twenty-five minutes since he'd watched Tayte go into Gillan Harbour. Now as he watched an orange inflatable dinghy power out of the harbour entrance, closely followed by Amy's teak motor launch, his hopes lifted.

But something about the scene wasn't right. The boats appeared to be racing each other as they turned the headland. Laity was too far out to see who was on board, but it was clear that there was only one person in each craft and neither looked like Amy or the American he'd just met. Anxiety returned like a clamp around his chest. He tried to make sense of the scene and realised he had no idea what to expect; he didn't even know if Tayte was supposed to bring Amy back out this way. For all he knew, Amy could be with Tayte right now, safe at St Anthony. He looked into Gillan Harbour again then back to the boats.

Then the explosion came.

The sound cracked out from the resting harbour like thunder after forked lightning. Laity shot to his feet, staring after the sound, but Gillan was a deep inlet, and the source of the explosion was too far in to see anything. He watched the boats chase into the Helford

River—seemingly oblivious—and he knew he had to act fast. His rationale was simple. If the explosion had anything to do with the American, he supposed he could do nothing for him, at least nothing more than anyone else in the area could do. If not, Tayte could look after himself. Either way, he saw no purpose in going into Gillan Harbour to find out.

Laity's focus was on Amy now, and his only link to her was racing into the Helford River, already distant. He needed to know who was in Amy's launch and where they were taking it, and as he pointed his bow towards the river and threw open the throttle in pursuit, he considered that he might even catch whoever was doing this. If things hadn't gone well for the American—if the killer still had Amy—there was still hope for her if he followed the launch.

The boats ahead of Laity had a strong lead. Had they been chasing the coastline, Laity knew they would have been impossible to catch. But on the Helford River things were different. There were other craft on the water, both active and moored. Consideration was expected and strictly enforced. So when his quarry reached a pool of sailboats, slowing at last as they became lost among them, Laity closed the gap, only throttling back when he arrived there himself.

Where are they? he thought. Then he heard the throb of Amy's launch, almost at idle. To his left he saw it, heading in towards the bank to the sailing club adjacent to Helford Village. He saw the orange dinghy there too. It was tied off at the end of a pontoon, one of two similar grey wooden platforms that stretched away from the club. He heard the man from the dinghy laugh at the other as Amy's launch went further in between the walkways.

Laity cruised out from the pack of sailboats, observing their behaviour as the man from the orange dinghy helped the other out of Amy's boat. Something was exchanged between them. *Money,* Laity thought. Whatever it was didn't look large enough to be the letter Tayte had taken to exchange for Amy. He pushed on the throttle, knowing he had to confront them.

The men were still out on the walkway as he came in between the pontoons, creeping towards Amy's launch. He could see them clearly now. One turned and looked out across the river. Laity knew him. He was a young lad, only fifteen or so. He'd seen him in his shop on occasion and often around the village. A nice lad, as he recalled. He wondered how he could be caught up in all this; he was no murderer or kidnapper to Laity's mind. He watched them move away, talking together in high spirits as they headed into the sailing club, not looking back, paying no further attention to Amy's launch.

Laity passed the motor launch, trying not to draw attention to his interest in it. A cursory glance revealed that the key was still in the ignition and his curiosity was piqued. He passed a few other boats; all were small craft that gave him no cover. He stopped, reminding himself that Amy was not there. If the lad was involved, any confrontation would only alert him to the fact that Laity was on to him.

The key is in the ignition...

The significance suddenly hit home. The boat's journey was not over. Amy's launch was going somewhere else today, and soon. *Why else leave the key?* Laity knew what he had to do. A quick blip on reverse sent his stern reeling into a free mooring space. Then he took off the way he'd come, back out into the cover of the nestled sailboats on the river. And there he would wait, like a cat in long grass, watching and waiting.

Developments that morning in the case of Peter Schofield's murder had left DCI Bastion in need of another rather more urgent chat with Jefferson Tayte. DS Hayne had been trying his mobile phone number for the best part of an hour now.

'Still no good, sir,' he said. 'Straight to voice mail again.'

Bastion turned away from the window in Tayte's room at St Maunanus House and drew a sharp breath. 'Well, I shouldn't bother leaving any more messages,' he said. He crossed the room to a single wardrobe and opened it. Two tan linen suits and a few white shirts hung above an old suitcase. He flicked a hand through the clothes. 'Doesn't look like he's gone far.'

'I'll leave a message with the landlady,' Hayne said. 'Have her call in when he shows up.'

Bastion's eyes interrogated the bed again, a bed that had clearly not been slept in. 'Where did he go last night?' He was reflecting on Tayte's condition when they left him at the hospital in the early hours. 'You'd think he'd have been straight back here for a good night's sleep.'

'Doesn't look too clever, sir, does it? You think he's a runner?'

Bastion had already dismissed the idea. 'Why would he? His alibi checked out. He's holding something back, but he's not our killer.' He flattened his hair down and went for the door. 'Maybe we'll find out when we get to speak to him.'

When they reached the bottom of the stairs, they found Judith waiting for them, wearing a polite yet wary smile.

'Did you find what you were looking for?' she asked.

'Not really, madam,' Bastion said. 'But thank you for your cooperation.'

Judith raised a quizzical brow. 'Is everything all right?' she asked. 'With Mr Tayte I mean. Anything I should know about?'

Bastion gave a tight smile. 'There's nothing at all for you to worry about, Madam. Just a few questions I was hoping he could help us with.' He continued towards the door. 'Sergeant Hayne will leave you a card,' he added. 'Perhaps you'd give us a call when you see him.'

By the time Hayne caught up, Bastion was on the drive, leaning on an open car door, listening to a call on his radio. His features were sharp and serious.

'Seems our man has turned up,' he said to Hayne when the call finished.'

'I take it he wasn't at the supermarket, then?'

Bastion winced. 'They fished him out of Gillan Creek earlier today.'

Chapter Forty-Seven

Watching the sailing club from the cover of the Helford River's mid-water moorings, Laity had seen few people come and go. A boat or two had gone out, another had arrived. Amy's launch was still there and no one had paid any attention to it.

'You won't catch anything there!'

The voice startled Laity. He looked away to the blue and white sailboat that passed close behind him. It was one of his regulars at the shop. 'Morning, Mr Brooks.' Laity laughed. 'Thought I might try for some crab. Nice morning for it.'

'It is that.' The man touched a hand to his denim sailing cap, drew on his pipe, and slunk by on a gentle breeze.

Laity watched him go then turned his attention back to business. His heart instantly picked up a beat. The young lad had come out at last, but he wasn't heading for Amy's launch as Laity had expected. Instead, he went to the side of the building where Laity lost sight of him for several seconds. When he saw him again, he was pedalling a mountain bike away from the club, out onto the road towards the village, and Laity was pleased to see him go. He couldn't discount his involvement, but it was clear now that the key to Amy's launch had been left for another.

As Laity settled again he saw a blue car arrive in a hurry at the club car park, kicking up gravel as it stopped. He froze and sank lower, watching. His nerves were in tatters. He saw the driver get out and open one of the rear passenger doors. He helped someone else out. Both wore hooded grey sweatshirts, and as they walked the driver put his arm around the other's shoulders, like they were out for a romantic trip on the river, but Laity could sense the tension between them.

His heart began to thump when he saw that they were heading for Amy's motor launch. Seconds later it fired into life and began to pull out from between the pontoons, heading directly towards Laity, who picked up an old mackerel line that needed untangling; anything to make it appear as though he had some purpose there.

As the boat turned its bow to the mouth of the river and Falmouth Bay, Laity looked up again and caught a brief flash of the faces beneath the hoods. He thought he recognised the man behind the wheel, though the launch was distant and the faces too shrouded to be sure. Then he clearly saw Amy's eyes above the gag at her mouth. He would have known those blue-green eyes at a crowded masquerade ball.

His first reaction was to storm in and save her, like the hero he wanted Amy to believe he was. But the risk was too high. According to Tayte, the man driving the launch had already killed, and Laity supposed he would have no dilemma over doing so again.

Just see where he takes her, Laity thought. *Then snatch her back.*

So Laity followed, and he was soon in open water east of the Helford River in Falmouth Bay. A fishing line stretched away from a rod hanging off the back of his boat into a calm sea, painting an everyday picture for anyone who might see him and creating a façade for his true purpose there. He slipped his olive-coloured fishing gilet on, the pockets of which bulged with spools of fishing line and other tackle, and sat by the rod, watching Amy's teak motor launch cruise around the low-lying Nare Point, heading south towards the coastal village of Porthallow with its grey quarry stone beach.

Laity was wary of getting too close. His aim was to lie offshore, where several small craft were already enjoying the morning. Out there he hoped to draw no lingering attention to himself. He would follow the serrated coastline as it rose to Nare Head and the cliffs beyond, just close enough to keep an eye on the launch and to know where they planned to go ashore. Then he would follow them in. He knew the Lizard's serpentine coast well, from land and sea. There were no other inlets or creeks to hide in even if he had to follow them all the way to Lizard Point.

But they did not venture far. Their pace was steady to Nare Cove—a particularly jagged tear of coastline—and there amongst the rocks they came to a full stop. Laity thought he must have been spotted, wondering if the launch had stopped just to see if he continued his course. So he passed them by, heading further south, knowing that on a clear morning like this he would have no trouble keeping them in sight.

The launch did not move. Ten minutes passed and still they remained at Nare Cove. Waiting. *But for what?* Laity wondered. He considered that they could be waiting for someone else. Then another reason struck him. *He's waiting for the tide.*

Laity was a walking tide table. He checked his watch. It was a little after eleven. High water had long passed, and the tide, though still above the median, was on its way out. It would be a few hours yet before low water, when Nare Cove would expose its sandy skin and its jagged claws.

Laity heaved a weighted sigh and relaxed for the first time all morning. He was confident that time was on his side, sure the launch would remain in the area for now. He took his boat back towards the mouth of the Helford River and the confusion of craft coming and going, then north towards Rosemullion Head, out of sight for a while to dispel any notion that he might be following the launch.

When he returned some time later, the launch was still there, and Laity kept going, pretending to fish that stretch of water as he often did. He continued down to Porthallow and waited several minutes before heading back for another sweep. As he approached Nare Cove again, peering over the side of the bow canopy for a better look, he knew he'd waited at Porthallow too long. The motor launch was gone, no trace of it to be seen.

Chapter Forty-Eight

She had been there no more than a few minutes, yet Amy could already feel the cold cave air creeping over her like an icy mist. Worse was the promise that the tide would soon return to drench her and she would be colder still. She stood staring at the bright slit of daylight at the cave entrance, knowing that by late afternoon when the sun fell into the west, what light it afforded her would be gone altogether.

The sand felt cool and damp against her clothing as her captor pulled her to the ground by the rusting chain around her waist. Behind her she could hear the familiar clanking of more heavy chains being fastened, securing her to the rock she was forced to sit against. She felt the chains yank, testing her bonds, pulling her uncomfortably close to him. The man paused as though savouring the intimacy. Then he stood away at last, crouching beneath the jagged cave roof, snatching up his torch, and turning the soft glow into a flickering beam that danced as he moved, lighting rough walls that were no more than ten feet apart.

As Amy continued to monitor the unchanging slit of light at the cave entrance, she reflected on what she'd seen back at Gillan Harbour: the rowing boat Tayte had been standing in one minute, then the shattered timbers raining down over the water like matchsticks the next. She felt hopelessly alone again, believing for the first time that she, like Gabriel, would never be found.

The man returned. 'I know this is uncomfortable for you,' he said, 'but it will all be over very soon now.'

Then what? Amy thought.

His torch beam was suddenly in her face.

'If today goes well,' he added, 'you'll be out of here long before the tide gets anywhere near that pretty head of yours.'

The light flicked away again, towards the back of the cave, and Amy watched the man follow after it, crouching low over broken beer bottles until he was forced to crawl. At the cave's tight and tapered innermost point, the light came to rest on a box Amy knew well. Her captor was lying prone in that cramped space. She saw him produce a letter, and the sounds he made while reading it told Amy that he liked what he read. But she quickly sensed the change in his mood. The man picked up the box and opened it, turning it in his hands. He felt inside it as if he expected it to contain something more than was evident. She knew his frustration had reached breaking point when he slammed the box down again and thrust the letter inside. Then he snapped the lid shut with such force that Amy thought she heard it splinter.

His bitter sigh lingered in the air and she smiled to herself. She knew this man was not getting everything his way, and all the while that was true she hoped to retain some value to him. She heard broken glass and the crunch of damp sand as he returned, then the torchlight was back in her face.

'It seems I might have been a bit hasty with your new American friend,' the man said. 'Do you think he knew what was so special about that box you found?'

Amy tried her best to ignore him. Even if she could speak through the tight gag at her mouth, she had no words for this man she had once trusted.

'Or did he keep something back?' he mused. He knew there had to be more.

He dropped to his knees and held the torchlight on Amy's face, forcing her to shut her eyes. 'I'd call him and ask, but of course I can't now, can I?' He pushed his face into Amy's as though he was going to kiss her. She flicked her head away, kicking out, stirring the sand at her feet.

The man laughed. 'I don't think you'd tell me if you knew,' he said, so close to her ear that she could feel his warm breath through the cold cave air.

He backed off. 'Who cares? It's payday! Time to start collecting.'

The torchlight flicked away and Amy willed it to return despite the hatred she felt for the man controlling it. Then like a wish come true, it did.

'Oh, I almost forgot,' the man said. 'I got you a present.' He produced a half-spent candle. 'Should keep you company for an hour or so.' He lit it and fixed it to the rock behind Amy. 'If the afternoon goes as well as this morning, I'll be back in time for tea with some dry clothes. I'm afraid it's fish and chips again.'

Amy watched the man's silhouette shrink towards the cave entrance where it paused. 'I'll move you out of harm's way for the night when I get back,' he said. Then he left.

——— ———

Just before the candlelight deserted Amy, leaving her to darkness and imagination, she caught the glint of something bright in the disturbed sand beyond her feet. She leant closer trying to make it out, kicking again to expose it further. As the object flicked into view, glowing in the fading light, she gazed upon it with unsettling recognition. She caught her breath. Then a silent scream burned in her chest until all light was gone.

Chapter Forty-Nine

It became necessary for me to kill you...

That was what Jefferson Tayte's adversary had told him in the car the night before, when he'd tried to cut his throat, and it was the last thought Tayte had before the blue and yellow rowboat he was standing in at Gillan Harbour blew apart. That thought had saved his life.

After being cheated out of Lowenna's letter, he'd watched the beat-up Mazda pull away from St Anthony, knowing he'd lost everything. He could see Amy's bound hands pounding at the window until the low morning sun hit the glass and she was lost to the glare. Then the car had stopped again. The nearside front window drew his eye as it opened and the glare dissipated. Set back inside the car, Tayte saw a face beneath a light grey hood that was too small to distinguish, but he'd known he was looking at the face of a cold-blooded killer.

Why has he stopped? Tayte had thought. *What's he doing?*

The glint of chrome-plated steel extending from the open car window like a swordsman's foil told him this game wasn't over. There had to be more to it, something he wasn't seeing. The killer had the box and the letter, and he had Amy. So why had the car stopped? What else did he want?

It had taken Tayte a few slow seconds to realise that he was watching an aerial extend from the car window. Sunlight danced along the length of the antenna, mesmerising him as it lengthened, causing him to wonder what the hell was going on. It was fully extended by the time he registered exactly what it was, and in that instant Tayte could only think of one reason why the car had stopped. The driver wanted him dead; he had told him so. Now there was a radio transmitter aerial hanging out of the man's car window.

Tayte understood then that he had to get out of that rowing boat. He leapt sideways into the water just as the boat erupted beneath him. He felt a searing pain in his legs, and the shock wave from the blast slammed him several feet through the water. The explosion boomed above him, dull in his submerged ears as he began to rise. At the surface, he was aware of debris falling around him. He felt something catch his head, knocking him under again. Then he'd blacked out.

He came to, lying on his back, blinking at a low white ceiling that was bright with overhead lighting. A face he didn't recognise stared down at him. A hand reached across and one at a time his eyelids were forced wide open and a bright light was shone into them.

'What's your name?' the stranger asked.

Tayte could feel movement beneath him; he'd sensed he was in a vehicle. 'JT,' he said. Medical equipment and a smiling face registered just before he began to drift again.

Tayte was sitting up on a firm bed in a private room at Truro's Royal Cornwall Hospital, patched up again and being held for observation after the concussion he'd received from the falling boat debris. He looked down at the bandages on his legs. They covered everything from his ankles to his knees, which were barely hiding beneath the hem of the pale green hospital gown he was wearing. It was hardly his style, but he was thankful to be out of that bloody suit at last.

Now with a clean bandage around his left hand and another around his neck to keep the replacement butterfly stitches secure, he looked like he was gradually undergoing some living mummification process. Fortunately, the doctor who'd examined him had told him the wounds beneath the bandages on his legs were largely superficial, and he was surprised at how little he hurt, which he put down to the strong painkillers he'd been given. DCI Bastion and DS Hayne were sitting to either side of him, making him feel more like a suspect than a victim.

Bastion stirred the contents of a stainless steel tray he was holding. 'You don't mind if we keep hold of these, do you, Mr Tayte?'

Tayte looked at the pieces of shrapnel that had been pulled out of his legs along with the splinters from the row boat. 'I don't care if I never see them again,' he said.

Bastion studied one of the pieces. 'It's amazing what devices people come up with,' he said. 'Primitive of course, but deadly just the same.'

'Hand grenades?' Tayte said, still coming to terms with this latest attempt on his life.

'That's right. Probably left over from the Second World War. Strap a few grenades together and wire them to a high-torque radio-controlled model servo. Then switch on the transmitter, push the control stick, and the servo turns, pulling all the pins at once.'

'Boom!' Hayne added, clapping his hands together.

Bastion winced. 'Thank you for the dramatics, Sergeant.'

'Sorry, sir.'

Bastion dropped the shrapnel back onto the tray. It sounded heavier than it looked. 'Now, Mr Tayte,' he said. 'Someone clearly wants you dead, and I want to know why.'

Tayte sat forward. 'First, I need my briefcase.'

The faces before him questioned why.

'When you first got here,' Tayte said, 'you asked where I was last night. I said I'd spent the night in the car you loaned me.'

'Yes, I got all that,' Bastion said.

'But I haven't told you what I was doing.'

'What *were* you doing?' Hayne asked.

'I was trying to find out who killed Schofield—who now has Amy Fallon.'

Bastion shook his head. 'We haven't established that anyone's been kidnapped yet, Mr Tayte.'

'*I* have. I spoke to Amy this morning. I was at Gillan Harbour trying to get her back.'

'And you think you've found out who this man is?' Hayne asked.

'I might have. There's a list on my laptop. That's why I need my briefcase. You need to check out the names.'

'How about I get someone to bring your car to the hospital with a change of clothes?' Bastion said. 'Then we can have a look at this list of yours. And while we're waiting you can tell me everything you know.'

Tayte reached across to the bedside table and picked up the keys that were there with the rest of his personal items: his notepad and wallet, which still needed to dry out, and his phone, which was now useless. He tossed the keys to Bastion, who raised a hand to the uniformed officer waiting at the door.

While Tayte waited for his briefcase and a clean suit to arrive, he gave Bastion and Hayne the full story, leaving nothing out. When he reached the part about the wild-goose chase he'd sent Schofield on, he wondered again what he'd turned up.

'I had Schofield checking out graveyards all day,' he said. 'When I called and asked him to go to Nare Point in my place, to meet the man who'd contacted me about James Fairborne's probate record, Schofield was excited about something. I wish I knew what it was.'

DS Hayne reached into a dark blue folder that was beside him on the bed and produced several photographs that were badly water-damaged. He flicked through them and Tayte watched him single out two images.

'Is this what he was doing, sir?' Hayne asked. He passed the photographs to Tayte. 'We found them with the rest of his belongings in the boot of his hire car this morning.'

'Shameful,' Bastion said, shaking his head. 'Lovely E-Type Jag, series III. It was pulled from the creek at Helford Village this morning, covered in all manner of filth. I'm surprised any of these photos survived at all.'

'V12,' Tayte said, recalling the throaty engine note he'd heard last night after the killer fled. He figured the man must have used Schofield's car after he killed him, leaving it nearby for a quick getaway when he returned for the box. *Very calculated,* Tayte thought, guessing that the killer might have continued his escape by boat after he dumped the car.

'All these photos are pretty much of the same view,' Hayne said. 'Something about it must have caught your colleague's interest. They were taken yesterday morning according to the digital time stamps.'

Tayte studied the photographs. The first showed a typical graveyard scene. There was no church in the picture, and Tayte supposed it must have been taken with the church behind the camera. Numerous headstones scattered the foreground leading to a low stone wall. Beyond that, the landscape diminished to the sea. He looked at the other photograph, which showed a similar view.

'That's a photo of a painting,' Hayne said in case Tayte had missed it.

Tayte could see the gilt frame just visible at the edges of the picture. It was a painting of the view he'd just seen in the first photograph, only this painting had fewer headstones in the foreground.

'It must have been painted some time ago,' Tayte said. 'The graveyard's filled up a bit since then.'

He continued to study the images, and he was close to handing them back when he saw what he thought Schofield was interested in. He tapped the photograph of the painting. 'Look at that,' he said.

Hayne leaned in. 'Looks like a memorial stone of some sort,' he said, failing to fully comprehend the significance.

'And it's not there now,' Tayte said.

They compared the photographs to confirm it. Where the memorial appeared in the painting—a tall stone pillar topped with a Celtic cross—the photograph of the scene as it looked today disclosed what appeared to be a spare plot.

'Could this be what your colleague was so excited about?' Hayne asked.

Tayte held the photographs side by side. The subject of interest was centred in each—the memorial on one, the space where it had stood on the other. 'I'm sure of it,' he said.

A double tap at the door announced the arrival of Tayte's briefcase and a familiar tan linen suit. They were a welcome sight now that he had a church to find, though he supposed it wouldn't be easy. The scene looked like a thousand other coastal graveyards, and he was sure Cornwall had more than its fair share.

Chapter Fifty

It was early afternoon by the time Jefferson Tayte managed to separate himself from Bastion and Hayne. Since he'd realised the significance of Schofield's photographs—that in some Cornish graveyard an empty space existed where once a memorial stood—all he wanted to do was find that graveyard. He felt like Schofield was reaching out to him, trying to tell him why he'd been so wired that day—his last day.

DCI Bastion had insisted Tayte answer a few more questions about the events that led up to the explosion at Gillan Harbour before they parted company. He took the telling-off he'd expected from Bastion as he told them about his telephone conversations with the killer and of his few words with Amy, and that he'd left Tom Laity waiting in the mouth of the Helford River. He'd suggested they put out a search for Amy's motor launch, and Bastion had been quick to assure Tayte that finding the launch was already a high priority, as was interviewing Tom Laity.

Against the advice of the hospital staff, Tayte discharged himself, insisting that he was okay and refusing the offer of DS Hayne's company for the afternoon. As far as Tayte was concerned, he figured the killer must have thought him dead after witnessing the explosion at Gillan Harbour, and he saw that as an advantage. He left with a warning to be careful and the loan of a mobile phone, which Bastion had insisted he keep handy.

The day had changed little while he'd been at the hospital. Now as he drove along a familiar country lane, looking ahead through a tunnel of canopied branches to the bright sunlight beyond, his destination was in sight. He needed to know what church Schofield's photographs were taken from, and he only knew one person who might be able to tell him. As he pulled the yellow Citroen into the parking area outside the parish church of St Mawnan, he hoped Reverend Jolliffe was there.

Tayte passed through the lych-gate and followed the shingle path around the church to his right towards the bell tower. A tunefully whistled rendition of Lizette Woodworth Reese's 'Glad That I Live Am I' immediately greeted him. The sound drew him into the graveyard to the rear of the church, where he saw Jolliffe clearing dead flowers from the cremation plots. The whistling stopped as soon as the reverend saw him.

'How good to see you again,' Jolliffe said, smiling. 'So many people drop by the once, never to return.'

Tayte almost felt guilty. 'I'm afraid I have another motive for being here,' he admitted.

The reverend met Tayte on the path. 'All reasons are accepted,' he said. Then he noticed Tayte's bandaged neck and hand and said, 'Whatever's happened to you?'

'It's a long story I'd be glad to share with you some day,' Tayte said. He reached into his jacket pocket and pulled out photocopies of the images Schofield had taken. 'I'm in a bit of a hurry just now though, if you don't mind.'

'Not at all,' Jolliffe said. His eyes followed the pictures in Tayte's hand. 'So how are you getting along with your work?'

'That's why I'm back,' Tayte said. He offered the images to Jolliffe who squinted at them then pulled away as he tried to bring them into focus. 'I was hoping you could tell me where this graveyard is.'

'I'll need my glasses,' Jolliffe said, reaching for them before he realised he didn't have them with him. 'Follow me,' he added. Then he marched off towards the blue south-facing door.

Tayte paused in the doorway and looked back at the view. Across the river he could clearly see part of the route he'd followed in Amy's launch earlier. He could see Nare Point and could even make out the rectangular shape of the observation hut. He couldn't seem to escape it, that place where Peter Schofield had met his bloody end.

Tayte caught up with the reverend as he was taking a glasses case out of from his fleece jacket, which had been resting over the pulpit.

'Now let's take a look,' Jolliffe said, squaring his reading glasses on his nose.

Tayte set the photocopies down on a nearby table, and he could tell the reverend was still having trouble seeing them clearly. One minute he was looking through the lenses, the next he was peering over the top.

'The originals were a little water damaged,' Tayte said, giving him an excuse.

'So I see.'

'I guess it looks like most churchyards around here.'

Jolliffe was bent double over the images now. Tayte sensed he was struggling and expected him to give up any minute. Then the reverend straightened and smiled.

'Definitely St Keverne,' he said. 'No question about it.'

Tayte moved closer as Jolliffe led his eyes to the scenery in the background. It was distant and indistinct, and he wondered how anything much could be drawn from it.

'See here,' Jolliffe said, pointing to the sea at the top of the photograph. 'Specifically this rock formation.'

Tayte could see something there in the distance, but he thought he'd need a magnifying glass to discern any detail.

The reverend put his glasses away, snapping the case shut. 'They're called the Manacles,' he said. 'There's only one church with that treacherous view. It's definitely St Keverne.'

Several hundred feet above Salisbury Plain, a blue and yellow Eurocopter was returning to Cornwall. Sir Richard Fairborne's official investiture as a life peer of the realm had passed well enough, though recent events concerning his right to even live at Rosemullion Hall had tainted the occasion. He knew he'd earned the honour he'd just received in London, but the question over his right to any hereditary claim was far-reaching. It all came back to that. Without the privileges of wealth and position afforded him through those he thought to be his ancestors, he knew he would not have had the opportunity to achieve what he had.

Sir Richard adjusted himself in his comfortably padded grey leather seat beside the window, which was one of four identical seats in a row behind the cockpit, and continued to gaze down over the aerial views of the mid-southern countryside. Celia Fairborne was sitting next to him with one hand resting on the back of his. The other two seats were empty.

They were passing into the airspace over Dorset when an amber light on the passenger radio phone began to flash; he'd put his mobile phone on divert to the onboard communications system before switching it off at the heliport. He froze momentarily as he felt Celia's hand squeeze into his.

'Richard Fairborne,' he said, his eyes locked knowingly with Celia's. He was conscious of his own voice suddenly, though the pilot seemed oblivious through his headset.

'I thought I'd keep things local for you,' the expected caller said. 'There's a boat tied up on the beach at Durgan. It has a blue tarpaulin cover stretched across it. You can't miss it.'

'When?'

'Be there at seven p.m. sharp. Slip the agreed package beneath the tarpaulin and walk away. It's that simple.'

'And that's the end of it?' Sir Richard said.

No answer came back.

He returned the handset to its cradle and fixed his eyes on Celia. 'He's gone,' he said. 'I'm to go to the beach at Durgan, tonight at seven.'

At that point Warwick spoke from the front seat. He'd only just made the flight to London. His mother had been pleased to see him; his father had not.

'You're not really going through with this?' Warwick said, twisting around to face them. 'He'll never go away.'

'Don't concern yourself,' Sir Richard said.

Warwick began to fidget; he didn't know whether to shut up or labour the point. 'Blackmailers are like stray cats,' he added, opting for the latter. 'Feed them once and they'll keep coming back for more. You can't do it!'

Sir Richard sat forward in his seat. 'I'll deal with it,' he said, firmly.

Warwick scoffed, offering a nervous smile that twisted his mouth. 'You'd rather support this criminal than help me out, wouldn't you?'

'I'll do whatever I decide is the right thing to do,' his father said. 'It's not your concern!'

Chapter Fifty-One

Tayte found the thirteenth-century parish church of St Keverne to the west of Porthoustock, between Porthallow to the north and Coverack to the south. He was standing in the grounds looking out over scattered headstones and memorials to a low stone wall. Beyond that, across an abstract vista of emerald countryside, he could glimpse the sea and the Manacle rocks that had betrayed the church's identity. Tayte raised Schofield's photograph in front of him again to confirm that the view he was looking at was the same as the one in the image. The stones were varied and distinct, and he had no trouble distinguishing them. The view was identical.

In his other hand was the photograph of the painting that bore the same view, and it was immediately clear to him where the memorial had once stood. He checked the image again and noted the pattern and type of headstones around the memorial, then he glanced back at the photograph and finally to the scene in front of him again. He could see the space he was looking for not fifteen metres away.

His eyes remained fixed on that space as he walked the path towards it, not wanting to cut across the burial plots out of respect. He arrived beside a fallen headstone that had cracked in two as it fell. It looked like it had been lying there a while; grass grew up through the crack like a thick ribbon of moss, and the engraving was all but gone. He stepped carefully beside it, moving further in until he came to a small stone cross, barely a foot in height. The space he was interested in was just beyond that.

As he arrived it became apparent that there was nothing spare about the plot of land before him. He saw a circular slab set into the ground, centred in what appeared to be a burial plot that was about four feet square. Long grass had since overgrown it, but he could still make out the relief lines that gave away its presence.

He squatted to get a closer look at the circular slab, drawing a deep breath as he parted the grass around it. Then he caught that breath and held it, afraid that if he let it go again the words before him might blow away. The inscription he read on the stone said very little, and yet it said so much. He read the words 'Betsy Ross' and beneath them a date, 'October 23, 1783.'

Inside the church, Tayte gazed up at the stained glass window that had caught his eye upon entering. The scene was poignant. It depicted a shipwreck on the Manacle rocks; in the scene, the lost souls were being delivered by St Christopher. Tayte drew closer, moving through arched stone pillars and then between red furnished pews ended with heavy oak carvings. At the base of the scene he read that the window was dedicated to the memory of the one hundred souls who lost their lives in the wreck of the *SS Mohegan* on the Manacles in October 1898. It set him wondering how many lives were lost when the *Betsy Ross* met with that same fate more than a hundred years earlier.

Tayte was looking for the painting in Schofield's photograph. It was the only record he had of the *Betsy Ross* memorial. The circular stone in the ground outside had confirmed the reference to the vessel he knew the Fairborne family had boarded in Boston, but it said nothing of the people aboard her. He needed to know who was buried there, and he hoped the painting might lead to some further clue; perhaps there was a dedication, or an inscription like those he could see on the walls around him.

At the opposite end of the church, past a young couple reading something on one of the pillars, he saw a table laid out with a white cloth before another stained glass window. A man was arranging candlesticks to either side of a golden cross. As Tayte made his way between the pews towards him, he saw the gilt frames on the wall beside the table and quickened his step. As he came closer, between regiments of wooden chairs, he was met with disappointment. The gilt frames did not border paintings at all; rather, they surrounded more words of comfort and remembrance. He turned away, scanning the walls again, but nothing he could see gave him any further hope.

'Can I help you?' a voice behind him asked.

Tayte spun around. The man arranging the candlesticks held an expectant smile. He wore stone-coloured trousers and a light grey check shirt—no clergy collar. He was thickset, about Tayte's age, with tidy brown hair combed in a side parting. His face was full and ruddy.

'I was looking for a painting,' Tayte said. 'Looks like I'm in the wrong place.'

'Or right place, wrong time,' the man said. 'If you were expecting to see an art exhibition, I'm afraid the fund-raiser finished yesterday.'

'Just my luck,' Tayte said. He offered out the photograph of the painting. 'I was looking for this in particular. Do you know if it was here?'

The man took the photograph and nodded. 'It was. It's by Joseph Horlor, painted in the mid-1800s. I know it well.'

'Do you know where it is now?' Tayte asked. 'Was it sold?'

'The painting wasn't for sale. It was one of the show pieces. It's back with its owner.'

'That's too bad,' Tayte said. He reached a hand to the photograph and pointed out the memorial he was interested in. 'I was hoping to find out more about this,' he said, running a finger along the image of the Celtic cross that no longer existed. 'Do you know anything about it? There's a plaque outside where this used to stand.'

'The *Betsy Ross*?' the man said, like he knew everything about it.

'That's right. I'm trying to find out what happened to her passengers.'

The man gave Tayte an amused smile. 'This has to be more than coincidence,' he said. 'I've been warden here for nearly twenty years and no one in all that time has shown any interest in the *Betsy Ross*—until yesterday.'

Tayte could almost hear Schofield's exuberant introduction. He supposed the warden would not have forgotten it so soon. 'Peter Schofield?'

The churchwarden nodded, smiling more fully now. 'Enthusiastic young man,' he said. 'You know him then?'

Knew him, Tayte thought. 'Yes,' he said. 'A colleague.'

'Did he miss something?'

'No, I'm sure he didn't,' Tayte said thoughtfully.

The warden handed back the photograph. 'He had me looking into things I haven't seen in years,' he said. 'I'm sorry there wasn't much information to give him. I doubt that I can add anything further to what I said yesterday.'

'Do you know who's buried in the plot?' Tayte asked.

'Ordinarily, I would,' The warden said. 'I catalogue all the plots. Bit of a hobby and it's useful to visitors.'

Tayte agreed. 'I wish every church did that.'

'Whatever happened to the *Betsy Ross* memorial,' the warden continued, 'happened long before I came here. When I began cataloguing, the plaque was there, bearing the name and the date, but little else. What records I managed to find at the time only gave a few names. I looked them up for your colleague yesterday. I think Grainger was one of the names. The others I don't recall, but those few I did find were all members of the crew.'

'Nothing about any passengers?'

The warden shook his head. 'All I know is that there are fifteen souls buried in the plot, and at least three of them were crew. Who the others are remains a mystery, but then I'm no professional. If you find anything more, I'd be glad of the information.'

'Of course,' Tayte said, distracted suddenly by his thoughts. When he'd looked into the *Betsy Ross* back home, he'd read that she carried a crew of fifteen. He supposed now that all the crew might have gone down with the ship and were buried in this plot at St Keverne. In which case, where were the passengers?

Tayte now knew that the *Betsy Ross* hadn't made it to England, but there had to be more to it than that. Why was there no record of the ship in the registers he'd checked? The wreck should have been recorded at Falmouth and there should be detailed lists of the victims and survivors. *More missing records*. He felt he had to be getting close.

As he made for his car, he understood that he had to return to his first line of enquiry; he had to find a way into the family crypt at Rosemullion Hall. A headstone bearing Eleanor Fairborne's name and the date of her death would tell him if she'd survived the *Betsy Ross* or not. Then all that would be left for him to figure out was why someone wanted to keep the family's history a secret from that point on.

Chapter Fifty-Two

Where is Tom Laity? Tayte wondered as he paced through Helford Village beneath a trail of bunting, heading for the ferry pickup. At the delicatessen, Laity's mother had told him she hadn't seen Tom all day and that it wasn't like him to be away from the shop so long. Tayte understood her concerns more than she knew. It was low tide now. Over the whitewashed stone wall to his right, the creek continued to bake beneath the afternoon sun. He looked for Laity's boat, but there was no sign of it. Tayte couldn't think why he'd still be out on the water.

The ferry pickup area looked deserted as Tayte arrived. He reached the bottom of the steps and checked his watch. It was almost three—plenty of time before the last ferry. An information board instructed him to raise a wooden disc to signal to the ferry on the other side of the river that someone wanted to cross. He hooked it up to reveal a bright yellow circle, and a few minutes later he recognised the twin hulled catamaran crossing from Helford Passage, weaving between the sailboats on the river.

Tayte still had no idea how he was going to talk his way onto the Fairborne estate. He figured he'd take the ferry across to Helford Passage and walk to Rosemullion Head. It was a trek and his legs were sore, but a slow walk would give him plenty of time to think of something. The way things were going, if he didn't have a presentable reason by the time he got there, he was about ready to help himself.

As the ferry came in, Tayte strolled along the concrete walkway to meet it. Behind the wheel he could soon see Simon's familiar face—minus the white iPod earphones and the reefer he'd been smoking when he last saw him. He was alone.

'Hi,' Tayte called as he came within earshot. He gave the kid a smile that was not returned. Instead, Simon turned his back to him.

'You okay?' Tayte added, stepping aboard. 'You look a little peaky.'

Simon eventually offered Tayte a guarded smile that was clearly not well meant.

'No help this afternoon?'

'Nope,' Simon said. He turned his back to Tayte again and left it there.

Too much weed, Tayte thought.

The boat dipped its stern under heavy acceleration, cutting an arc through the water as it turned and headed back across the river. No further words were exchanged until they were halfway across. Then Simon slowed the engine, turned to Tayte and said, 'This is all a bit weird for me, you know. No one's seen Amy for the last two days.'

'I know,' Tayte said.

'I bet you do!'

'What's that supposed to mean?'

Simon stopped the engine. 'I mean, a stranger turns up one evening and tells me Amy's in danger. He asks me to take him to her house or he'll report me for smoking weed. Next evening Amy's not around. Then the law turns up asking me where I was last night and if Martin was with me.' Simon snorted. 'Then they tell me a dead body's been found at her house and she's gone missing.'

Tayte had to admit that under the circumstances he'd have thought himself suspect too. 'I was on a train,' he said, knowing what Simon was driving at. 'You want to see my ticket receipt, too?'

Simon turned back to the wheel. 'Just don't ask me for any more favours,' he said, taking the boat in towards the pontoon at Helford Passage.

They were less than a hundred metres out when Tayte saw something that made his pulse race. He stood up, drawing an excited breath through flared nostrils. He was looking to shore, to the left of the jetty, further back where a road led away before a line of houses. A man of medium build with mid-length brown hair was getting out of a car he recognised. He'd seen it that morning at St Anthony. It was the same beat-up blue hatchback the killer had been driving.

'Who's that?' Tayte said, pointing to shore like he expected Simon to know. 'Over there, getting out of that blue car.'

There was only one blue car there. The dark-haired driver was around the back, opening the hatch. Simon knew him very well. 'That's Martin Cole.' he said. 'The guy I work with. Looks like he's been out for groceries.'

Tayte was right behind Simon now, as close to the bow as he could get. 'Can you get us in faster?'

'I told you, no more favours—and I don't care how much you offer me.'

The man by the blue hatchback began to unload carrier bags from the boot.

'And you say Martin's not been working today?' Tayte asked, already sure of the answer. The big picture began to fall into place like a police photo-fit.

Before Simon could answer, the phone in Tayte's pocket played an unfamiliar tune. He answered it. It was DS Hayne. Tayte couldn't have hoped for better timing.

'Mr Tayte,' Hayne said. 'Your list of suspects…Good work.'

Tayte already knew the name Hayne was about to give him. He didn't know how Hayne had worked it out, but he knew he was staring at the killer right now, going about his business, keeping up appearances like nothing had happened.

'It took a bit of digging,' Hayne said. 'One of the people on the list changed his name a few years ago. Threw me off for a while.'

Changed it to Martin Cole, Tayte thought as the ferry brought him closer; they were less than fifty metres from the shore now. Then the revs dropped as the ferry slowed for the approach and Tayte wheeled towards Simon, suddenly aware that they were slowing. He wanted more speed, not less. He wanted Simon to ram into the beach like he had when he'd taken him to Amy's house. Tayte watched Simon bend down to pick up a coil of rope and his words lodged in his throat.

'If he hadn't been a naughty boy when he was sixteen,' the voice in Tayte's ear continued, 'and landed himself with a caution for cannabis possession, I might never have spotted it.'

Hanging from Simon's neck, suspended by a thick leather cord, Tayte saw a bright silver crucifix catch the light. He recognised it from a drawing at the exhibition at Bodmin Jail and the hairs on the back of his neck stood to attention.

Simon froze, one hand on the rope as the other reached up and slipped the crucifix back inside his t-shirt. His head turned slowly towards Tayte as he rose, dead eyes staring.

'He changed his name to Simon Phillips,' Hayne said on the phone. 'We're on our way to his flat at Porth Navas now. Another car's on its way to the Helford Ferry.'

Tayte lowered the phone from his ear and in that split second it all kicked off. He saw Simon reach a hand towards his jeans pocket, and he didn't wait to find out what he was reaching for. He dropped the phone and lunged at him, throwing Simon back into the steering wheel, spinning the vessel away from the pontoon as the boat began to wheel away from shore in a wide arc. As Tayte crashed into Simon, he felt the kick against his sore, bandaged legs. It forced him back, but he managed to stay on his feet. This time the kid's hand reached his pocket unhindered and eight inches of broad polished steel flashed into view.

'I think you two have met before,' Simon bragged, waving the knife in front of Tayte.

Then he went for him.

Tayte didn't think about it. He saw the coil of rope on the floor, grabbed it, and swiped it across the arm brandishing the knife. The blade went spinning across the boat, caught the canopy, and landed on the seat moulding, sliding all the way to the rear of the vessel.

Simon shot after it, passing Tayte before he could recover from the momentum as the rope swung him around. On the rebound, Tayte threw the rope at Simon's feet and Simon tripped, reaching for the blade as Tayte arrived with all his weight, crashing down on him like a wave. Tayte knew he'd knocked the wind out of him. He heard Simon's breath escape in a rush as he went for the knife, sliding it back along the seat moulding and out of harm's way as he pinned the kid face down on the deck.

'Get the fuck off me!' Simon yelled.

'No chance. Where's Amy?'

'Where you'll never find her.'

Tayte picked Simon's head up by the hair and slammed his face into the gritty deck. *One for Schofield,* he thought. In his mind he was tearing Simon to shreds with his bare hands. 'Who are you working with? Who took Amy's boat this morning?' Tayte thumped Simon's head into the deck again, harder this time. In the background he heard that unfamiliar ringtone again.

'He was just a kid I paid to pick up the boat,' Simon said. 'We never even met. I left a twenty under the seat for him.'

Tayte lifted Simon's head off the deck again and turned his face around. His teeth were dripping blood. 'Now where's Amy!'

A spiteful grin crossed Simon's face. 'You can't hurt me.'

Tayte slapped the exposed side of Simon's face with the hard end of his palm. 'I can take a long time finding that out,' he said. 'Now where is she?'

'It's funny,' Simon said. He sounded calm now, coming right back at Tayte like he'd barely felt it. 'I could see this going wrong when you spotted the car.'

'Yeah, that must have been a real blow.'

'Lucky you saw the crucifix and realised it was me.'

'Really?'

Simon laughed. 'I couldn't have let you off the boat alive,' he said. 'Martin would have told you it was my car, that he just borrows it now and then. The game would have been up anyway, wouldn't it?'

'It's already up,' Tayte said. 'The police know who you are.'

The persistent ringtone had not long stopped. Tayte looked for the phone and noticed that the boat had wandered away from shore. Now it was running in circles, fortunately clear of other craft for now. He saw the phone at the other end of the boat, towards the wheel. He knew he couldn't get to it without letting Simon up, but he figured someone would soon spot the ferry's unusual behaviour and come out to see what was going on. The police were on their way, coming for Simon. He just had to wait.

'We work in shifts,' Simon announced. 'In case you were wondering.'

'I wasn't,' Tayte said. He began to wave his arms above his head, trying to get someone's attention.

'Martin was on this morning while I was busy blowing you up. Now I'm on for the afternoon shift. It was working out really well.' Simon let out a scornful laugh, like he couldn't quite believe the unexpected predicament he now found himself in. 'You're supposed to be dead!' he added. 'So much for third time lucky. I should have knifed you after I gave you that lump on the back of your head. I knew it had to be you when I saw you down by the ferry that morning—when you spoke to Martin. After I followed you onto the Fairborne estate, I had no doubt.'

Tayte leant forward and pressed down on Simon's head like he was trying to crush his skull into the deck. It was an act of pure frustration. 'Unless you're going to tell me where Amy is,' he said, 'just shut your mouth!'

'Amy? Oh, yeah...'

Simon was laughing again. It unnerved Tayte. He could have wrung his neck there and then just to silence him.

The laughter stopped. Simon was still grinning. 'I haven't worked out why that box was so valuable,' he said. 'Perhaps you can help me.'

That suggestion almost made Tayte laugh.

'Oh, I think you're going to help me, Mr Tayte,' Simon said, forcing his voice into tones that Tayte recognised from all those phone calls.

The words made his skin crawl. He heard Simon laugh again, spluttering into his own blood and spittle on the deck.

'It doesn't sound as good without a spliff to drag on,' he said. 'Can't quite get the squeaky notes.' He seemed to be enjoying this. Then his tone changed, adopting a more serious air. 'If I don't get back to Amy by nine-thirty tonight, she'll drown,' he said. 'We all need a little security, don't we, Mr Tayte?'

Tayte felt like he was playing noughts and crosses; he couldn't win. He eased off, thinking about his next move. He didn't like the way this was going.

'Irony's a funny thing, isn't it?' Simon said. 'Turn me in and you kill Amy. The very person you want to save. You have to save me from the police now in order to save Amy.'

Tayte couldn't miss the mocking smirk on Simon's face. 'I'm through playing your sick games, you hear me? You'll tell the police where she is or...'

'Or what? They'll lock me up for murder? Too late. I'm already up for two recent counts. What have I got to lose?'

'Two counts?' Tayte said as the inference of Simon's statement hit him.

'That's right,' Simon said. 'Oh, you don't know, do you?'

'Know what?'

'That deli owner…'

Tayte went limp.

'I told you not to get anyone else involved.'

Tayte looked around for anything he could use to smash this kid's head with. If something suitable had been within reach he might well have used it.

'Then there's Gabriel Fallon,' Simon added. 'I saw him at the cottage through the dining room window one afternoon. I was sure he'd found the box—it looked like a box. Next day he came strolling out looking pleased with himself. He was carrying something in an old towel, so I followed him onto the river. I figured he was taking it to show someone. It must have been important to him—the weather had turned to shit by the time we reached Toll Point. I mean, he must have had a good reason to stay out there, right?' Simon laughed through his nose. 'Well, I couldn't let the opportunity go, could I?'

Tayte could feel his breath catch in his tightening chest as adrenalin began to pump through his veins. His hands formed tight knots beside him.

'I slit his throat for a tackle box!' Simon added. His laugh was sickening. 'The idiot was out fishing, and he didn't even have the sense to turn back when the storm hit. What was I supposed to think he was doing out there? A fucking tackle box! So don't think Amy's life means more than piss to me, because it doesn't.'

Tayte had heard enough. He raised an arm above his head, ready to end this. Then through his rage he saw an image of Amy, cold and alone. His only thought was that he had to help her if he could. He let out a frustrated roar and slapped the deck hard beside Simon's face.

Simon glared back at him. 'So here's the new game,' he said. 'Get your fat arse off me. Find out what's so valuable about that box. Then meet me on the beach at Durgan tonight at eight o'clock with the answer. If I like what I hear, I'll tell you where Amy is so you can be the all-American hero and go save her.'

'What if I can't find the answer in time?'

'It's a gamble, but that's all the time you have. At the risk of sounding like a broken record...' Simon slipped into his alternate voice again. 'If you don't find out by eight o'clock tonight, Mr Tayte—Amy dies!' He laughed at himself then stopped abruptly. 'Or you can just turn me in now and she dies anyway. It's up to you.'

That was really all it came down to and Tayte knew it. He could turn Simon in and risk having Amy drown if he couldn't find her in time. Or he could let Simon go, in which case he had five hours to find out what dark discovery Lowenna Fairborne had made back in 1803. Five hours to find out what Lowenna knew that was so valuable she thought she could use it against her father to protect herself. Tayte assumed that Simon wanted this information to use against the Fairbornes himself, all these years later.

'So that's all this is about?' Tayte said. 'Revenge?'

'More or less,' Simon said.

'Revenge for Mawgan Hendry?'

'For Mawgan...' Simon nodded. 'And for me. I need to set things right.'

'And I suppose you'll get rich along the way?'

Simon mocked him, like he resented the suggestion that this was all about the money. 'The chat's over,' he said. 'Time to choose.'

Tayte sat there a moment, although he already knew what he had to do. He shook his head and pushed himself up off Simon's shoulders, knowing he had to take the chance. If he turned Simon in, Simon would deny knowing anything about Amy's whereabouts until it was too late. He stood back and let him up. He could barely look at the kid now, grinning as he rose from the deck, smug in his moment of triumph.

'Enjoy your freedom,' Tayte said through gritted teeth. 'It won't last.'

The two men circled one another warily as Simon went to the wheel and regained control of the boat, guiding the vessel back to shore but away from the ferry pontoon.

'So you're a descendant of Mawgan Hendry and Lowenna Fairborne,' Tayte said as the boat took him in.

'Once a bastard, always a bastard, eh?' Simon said, still wearing that grin. 'I'm glad you worked it out,' he added. 'It's good to know someone else knows the truth, and the letter you gave me this morning proves it.'

'Not much good to you now, though, is it?' Tayte said.

'Not much,' Simon agreed. 'I can't exactly tell anyone, can I? When this is all over, I can hardly turn up as the rightful heir to claim the spoils. That's why the rest of the puzzle is so important.' Simon lined up the craft for the landing. 'Looks like you've won yourself a victory after all,' he added. 'Still, it's important to know who we are, don't you think?'

Tayte gave no answer as the catamaran slid into the shingle. He went out onto the bow and lowered the ramp, wondering what Simon meant by 'rightful heir' as he watched the kid collect his knife from the seat moulding.

'Don't forget this.' Simon tossed Tayte his phone. 'You might need it.'

As Tayte jumped clear of the craft, he was aware of a police car arriving along the road towards the Ferry Boat Inn. He turned back to the river and watched the catamaran pull away as he stared after it. He felt sick to his stomach.

Chapter Fifty-Three

Five hours... Tayte couldn't get that number out of his head. He knew he had plenty to do in that time if he was going to save Amy, and he knew where he wanted to start: Rosemullion Hall. Eleanor Fairborne and her children had to be buried on the estate. Their headstones would tell him if they survived the *Betsy Ross* or not, and he was sure that the circumstances of their deaths and Lowenna's dark discovery had to be connected—find one, find all. If only he knew how.

Tayte *wanted* to go to Rosemullion, but he couldn't. The police car that had arrived at Helford Passage to take Simon Phillips in for questioning had left instead with Jefferson Tayte. Now he was on his way to see Bastion and Hayne at an address a few miles away in Porth Navas—Simon's flat.

As the car arrived along a tight single lane, sandwiched between a terrace of cottages on the left and a tree-lined creek on the right, Tayte supposed that police boats would be out on the river and the surrounding coastline by now, looking for the distinctive catamaran that Simon had made off in. He found himself hoping that Simon had had sense enough to ditch it, and it pained him to think like that—like he was on the killer's side, rooting for him. And he knew he would have to lie to Bastion and Hayne. He'd been picked up at Helford Passage, having crossed the river on the most-wanted ferry in England with the man *his* list had led them to. He was ever aware that he'd helped the killer evade the law; he would have to watch what he said.

'This way, sir.' A uniformed officer was standing by the car; another was already at the door to a stone cottage that faced the creek. There was no garden as such, just a bench that sat in a three-foot-deep border with large red and pink hydrangeas to either side. The officer at the door led Tayte in and up a short flight of stairs to the upper flat. He announced Tayte and then left.

'Mr Tayte,' Bastion said. He offered his hand and Tayte shook it. 'Keeping out of trouble, are we?'

If only you knew! Tayte thought. 'So far,' he said, staring into the room, intrigued by what he saw.

'I must ask you to stay by the door and not touch anything,' Bastion said. 'You shouldn't really be here, but given what we've found, I could use your professional opinion. See if you think we've got the right man.'

Tayte already knew they had. 'Of course,' he said.

Across the room DS Hayne was arched over a teak sideboard that had several stacks of A4 paper piled neatly on top of it. He looked up and gave Tayte a nod. They were in a sitting room of minimal comforts: a television in one corner, a thin-legged table by the window. A dark brown sofa and two matching armchairs rested against white walls, and the sage carpet looked like it was long over-due for replacement.

The thing about the room that had Tayte mesmerised was be-hind DS Hayne, on the wall. He was looking up at a neatly con-structed family tree. Short lines linked a muddle of names written in tidy boxes in black felt pen. At the top of the chart were James and Susan Fairborne. On the left it traced down to Sir Richard and Lady Celia Fairborne, and below that was their only dependant, Warwick. Lowenna Fairborne and Mawgan Hendry appeared to the right, beneath which he saw Mathew Parfitt and other names that were familiar to him from last night's research. Circled in red at the bottom of the family tree, opposing Warwick's, was a name Tayte recognised from his list of suspects: Daniel Hawthorne.

So that's your real name...

Hayne picked up another pile of papers and began to flick through them. 'What happened to that phone call?' he asked. 'I thought you'd like to know about that list you gave me.'

'The line was bad,' Tayte said. The lie sounded natural enough. His eyes were back on the wall like it was no big deal. 'We must have gotten cut off. Then I couldn't get a signal.'

'Reception's a bit like that around here,' Hayne said. 'Funny though, I got a ringtone when I called back.'

Tayte made no further comment. Hayne went back to the papers he was looking at.

Bastion eyed Tayte quizzically. 'They tell me you were at Helford Passage when the car arrived to bring Phillips in.'

'That's right.'

'What were you doing there?'

'I went to look for Tom Laity. Did you speak to him?' Tayte wanted to change the subject.

'No one's seen him,' Bastion said. His eyes squinted at Tayte. 'But you were on the wrong side of the river, weren't you? His shop's in the village.'

'I was planning to catch the ferry across,' Tayte said, hoping they didn't check where his car was parked. 'Only it wasn't there.' His brow lifted and stuck there. 'Now I know why. You didn't get your man then?'

Bastion shook his head, brushing a hand through his wiry hair. 'No,' he said. 'Looks like he knew we were coming, and judging by what we've found here, he had good reason to run.'

Bastion crossed the room to Hayne and indicated the piles of paper Hayne was going through. 'These all appear to be copies of certificates and other records,' Bastion said. 'Records for all the names that appear on the wall here. Births, marriages, and so on.'

Bastion picked up one of the records from the sideboard. It was separate from the rest of the pile, sitting alone. 'This is the only document that's not a photocopy,' he said, crossing back to Tayte inside the doorway. 'Looks like the original.' He handed it to Tayte. 'You said Schofield's killer baited you with the promise of seeing a probate record, didn't you?'

'That's right.'

'Well, I need to know if this is the document you expected to see, and if you'll testify to that in court once we've brought in Simon Phillips—aka Daniel Hawthorne. I could make out a few words, enough to know what it is, but the rest of it might as well be in Swahili.'

Tayte opened the document. The text it contained was written by a wavering hand in a form that to most would be considered hard to read. To Tayte's experienced eyes, however, no transcript was required. He scanned the opening lines: 'This is the last will and testament of me, James Fairborne of Rosemullion, within the parish of St Mawnan in the county of Cornwall.'

'This is it,' Tayte said. 'The document was missing from the record office in Truro. I've wanted to see this from day one. How did Simon get hold of it?'

Bastion and Hayne looked at one another, like they were questioning how much of the case they should share. Then Bastion gave Hayne a nod.

'It seems that working the ferry wasn't Simon's only job in the area,' Hayne said. He crossed the room and flashed a plastic passcard at Tayte, an ID that bore the Cornwall County Council's logo and the words 'Cornwall Record Office' above a passport-sized photograph of Simon Phillips.

'That explains a few things,' Tayte said, recalling the phone call he'd made to the record office on his way back from Devon and the uncooperative assistant he'd spoken to there, whom Penny Wilson had said worked in the office part time. He could have found so much out from Penny. She knew Tayte's agenda and knew that he was coming to England from all the times he'd called her. And she had his number—Simon could easily have obtained that from her. Simon would have been on the lookout for him from the moment he'd arrived in England. 'An easy job for an insider,' he mused.

'And I should think his position there helped him no end with all this,' Bastion said, throwing an arm towards the chart. 'What does it all mean, Mr Tayte? What's he up to?'

Tayte studied the wall again. 'He's clearly made a connection to someone in the past he thought he was related to—someone very wealthy.' Tayte pointed to the name at the top of the chart. 'That would be James Fairborne,' he added. 'Then he's set out to prove his lineage, which is where our paths crossed.'

Tayte paced the room towards the chart. 'I was looking into Mathew Parfitt here,' he said, pointing at the corresponding box on the wall. 'A letter turned up proving that Mathew Parfitt was Lowenna and Mawgan's son.' He raised his arm to indicate them on the chart. 'It gave Simon all the proof he could want. That's what I gave him this morning when I was trying to get Amy back.'

'But why try to kill you over it?' Bastion said. 'What does it matter who knows? Surely he wants everyone to know he's part of such a family. Sir Richard Fairborne's a baronet after all and very well connected.'

'I'm sure he wanted the world to know about it in time,' Tayte said. 'But not just yet.'

Hayne interjected. 'So there's more to it?'

Tayte spun around to face them. 'There is,' he said. 'Simon had to kill me because I was getting too close. There was a risk that I would discover the same thing he's looking for. Maybe even beat him to it.'

'And he's kidnapped Amy Fallon for insurance?' Hayne said.

Tayte nodded. 'And all because of the box she found. Simon st have known she had it. He just needed to be sure.' He thought about the clue that had been left under his wiper blade at Bodmin and how it had led him straight to Amy. 'I helped draw the box into the open where Simon could see it,' he added. 'When I left Amy that night he must have gone in after it.' He knew well enough that Simon was at Ferryman Cottage the night Amy disappeared, and it didn't sit well on his conscience that he'd paid the kid to take him there.

'Only Amy no longer had the box,' Hayne said.

'That's right. I was taking it to London next morning.'

'So the killer revealed himself to Amy,' Hayne said. 'He couldn't have just apologised and left again. He had to take her with him. Then he came up with a plan to get the box from you at Nare Point.'

Bastion winced. 'It's a good thing for Amy that she *didn't* have the box,' he said. 'Or that might have been her body we found at Treath.'

The truth of that hit Tayte hard. Life or death, it seemed, balanced by a fine silk thread wherever the box was concerned. 'The writing box is the key,' he said. 'It holds the secret to a truth we're both searching for.'

'Something to do with the Fairbornes?' Hayne asked.

'I'm sure of it.'

Bastion threw Hayne a puzzled look, and Hayne returned a self-conscious smile. 'Why else would Simon Phillips want to hide James Fairborne's will?' Hayne said. 'It has to be related.'

Tayte turned his attention back to the probate record in his hand. He read the date, noting that James Fairborne's will was proven in 1829, which would have been the year it was made official, but not necessarily the year James Fairborne died. It was a short will for one of such magnitude, and the reason promptly manifested itself. Tayte read the words 'sole beneficiary' and then skipped the wordy formalities to the part that revealed the fortunate recipient and heir: 'That is to say, I give and bequeath unto my brother William Fairborne of Rosemullion in the Parish of St Mawnan...'

'Everything!' Tayte said. 'Nothing to any servants or children? It all went to his brother, William.'

The significance of what he'd just read took a while to register. When it did, he had to sit down. He lowered himself into the nearest armchair. His eyes remained on the words 'William Fairborne.' 'This can't be,' he said.

Bastion and Hayne came closer, like a pair of aroused sniffer dogs that had just picked up a new scent.

'I'm working for the descendants of William Fairborne's family now,' Tayte said. 'I know he never came to England. My research suggests that James and William didn't even get along. Whoever benefited from James Fairborne's will sure wasn't his brother.'

'So this family weren't the legal heirs?' Hayne said, running a hand down the chart to Warwick Fairborne.

Bastion glared at Hayne. 'Steady, Sergeant. That's dangerous talk without the evidence to back it up.' He took the probate record from Tayte and read the name of the beneficiary for himself. The name at least was clear. 'Are you sure?' he said.

Tayte looked Bastion in the eyes and nodded like he was never so sure of anything in his life. 'I've got a copy of William Fairborne's death record,' he said. 'He was buried alongside his wife in America, and I can tell you that his wife was not the lady on the wall here.'

Bastion sat down himself. 'Then who's the fella this James Fairborne left his fortune to?'

'I don't know,' Tayte said. 'But he must have had some hold over him.'

Chapter Fifty-Four

Gazing up at the family tree in Simon's flat, Tayte was curious again to know why Mathew Parfitt had dropped his claim against James Fairborne's will. It seemed all the more unusual now Tayte knew that Mathew had a valid reason to contest it. Mathew was related by blood to James Fairborne through Lowenna; it seemed fairly certain that whoever the man was who was calling himself William Fairborne, the man to whom Mathew's grandfather had left everything, was not the estranged brother James Fairborne thought him to be. Tayte supposed Mathew must have known that, or he at least suspected that James's will had been influenced.

A thought crossed Tayte's mind that had been there before. It concerned someone he'd given little thought to as he researched this assignment, purely through a lack of information about him. Lowenna had died young; that much he knew from Emily Forbes, from that fateful story she'd told him. But her brother, Allun Fairborne—what had become of him? He would have been a relatively young man at the time of his father's death. Why hadn't *he* contested the will? The most likely reason was that he had died before his father, and Tayte began to wonder at the circumstances that surrounded Allun's death.

He looked down at the stacks of paper on the sideboard, to the photocopies of Simon's family history records. Then he looked back to the wall and across the top of the chart. There were entries for as yet unexplored family lines. To the right of Lowenna was an entry for her brother, Allun. No further names appeared beside it or below it, but he realised there could be information on those record copies that might tell him more about Allun Fairborne's fate.

He turned to Bastion and Hayne who were right behind him, watching him think. 'Grab a pile,' he said, reaching for one of the stacks. 'I need to find anything in here relating to a guy called Allun Fairborne.'

Bastion and Hayne each took up a handful of papers. They were ordered, and Tayte soon knew where he was relative to the wall chart. Allun's records, if there were any, would be close to Lowenna's and their father's, towards the bottom of one of the piles. He riffled through the papers, finding nothing that dated that far back. Then Bastion interrupted his flow.

'Here you go.'

Tayte leaned in over Bastion's shoulder. He'd seen the record before; he had a copy in his briefcase. It was Allun Fairborne's birth record. 'Anything else there?' Tayte said.

Bastion shook his head. 'Just this.'

'So, Simon couldn't find the old records either,' Tayte mused, concluding that the missing death record information must have been removed many years earlier, when they were still maintained by the church, not stolen by Simon Phillips. Even if Simon had access to the original records, Tayte knew he couldn't get to all the indexes. References to the documents would have existed in too many places. When the records had been stored in a local church registry however, before they were centralised and catalogued…they would have been easy enough to get at then.

'What about James's wife?' Bastion said. 'Wouldn't Mrs Fairborne have had something to say about all this?'

'Susan?' Tayte said. The suggestion had merit. 'Let's take a look.' He went to the stack of records where Bastion had found the copy of Allun Fairborne's birth record. Behind that he found the records for

James and Susan Fairborne. He pulled out Susan's death record copy and glanced over it. 'According to this, she died a couple of years before James. She wasn't around to contest the will herself.'

Hayne still had his head buried in the stack of records he was checking. He was smiling. 'Lavender Parfitt,' he said with obvious amusement. He held up a copy of Lavender's record of marriage to Jane Forbes. 'I bet he got picked on at school.' His eyes wandered to Lavender's death record and his smile faded as he added, 'Died, Monday the 22nd of June, 1829.'

That got Tayte's full attention. He practically snatched the death record copy from Hayne's hands and checked the date again to make sure he'd heard it right. He reached into his jacket and took out his notebook. Several of the pages were stuck together from their earlier soaking at Gillan Harbour. He flicked through them carefully, looking for the pages he'd used to write down the information he'd found in *The Times* articles. When he found the date he was looking for, the mystery surrounding Mathew's contest of James Fairborne's will dissipated like midday fog.

'That was two days before Mathew Parfitt dropped his claim,' Tayte said.

Bastion and Hayne looked a little lost.

Tayte had the picture clear in his head now. 'Don't you see? The man claiming to be William Fairborne got to him. He got to Mathew here.' Tayte flicked a hand up to Mathew's name on the chart. 'He warned him off by killing his father.'

'That's pure conjecture,' Bastion said.

'Maybe so, but the coincidence is too big to ignore.'

'He might have a point, sir,' Hayne said. 'Looks fishy.'

Bastion scratched at the hair above his left ear, causing it to spring out. 'Why not just kill this Mathew fella?' Bastion said. 'That would have made him drop his claim soon enough.'

'It was a high-profile will contest,' Tayte said. 'There was a fortune at stake, and if the claimant had been killed, or had otherwise been seen to die suddenly, the death would have drawn too much attention.' Tayte shook his head. 'No,' he added. 'Killing Mathew would have been too risky a play.'

DS Hayne knew exactly what Tayte meant. 'The finger would have pointed straight at the man who stood to gain the most from Mathew's death,' he said. 'Killing Mathew's father and maybe even threatening to do the same thing to his mother on the other hand… that would have shut him up tight as a coffin.'

Tayte quickly found Jane Parfitt's death record from the records Hayne had been checking. 'She lived to a ripe old age,' Tayte said a moment later.

Bastion drew a long breath and paced to the window, where he looked out through a stretched film of net curtain over the creek below. 'This is all very interesting,' he said. 'But where is it taking us? You've given us Simon's motive and confirmed the means by which he lured Peter Schofield to his death. Everything we need to get a conviction is right here.' Bastion turned back into the room. 'All we need now is Simon Phillips.'

'There's still a kidnap victim to find,' Tayte said, thinking about Amy and where these latest clues fitted into the puzzle he had to solve before high tide.

'We'll find Amy once we've brought Simon in,' Bastion said.

Tayte wished he could believe that. Part of him wanted to tell them exactly where and when they could pick Simon up. It would be so easy. And if he thought there was any chance that Simon was bluffing about letting Amy die at the hands of the tide, then he would have. But Tayte knew Simon was deadly serious. He'd seen it branded in his eyes. He had to remind himself to watch what he said. If he let it slip that he needed to solve the riddle of the box in order to find Amy, Bastion and Hayne would question why, and with Tayte's track record he knew they wouldn't need Sherlock Holmes to tell them that he had his own plan to save Amy again.

With all that Tayte had discovered at Simon's flat, a terrible image was beginning to form in his mind, like a sliding picture puzzle whose jumbled pieces were right under his nose and were at last coming together. But there was still a piece of the puzzle missing, and without it he couldn't quite make sense of what he was looking at. He headed for the door, certain that he knew where to find that missing piece. He just had to get onto the Fairborne estate at Rosemullion Head.

'I'm sure you're right,' Tayte said. 'I don't think I can add anything more to this.' He excused himself with a polite smile and wished them good luck.

'Thanks for your help,' Bastion said. 'I'll have you dropped back to your car.'

My car... Tayte's mind tripped over the words. He knew he couldn't let them drop him back there; they would know he'd taken the ferry and would realise he'd seen Simon. 'Great,' he said. He checked his watch and knew he was running out of time. The afternoon was already spent, and now in a little more than two hours he had to meet the man who held Amy's life in the balance with answers he had yet to find. On top of that he now faced being stranded at Helford Passage with no car and no ferry to take him across the river to pick it up.

Tayte passed through the doorway knowing only that he needed to get to Rosemullion Head, and fast. He had to know if Eleanor and her children were buried there, and he had to know when they died. As he hit the first step on his way out of the flat, he realised he still didn't have a sure-fire angle that would get him onto the Fairborne estate, even if he could talk the driver of the police car into dropping him at the door.

That gave Tayte an idea.

He stopped halfway down the stairs and spun around to Bastion, who was right behind him. 'How long would it take to get a search warrant to go over the grounds on the Fairborne estate?' he asked.

Bastion looked wary. 'We'd only need one if we were refused access,' he said. His questioning eyes tightened to a squint. 'Why?'

Tayte suddenly saw his way in. 'Gravestones,' he said, giving nothing away.

'And how would it help the case?' Bastion asked. 'Despite the implications of that will, the Fairbornes still pull a lot of strings around here. If we go disturbing them without a bloody good reason...' He looked over his shoulder to DS Hayne and scoffed. 'Heads will roll,' he added.

'Anything to do with those churchyard photos we found in Peter Schofield's bags?' Hayne said.

Tayte nodded. His angle had arrived.

Chapter Fifty-Five

The light was beginning to fade as Rosemullion Hall came into view. Tayte was riding up front with DS Hayne in an unmarked silver BMW 3 Series. The mention of unsolved past crimes relating to the case had appealed to Bastion's ego enough to send Hayne along with Tayte while Bastion orchestrated the hunt for Simon Phillips. Tayte had made it seem like they were scratching each others backs: Bastion wanted results and Tayte wanted to finish his assignment and go home. That's how it seemed, but saving Amy was his only priority.

The car turned onto the headland along a private road towards Rosemullion Hall, and across a settling field laid to pasture the grand Elizabethan manor house came into view. It was already lit up for the night, and what remained of the early evening sun splashed a burnt orange glow across the stone, lending it a fiery sense of drama.

'Looks like they're having some sort of party,' Hayne said as they approached.

Ahead, the main gates were fixed open. They passed between them and along the smooth slate driveway towards what looked like a prestige car show. There were about twenty cars in all, the majority in varying shades of silver or black, with the occasional shock of Ferrari red or Lamborghini yellow. Hayne pulled up beside a Bentley Continental Flying Spur and both men got out.

Tayte had trouble keeping up with Hayne's authoritative march as they made their way towards the house. He thought it looked odd seeing Hayne without Bastion; they seemed so interdependent, like a double act. He watched Hayne push the knot up on his tie as he stepped between the pillars that framed the gilt-dressed doors. One half was already open, spilling soft light and the delicate plink of a harp from within.

By the time Hayne reached the entrance, his identity badge was out, ready to announce himself. Then a man Tayte recognised appeared in the door frame and studied them both curiously. It was Manning, the Fairbornes' butler. Tayte caught the recognition in the man's eyes as Hayne began the introductions.

'Could I see Mr Richard Fairborne?' Hayne said, offering out his badge.

Manning scrutinised Hayne's ID with raised brows for several seconds then snootily said, 'I'm afraid *Lord* Fairborne is otherwise detained.' His forced smile served only to patronise. 'Perhaps you could call back another time?'

'What about the lady of house?' Hayne said.

Manning stepped forward and pulled the door to behind him. 'As you can see,' he said. 'Lady Fairborne is entertaining this evening. I really don't think your presence here tonight will be welcome, whatever your business.'

Tayte thought the man more than a little presumptuous for a butler. He took a step closer. 'How about you go get her and let her decide, eh buddy?' He locked eyes with Manning longer than he cared to. 'Or do you want to be responsible for the scene that's about to follow if you don't?'

Hayne squeezed his eyes shut and winced.

Manning did not hide his irritation. 'Wait here,' he said. Then he turned back into the house and closed the door.

Hayne shook his head. 'Better let me do the talking, Mr Tayte.'

'Sure,' Tayte said. 'Lady F's all yours.'

Both men turned away from the door and looked across the driveway at the expensive cars.

'Nice,' Hayne said.

'Very,' Tayte agreed. 'So do you two always work together?'

'Me and Bastion?'

Tayte nodded.

'Three years now,' Hayne said.

'Still call him sir though, right?'

Hayne flashed Tayte a serious-looking affirmative. 'On *and* off duty,' he said. 'I just can't hear myself calling him Leonard. Doesn't feel right somehow.' A moment later he added, 'So, genealogy? Is it always like this?'

Tayte could see the detective's eyes flitting between his numerous bandages. 'Not always,' he said. 'But it's not all archive rooms and microfiche, either.'

'Sort of like Indiana Jones, then?'

Tayte returned Hayne's playful smile. Then the plink of harp music returned and both men wheeled in unison towards the door to see an attractive middle-aged woman. She was shadowed by Manning, who stood in the doorway like a fixture.

'Lady Fairborne?' Hayne said.

The woman nodded.

Hayne stepped closer. 'I'm sorry to trouble you, madam,' he said, offering his badge up for scrutiny again. 'With your permission, I'd like to take a look around the grounds.'

Lady Fairborne gave Hayne's badge a cursory glance. 'Whatever for?' she said.

'I believe it might help us with our investigation. An American gentleman was murdered last night just across the river. You might have heard about it?'

Lady Fairborne shook her head. 'We've been very busy,' she said. 'But you don't think it has anything to do with us, do you?' She looked shocked at the idea.

'No, of course not, madam. It's just routine. We're following a line of investigation that concerns the suspect's motives, that's all.

Specifically, we'd like access to the family burial plots. The family crypt, I suppose you'd call it.'

Lady Fairborne flashed a wary smile at Tayte. 'And is this man a policeman too?' she asked. 'I don't believe I caught your badge,' she said, addressing Tayte directly.

Hayne intervened before Tayte could get a word out. 'Er, no, madam,' he said. 'He's a specialist helping with the case.'

'Is he indeed?' Lady Fairborne paused long enough for Tayte to think she had him rumbled. 'I could be wrong,' she added, 'but don't you need a warrant for this sort of thing?'

Hayne smiled. 'Do you have something to hide, then?' He laughed to make light of the suggestion.

'Certainly not.' She laughed with him. 'They always say that on television programmes though, don't they?' She looked suddenly satisfied with herself. 'It *is* true, though, isn't it?' she added. 'You do need a warrant.'

Tayte was losing his patience again.

This time Hayne didn't give him the chance to cut in. 'I can get a warrant and be back here within twenty-four hours,' he said. His smile was gone. 'And I can bring a very large team with me,' he added. 'Discretion could not be guaranteed under the circumstances.'

Touchdown! Tayte thought as he watched Lady Fairborne's resolve collapse.

Celia Fairborne shrank back into the doorway with her deflated smile. She drew a deep and thoughtful breath. 'Very well,' she said. 'But I want no interaction with the guests, and you're to leave quietly as soon as you've finished. I'll have Manning meet you at the back of the house with the key.'

Chapter Fifty-Six

By the time Manning reappeared at the back of the house, the last of the party guests had moved off the manicured lawn and were now inside enjoying hors d'oeurves and cocktails. Tayte had looked at his cheap digital watch too many times; it was almost seven and he had just over an hour now to find what he was looking for and get himself to Durgan. Before then he also had to lose DS Hayne, and that meant he needed enough time to get a lift back to Helford Passage where his hire car was supposed to be and walk to Durgan from there. It wasn't far by the coastal path, but it would be dark by then.

'Follow me, gentlemen,' Manning said as he arrived with a bunch of old keys. He passed them and kept going, heading down through the gardens towards the sea.

They followed Manning's jangling keys almost to the edge of the grounds, to the far righthand corner of the gardens and beyond, through high and thick gorse that served to conceal the structure they were looking for. Manning finally stopped at a barely visible cobbled pathway that wound through a tangle of overgrown rhododendron bushes and other unkempt shrubbery. It was clear to Tayte as he followed Manning along the path, pushing aside the foliage as he went, that this was not a place frequented by the family with any regularity.

A defunct water fountain marked their arrival at a heavy granite structure, which over the years had become a frame for climbing roses and ivy. Apart from that it reminded Tayte of Grant's Tomb—the General Grant National Memorial—in Manhattan, New York City. It was smaller in scale, incorporating a purely aesthetic conical dome rather than the great dome that housed the commemorative mosaic murals of Ulysses S. Grant and Robert E. Lee, but it shared the mighty, pillared exterior at the front of the structure's base.

Manning must have anticipated their interest in the architecture. 'It was modelled after the Mausoleum of Maussollos,' he said, as if he was giving them a guided tour. 'One of the seven wonders of the ancient world.'

Several granite steps as wide as the structure led to a row of five broad pillars. Tayte walked the steps between them to a carved oak-panelled door, framed by granite sculptures of nameless saints. Manning was close behind him with the keys, and Tayte noted he had no trouble choosing the correct one from a selection of many.

As Manning pushed the door silently open, Hayne produced a Maglite torch, testing the beam as Manning stepped boldly through. Tayte felt his heartbeat quicken as he followed them in, wondering what revelations awaited. He heard a switch click. Then the main lights came on, and the illusion Tayte had in his head of some dusty old chamber evaporated like a waking dream.

They were standing in what Tayte thought looked like a chapel. It was adorned with white marble engravings and was nothing like the dingy place Tayte had imagined it to be from the outside. It hadn't been used in a while, though; there were no pews and no other adornments that were not literally set in stone.

'I keep the cobwebs at bay,' Manning said, as if he'd registered the surprise on Tayte's face. 'You never know when such a place might be called upon again.'

To the side walls, Tayte saw several recessed chambers—the sepulchres in which the sarcophagi of past members of the Fairborne family rested. Directly ahead of him, the room recessed into a wide space that housed a larger, highly sculpted sarcophagus that instantly demanded Tayte's attention. He moved instinctively towards it, past the floor-to-ceiling cinerary urn niches on either side, and then up a single white marble step to the sarcophagus that had drawn his eye.

'The resting place of William Fairborne,' Manning said before Tayte had chance to read the inscription.

Tayte fired a look at Hayne that said, *Yeah, right!* But this wasn't the time or the place to argue the paradox of how William Fairborne could be buried both here *and* back home in the States.

Manning approached Tayte, leaving DS Hayne to continue reading from the many inscriptions on offer. 'The building was designed and part built by him, so I'm told,' Manning said. 'On the plaques behind you, you'll find everything you're looking for.' He pointed past Tayte to the end of the chamber, where white marble slabs engraved with gold lettering rose to the ceiling. 'All the family interred here are listed on that wall.'

Tayte loved organised lists. A simple list could save so much time, and he was never more thankful for such a list than now. He went to the nearest plaque first. Separating them was another thicker slab that bore no engraving. He could see there was room on this plaque for more names at the bottom. He quickly scanned the dates. The oldest entry was at the top of the list—1903. Too late.

He moved across the wall, past the nondescript central slab to his left, and saw that this list was full. A quick glance at one of the dates somewhere in the middle read '1882.' *This has to be the one,* he thought. His eyes quickly scanned up the list and his hopes lifted with his eyes, but he was running out of names, and the years were not receding fast enough. He reached the top of the list and read a name he knew well. There were no entries dated before that of William Fairborne—1841 was as far back as they went.

'There's nothing here for James Fairborne,' Tayte said, speaking the words softly to himself as a disbelieving murmur. 'Nothing even for his last wife, Susan, or their children, let alone the family he arrived from America with.'

Tayte turned to Manning, hoping for some enlightenment. 'Nothing before 1841?' he said. Then his eyes caught the date engraved in prominent if faded gold numerals over the doorway. He read, '1830' and realised why; that was the year after this man calling himself William Fairborne inherited everything James Fairborne ever had. And it appeared that one of the first things he'd done with his new wealth was to build himself a mausoleum.

Manning and Hayne stood beside Tayte, looking up at the faded date over the door.

Tayte still couldn't believe it. 'You said William Fairborne had this place built?'

'That's right,' Manning replied. 'In 1830, as it says there. Eleven years before he died.'

'Well, what did he do with James Fairborne?' Tayte asked. He got a blank look. 'His benefactor?'

Manning continued to show nothing but vacant incomprehension.

What Tayte couldn't believe was that the man who claimed to be James Fairborne's brother could take everything from him and not even bury him in the family crypt. *Wait a minute...* Tayte paused to check his understanding. *This man wasn't really a Fairborne.* It suddenly made perfect sense. Why would he want a real Fairborne in there alongside his own family? He'd taken the name and the baronetcy, along with everything else. He probably wanted to forget where it all came from. How could he sustain the illusion if James Fairborne was always there under his nose to remind him?

So he built a mausoleum...

Tayte smiled to himself. 'He probably built this place right on top of the old family's graves,' he said.

Hayne edged past Manning and flicked a casual glance at some of the names on the plaques. 'What better way to hide something?' he said.

Tayte turned to Manning. 'Was there anything on this site before the mausoleum was built?'

Manning threw Tayte a bewildered stare. 'I may look old,' he said. 'And I may have been with the family for over thirty years, but that's hardly long enough to know that now, is it?'

Tayte shrugged. 'People can do a lot of talking in thirty years.'

'Well, not to me they don't. This place is private. Everything about it is the family's business and no one else's.'

Hayne scoffed. 'That all depends on what they've been up to.'

'I believe you've seen all there is to see here,' Manning said, jangling his keys as he went for the door.

Tayte couldn't argue with him. He was standing in a marble tomb with sarcophagi and cremation urns all around him, and a list on the wall told him that what he was looking for wasn't there—simple as that. If there were bodies buried beneath the marble that someone didn't want anyone to know about, then they'd made a good job of it. Without an inscription somewhere, short of digging the place up, how would anyone know? And Tayte hardly had enough proof to warrant that.

Hayne was already at the door with Manning, who stood looking at Tayte, waiting with one hand on the door, the other on the keys.

'I'd like to take a quick look outside,' Tayte said as he reached the door.

Manning sighed deliberately as Tayte passed him to meet the onset of night.

The fading light was a sullen reminder to Tayte that he had little time left if he was to make his lifesaving appointment with Simon Phillips. He didn't know what he expected to find outside the mausoleum—just that he had to find it soon. His best hope now was to discover some long-forgotten burial ground nearby, a resting place for the family before the mausoleum was built. As he moved around the side of the building, however, it was immediately apparent that even if such a plot of ground existed, in this low light, amidst such overgrown vegetation, he had no hope of finding it. He sighed and scuffed a loafer through the dirt.

'Perhaps we could come back when there's better light,' Hayne said.

Not an option, Tayte thought. He left Hayne and began to walk around the back of the mausoleum, trampling beside an unfussy granite wall until he reached the corner. He looked back. Hayne seemed distant. Then something caught Tayte's imagination. Hayne was too distant. The building was too deep. The plaques on the wall inside hadn't seemed as far away as Hayne was to him now, and he was sure it hadn't taken him anything like as many steps to reach them.

Tayte thought about Gerald Braithwaite and the writing box, reminding himself of one of the procedures Gerald said he used to determine if a box had anything to hide. The Fairborne mausoleum was nothing more than a big box after all, and from where Tayte was standing, this box was definitely hiding something.

He paced deliberate steps back to Hayne. 'Twenty-four,' he said as he arrived.

Hayne looked bewildered.

'Hold it!' Tayte shouted to Manning as he arrived back at the entrance to see him reaching a key towards the lock. He rushed up the steps with Hayne in tow. 'I need to go back inside.'

Manning froze as Tayte grabbed the handle and threw the door open. He walked into darkness and a torch flicked on behind him, shortly followed by the main lights. Tayte stared at the marble slab on the far wall, beyond the sarcophagus in the central recess. It had struck him as being a little too plain for its surroundings; it had no engravings and seemingly no functional purpose. He counted his paces towards the slab, and when he arrived he knew he was right.

'Only seventeen,' he called back. 'It's seven paces short. There must be another chamber.'

Chapter Fifty-Seven

With just under forty minutes to spare before his scheduled meeting with Simon Phillips on Durgan beach, Tayte wasn't sure whether his pulse was hammering because he thought he was going to be late or if it was just because he'd arrived at one of those rare defining junctures that made everything he ever did worthwhile. He was standing at the marble slab, running his fingers along the edges, looking for a way through into the chamber that every instinct in his body told him had to be on the other side.

Hayne joined him. 'Looks pretty solid,' he said. 'Are you sure you counted right?'

Tayte didn't turn around to answer him. He was on his knees now, brushing his hands along the floor where it joined the slab. 'There's a raised lip,' he said. He looked up at the ceiling and pointed. 'There's another,' he added. 'They're holding the slab in place, like it's on runners.'

'A sliding door?' Hayne said.

'Why not? Whoever sealed the chamber off might have wanted access again at some point.' Tayte fixed his hands on the right side of the slab and began to push. It was like pushing against a brick wall—nothing gave.

Hayne was directly in front of the slab. He gripped the edge with Tayte, ready to pull. 'Three, two, go!' he said.

This time Tayte felt something move. 'Again,' he said, and now he felt the slab slide a little further. A dark crack appeared and he could feel the draught as he put his face to it, drawing the air in. It wasn't the best fragrance he'd ever sniffed, but it was all his—he'd discovered it. They heaved again, and Tayte could tell by the look of disgust on Hayne's face that the time-locked reek was far from his liking.

'Urgh! What's that?' Hayne said. He shied away. 'Smells stale—like that musk aftershave I always got off my gran at Christmas.'

Tayte smiled at the idea that anyone would deliberately manufacture anything that stank like the air that was coming out from behind the slab. 'Earthy too,' he added, shoving at the edge of the slab again. 'Two key ingredients that go into making a great find.'

Manning was still with them, though he kept his distance. 'I'm sure her Ladyship would not approve of this,' he said.

Tayte was too focused to pay him any attention. The gap was a few inches wide now and growing by the second until Hayne was able to squeeze a shoulder in. He put his back into it and Tayte nearly fell over as the momentum picked up and the slab slid a couple of feet at once.

Hayne's Maglite lit the way. 'After you.'

The gap, which was plenty wide enough for Hayne to fit through, was not so accommodating for Tayte. He sucked everything in and squeezed through into a narrow tunnel-like space that was dark until Hayne joined him with the torch. They were standing beneath a stone door lintel. Rotten wood littered the floor, and the rusty hinges where the door used to be still hung out across the opening. Tayte pushed the upper hinge and it broke away, falling with a dull clank onto stone steps that gave way to soft earth partway down. He was convinced he'd caught the ground moving at the edge of the torchlight.

Hayne shone the torch to the back wall, revealing a two-by-four matrix of empty recessed chambers. The beam wandered higher then until it caught a stone angel looking down on their arrival with an uncharacteristically malevolent stare. Hayne flicked the light away again to a large central granite sarcophagus that was plain sided and carried no decorative detail. Both men followed the light towards it.

Standing over it they could see that the lid was covered with engraved lettering; several names and dates appeared around a central inscription.

'Now lie with them in death,' Tayte read aloud.

'Cryptic,' Hayne said. He set the torch down on the sarcophagus lid with the beam facing the ceiling. Dull light spread and faded across the room, reintroducing the angel who continued to watch them through unsettling eyes. Beyond the point of light directly above them, the room was barely illuminated; it was like looking through a dark veil.

Around the inscriptions were the names of the interred: James and Susan Fairborne, their children, Lowenna and Allun. Tayte scanned the dates and their ages at death, confirming that Lowenna had died in 1803 at the age of seventeen, giving further credence to Emily Forbes's story. Yet something about that story bothered Tayte.

'Lowenna's child was to remain in the family,' he said, as much to himself as to Hayne. 'She would have known where her aunt and uncle lived, and from what I've learnt about Lowenna, I'd say she was a very determined girl.'

Hayne's eyes remained on the sarcophagus, taking in the details, saying nothing.

Tayte shook his head. 'I just can't believe she'd kill herself and leave her child like that—her lover's child. Hendry's murder must have been hard to take, sure, but leaving the child? How could she make that decision?'

Hayne looked up at last. 'Believe me,' he said. 'It happens.'

Tayte couldn't argue the point. Checking the dates further, he was not surprised to learn that Lowenna's brother, Allun, had died just two years later. After seeing Lavender Parfitt's death record at Simon's flat and noting the 'convenient' timing of his death, he'd already formed his opinion about what had become of Allun; that he died soon after Lowenna just helped to confirm it.

Were they both murdered, with Lowenna's death made to look like suicide?

Tayte had no trouble convincing himself that he was right. He now knew that James Fairborne left no heir from his marriage to Susan Forbes. None of his immediate family were alive to contest his will, and that made things very convenient for the man who claimed to be his brother. He wondered for the first time whether this man had also ensured that James's family by his first marriage to Eleanor would cause him no trouble as well.

'Now lie with them in death,' Hayne said, still pondering the meaning. 'It's almost like there's something missing. Something only the person who wrote it understood.'

Tayte rolled the words around in his head and suddenly got a buzz along his spine. 'They're here!' he said, grabbing the torch and throwing Hayne into darkness as he flashed the beam down at the earth, scattering a confusion of bugs.

'Who's here?'

'All of them,' Tayte said. 'The family I came to find.' The torch beam continued to scan the ground. 'Now lie with them in death. It can't be about the people in the sarcophagus with James. Of course he's lying with *them.* That only leaves his first wife, Eleanor, and their children. Apart from a sister and brother-in-law, James had no other family in England.'

Hayne watched the focused torch beam cut across the earth like a laser. 'You think we're standing on them?' he said. He picked up his feet like he was checking his shoes for gum.

'It makes perfect sense,' Tayte said. 'Stick James Fairborne in here with all *his* family, out of the way and forgotten, while this other man who took everything James had keeps the penthouse.'

He recalled Lowenna's note to Mawgan Hendry. *It's what is inside that counts,* he thought. It wasn't just about the child she was carrying as he'd supposed, or the letter Gerald Braithwaite had found. There was something else inside that box. To Tayte's mind, with all that had passed, he could see no other explanation.

But why? That one question still troubled him. Tayte hoped to find some other truth—something that would absolve James Fairborne of all the unthinkable sins his mind had already convicted him of. Yet, he somehow doubted he would. Unless he recovered the writing box, he knew he would never find the truth.

'So this character calling himself William Fairborne,' Hayne said as they headed down Grove Hill. 'He built a mausoleum around the old site, presumably to hide it. Why not just build over it? Less chance of anyone finding them if he had.'

'I wish I knew,' Tayte replied. 'He must have had his reasons.'

Hayne nodded. Then after a pause he laughed and said, 'I should think we'll get a complaint in the morning for shifting that slab.'

Tayte's thoughts wandered to the impostor who put it there and the implications of what they had found behind it. There would be more than enough DNA in that room to prove that the man who inherited the Fairborne legacy was not who he claimed to be.

'I'm sure that's going to be the least of their troubles,' he mused. It was already the least of his. This night's work was far from over, and he was keen now to be elsewhere.

The glowing red digits on his watch told him he was already out of time. In ten minutes he had to be at Durgan to meet Simon Phillips, and he knew he would never make it, even if Hayne drove him straight there, which was out of the question. He had to hope Simon wanted answers more than he cared about the rules of his game. And he had to hope he would give him enough time with the writing box to prove his suspicions—even if that meant destroying it.

It was eight o'clock when Hayne passed the Ferry Boat Inn and pulled up outside the ferry kiosk at Helford Passage. Across a gloss black river that was given away only by the stirring of shingle at the shoreline, the scant lights of Helford Village and Treath looked distant above their reflections. Tayte jumped out of the car as soon as it stopped.

'Thanks,' he said, 'I guess I'll see you tomorrow.' He was already backing away as he watched Hayne half climb out of the car after him. Tayte forced a smile. 'Lot of thinking to do tonight, and boy, do I need some rest.' He felt tense as he turned away and increased his pace, filling his lungs with evening air that was redolent of drifting honeysuckle.

'Where's your car?' Hayne called after him.

Tayte turned but kept walking, palms sweating. 'It's just off some lane back here,' he lied. He threw a thumb over his shoulder to indicate roughly where he meant. 'It's not far. I'll be fine.'

Tayte could see the start of the coast path ahead. Not far to go. The gap was closing. Under his breath he willed Hayne to get in his car and drive away; he didn't have time for explanations. He slowed his pace. He could almost feel Hayne's professionally inquisitive eyes boring into his back. Then he heard a car door close and a familiar engine note start up. He didn't chance a look. He heard the car pull away, and as he reached the start of the coastal path, he began to run.

Tayte arrived at Durgan out of breath and almost fifteen minutes late for his rendezvous with Simon Phillips. He'd jogged all the way there, passing no one as he followed the beam of Hayne's Maglite along the coastal path, willing his sore legs to keep him going. He took another chestful of air and pushed against his knees, straightening himself up. He was standing in the centre of Durgan, a tiny junction with an old-style red phone box on one side and a stone-built public shelter on the other. Behind him, looming like storm shadows, the gardens of Glendurgan stretched away from the diminutive hamlet that nestled at the edge of the river.

It was too dark and too quiet for Tayte's liking. He looked around at the few stone fishing cottages he could see and noted that all were in darkness. As he made his way between two of the cottages towards the river, he began to wonder if anyone actually lived in Durgan. He supposed the solitude was why Simon had chosen the place.

He followed a boat access ramp between high stone walls that continued along the beach like sea defence barriers. His torch picked up shingle ahead, and he could soon feel it crunching underfoot. He shone the torch to either side of him, pushing light along the shingle as far as the Maglite's limited power would allow before darkness overwhelmed it. To his right he could see that the beach petered out to what looked like rocks, and higher up to the shadows of surrounding foliage. To his left the beach was too wide to see where it ended.

Tayte drew the beam back along the wall, picking out a few small boats. He made his way towards them. The first was a dinghy, and beside that was a larger craft topped with a blue tarpaulin cover. When he reached them he knew that Simon had not waited. He could see now where the beach ended, and there was no one out there. He'd blown it; that much was clear to him. He'd failed Amy for want of no more than fifteen minutes.

As he turned away from the boat with the blue tarpaulin cover, distracted by thoughts that asked how the hell he was going to find Amy before high water now, he caught his shin and almost fell into the dinghy beside him. His hands instinctively came around to steady himself, swinging the torch around with them, splashing light into the boat like yellow paint. He startled and spun away again so hard that he slipped in the shingle and fell onto his elbows. What he saw in that brief flash told him that things were far worse than he could ever have imagined.

Chapter Fifty-Nine

In the darkness on Durgan beach, Tayte staggered to his feet, knowing that his problems had just become more serious than ever. He shone the torch back into the dinghy, and this time he held it there. He glanced away briefly to check the time and registered with startling clarity that unless he found Amy within the next hour and ten minutes, she would die, drowned by the tide wherever Simon had left her. The problem was that he was now looking at the only man in the world who could tell him where she was, and the face in Tayte's torch beam was as ashen as the grey hooded sweatshirt he wore. The two glistening bullet holes and the dark stains on the man's chest left Tayte in no doubt that he was looking at a corpse.

Simon Phillips was dead.

Tayte was too caught up in the moment to consider that whoever killed him might still be nearby. The realisation that this murder was still as fresh as the blood on Simon's sweatshirt only registered when he heard the shingle crunch over by the boat access ramp. And there was Tayte, brandishing a torch in otherwise total darkness beside the body of a dead man. He might as well have had a flashing target on his chest.

He flicked the beam towards the sound, which was closer now, maintaining the same steady tempo. He caught a glimpse of a dark trouser leg and the brief gleam of a shoe, and it occurred to him that anyone with an innocent reason for being there would have a torch of their own. Only then did he think to switch off the Maglite and run for cover. As the torch beam died, he heard the shingle stir excitedly then stop.

'Mr Tayte?'

Tayte flicked the torch on again, and this time it shone straight into DS Hayne's face, causing him to raise a hand to shield his eyes from the glare. 'It's a serious crime to take a policeman's torch without permission, you know.'

Tayte came out from his cover and stood beside the dinghy. He was pleased to see that Hayne was smiling, though he knew it wouldn't last.

'What are you doing down here?' Hayne asked. 'You weren't very convincing when I dropped you off, so I followed you.'

'I came to meet Simon Phillips,' Tayte offered. 'Another exchange plan I couldn't tell you about. Amy's whereabouts for some information he wanted.'

'And did you? Did you meet him?'

'Sort of...' Tayte shone the Maglite into the dinghy, illuminating the body that lay awkwardly across the centre seat board.

Hayne's eyes widened as he went for his radio.

Within thirty minutes Hayne knew everything that had transpired on the ferry boat that afternoon between Tayte and Simon Phillips, and the pair were now lit up on Durgan beach like actors on centre stage. The light source came from the Aquastar police launch that had diverted to Durgan after Hayne had placed his call. Tayte walked towards the light—which seemed to hover several metres above the river—squinting through the white glare as he watched a powered inflatable come ashore. Seconds later DCI Bastion stepped out, accompanied by a marine officer who dragged the craft further in.

Bastion strode up from the shoreline with fitting authority. 'I'm beginning to wish I'd had you deported after the first murder!' he called to Tayte who was still trying to shield his eyes from the glare. 'Death seems to follow you around like the plague.' He passed Tayte, heading straight for Hayne who was still beside the dinghy at the top of the beach. 'And Mr Laity might well be joining them before the night's out.'

'You found Tom Laity?' Tayte said, following after him. 'I thought he was already dead.'

'A returning fishing boat reeled him in off Porthkerris Point about an hour ago.'

'What was he doing there?'

Bastion shrugged. 'No idea. The man was senseless by all accounts. Had a nasty gash to his head.'

'Where is he now?'

'Hospital, Mr Tayte. Intensive care at Truro. He was rambling when they picked him up. Something about mackerel fishing for heaven's sake. Obviously delirious. He's been out cold ever since.'

Bastion turned his attention to the fresh body in the dinghy. 'What've we got now then, Sergeant?' He leant in over Simon's body, clicked on his torch and began to study the scene. 'Anyone touch anything?'

'I don't think so, sir.'

'No,' Tayte said.

'Good. I don't suppose you can help us with a motive this time can you, Mr Tayte?'

Tayte could barely pull his thoughts away from Amy long enough to try. 'I don't know,' he said, shaking his head, not really thinking. 'Simon obviously knew plenty about the probate record you found at his flat. He had enough there to piss a few people off.'

'People like Sir Richard Fairborne?' Bastion said.

Tayte nodded. 'I guess. Did Laity say anything else?'

'Nothing intelligible. The man was barely breathing.'

Tayte thought back to his earlier conversation with Simon, when the kid had boasted about killing Laity. 'Laity might have found Amy,' Tayte thought aloud.

Bastion turned away from the dinghy. 'Mr Tayte,' he said impatiently. 'I have another murder to investigate here.'

Tayte sensed that Bastion was close to throwing him off the beach, but what had he to lose? 'And if we don't find Amy before high tide,' he cut in, 'you'll definitely have a third.'

Hayne offered a few words in Tayte's favour. 'Mr Tayte had a bit of a struggle with our late Mr Phillips here this afternoon that he neglected to tell us about, sir.'

Bastion sighed. 'And why doesn't that surprise me?'

'I couldn't take any chances,' Tayte said. 'But when I left him I was assured that Amy would drown unless he got back to her by high tide.' Tayte checked his watch again. 'That's about thirty minutes from now, and all I know is that she's someplace where the tide can drown her. That's gotta be along the coast somewhere, right?'

'Or the river,' Hayne corrected. 'The Helford's tidal.'

Tayte squeezed his temples, thinking the search area was too big given the time they had left. Then he realised that if Laity *had* found Amy...

'She must be somewhere close to where Laity was picked up,' he said.

Bastion sighed. 'Mr Tayte. A body can drift for miles along this coastline in a very short time.'

'I'm sure it can,' Tayte said. 'But we don't know how long Laity was out there. It's gotta be Amy's best shot.'

Hayne interjected. 'I could take the boat out and have a look, sir. The sea's calm tonight. He might not have drifted far.'

'If we do nothing,' Tayte said, 'she's dead for sure.'

The beach fell silent. Bastion seemed to ponder his options. Then at last he gave Hayne the nod. 'The rest of the team should be along soon. I'm sure I can manage without you a while longer.'

'Right, sir.'

As they ran for the inflatable at the shoreline, Tayte heard encouraging words from DCI Bastion in the background. He was talking to the marine officer who'd come ashore with him.

'Get on to the Coastguard,' he said. 'Let's see if we can get a few more boats out to join in the search for Mrs Fallon.'

———————

Porthkerris Point was located approximately one kilometre southeast from the coastal village of Porthallow on the Lizard Peninsula, three kilometres south of the Helford River. Tayte and Hayne were aboard the Aquastar police launch being powered towards Porthkerris under a dark sky and the capable command of the marine unit sergeant.

From the single seat on the exposed upper deck, Hayne stabbed a finger through the cool night air towards the headland where Tom Laity had been picked up. 'There it is!' he shouted over the rush of the twin 400-horsepower diesel engines. He swung the spotlight beam away from the land on their right, across Porthallow and along the coastline to Porthkerris Point.

With him on the upper deck, above the main cabin that housed most of the controls, Tayte looked out portside. His eyes followed the light, but as far as he could see, the only clue that they were heading for land at all was that the headland appeared subtly darker than the sky above it. Then gradually he became aware of the stars that framed the land mass which appeared to him now as a dark void.

They arrived in a hurry and slowed to a sudden crawl, pitching the craft and forcing Tayte to grab onto the rails. As they came in towards the rocks, as close as they dared, Hayne lit up the cliff face and the Aquastar patrolled alongside, searching. Tayte was pessimistic about their chances. He knew as soon as they arrived that the police launch was too big a vessel to be effective. Bright as the spotlight was, the Aquastar couldn't get close enough. He considered that Simon would have been careful with his choice of hiding place for Amy. He supposed she would be somewhere that no boat this far out could easily see.

He looked back towards the Helford River and Falmouth Bay, and it suddenly struck him just how dark it was out there. It was too dark, and they were too far out. The tide was almost in now, and try as he might to fight his rising inner voice of despair, Tayte's hopes for Amy began to sink. Time was running out.

'I'm taking the inflatable,' he said. He pulled Hayne's Maglite from his pocket, gripped it between his teeth, and part slid, part fell off the upper deck and down the steel ladder, heading for the dinghy that was raised off the Aquastar's stern.

'Bastion'll have my badge!' Hayne called.

Tayte took no notice, and Hayne made no effort to stop him. Instead, he reached into a locker beneath his seat. 'Here, take this,' he said as he threw Tayte a halogen dive lamp.

Tayte flicked it on and sent a piercing column of light ripping into the night. He climbed into the inflatable and lowered himself behind the launch until he was hovering inches above the water. Then he let the rope go and splashed down. Seconds later, the outboard motor buzzed into life and he was away, one hand on the dive lamp, the other on the throttle arm which also served as the tiller. With the tide almost in, Tayte knew he could get the inflatable right in among the rocks. It lifted his spirits. He felt like Amy had a chance now as he began to search for what he figured must be a cave entrance of some sort; somewhere out of sight of the open water.

He ventured back towards Porthallow first, cutting in close to its grey stony beach before crossing between dark hills, catching the odd breaking wave as he went. The sea was no longer as hospitable this close to the rocks; the swell began to shove the inflatable around, reminding Tayte who was boss.

He ran the inflatable back towards the Helford River, thinking the Aquastar had passed that section of coastline far too quickly to have been effective. Always in the back of his mind he knew that things must be desperate for Amy by now. Maybe it was already too late. He pushed on and very quickly one rock formation came to look like the last. He was soon past Nare Cove, then off Nare Head. *Too close to the river,* he thought as he spun the inflatable around and headed back for another sweep.

Tayte conceded that Bastion might well have been right. Laity could have drifted a long way before he was picked up by that fishing boat. And he could have drifted in either direction. To Tayte's frustration, he didn't know enough about sea currents or the area he was in to know which way or how far Laity had been carried before he was found off Porthkerris Point.

He was back at Nare Cove now. The inflatable had drifted a little with his thoughts, and he was suddenly aware that he was too far out. He turned the tiller in and blipped the throttle to get back amongst the rocks and the cliff face. Then as the revs rose, there was a whir and a slap from the water behind the motor and it fell instantly silent.

The engine had stalled.

Tayte pulled at the starter cord to revive it, but the motor felt like it was jammed solid. He tilted the outboard motor up on its hinges, shone the lamp over it, and immediately saw the cause. The prop blade had choked on a length of fishing line. It was a tangled mess.

Chapter Sixty

The low hum of a mobile generator was busy in the background on Durgan beach, powering a series of floodlights on tall stands around the crime scene. The entire beach was alight, although nowhere was brighter than at the scenes of crime officers' interest epicentre: the body of Simon Phillips and the dinghy where Tayte had found him.

The cameras had finally stopped flashing; the scene sketches had been made. The people in white paper suits were now busy collecting evidence and dusting for prints—and the smooth tarpaulin cover on the larger of the two boats was proving a rich source of forensic information. One of the white suits—the SOCO supervisor—finished with the last of Phillips's personal effects and bagged it; it was yet another mobile phone to complement the others they had found on him. The supervisor left the dinghy and brought a collection of clear plastic bags with her beyond the perimeter of lights to where Bastion waited at the shoreline, gazing across the Helford River, deliberating.

As she arrived beside him, the SOCO supervisor pulled the hood back off her tidy red-brown hair and lifted the bags up for Bastion to see. 'Here you go, Chief,' she said. 'All done.'

Bastion wheeled around in the shingle and smiled. 'Thank you—' He paused. She was familiar, but he couldn't place her.

'Gillian McDowd, sir.'

'Yes, of course. McDowd.' Bastion flashed her another smile, more out of embarrassment than sincerity. He turned his attention to the bags McDowd was holding. The outline of a sheath knife flashed a violent image of Peter Schofield through his mind.

'It was velcro'd into his jeans pocket,' McDowd said, clearly having noticed his interest.

Bastion's fringe twitched. 'Concealed, yet convenient,' he said. He led McDowd back into the floodlit arena, towards the stone wall at the top of the beach where a folding table waited.

'I'm sure you've been thorough?' Bastion said as they crunched their way towards the table.

McDowd's smile looked forced. She spread the bags across the table and produced a fresh pair of latex gloves. 'Better put these on if you insist on touching anything before the lab's done with them.'

Bastion snapped the gloves on without taking his eyes off the contents: the knife, a few fat roll-ups, three mobile phones, a silver crucifix, and an old leather-bound book. He removed one of the phones and switched it on, navigated to the last call list, and re-dialled the number Simon Phillips had called that morning at an indicated ten minutes past ten. The call went straight to Jefferson Tayte's voice mail.

Bastion cleared the call, thinking it would have been the last call Simon Phillips made to Tayte before he'd tried to blow him up. He switched the phone off and slipped it back into the protective bag. Then he moved on to the next phone and repeated. The last call from this phone was later, and obviously not to Tayte since Tayte's phone was out of action by then. The displayed time read 13:39. Bastion redialled the number, another mobile phone. This time the call rang, and after several seconds it was answered.

'Richard Fairborne,' the voice announced.

Bastion was speechless. His head buzzed with the implications. He had not expected this. Thanks to Tayte, he already knew Sir Richard Fairborne had motive enough to want Simon Phillips dead.

Now it transpired that Phillips and Sir Richard Fairborne had spoken together that very afternoon.

Bastion could still hear Sir Richard's voice in the earpiece. 'Hello...who is this?' Bastion ended the call. 'I wonder if he's got an alibi,' he said to himself. Then to McDowd he added, 'I'm bringing someone in for questioning. I need as much of this processed tonight as possible.' He reached for his radio, about to make a call that would end the celebrations at Rosemullion Hall. 'If we can place Sir Richard Fairborne at the scene, maybe we can keep him in on suspicion.' He scoffed. 'Might even get a charge out, the way things are stacking up.'

Floating adrift in the swell at Nare Cove, by the light of the dive lamp DS Hayne had thrown him when they parted company, Jefferson Tayte was on his knees, bent over the back end of the police inflatable he'd semi-appropriated from the Aquastar. He was staring in disbelief at a prop blade that looked like it would never turn again.

The timing sucked.

He reached a hand out to the prop and tugged hopelessly at the thick orange fishing line that had snagged it. He wished he had a knife. He looked back towards Porthkerris Point for the Aquastar's search light, but there was nothing. The sea and sky merged as one dark eternity. The coastline too was barely discernible in the void, and Jefferson Tayte was stuck somewhere in between. He figured Hayne must have gone further south, beyond the headland. He silently wished him better luck.

Some good I've been...

Tayte eyed the backup oars clipped to the inner walls of the inflatable. Maybe he could row along the coastline—anything would be better than just sitting there. But he realised the oars were useless.

Without a spare hand to hold the dive lamp, he wouldn't be able to see a thing. He turned back to the motor and tried to rotate the prop blade by hand to see if there was any play in it, hoping to work it loose enough to be able to turn it over more forcefully with the starter cord. It wouldn't budge. Without something sharp to cut the tangled line away, Tayte knew he'd be there until the Aquastar came back.

Out of frustration he snatched at several strands of line with both hands and began to vent his anger on them, pulling back and forth with all his weight until the pain across his fingers felt like he was close to losing them. As he let go and went to cool his hands in the salt water he saw a single strand of orange line stretching away.

His first thought was that he might be able to push the loose end back through the tangle and in doing so, gradually unravel it. It would take time, but he saw no obvious alternative. He grabbed at the stray line and pulled it clear of the water, but instead of finding a loose end, the line went taut and twanged out from the sea. It ran all the way to the cliff face.

Tayte knew his luck had just changed. He couldn't stop smiling as he unclipped an oar and began to row the inflatable awkwardly towards the cliff, following the orange fishing line with the dive lamp between his knees.

Is this what Laity was trying to say?

He recalled Bastion telling him that Laity had said something about mackerel fishing when they picked him up. *Maybe this was the line he used.*

Closer in, the swell shoved the inflatable around harder than Tayte liked, and more than once he felt the scrape of a rock beneath the inflatable's soft underbelly. The fishing line led him to a sheer wall of rock that at first he thought was literally the end of the line. Then he saw a towering split in the cliff face that he hadn't noticed before. He passed uneasily beyond it, through a tight gap that barely accommodated the craft until he vanished from the eyes of the world, hidden now behind a curtain of rock. Around him in that tight space, the sea began to break over every inch of exposed surface it touched. Salt spray soaked him, and Tayte instinctively knew that this was not a good place to linger.

The fishing line ended abruptly in the middle of a hidden pool where it sank below the water. Tayte could still feel resistance as he tugged it. It was attached to something, but he could no longer see it. He shone the dive lamp down through the water and his eyes followed the line until it dropped too deep to see. He realised then that to follow the line further he'd need the services of a diver with scuba gear.

Or some guts.

Tayte already had the dive lamp. His lungs would have to provide the oxygen. He shook his head at the idea, knowing what he had to do, yet barely able to believe he could. It was like someone else was inside his head with him, suddenly calling the shots. Only that other guy was plain crazy.

Tayte was over the side before his sensible self had a chance to argue. He drew a sharp breath against the cold water as it filled his clothes and pricked his skin. He took another, deeper breath, and then followed the dive lamp beneath the surface.

Chapter Sixty-One

Beneath the sea, without a dive mask or goggles to put any air space between his eyes and the water, Jefferson Tayte's vision was blurred. In the halogen light, he could see a white sand bed rising as it came in towards the cliff. He blinked and followed the incline to a dark slit in the rock. The orange fishing line, which seemed to glow now as he shone the dive lamp along its length, vanished again into that narrow space. He felt a twist of nervous excitement as he realised he was looking into a cave and that Amy might be on the other side. The opening looked tight. He bobbed his head up for a last breath of air before going on. Then he sank below again, following the line.

It only took a second for him to realise he might not make it through. The gap was closing. His suit began to snag and tear, and he wished he'd left his jacket in the boat. He reminded himself that he didn't even know if Amy *was* on the other side. Yet at the same time it occurred to him that someone must have fixed that fishing line in there. So he wriggled and squeezed, forcing himself further in, millimetre by millimetre it seemed, until it was suddenly all or nothing. Then a swell surged in and gave him the push he needed.

As Tayte burst through the gap, he realised the tide must still be coming in. There was still hope. He fell through the water to his hands and knees, still submerged, kicking up sand that clouded his view. He began to float and his feet scrabbled for purchase. When they found it he kicked into the sand and shot clear of the water, gasping for a long starved breath.

It was then that he saw her. 'Amy!'

At least, he thought it must be Amy. He didn't recognise her at first and she gave no response. She looked dead. Her eyes were wide and staring. Her bottom lip and what was visible above the water line of her lower jaw were moving in a perpetual shiver. Her chin was all but submerged and Tayte couldn't understand why she didn't get higher. There was still plenty of air space above her, and further into the cave it was shallow enough to see breaking water, becoming more pronounced towards the tapering end of the cave where sea foam danced with abandon over the exposed and jagged rocks.

Why doesn't she move?

Tayte surged towards her, ducking as he went. He almost had to crawl to reach her. 'Amy!' he called again. She didn't seem to notice he was there. From his jacket he pulled out the phone Bastion had loaned him. Water dripped from its insides, and the screen was tellingly blank. He dropped it, doubting he would have a signal anyway. Now that he was close to Amy, everything about her looked odd. Her body leaned forward, tilting to her left, bringing her head lower in the water than it needed to be. Dangerously low. The water brought a kiss of death to her bottom lip now, and it was rising with every surge.

Tayte set the dive lamp down on a nearby rock and took hold of Amy's shoulders. He tried to sit her up to get her head higher, but he couldn't move her. Her body felt rigid and so very cold. Then he noticed her left arm reaching out beneath the water. He held his breath and went under with the lamp. She was definitely reaching for something. He went closer until he began to make out her hand, and the Celtic ring she wore caught the light, drawing his eye. As the sand began to clear, his eyes suddenly widened. He wrenched away, coughing and spluttering and almost filling his lungs with water.

Tayte was looking into the empty eye sockets of a human skull, part buried in the sand, showing just enough to return his stare as his eyes fell upon it. Close by was a pile of small bleached bones, one with a gold ring still attached—a ring identical to Amy's. Her arm reached past them, to the stubby ends of two larger bones protruding from the sand. It looked like she was trying to pull them free and could not let go. Tayte forced her hand away and he saw movement at last as Amy's fingers autonomously clutched for the bones again, trying to re-establish the connection until, in sudden panic it seemed, she pulled away.

Amy screamed his name. 'Gabriel!'

Tayte saw her fall back into the water. He rushed in, lifting her head above the rising tide. She spluttered, coughing up sea water, thrashing in Tayte's arms.

'Hey! It's JT!' He slipped his jacket off and pushed her arms into the sleeves, holding her head steady as he locked eyes. 'Amy?' He tapped her cheeks. They felt ice cold. He cupped her face between his palms and rubbed them. 'Amy, it's me.'

Amy's brow furrowed. Then Tayte caught the faintest trace of a smile, and beyond his hopes, Amy spoke.

'Thank you,' she said, her words shivering slowly free.

Tayte returned the smile as eagerly as he knew how. 'Let's get you out of here.' He was already trying to carry her to the cave entrance, but something still restricted her.

'Chains,' Amy said.

Tayte shone the dive lamp behind her and saw the rusty quarter-inch link chain around her waist. In the lamplight he could see that it was cinched tight, secured by a heavy padlock that looked new. From the shackle he followed another length of chain that led away to either side of the rock.

'Stay with me, Amy!' he said.

He could see that she was struggling to remain conscious and it was clear that she was as much in danger of hypothermia now as she was from drowning. He propped her up against the rock, as high as the chains would allow, tilting her head back to keep her airway clear. Then he followed the chain further into the cave.

Rust had stained the granite. It looked like an ancient snake fossil, suggesting that the chain had been there for some time. The rising sand bed, more pronounced on this side, meant that he was now in shallower water. The chain was just visible above the water line, and Tayte noticed how eroded the links were. Under closer scrutiny he thought they had to be weak enough to give out with the right persuasion. If he could find a lump of rock big enough, then maybe he could break one of the links apart.

He looked around, his vision blurring as he flicked his head one way and then the other. Then his eyes fell on something he hadn't expected to see again. The writing box was at the back of the cave. The swell was playing with it, lifting it and tossing it among the rocks like a mouse at the mercy of some tireless cat. He hadn't heard its hollow clatter before over the sound of the breaking water, but now that he could see it, it yelled for his attention. The box looked damaged. The lid appeared to be loose—part hanging off. He crawled towards it, catching his knee on a rock, reminding him of his priorities.

Amy…What am I thinking?

He pulled the rock out from beneath the water and with both hands he flew at the exposed length of chain. It landed right on target, sandwiching rusty steel between hard rock and the chain exploded, sending the remaining links crashing into the water. He crawled back to Amy to find the rising water lapping at her mouth and nose. With the chain broken she was slipping forward. She seemed to stir as he caught hold of her and pulled the chain through the shackle until he was able to lift her clear.

Thank God, he thought. Then still on his knees he made for the exit with Amy cradled in his arms. His touch must have reached her. Amy's eyes very slightly and very slowly opened.

'The box,' she said, like she could read his mind.

Tayte had already dismissed the idea. 'I can't chance it,' he said. 'We need to get out of here.' He kept going.

'Please!' Amy's eyes were staring again. 'Or all of this is for nothing.'

Her words stopped Tayte in his tracks. He understood. Amy needed to know why Gabriel had been murdered, why Simon Phillips had taken her husband's life from her so abruptly and now so definitely. Tayte understood, just as he knew he owed it to Schofield to finish what he'd started. The writing box's final secret had to be told to make any sense of his bizarre few days in Cornwall. For Amy it meant everything now. They had to win unequivocally, whatever the consequences.

Ahead, Tayte could no longer see the slit in the rock; the cave entrance was completely submerged now. Getting out again would be difficult at best and to compound the problem, the chain that was still locked around Amy's waist by the padlock would act like a dive belt as soon as they hit deeper water. It would drag them both down.

One step at a time, Tayte thought. He carried Amy back, past the rock where she'd spent the worst part of the last two days, and set her down towards the back of the cave where the sand bed rose. Over a clutter of broken bottles he could see the box again. As he crawled through the tapering innermost reaches of the cave, holding his breath each time the swell washed over him, he could see that the box was definitely breaking up. Returning for it in the morning when the tide was out—a thought that had crossed his mind—was not an option.

He threw a hand out for the box as soon as it was within reach, catching the lid as the swell surged into the box and ripped the main body away. He watched the swell cast it over the rocks on a bed of frothing sea foam until it finally smashed against the back of the cave. The pieces drifted on the backwash, suddenly insignificant and unrecognisable. The box that had caused so much pain to all who encountered it was no more. A fold of paper floated among the pieces briefly—Lowenna's letter, Tayte supposed—then it dissolved in the water like wet rice paper.

Tayte's heart sank. But as he looked down at the lid in his hand—at the ivory carving of the lady reclined on a chaise—hope returned. The left edge of the lid was cracked, revealing the damp corner of another fold of paper. He tried to pull it free but it broke away as soon as he touched it. Something, however, had moved. The inner lining with the ivory rose dial slid away slightly from the carved outer piece and despite being cold and wet, he felt his palms flush.

The box was giving up its final secret.

Inside that lid Tayte was sure he would learn the truth about what happened the night the *Betsy Ross* arrived from Boston; he would know at last what really happened to Eleanor and her children. Lowenna knew, as did her father and the impostor who called himself William Fairborne. Clearly he carried that hold over James Fairborne to his grave.

Tayte hurried back to Amy, cutting his hands and knees on the bottle remnants in his haste. He took a piece as he returned, thinking about that snagged propeller blade on the incapacitated inflatable. When he reached Amy he saw no improvement; she was still that same blue-grey colour; still drifting in and out of consciousness. He held up the lid like a trophy for her to see, trying to keep her eyes open and interested. Then he slid the two sections apart and lifted out the papers that were folded in between. They were damp, but not excessively so. The space in the lid must have been tight, compressing the paper and keeping it dry. Now he just had to figure out how to keep it that way.

He flashed the dive lamp around the cave to see if there was anything suitable, thinking it ironic that of all the plastic bottles that end up floating in the sea, there was never one around when you needed one. He was starting to think that the lid itself might be the best place. It had served well enough all these years. But it was broken now. He couldn't be sure that the paper would be any good by the time he got back to the inflatable. He thought about reading it aloud to Amy, in part just to try and keep her awake; he felt sure she would have insisted if she knew there was any chance of losing it. But he suddenly saw the answer. He needed something with a waterproof guarantee and it was right there in his hand: the dive lamp.

'Hang on,' he said, studying the lamp while he could still see it. Then he switched it off and darkness was as sudden as it was absolute. He unscrewed the base of the lamp to access the rechargeable cell, slipped it out, and wrapped the papers around it. Getting the cell back in was tight, and he only knew he'd managed it when he flicked the dive lamp back on.

The first thing Tayte saw when the light returned was Amy. In the brief darkness he'd remembered her as he'd seen her that night at her house when he'd first seen the box. Now in the light again the stark contrast was too sudden a shock. Her eyes were closed tight on a still and expressionless face that was ashen as death. He pressed two fingers to her neck to check her pulse. It was slow and weak. He knew there was no way he could get her out unaided; he couldn't even keep her conscious long enough to make the exit. Then there was that chain belt to contend with. He knew what he had to do, but he didn't like it.

Tayte closed the two pieces of the writing box lid together and slipped them down the neck of his shirt. He took a last look at Amy then made for deeper water and the exit, thinking about the Aquastar and the Coastguard, knowing that help wasn't far away.

Chapter Sixty-Two

The night felt cold on Tayte's back as he tossed the dive lamp into the inflatable and climbed in after it like a struggling seal. A wave of goose bumps broke over his skin at the first hint of a barely discernible breeze, and he could only imagine what it was like for Amy. He clutched at a sore but minor gash to his stomach—a parting gesture from the jagged walls inside the tight cave entrance. He'd forgotten how choppy the water was in this enclosed space, hidden away in its own lost world behind that deep split in the cliff face. He steadied himself, and through the restricted view offered by the gap in the rocks, he looked out for any sign of Hayne and the Aquastar.

Where is he? Tayte thought.

The Aquastar's light was nowhere to be seen. His only thought then was that he had to get the inflatable running again. He had to find the help Amy so desperately needed. He felt the sharp outline of broken glass in his trouser pocket, took it out and threw himself over the back of the motor. He grabbed a handful of tangled line, and as he went to hack into it, before a single strand had been cut, he heard a promising call.

'Hello!'

The voice was close by. Tayte turned to see a mid-sized craft entering his field of vision to his left, not twenty feet away. It had no light, so he hadn't seen it before. *Bastion's call to the Coastguard,* he thought. *They must have rallied the locals.*

Tayte flashed the dive lamp across the approaching craft's canopied bow. 'I need help here!' he called. He grabbed an oar, pushed the inflatable towards the gap, and paddled through.

The other craft met him as he cleared the gap. It arrived bullishly and barely managed to stop in time. The engine sounded erratic, rising and falling in pitch and power like whoever controlled it didn't know forward from reverse. Tayte didn't much care as long as the skipper had a radio or a phone that worked. He shone his lamp onto the settling craft and confused recognition washed over him.

He was sure he knew that white boat with the walk-in bow canopy. It looked identical to Laity's fishing boat. When he shone his light into the craft, to the man he was about to greet as Amy's saviour, he knew just about everything in the picture before him was wrong. After all the surrealism he'd experienced in the past few days, the cherry had just landed on the cake. Tayte was incredulous.

We're being rescued by James Bond, for Christ's sake!

The canopy guarded the man's face, but beneath it Tayte could see the contrasting sheen of a glossy black lapel and bow tie crowding a crisp white shirt. He'd seen that attire earlier this evening on the guests at Rosemullion Hall. He knew it had no place out there tonight on a lone fishing boat of dubious identity.

As the figure stepped out from the canopy, the barrel of a silencer demanded Tayte's full attention. His eyes flicked up to a face he recognised from his first morning in Cornwall, and suddenly everything on Durgan beach fell into place. The image of Simon Phillips sprawled back in the dinghy where he'd found him flashed in Tayte's head like a single frame of subliminal advertising. *That is Laity's boat*, he thought. He figured Simon must have used it to get about in after he'd ditched the ferry, taking it to Durgan. Then it changed hands again—clearly not part of Simon's plans.

Warwick Fairborne edged closer, his gun hand brandishing the black market Bulgarian Makarov he'd acquired for the occasion, a gift from his creditors to help secure the debt. 'Sorry to see you're still running about,' he said.

Tayte eyed the gun and the nervous look on Warwick's face, registering that the two didn't mix well.

'Find anything out here?' Warwick added.

'Like what?'

'Oh, I don't know. Like a woman who probably knows as much about my family history as you do?'

Tayte swallowed hard and shook his head. 'Nah...still looking.'

'That's a shame. Still, the tide's in. I heard she'd be drawing her last breath about now anyway.'

It was clear to Tayte that Simon must have done a little plea bargaining before Warwick shot him. He wished he had something to fight back with, but a piece of broken glass against a bullet was no fair contest. All he had were words—they had served him well before.

'Don't you want to tell me all about it?' he said. 'How you're going to kill me to protect your family's interests? Anyone would have done the same, right? Survival of the fittest and all that crap!'

Warwick's smile looked uncomfortable. 'That's very amusing, Tayte, but Darwinian theory's not really my bag, and I'm afraid you'll get no megalomaniacal drawl from me about protecting my *family's* interests.' He cocked the gun like he'd practiced it a thousand times. 'This isn't personal. You're just an unfortunate side effect. A loose end in a game that's gone too far.' He levelled the gun at Tayte's chest. 'Now it's time to end it.'

A split second later, a 7.62 calibre round hit home and Jefferson Tayte fell back into the inflatable.

Chapter Sixty-Three

DCI Bastion was with Hayne's uniformed stand-in at Rosemullion Hall, company for an arrest that was now on hold. He was sitting, curled over his radio, waiting for news like an expectant father while Sir Richard and Lady Fairborne were detained in a room along the hallway.

When Bastion had arrived at Rosemullion Hall, Sir Richard had thought himself ready for him. His political years had prepared him well enough for a little police banter, and he understood his rights. He knew from Tayte's earlier visit with Hayne that the American was still alive, so that was off his conscience, and if the money had turned up and had been traced back to him, then so what? He'd get his money back. What had he done wrong? Once Sir Richard knew why Bastion was really there, however, his steely façade had buckled, and it wasn't until the policeman was partway through explaining the situation that he realised the terrible truth of what he was indirectly suggesting.

Sir Richard had moved the conversation from the entrance hall into a private room off the first floor gallery. He looked like he was scrutinising something on Bastion's face that he could barely see. 'Murder?' he said, still unable to comprehend how it was possible.

'That's right, sir,' Bastion said. 'Simon Phillips. Young lad. Works the ferry down at Helford Passage. He was shot twice in the chest. Did you know him?'

Sir Richard curled his lower lip and shook his head. 'No.' It was an honest reply.

'Well, he seems to have known you. Your mobile was the last number he called, about one-forty this afternoon. The call lasted a few minutes.'

'I was flying back from London. We were halfway through the journey by then.'

Bastion threw Sir Richard a raised eyebrow. 'I do hope you're not going to tell me it was a wrong number, sir?'

'No, I'm sure it wasn't.' Sir Richard pulled at his bow tie and let the silk unfold. He rubbed his neck as if his collar had been too tight. 'Truth is I didn't know who the caller was.'

'Anonymous, then?'

'No. Not exactly anonymous either. You see, that wasn't the first call.' Sir Richard paused, still unsure whether he was ready to unleash the nightmare he knew would follow if he continued.

'Go on, sir.'

Sir Richard took the deepest breath of his life and sighed. Then he said, 'I was being blackmailed.'

It was out.

Bastion shifted in his seat, his brows rising as though to the welcome ring of familiarity.

'I was at Durgan tonight making a payoff,' Sir Richard said. 'A man called a few days ago. Said he had information that would destroy my career—perhaps even my family. He sent proof. Part of it, at least.'

'James Fairborne's last will and testament?' Bastion said. He looked proud of himself.

Sir Richard nodded. It surprised him that Bastion knew, but it eased the pressure of talking about it. 'I couldn't afford the scandal,' he said, 'even if the implication was a lie. I suppose it will all be looked into now anyway?'

'I couldn't say just now, sir,' Bastion said. He turned the conversation back to the beach at Durgan. 'So you dropped the money off and left, did you?'

'That's right. I was there no more than five minutes. Did you recover the suitcase?'

'Suitcase, sir? We found no suitcase. Just Mr Phillips's body.'

No suitcase, Sir Richard thought.

'Did anyone else know about this payoff?' Bastion asked.

And there it was.

Warwick knew. And I've led the police to him.

No one had seen Warwick since the guests began to arrive at Rosemullion Hall. It was clear to Sir Richard that Warwick must have followed him to Durgan, that he'd waited for the blackmailer to show. Then he'd killed him to protect his future and taken the money to clear his debts. Sir Richard might have played things down even now, suggesting that the blackmailer might have had an accomplice who'd turned on him. But with Tayte still alive and Warwick on the loose, he understood that Warwick could not let Tayte live now he'd gone so far.

And it was all *his* fault. He could see it no other way. *Systems fail. Sir Richard Fairborne does not.* He knew that maxim now for the lie it was. He'd failed his son. Every bitter discourse between them had pushed Warwick further away. And now it had pushed him to this. He knew he had to end it before anyone else was killed.

'Where is Mr Tayte?' he asked.

Bastion related Amy's situation. 'And Mr Tayte's out with my sergeant looking for her now,' he finished.

'I believe they're both in danger,' Sir Richard said.

———

Soon after the conversation ended, a high-speed police response rigid inflatable boat launched out of Falmouth. It cleared Falmouth

Bay and passed the mouth of the Helford River in under two minutes, heading for a rendezvous with the Aquastar. Hayne had told them they should expect to find Tayte somewhere in between, and the bright beam of Tayte's dive lamp had been easy to locate. But the situation was already hot as they came in sight of him.

Now, in a room off the first floor gallery at Rosemullion Hall, the radio Bastion was cradled over suddenly crackled into life. 'We have confirmation, sir. The subject has been taken down.'

Bastion sank his head into his hands. 'Thank you,' he said, though he wasn't sure he meant it. It was not the result he was hoping for. It never was to his mind, regardless of the things people did that led to the need for an armed response unit. He'd promised Sir Richard that they would, as always, use as little force as was deemed necessary.

They would have had no other option, Bastion told himself as he left the room to tell Sir Richard and Lady Fairborne that their son was dead, killed long distance by a 7.62 calibre sniper round.

Chapter Sixty-Four

As the bullet hit its mark at Nare Cove with a dull thump, Jefferson Tayte fell back into the inflatable. He watched the impact explode from Warwick's chest, staggering the man forward, jerking his gun closer, and the shock of Warwick's sudden advance under those heightened circumstances sent Tayte reeling and tripping over the seat board. Were it not for the blood spattering off Warwick's dinner jacket, Tayte would have been checking himself for holes. As it was, Warwick's plans had been terminally interrupted before he'd squeezed out a single shot.

The gun fell to Warwick's side like it was suddenly too heavy to hold. Tayte heard it clatter onto the deck with focused clarity as he watched the nervous grin on his adversary's face turn to disbelief. His wide eyes stared at Tayte, lost and child-like in the lamplight. Then Warwick dropped, and Tayte didn't know if he was shaking more from the cold or the shock. As he sat up he saw a searchlight off to his right; the Aquastar had turned the point. To his left, the rapid response RIB approached, skimming another bright light low over the water.

—⁀—

Within twenty minutes Tayte was sitting in the RIB with two grey blankets around him. He was watching Amy being winched like a giant foil wrapped sub sandwich into a pillar-box red air ambulance. She was still alive, but it was too soon to tell how the next few hours would go; too soon to know if any damage had been done. Her core temperature had dropped dangerously low.

DS Hayne was with him. 'She's in good hands,' he said as the helicopter dipped its nose and headed back.

Tayte nodded. He believed him. Amy would get the care she needed now. He watched until the helicopter banked inland and passed out of sight. Then he turned an absent gaze back past the Aquastar to the cave that could so easily have claimed her. Police divers were still in the water and Tayte knew they couldn't have done a better job. With all the gear and their expertise, they made getting Amy out of there look easy. Tayte knew it wasn't. Now that Gabriel was off the missing person's list, the cave was yet another crime scene. The divers would be there a while, Tayte supposed, as the RIB fired up.

'Are you going to keep that torch, too?' Hayne asked, indicating the dive lamp.

Tayte returned his smile. The dive lamp had become such a part of him that he almost forgot he was still holding it. He studied it briefly, relaxing his grip at last, knowing what was inside. 'Can I?' he said.

'I'd expect a good reason. Like super glue or something.'

'Super glue,' Tayte repeated. He nodded. 'Yeah, you could say there's a bond between us that can't be broken just yet.'

Hayne shook his head. 'Don't tell the Chief, will you?'

———

A growing assortment of craft had gathered in the bay at Nare Cove, a community of well-intending locals who had come out from the river to help if they could. At the head of the fleet, Martin Cole watched the proceedings with renewed hope. He'd been among the first there, close behind the Coastguard, which by now had stood down. Martin had spearheaded the recruitment of volunteers as soon as he'd heard about Amy. But it had taken time for word to get around.

He lit a roll-up and watched the RIB approach the anxious gathering. His eyes were on the man in the grey blankets, and he knew he had a lot to thank him for. As he caught Tayte's eye and subtle nod of recognition, Martin raised his hands above his head and slowly began to clap until that one gesture was joined by many—and then the RIB was gone.

Chapter Sixty-Five

Sunday.

It was mid-morning when Jefferson Tayte returned to the Royal Cornwall Hospital in Truro. After watching the air ambulance rush Amy away from Nare Cove little more than twelve hours ago, the police RIB had taken him to Helford Passage where Hayne's car waited to take him the rest of the way to the hospital himself. More clean dressings for his earlier wounds and another to cover the gash on his stomach saw Tayte heading for his bed, but not before he'd stuck around long enough to learn that Amy was out of danger. He'd left knowing that she was expected to make a full and speedy recovery.

Tayte was looking across the hospital bed in Tom Laity's room at the evidence of that recovery now. He watched Amy smile again. Then he looked at Laity sitting up in bed and he was scarcely able to believe the scene possible. Beside him on the floor, his tired cases were packed and ready to go home with him, but not before he'd concluded his business in Cornwall.

The dive lamp already had their attention. Tayte had watched their eyes flitting to and from it all through his update on what had happened since he'd last seen them. Then Laity told him how he'd followed the launch until he'd lost sight of it, only to see it again as it came out from the cover of the cliffs a short while later.

'When I thought the coast was clear,' Laity said, 'I went in for a closer look.'

'I couldn't believe it,' Amy said. 'I thought Simon had come back, but there was Tom Laity. I was saved.' She frowned. 'Or so I thought.'

'He must have spotted me,' Laity said. He put a hand to the wound on his head. 'He came at me while I was busy trying to free Amy; thumped me with a rock and left me for dead.'

'I thought you *were* dead,' Amy said.

Laity chuckled. 'I'm made of tougher stuff than that.'

'What was the deal with that fishing line?' Tayte asked.

Laity chuckled. 'The rising tide must have brought me round,' he said. 'I crawled over to Amy and pulled a reel from my pocket: bright orange line I use for mackerel. When Amy tied it off I half swam, half floated out. I must have got separated from the line, drifting until that fishing boat picked me up.'

'Knots aren't really my thing,' Amy said in her defence.

'Well, I'm glad things turned out okay,' Tayte said. He lifted the dive lamp from his lap at last, refocusing their attention. 'I couldn't open it,' he said, thinking how he'd wrestled with his conscience all night, contemplating the lamp and its contents until its image was burnt on his retina like a bright object stared at too long. 'It didn't seem right somehow,' he added. 'Not after all you've been through.'

Amy didn't recognise the lamp from her ordeal in the cave, and beyond his fixed smile Laity just looked confused.

'The box was destroyed in the cave,' Tayte added. 'The lid's in my briefcase, but that's all there is.' He imparted a knowing smile. 'Apart from what I found inside the lid. That's now in here.' He tapped the dive lamp.

'Answers?' Amy said.

Tayte nodded. His hands were shaking with anticipation as he unscrewed the base of the lamp. 'I hope so,' he said.

The cell pack was tight inside. Tayte took a pen from his jacket pocket and prised it free, and as it fell onto his lap, the papers un-furled. He studied them, carefully separating the pages, taking his time now the moment had arrived. There were two different types of paper: two letters. The first was thick and rough to the touch. Its edges were tattered, and the words were blurred and smudged in places. It was dated October 23, 1783—the day the *Betsy Ross* went down.

Tayte's palms were sweating again. He read out the title on the first page: 'Journal of Katherine Fairborne.' He bowed his head and silently followed the words, noting that the style changed part way through. It looked suddenly rushed and the smudges became more frequent. He took a deep breath. 'Here goes then,' he said.

It is early evening and we are caught between a raging sky and a tumultuous sea as we reach our destination at last. It is dark as midnight in a place without moon or stars, giving no distinction to our eyes. Yet hope greets us in the form of a single light in the darkness, another ship that Captain Grainger hopes we may follow into Falmouth, skippered perhaps by one who may better know these waters.

Tayte paused. A long sigh slipped unheard from his lips as his eyes scanned ahead, though what he read next he already knew.

Disaster! We have run aground! Such a crack shook the cabin that I can only believe the hull has split in two. The Betsy Ross *is listing. We are taking on water.*

Tayte's mood darkened with every word, reflecting Katherine's anguish like he was aboard the *Betsy Ross* with her in its last moments. He continued to read the journal.

Mother is fussing over Clara and is greatly concerned for her condition. Little George clings to her like a limpet, and Laura has curled into a tight ball beside me. I fear that panic is upon us all.

Tayte had trouble reading the next line. The paper was folded through it, distorting the words. He flattened the sheet and then slowly determined each word until he could make sense of it.

Father has come for us. One by one we are leaving what must otherwise become our watery tomb...

October 23, 1783. Aboard the *Betsy Ross*, off Godrevy Cove, Cornwall.

The hatch burst open and Katherine watched her father slide down the ladder rails, bringing all the elements into the great cabin with him.

'Quickly!' he called. 'On deck, all of you. She's going down!'

Katherine was sitting in shadow at the back of the cabin, recording the scene of fear and panic as the rest of her family cleared their cramped accommodation. Her father went last, and she did not run after him. Not yet. The lamp was still lit and secure on the table. She had to get all of this down while there was still time, and she was nearly done.

The brig lurched again, creaking and cracking around her. The hatch flapped and banged, loose in the vicious wind, adding to the chaos. Then the cabin's rear wall suddenly split across and the wind ravaged the timbers, opening up the room like it was nothing more than a paper bag.

It brought Katherine to her senses.

She grabbed the box, threw her quill and journal inside, and ran for the ladder. 'Wait!' she called. She felt her heart begin to pound in her chest, quickening her breath as if she had suddenly emerged from the story she was writing and knew how it would end. She reached for the rails as another crack ripped across the cabin and knocked her to the floor. The brig was breaking up. She had to get out. She tried to stand, but could only watch in horror as the ladder broke away and fell towards her, smashing into the table and throwing the room into darkness.

The *Betsy Ross* was disintegrating rapidly with every tidal assault that came in regular foaming barrages of such destructive might that the 110-ton vessel had no more strength against it than if it were made of balsa wood. In the darkness inside the great cabin, Katherine began to pick out distant and unfamiliar voices over the panic of her family and the brig's crew who by now were clear of the wreck. She scrabbled to the gap where the timbers had earlier cracked open, knowing only that she had to get out before the brig suffered further damage or was washed off the rocks and down into the depths, where she knew it would ultimately rest.

Has help arrived already? she wondered.

There was little to see in the continuing darkness outside. She was aware of people in the water, though, and of others clinging to the rocks. She thought she heard her mother crying for a moment, but the lashing wind carried the sound off again all too soon to be certain. Then a light caught her eye, drawing her gaze away from the rocks beyond the shoreline. There was a house. A light blazed in the window. Had they seen the vessel in danger and raised the alarm?

As Katherine's eyes became accustomed to the dark, she began to notice other lights, small and distant, between the house and the rocks. They were drawing closer. She clapped her hands and smiled. 'We are saved!' she called for the benefit of anyone beyond the wreck who might hear her. She swung a leg awkwardly through the opening, catching her loose undergarments and wishing then that she had taken to dressing more like the crew as Laura had since their first week at sea.

Katherine cursed and tugged at the pathetically inappropriate costume she wore, which was as pink as her first blush at meeting the man she had since worn it for. She despised herself now for allowing herself such arrogant vanity.

And where is my helmsman now? she wondered. *Where is Jack when I need a strong arm to lift me down and help me safely ashore?*

She pulled at the material again, harder this time, until it tore away, unsteadying her to the extent that she nearly fell into the sea below. The brief sight of spitting sea foam as she tipped over told her she would have to time her exit well. There were rocks below, and the wreck was shifting and tilting in time with each new crescendo of waves. It would be difficult to miss them.

The lights were at the shoreline now, several figures with lanterns held out before them, giving each an isolated glow in the darkness, like spectres come-a-haunting. She watched one of the lanterns throw its light onto a crew member as he made it to shore. Then in that same moment she became both confused and horrified. She clasped a hand to her mouth to silence any scream that dared to rise, unable to take in the truth of what she had just seen.

The subsequent violent blows, however, served well to convince her. Katherine looked on, terrified as the helpless man was beaten repeatedly with what looked like the rough form of a rock; he was beaten back into the sand as he tried hopelessly to claw himself to his feet. She watched it all unfold by the light of that single lantern, like a spotlight on the stage of some macabre play.

Several more lanterns quickly joined the first, lighting the entire stage as another of the crew rose exhausted from the sea, apparently unaware of his shipmate's end. The sailor's arms were extended to the gang, clearly mistaking them for their saviours as Katherine had. She watched a brute of a man leave the pack then, charging and splashing into the sea with enthusiasm, dwarfing the company around him and carrying no rock or blunt implement other than his own clenched fists, which he brought down onto the crewman's shoulders, smashing him to his knees. Then the brute held him by the throat under the dark water until he was still.

Katherine could not move. Her eyes followed another man as he stepped out from the gathering, another goliath whose hands punched the air above him, demanding attention.

'Remember!' the man cried. 'Only by drowning or beating. No blades. It must appear as if the sea took them.'

A cheer went up from the gathering, displaying in their raised hands an assortment of bludgeons. Then the gang broke, spreading light along the shore again and into the sea as each man searched for the next victim.

Katherine at last fell back into the cabin. Her hands were shaking as she found the table and laid her writing box down. She fumbled around the edges in darkness, feeling for the drawer where she knew the tinderbox and spare candles were kept. She had to record what she had witnessed, and it occurred to her now that the light the crew had been so exultant to see as they came through the Channel was no ship at all, but the light of the wreckers who had succeeded in bringing them onto the rocks.

Her hand caught against the drawer handle. She opened it and removed a brass tinderbox and a single candle. On the fourth strike the dry shreds of hemp caught, and when the candle was fixed and glowing, Katherine opened her writing box and took up her quill. Before dipping into the ink, she went back to the opening to gauge how long she might have. She knew the light would draw attention. She would have to be quick.

Quicker than she hoped.

A small boat was in the water now. Several lamps were lit aboard it. They were coming to the rocks—to the *Betsy Ross*. Ahead of it she noticed that others from the gang had already made their way around the rocks at the base of the shoreline cliffs. Lanterns danced and bludgeons fell and she knew that all hope was surely lost for herself and for her family. She thought of her mother, kind as a saint, then of Laura and whether she had been a good sister to her. She had to fight to hold back her tears. Then unsolicited images of little George forced themselves into her head and sent those tears flowing unrestricted until she could do no more than bury her head in the ruffles of her gown.

When she looked up again the small boat was closer, but its advance had stopped. It pitched and rolled on confused waves that seemed to have no respect for nature, flowing into the shore and out from the rocks in all directions.

It was then that Katherine saw why the boat had stopped. A man was being pulled from the sea, a man she knew and loved so well. It was her father, James Fairborne. She looked away as the first rock struck him. Then every arm on that boat rose and fell like hammers striking a blacksmith's anvil.

'Father!' she called, ready to jump to his aid and to her certain death. But she knew she could not. She knew only that she had to record what she had witnessed. She ran back to the table and hurriedly began to write, smudging the words with her tears.

.

Chapter Sixty-Six

Tayte stopped reading. He looked up through troubled eyes, first to Amy, and then to Tom. 'My father is dead!' he read again.

Amy got up and read it for herself. 'That can't be right.'

Tayte could scarcely believe it either. 'You don't make up stuff like this,' he said. It wasn't the answer he expected to find, but he could not refute it. He expected to learn that James Fairborne had set up the whole thing, only to spend the rest of his days living in fear of someone finding out, finding Katherine's writing box and the iniquitous secret it harboured.

'So they were *all* murdered that night,' Amy said.

'Wreckers!' Laity added, flashing his eyes.

'More than that,' Tayte said. 'They took everything James Fairborne had: his life, his family, and his identity.'

The answer to the mystery surrounding the sole benefactor named in James Fairborne's last will and testament was suddenly clear. Tayte understood now that they were both impostors, the man who had called himself James Fairborne *and* the man who claimed to be his brother. They had stolen their fortune through their own murderous machinations and taken all necessary precaution via the will to ensure that their lie perpetuated beyond their own lives.

Tayte turned back to the letters and read on. 'My father is dead! Now the candle has drawn them, but they are no weak moths come to perish by its flame. I hear their boots on the boards above me now. They are here for me.' He stopped reading. 'That's all there is,' he said, wondering as he supposed everyone else was how the rest of the Fairborne family had died.

In 1783, Katherine's words were written with no time to spare. She tore the pages from her journal and sealed them tight into the box's lid. She had barely finished putting the box back together when a bearded face that was wild and hateful as the night appeared inverted at the hatch.

'What's this?' the man said.

He forced a menacing grin, obviously pleased with his find. Katherine saw his boots dangle in, quickly followed by the rest of him as he dropped heavily through the hatch and sprang to his feet. His grin remained, though changed now to a leer as he eyed her up and down like she was some prize he'd just won.

'And you dressed up for us,' he said, circling the table as Katherine edged back towards the opening. 'Very pretty you look, too,' he added. He lunged for her and laughed as she flinched away. Then as she made towards the opening, he blocked her, pinning her to one of the bunks. 'This is a little extra the boss didn't say about.'

Katherine could find no words, useless as she knew they would be. She kicked and lashed out, but she was no match for him. She felt him pull her closer, pressing himself against her. She heard her dress rip and felt the tug at her chest. Then the man was drooling, so close to her that she could taste his stale tobacco. She was barely aware of the second man who dropped in through the hatch.

Her attacker reeled and bellowed, 'Get in line! I go first!'

'This says otherwise!'

A wooden beam connected with his head and he fell aside like a discarded rag.

Katherine found herself staring into Jack's eyes. Her helmsman *had* come for her. He grabbed her by the wrist and pulled her from the bunk—pulled her into his arms and held her there for as long as he dared. A moment later he pushed her towards the opening.

'Go!' he said, and his eyes begged her to obey. Above them, the sound of heavy footfalls rattled the planks as the wreckers scurried over the ship like the rats they were.

Katherine was shaking her head as she retreated, still clutching the box, unable to bear the idea of parting with Jack again so soon, unable to suffer the thought of what might happen to him if he stayed. She reached the opening and he turned away from her at last, distracted. 'Please!' he said.

And Katherine was falling.

———

She had no idea how she came to the shore, or even why she was still breathing. Katherine felt she had no right to either, but the sensation of wet sand tickling through her fingers was as welcome as any pillow after a long and arduous day.

Jack...

Her delusion of being somewhere else was over. Katherine rolled weakly in the sand and looked back to the *Betsy Ross,* knowing in her heart that her helmsman could not have made it. The brig was awash with lamplight, as were the exposed rocks. The wreckers had all but finished their night's devilry.

Are they all out there? she wondered.

The lanterns were as many as she'd seen all night. She considered her chances, remembering the house she'd seen earlier with the light blazing in the window. Was there any hope that she could raise the alarm? She turned away from the wreck to look for that light again and knew at once that all hope was lost.

A lantern approached along the shore, another was close behind. Between her and the first lantern a body drifted face down, not six feet from her, floating lifeless with the surging tide, catching in the sand as the waves receded, and then washing further in as they returned. *Another poor soul from the crew,* Katherine thought from the attire, knowing her own end was close. But the body was too small, the hair too long and too familiar. It was Laura.

Katherine made no effort to rise from the sand as the first figure approached. She was too weak to struggle, physically and emotionally. What hope did she have against the brute of a man who came out from behind his lantern and dragged her from the edge of the sea by her hair? She made no sound, despite the pain. Her writing box tumbled at last from the folds of her soaked gown and spilled its contents onto the shore, washing ink into the sand, black as his blood.

The brute stooped to retrieve it, admiring it.

'Let me go,' Katherine pleaded at last. 'Take the box. I give it to you.'

The brute smiled. He snapped the lid shut and then took her supple young neck in one calloused hand and wrenched her closer. 'It is already mine!' he seethed.

The other lantern arrived in time to stay his brutality. 'Do not tarry here,' the second man ordered. He stepped into the light and the hand around Katherine's neck dropped her, as a hunting dog drops game at its master's feet.

'Bring me James Fairborne's body,' the man ordered. 'It must never be found.'

The brute turned away and his master caught his arm. 'What's this?' His eyes were on the box. 'Nothing leaves the beach! I made that very clear.' He snatched the box away, admiring it as he turned it in his hand.

The brute's back was to him now. His shoulders slumped as he made off.

'No witnesses!' his master called after him. 'Not a soul,' he added, as though affirming some previous assignation. He admired the box again and without taking his eyes from it, he said, 'And when I am found in your father's place, battered and close to death myself, this will make a fitting trinket to be clutching. Something precious to me, James Fairborne, after the sea has claimed all else.'

His eyes lowered and fixed on the edge of Katherine's gown, washed into the sand at his feet. He followed the flowing lines only so far, never once looking upon her face. Then he forced her prone and Katherine felt his heavy boot on the back of her head, pressing her face into the sand until her muffled cry fell silent and her thrashing body at last accepted death's cold embrace.

Chapter Sixty-Seven

Jefferson Tayte shook his head, thinking about the ill-fated Fairborne family, wondering how anyone could conceive such a murderous plan, let alone carry it through.

'Who did this?'

He placed Katherine's journal extracts onto the bed and saw that Amy shared his anger and that Laity's smile had succumbed to glistening eyes. Tayte held up the remaining pages. The writing was clear, the paper otherwise unmarked.

'Maybe the answer's in here,' he said.

The letter, signed by Lowenna, was dated Monday, May 16, 1803—the day before Mawgan Hendry was murdered. Tayte cleared his throat and continued.

That my father is not the man he claims to be, I am certain. That James Fairborne was murdered even before he reached Cornwall's shores in 1783, I have no doubt. These past few days have left me guessing as to who I really am, although I surely have no right to call myself Fairborne. Today, just one day after discovering that Katherine's journal bore a startling truth, I have learnt enough of my father's past to give us both our rightful name.

Since hearing my father breathe the lie that would have me believe that Katherine Fairborne was his daughter—after reading in Katherine's own hand that she had witnessed the murder of her real father—I had determined to make my own plans to protect my future and that of my as yet unborn child. Success would lie in simplicity. I would again become congenial and conform to my father's wishes. I would go about my routine as though the episode that passed between us after yesterday's morning ride had been nothing more than childish folly.

The following morning I returned to the stables in search of my father. In place of my usual riding breeches and tunic, I wore my brightest yellow gown and an even brighter smile for his benefit. But I was late—or rather he appeared to have gone out early. His mare was away and although not to my devise, I was happy to see Gwinear standing alone, happy that I had been spared the morning ride. I had at least made my appearance at the expected time, and I would be there feigning disappointment when he returned.

But the scene today was not quite correct, and it was not until I first began to hear those heavy hooves returning that I realised why. The stableboy was nowhere to be seen. My father would have taken the skin off his back had he not been there to take his reins. Where was he? The answer came to me as unannounced and as unwelcome as the onset of a fever. It came in the brutish form of the man in my father's pay as he appeared beside the stable, striding out to meet my father in the stableboy's stead.

Why I could not stand my ground against him I do not know. I knew him then as nothing more than a servant of my father's, although his duties were never known to me and he was rarely seen. We have never been introduced and we have never spoken. And yet I know very well why I fled, tumbling into the cover of hay at the back of the stable. To look upon that man at such close quarter is to become irrational with fear. As it transpired, this was to be to my advantage.

I lay there, hidden in the confusion of hay and the folds of my yellow dress, praying that he had neither seen nor heard me. Then as I looked out to see the brute greet my father's return, I knew that my prayer had been answered. I watched my father dismount and walk with his mare as it was led towards me, and I dared not stir in my cover *for fear of my life if I were discovered. From that place of hiding I came to discover my father's true identity and the reason my father kept this disagreeable brute of a servant so close at hand.*

That morning in May 1803, as Lowenna lay tangled in hay and still as death itself, her senses sharpened. She watched and she listened as the larger of the two men spoke first, their voices hushed beneath the morning birdsong. He was clearly agitated.

'I tell you, if she knows anything of Katherine Fairborne then she already knows too much!'

'She knows nothing!'

The brute scoffed. 'Good living has softened your head, Ervan.'

Lowenna saw the rage flare in her father's cheeks. 'Do not speak that name here,' he said. 'Do not speak it anywhere!'

'And why not? Are you so ashamed of it already?'

'It is a past best forgotten, that is all.'

The brute's head sank to his chest, slowly shaking as though denying his own ears. 'What happened to us? Men once feared our name.' His head shot up again and their eyes locked. 'Look at us now,' he said. 'You, a respectable *gentleman,* and me...What am I Ervan? Tell me, brother. What have *I* become?'

Lowenna's father fell silent and she sensed the temper welling inside him; she knew it well enough.

'I am nothing,' the brute continued, heaving himself closer. 'I am a shadow, more now than I was when I could proudly call myself Breward Kinsey.'

Lowenna startled in her cover then as she watched her father let loose his rage.

'You go too far!' he said, his voice no longer hushed as he charged the brute with his fists and pinned him to a support beam. Lowenna was surprised to see no retaliation. The brute appeared suddenly submissive, like a child, though he had every advantage in size and strength.

'Did I not look after you?' her father said. 'Have I not told you that your time will come?'

The brute shifted against the beam as though to shake himself free of the situation. 'It already comes too late!' he said.

Lowenna saw her father push himself away then. His muscles relaxed and his hands reached up to the brute's rough face, cupping his jaw. 'Have I not always looked after you?' he said. 'Or have you forgotten how it was with our own father?'

Breward Kinsey began to shake his head.

'Has your mind locked away those vile times since our mother died, perhaps to spare your pain?' Ervan added.

'I remember them too well.'

'As do I.' Ervan Kinsey brought his face close to his brother's so there could be no distraction between them. 'I killed him for you, Breward. I killed him with these very hands to end your suffering at his. And I've been there for you ever since that day—since we fled into hiding.'

Breward nodded.

'Well, I was sick of hiding,' Ervan said.

The brute was quick to return. 'And how do you think I felt all these years? How do you think I *still* feel?'

'The plan was laid out and agreed,' Ervan said. 'And you must continue to wait for your time. Do not forget why we have done this, Breward. It was never about us. It was all for our children, so they might have everything in their lives that we did not. You will be provided for, and your children will reap the rewards along with mine after we are but bones in the ground, and the legend of our former lives is nothing more than a whisper in the dark or a puff of smoke from the pipes of men too afraid to speak of it.'

'You preach so proudly of your plans, Ervan,' Breward said. He threw his weight off the beam at last, forcing his brother back. 'But your plans are for nothing if the truth is uncovered. How do you suppose your daughter has come to know of Katherine?'

Ervan was silent. Then he said, 'I have not spoken Katherine's name to a living soul.'

'And what of the crypt?' Breward asked. 'Have you been careless with the key? Has she uncovered their headstones, perhaps?'

Ervan denied the possibility with a firm shake of his head. 'The place remains sealed.'

'Then how? What has she discovered to put that accursed name on her lips?' Breward looked suddenly wary. 'Tell me everything from that ship went down with her. I remember your own words well enough. Nothing leaves the beach, you said. Tell me nothing did.'

Ervan Kinsey fell silent, his head bowed. 'The box,' he said. 'I kept the box for myself, and I gave it to Lowenna on her fifth birthday. I should have listened better to my instincts.'

Breward turned away, pacing towards the back of the stable, to the pile of hay where Lowenna was hiding. He stopped at the edge, staring into space. A moment later he turned on his heels. 'Then she knows,' he said.

'We cannot be sure of *what* she knows.'

'Then you must ask her. Force her to tell you what she has learnt from that box.'

'And if she knew nothing before, she will surely know plenty after I have questioned her.'

'She must be silenced,' Breward said. 'I cannot live like this for another day unless I can be sure of my reward at the end of it.'

Lowenna watched her father come at Breward again with a raised finger stabbing like a dagger at his heart. 'If any harm comes to my daughter, you will get nothing!' Ervan said. 'And your children will get nothing!' he added. 'Do you understand? Lowenna will not be harmed!'

Lowenna watched her father turn away then, anger forcing his pace as he made towards the house. The brute's nod acquiesced agreement, but as soon as her father was beyond earshot, his features darkened to contradict.

'You are not the brother I once knew,' Lowenna heard him say. 'You have grown as soft as the bed linen you have become accustomed to.'

She watched him take a steel horseshoe in his hands, twisting it until it snapped in two. 'My blood will prevail, brother,' he said. 'Not yours.'

Chapter Sixty-Eight

The nurse at the door reminded Tayte that Tom Laity was still under the hospital's close care. 'Your consultant's on his rounds,' she said to Laity. Then to Tayte and Amy she wrinkled her nose and said, 'You've got a few minutes.'

'Thank you,' Amy said.

Tayte was still bowed over the story that had waited more than two hundred years to be told. *Now lie with them in death,* he thought, recalling the inscription on the sarcophagus that was hidden inside the Fairborne mausoleum. It made perfect sense to him now. Ervan Kinsey had lived James Fairborne's life, and his brother, as some final act of retribution, had made sure he would remain with them in death.

'So these Kinsey brothers,' Laity said. 'Surely they had to know the ship was coming?'

Tayte looked up from the letters. 'Falmouth was a busy port back then,' he said. 'Plenty of traffic coming and going, and it wouldn't have been difficult to access the registers—they were clearly very persuasive people.'

'But how could they have known who these people were in the first place?'

'That would have been easier still. News of a wealthy family fleeing war-torn America and arriving to take up residence on such a valuable estate in Cornwall would have been hard to keep a lid on.

And he arrived to a baronetcy, don't forget. That would have been widely discussed in a tight-knit place like this.'

'But surely they were leaving a lot to chance,' Amy said. 'Lady Luck would have had to play her part.'

Tayte thought about it. 'Maybe luck did play its part. You never hear about the ones that get away,' he said. 'They might have tried before, and they might have kept trying if this hadn't come good for them.' It occurred to him then that the year the *Betsy Ross* came to England was familiar to him for other reasons. 'They left Boston in 1783,' he mused. Then it registered. 'That was also the year of the Laki eruption in Iceland.'

Blank faces told him he would have to elaborate. 'You'd be surprised how many of my British assignment trails turn up a death record for that year. They reckon when Mount Laki erupted, it killed twenty-three thousand people in Britain alone from airborne sulphur dioxide poisoning. It had a crazy effect on the weather here, too. Raging thunderstorms and a lingering haze that reports say made the sun look blood red. I don't know how long the haze lasted, but I read that there were hailstones that year big enough to kill cattle. Taking a gamble that an arriving ship would hit a bad storm in the latter half of 1783 was a pretty safe bet.'

'And the rest was easy for them,' Laity said.

Tayte agreed. 'I'm sure they knew a thing or two about the wrecking business, and you've sure got the rocks for it around this coastline.'

The nurse appeared at the door again. This time an entourage of white coats accompanied her.

Tayte got up, slipped the letters into his briefcase, and shook Laity's hand. 'Well, thanks for everything,' he said. He collected his cases and the dive lamp he'd promised to return to DS Hayne, then he followed Amy into the corridor.

'When are they letting you out?' he asked her once Laity's door had closed.

'Soon, I hope,' Amy replied. 'I expect they'll be in to see me next. Better get into bed quick!' She feigned an exaggerated sprint to her room a few doors down, then turned back and laughed.

Tayte found her smile pleasantly contagious, even in that green hospital gown.

They passed the door to her room and walked together along a busy corridor, passing a medley of medical staff talking into their patient reports. The pace was deliberately slow.

'So how are you coping?' Tayte said. He began to fish around in his pocket for something. 'Finding your husband, I mean. I know you don't remember much about what happened in that cave last night.'

Amy took a moment to think about it. Then she said, 'At least now I know.'

Tayte's hand fell onto what he was looking for. 'I knew you'd want this,' he said. He held out a gold ring: Gabriel's matching Celtic wedding band.

Amy smiled as she took it. 'We'll have a small service for Gabriel when everything's settled down. I suppose there'll be an inquest.'

'I think that's usual,' Tayte said. 'Sorry I can't stick around.'

Amy nodded as though she would have liked that.

'So what are your plans?' Tayte asked. 'Might seem a little dull around here after all this.'

'You mean after you've gone?' Amy said.

Tayte laughed. 'I didn't say that.'

'You might as well have,' Amy said. 'And it wouldn't be far from the truth. Hey, I bet the police will be glad for the rest.'

Tayte laughed again and knew then that he would miss Amy as soon as he left. 'What about the ferry business?' he asked. 'You gonna keep at it?'

Amy shook her head. 'No. Too many memories. But it's the good ones I'll be running away from.'

'Where will you go?'

Amy shrugged her shoulders. 'I've no idea. It'll take a while to sell up. That'll give me some time to think. I guess I just want to pick up my life again. Move on, you know.' She stopped in her tracks and locked eyes with Tayte. 'I think I can do that now,' she said. Her eyes narrowed. 'Did I thank you yet?'

'I'm sure you did,' Tayte said. 'There's really no—'

Before he could finish, Amy put her hands on his shoulders, rose up onto her toes, and kissed him. 'Thanks.'

Tayte's whole face felt like it was on fire. 'Got any hobbies?' he said, changing the subject. 'Anything to distract yourself with?'

'I might take up fishing,' Amy said, settling back into a lazy stride. Tayte scoffed.

'No, really. I promised Tom he could take me out in his boat again when he's ready. And if I know Tom, that should get him up and about again pretty quickly.' Amy eyed Tayte's packed cases for the umpteenth time. 'And what about you?' she said. 'Your assignment's all wrapped up, I suppose.'

Tayte nodded. 'Pretty conclusively. I came here to find James Fairborne's family, and now I can put a big line under 1783 for all of them, including James. I'm booked on a flight out of London later today. That gives me the whole of tomorrow free to tidy up my work before the deadline.'

'How will your client's family take the news?'

'Oh, they'll be sorry to hear they've no living family in England, that's for sure.' Tayte recalled some of the emotional scenes he'd started in the past. 'I expect there'll be a few tears shed when they hear what I've got to tell them. It doesn't seem to matter how long ago a thing like this happened. If they were family, you feel for them—especially when children are involved. It's almost like time slips out of the equation briefly, and you're telling them about their own.' He reflected on those poor Fairborne children: their unfulfilled expectations, their unimaginable terror. 'Mind you,' he added, 'I should think Walter Sloane will cheer up when I drop the letters proving all this on his lap. The probate record names William Fairborne sole beneficiary. I think his real descendants have a good deal of money owed them.'

Amy went quiet. Then she said, 'It'll destroy the family here, of course.'

Tayte nodded. 'I guess it will.'

'And it's not like they had anything to do with those terrible things that happened all those years ago.'

Tayte agreed. Generations of false Fairbornes had come and gone, oblivious to the origins of their wealth. And by all accounts they'd made a good show of it until now—until Breward Kinsey's seed had risen again in Warwick.

'Ironic, isn't it?' Amy said.

'How do you mean?'

'Well, that's just what Simon Phillips wanted.'

Tayte hadn't thought of it like that.

They arrived at a set of double doors that led out into the main waiting area. Tayte could see DS Hayne sitting on the other side. He hadn't spotted them yet. *So soon,* he thought. He checked the time and noted that his train was due in less than an hour.

'Well, there's my ride,' Tayte said. 'Not bad, eh? A free ticket to the train station in an unmarked cop car.'

Amy smiled. 'They probably want to make sure you leave the county!'

Tayte snorted and said, 'You could be right.' He was about to say goodbye when he remembered something he needed ask. 'If you don't mind,' he said. 'I still have the lid from the writing box. I thought I could return it to the family it belonged to, but it's your call. You found it.'

'Keep it,' Amy said. 'I don't want anything more to do with it.'

'Thanks. I'm sure they'll appreciate it.' Tayte stood back from the doorway, not wanting to draw Hayne's eye just yet as something else occurred to him. 'What happened to the silk heart?'

Amy had lost track of it. Then she remembered she'd taken it out of the box the night Tayte called on her. 'Must still be at the house,' she said. 'I'll hang on to that. It was Lowenna's heart, and she gave it to Mawgan. I like that part of the story even if things didn't turn out for them. I think I'll put it back in the room where I found it. Lowenna only meant it for Mawgan's eyes.'

Through the double doors Tayte could see that Hayne was growing restless. 'Well, good luck,' he said. He leaned in and gave Amy a peck on the cheek. Then he took four backwards steps, gave her a final wave, and turned away. Before the doors had closed, he thought he heard Amy say, 'Don't forget to write.' But he couldn't be sure.

Chapter Sixty-Nine

The departure lounge inside Terminal 3 at Heathrow Airport frothed with nameless faces and blank expressions, and by the time Jefferson Tayte had finished his succinct pay-phone call to Walter Sloane and fought his way back to his seat, he was missing Cornwall already. He sipped at the edge of his paper coffee cup, reflecting on the past week and wondering if life was all just another rerun on a channel you couldn't change; whether we're all destined to follow the genetic plans that define us. Time and the nature of our existence may alter the surroundings, he considered, but are we capable of breaking free from such fundamental triggers as our own imbedded instincts?

Simon Phillips and Warwick Fairborne weren't, that's for sure.

As Breward Kinsey had murdered Mawgan Hendry in 1803, so now had their descendants come violently together to replicate that same fate—two people chasing a stolen legacy neither of them had any right to.

History repeats...

Tayte found himself questioning whether things could really have been any different. Once those genetic instincts had been awoken, could either of them have reacted any differently to the stimulus? He doubted it. It was in their blood.

He looked up from his coffee, scanning the myriad faces he couldn't avoid. He checked his watch; not long now. His briefcase was open between his feet, reminding him that something was missing. *Have I done the right thing?* he questioned. He knew DS Hayne must have found the envelope by now, and he'd probably read the letters. *Is it enough that the truth's been discovered and the Fairborne story's been told?*

Tayte didn't have the answer. He only knew that he owed it to Schofield not to let his killer succeed if he could help it, posthumous though any victory might be. And he owed it to Amy, for Gabriel and for what Simon Phillips had put her through. Yet he couldn't bring himself to destroy the letters any more than he could wilfully fulfil Simon's plans for revenge and wealth. While the letters survived, so too did the Fairborne story and the truth of what happened to that family. In being the first to tell it, Tayte felt he had a certain duty of care. His accompanying note to DS Hayne was clear; the letters should be filed as case evidence. Beyond that, Hayne was to use his own judgement.

The decision to leave them with Hayne became easier when, on the way to the train station, Hayne had explained how Sir Richard Fairborne had broken down during the night and confessed to sanctioning Tayte's murder. Tayte knew the implications would be punishment enough for a man in his position, and while it angered him, it also came as no surprise. Tayte wasn't out to get anyone for the sins of their ancestors; Amy had been right there. But they weren't exactly getting away with it either, and since Warwick was their only child, the stolen Fairborne dynasty had all but died with him at Nare Cove.

An announcement told Tayte that American Airlines was now ready for him to board. He snapped his briefcase shut, collecting it as he stood. He felt strong again, ready to have another go at tracing his own origins, ready to give that all-consuming hunger its last meal. He looked around at all the faces again—all the family history.

I'm a genealogist, he reminded himself. *And a damn good one.*

Looking out the windows, Tayte couldn't miss the sunset shimmer of the polished steel plane that waited to take him home.

After all he'd been through, it didn't look so intimidating this time around—at least, not from the safety of the departure lounge. But he could already feel his hands getting clammy.

Gotta face your fears, JT, he thought as he headed for the boarding desk. *When you fall off, you gotta keep getting back on.*

His eyes were still busy taking in all the faces. Scanning… *Where is she?* She was cutting it fine, and Tayte was surprised at how he felt at the idea of her not making the flight. Was he really ready to try his hand at romance again after all this time? He couldn't quite believe it possible, but why did he feel like he was back in high school again, getting ready for prom night? *Maybe she's not coming…* She'd made no promises when he'd called her with his flight details. He'd been true to his word: Larry Hagman for his flight number. That was the deal. But she'd said she had a busy schedule; Sunday was no excuse to sit back and take it easy in her business.

But who was she kidding? Tayte knew Julia Kapowski wouldn't have missed that flight, not even for a promotion. He heard her before he saw her.

'JT!'

A petite figure in a fitted black trouser suit asserted her way through the masses, clearly in a hurry to get to him. An amused smile spread across Tayte's face, though he tried to guard it.

'JT, honey!'

Kapowski was almost running now. When she was no more than a few feet away she stopped hard in her tracks. Her eyes were big as a panda's and radiated twice the sentiment.

'My God…sweetheart…' she said, eyeing the hospital dressings. 'What happened to you?'

'I don't suppose I can get away with it being a long story?' Tayte said.

'Not a chance!' She threw herself at him. 'We've got eight hours to kill, and look at you…you're gonna need someone to hold that *poor* hand of yours all the way to Boston!'

Acknowledgements

I can take no credit for the verse 'Of all the mortals…' reproduced here as part of the public domain. I came across it in a National Trust pamphlet while visiting Cornwall. It was written by an unknown Cornish farmer in the nineteenth century about the often tardy and drunken ferrymen who operated the Helford ferry service at the time.

My thanks to Tina Betts at Andrew Mann Ltd and to Cornerstones Literary Consultants for helping to shape this story, to Inspector Pat Rawle for assisting with my enquiries, to Mary Kemp for her encouragement and the pamphlet that started it all, to Emilie Marneur for inviting me to join Amazon Publishing, to my copyeditor Julie Hotchkiss, and everyone else at Amazon Publishing who has contributed in any way to this work, and to my wife, Karen, for everything…

About the Author

Credit: Karen Robinson

Steve Robinson drew upon his own family history for inspiration when he imagined the life and quest of his genealogist-hero, Jefferson Tayte. The talented London-based crime writer, who was first published at age 16, always wondered about his own maternal grandfather—'He was an American GI billeted in England during the Second World War,' Robinson says. 'A few years after the war ended he went back to America, leaving a young family behind and, to my knowledge, no further contact was made. I traced him to Los Angeles through his 1943 enlistment record and discovered that he was born in Arkansas …'

Robinson cites crime writing and genealogy as ardent hobbies—a passion that is readily apparent in his work.

He can be contacted via his website www.steve-robinson.me or his blog at www.ancestryauthor.blogspot.com.

21358379R00229

Printed in Great Britain
by Amazon